Tho

Thomas, Craig
    Sea leopard.

Sea Leopard

CRAIG THOMAS
Sea Leopard

NELSON CANADA LIMITED

Published in Canada in 1981 by Nelson Canada Limited
1120 Birchmount Road, Scarborough, Ontario M1K 5G4

ISBN 0-17-601513-2

Printed and bound in Great Britain

for MIKE, *agent and friend*
and in memoriam
ANTHEA JOSEPH
a kind and courageous lady

Acknowledgements

I wish to thank particularly my wife, Jill, for her strict and expert editing of the book, and for her initial suggestion that I attempt this story.

My thanks, also, to GH who acted as captain of the submarine HMS *Proteus*, and to the Royal Navy, without whose assistance, given so freely and willingly, I could not have completed the book. Gratitude, too, to TRJ for coming to my assistance in developing the "Leopard" anti-sonar equipment on which the story hinges.

As usual, I am indebted to various publications, particularly to Breyer & Polmar's *Guide to the Soviet Navy*, Labayle & Couhat's *Combat Fleets of the World*, and *The Soviet War Machine*, edited by Ray Bonds.

Any errors, distortion or licence for dramatic purposes is my responsibility, not that of any of the above.

Craig Thomas,
Lichfield 1980

Principal Characters

Kenneth de Vere AUBREY	:	Deputy Director, British Intelligence (SIS)
Patrick HYDE	:	a field agent of SIS
Ethan CLARK, USN	:	on liaison to the Admiralty
QUIN	:	an eminent electronic engineer
Tricia QUIN	:	his daughter
Col. Giles PYOTT, R.A.	:	a member of the NATO StratAn Committee
Comm. Richard LLOYD, R.N.	:	captain of the submarine HMS *Proteus*
Lt. Comm. John THURSTON, R.N.	:	first lieutenant, HMS *Proteus*
Sir Richard CUNNINGHAM	:	Director of British Intelligence ("C")
Peter SHELLEY	:	assistant to the Deputy Director, SIS
Sqn. Ldr. Alan EASTOE, R.A.F.	:	Nimrod pilot
Valery ARDENYEV, Red Navy	:	O/C Underwater Special Ops. Unit
DOLOHOV	:	admiral of the Red Banner Northern Fleet
Tamas PETRUNIN	:	KGB Resident, Soviet embassy in London
Viktor TEPLOV	:	petty officer to Ardenyev's unit

PLESSEY **The Plessey Company Limited**
Millbank Tower, 21-24, Millbank, London SW1 4QP
Telephone: 01-834 9641 Telex 917530

INTER OFFICE MEMO

from: Head of Project L

to: Head of Research

ref: 'LEOPARD'

I quite realise the pressure you must be under
from the Board to achieve results.   You may,
when you report to them, inform them of the
following:-

The broad effect of 'Leopard' is already working.
We have progressed to the point where we can
prevent an enemy sonar signal registering the
presence of a vessel using 'Leopard', and we
can also, after nullifying that signal with the
equipment, return to the enemy a false echo as
if from the sea bed below the submarine.

The remaining problems are related to the
variable quality of the false signal.   I am
confident the improvements can be made.

Registered in England and Wales at Vicarage Lane, Ilford, Essex IG1 4AQ Number 203848

1974   1976

9

PLESSEY ⬛〰️ **The Plessey Company Limited**
Millbank Tower, 21-24, Millbank, London SW1 4QP
Telephone: 01-834 9641   Telex 917530

Commodore D. N. Blackshaw, R.N.,
Senior Projects Officer,
Royal Navy (Projects),
Old Admiralty Building,
Whitehall,
LONDON.

Dear Commodore,

In considering your urgent request to the company
to accelerate the final stages of development of
the field prototype of our 'Leopard' project, I
am advised by the project head, Dr. A. J. Quin,
that it is possible to shorten the time prior to
full sea trials, only by a matter of a few days.
I respect the urgency of the matter, and understand
the kind of mission on which 'Leopard' would be
of inestimable value, but I am afraid that is the
best we can do.

Yours sincerely,

R. M. Bennett

R. M. Bennett,
Deputy Chairman.

 Registered in England and Wales at Vicarage Lane, Ilford, Essex IG1 4AQ Number 203848

1974   1976

10

FROM: Peter Shelley

TO: Kenneth Aubrey,
Deputy Director, SIS

You requested a copy of the accompanying report on the
sea trials of the LEOPARD anti-detection equipment as
soon as possible, together with a summary in layman's
terms.

As you know, a specially equipped Nimrod and a Sea King
helicopter were used in the sea trials with HMS Proteus.
They could not effectively detect or pinpoint the submarine
on any single occasion.

The full report is complex and highly technical, as well
as being liberally sprinkled with service jargon!
However, I have discussed it with the Director of
Technical Services Section, and he has summarised the
sea trials in the following terms:-

   i.   No problems were encountered with the hull sensors;

   ii.   The 'noise generator' unit effectively cancelled
       all external acoustic emissions, and dealt
       successfully with all attempts to detect the
       submarine using sonar;

  iii.   In shallower waters, the unit's delayed response
       system effectively transmitted a sonar echo
       which accurately simulated a 'seabed' response -
       in other words, the vessels seeking out HMS Proteus
       only registered the seabed and not the submarine.
       She was effectively 'invisible', as expected.

DEFENCE DEPARTMENT (NAVY)

UNITED STATES NAVAL INTELLIGENCE

USN (Intelligence) Form TAL 1

Our Ref	Deputy Director
Your Ref	Capt. E. V. Clark, USN
Date	

page 2 of 2

so I don't have to tell you how much of a threat
to the British, to ourselves and to the whole of
NATO the new Soviet sonar buoy carpet in the
Barents Sea represents. Unless it is fully
mapped, and therefore neutralised as a threat,
the Soviet Navy can close the Barents Sea at any
time, and that would mean the loss of NATO's
northern flank without a shot being fired.

For the reasons I have outlined, it was decided
that the Navy Department ask the British Royal
Navy to investigate and chart this new sonar
carpet, codenamed CHESSBOARD, using the submarine
Proteus, with the new LEOPARD equipment. The
submarine, if your reports on her sea trials are
accurate, should remain undetected throughout
the time she is in the area of the Barents Sea.

Your brief is liaison and observation, both for
the Navy Department and for NATO. Don't overstep
your mission orders, but get back to this office
immediate and direct through the embassy if
anything happens you don't like. Neither the
Director nor myself are really happy about risking
this LEOPARD equipment, if it's as good as they
say. But, we don't have much choice.

Adml. J. K. Vandenburg, USN,
Deputy Director,
US Navy Intelligence.

SIS
F. TTR 1a
TAPE TRANSCRIPTIONS

FILE REF   SIS/26554/3A - PH/Aubrey

TAPE No   B/163487/82/4/23

DATE

REFERS   QUIN - DISAPPEARANCE

Tape
Mark

.......continued

furthermore, none of his personal effects appear
to have been removed from the flat.   There was
still mail behind the door, dating back more than
three weeks.   There have been no subsequent
sightings.

In conclusion, I think the bird has flown.   On
the other hand, I don't believe it was his decision.
There was no pre-planning.   Coupled with the
information regarding the 'Trade Mission' arrivals
and departures at the Soviet embassy during the
relevant period, I am certain that Quin was snatched
and is now in Moscow.

I am inclined to believe that his daughter is with
him, since Birmingham Special Branch haven't had a
peep from her since the time of Quin's disappearance.

I have ordered the continuance of 24-hour
surveillance on the flat Quin occupied in Bracknell
and on his estranged wife's home in Sutton Coldfield.

P.H

Patrick Hyde

PART ONE

A GAME AT CHESS

ONE:

Bait

The office of Tamas Petrunin, Trade Attaché at the Soviet embassy in London, looked out upon Kensington Palace Gardens, across the lawns of the embassy grounds. The straight lines of bare plane trees marked the boundary between himself and the western city he both despised and coveted. A fierce early spring wind searched for, and found, the remains of last autumn's leaves, and hurried them along the road and beneath the wrought-iron gates into the drive of the embassy, finally scattering them like burnt secret messages and papers over the gravel and the grass. The sky was unrelievedly grey, and had been threatening rain all morning. Tamas Petrunin had leisure to reflect, as he listened angrily to the tape cassette from the duty room and its recorded conversation, that London irritated him particularly at that time of year. *There was no snow.* Wind, and rain – an umbrella threatening to turn inside out carried by an old man passing the gate, unceremoniously jostled by the wind – wind and rain, but little snow. Only sleet in the evening air sometimes, turning instantly to slush in the gutters, like a promise broken. In Moscow, there would be inches of snow, and everyone rotund and animalised in fur coats and hats.

The Scotsman's recorded voice enraged him. Almost always it did. Now nasality and meaning combined to grip his stomach with an indigestion of rage.

"We have been trying to contact you for two days," the authoritative Russian voice insisted. Ruban, the Naval Attaché who worked under the auspices of Petrunin and the KGB at the embassy. "You fully understand how difficult movement outside London is for our people here. Why have you not contacted us on schedule? Now you say the submarine has sailed."

There was an additional nasality, and a promoted, cultivated cough in the Scot's voice when he replied. "I've been in bed with the flu. It's no' my fault. I havena been to work all week. I've been in my bed, y' understand?" The whine was almost rebellious.

"We do not pay you to be ill, MacFarlane."

"I couldna help it. I still feel lousy. I got up to come to the phone.

17

There's fog, too." A small, projected bout of coughing followed the weather bulletin. Petrunin, in spite of his anger, could not suppress a smile.

"When did the submarine sail from Faslane?"

"Three nights ago, early hours."

"What? *Three* nights? What else did you learn?"

"I couldna ask, could I? Just that she sailed three nights ago."

"You are useless to us!" stormed Ruban on the tape behind Petrunin. One of the embassy chauffeurs was walking, leaning against the wind, towards a parked black Mercedes saloon. His black uniform trousers were flapping around his legs, and he was holding his peaked cap firmly on his head.

"I couldna help it – it was no' my fault if I caught the damn flu, was it?"

"Was the equipment on board? Do you know that much for certain?"

"I heard it was."

"You don't *know*?"

"Yes, dammit, it was on board!" The Scot sniffled on the tape. Petrunin pictured him. Pale, rat-faced, unshaven, untrustworthy. Trash. He was poor material with which to start a blaze. Ruban thought so too, by the sound of his voice. Ruban would have to report to Murmansk, via himself, and they would have to decide, on Mac-Farlane's word alone, whether the British submarine *Proteus* was carrying the "Leopard" equipment or not when she slipped out of Faslane into the Atlantic three nights before.

"You're guessing," Ruban said after a pause. "You can't know for certain."

"I'm sure, dammit! Nothing was taken off the ship after she returned from sea trials with this 'Leopard' stuff!" MacFarlane had forgotten his habitual ingratiating manner. "I found out that much. Nothing came off the ship."

"And where is she now?"

"I dinna know." MacFarlane retreated from anger into surliness.

"And that ends your report?"

In the silence that followed, Petrunin moved to his desk and switched off the cassette player. Then he returned to the window of his office, rubbing his chin. In no more than thirty minutes, he would have to summon Ruban, and they would have to make a decision before five or five-thirty as to the nature of the signal they would send to Moscow Centre and to Red Banner Northern Fleet HQ, Murmansk, EYES ONLY Admiral Dolohov. Damn MacFarlane and his attack of influenza.

"Leopard". Was it on board? If so, then the likelihood that *Proteus*

18

was on her way to map the location and extent of the newest Soviet sonar-grid across the Barents Sea from North Cape to Murmansk was transmuted into a virtual certainty. The only way to do that was by means of a submarine indetectable by sonar; which would mean *Proteus* using the "Leopard" equipment. Ethan Clark, the American expert, was in London on liaison work, *Proteus* had sailed on secret orders to an unknown destination as soon as her sea trials were complete. It was a likelihood – was it a certainty?

Petrunin paced the room carefully, keeping to the border of the patterned Turkish carpet, studying his footsteps with apparent intentness, rubbing his chin lightly with thumb and forefinger in a ceaseless motion of his hand. *Proteus* had to reach North Cape in order for the Red Banner Fleet's cock-eyed plan to be put into operation. If she were sailing elsewhere, all the preparations would have been a waste of time and effort.

Petrunin found himself before the window again. The newly-imprisoned leaves seemed to be scurrying aimlessly across the embassy lawns, seeking escape. He shook his head. *Proteus*'s target had to be "Chessboard". The development of "Leopard" had been violently accelerated during the past six months, the sea trials had been conducted with maximum haste; both facts implied an urgent task for the equipment. After all, there were no other "Leopard" units as yet, none fitted to any submarine or surface ship in the Royal Navy. Just this one priceless example of anti-sonar equipment, being used for one special task –

Yes. He nodded vigorously. He would go over it again with Ruban in fifteen minutes or so, but he had decided. They would signal Moscow and Murmansk that *Proteus* was on her way north, making for North Cape. Then it was up to the Red Banner Fleet.

And, he reminded himself, not for the first time that afternoon, there then devolved upon himself the task of finding Quin. Quin, the inventor and developer of "Leopard". Disappeared without trace. Not under protective custody, because British Intelligence, the Directorate of Security and Special Branch were all looking for him. Quin. More important – at least in Petrunin's estimation – than "Leopard" itself. Where was he?

He realised, with a mounting disappointment, that his decision with regard to *Proteus* was no decision at all. Merely a side-issue, a piece of self-indulgence, a war-game for sailors. Quin was what mattered. And Quin could not be found.

It had become routine, watching the house in Sutton Coldfield, in a quiet, residential street between the roads to Lichfield and Brownhills. A pre-war detached house, standing a little back from the road and elevated above its level, partially screened by a stone wall and a dark hedge. Leaded windows, trained ivy like an artificial ageing process climbing wooden trelliswork around the front door, and cherry blossom trees waiting for the spring. The street was still stained from the recent rain, and the slim boles of the trees gleamed green. Routine, boring routine. The young officer of the Special Branch unit attached to the West Midlands constabulary knew the façade of the house in which Quin's divorced wife lived with a familiarity that had become sour and stultifying. She worked part-time in the elegantly refurbished premises of an antique shop a hundred yards away. She was there now. The Special Branch Officer had parked his unmarked Ford Escort so that he had a clear view of the house and the entrance of the shop. He had observed well-dressed women, the occasional couple, a small delivery van, but no sign, none whatsoever, of Quin or of his daughter who had disappeared from her teacher training college in Birmingham at the same time that he had vanished. And there had been no visitors to the house except the milkman, the grocery delivery on a Thursday, the fish van on Wednesdays –

Sugden found himself idly flicking through the leaves of his notebook, rehearsing the boredom of two weeks' surveillance of the quiet street in a quiet suburb, shook his head, and snapped the notebook shut on the seat beside him. He put another cigarette to his lips, lit it, looked at his watch – Mrs. Quin would be coming home for a salad lunch in another half-an-hour – and slid lower in the driving seat, attempting to stretch his legs. He yawned. He and Lane, day and night for two weeks, just in case the missing man contacted the wife he'd left four years before, or in case the daughter turned up.

No chance, he told himself with a spiteful satisfaction that seemed to revenge him on the London superiors who had placed him in his present limbo, no chance at all. It was even duller work than preparing for the visit of the Queen to a Lichfield school a couple of years before, or Princess Margaret's opening of another Lichfield school before that, just after he had joined the Branch in Birmingham. Dull, deadly, dead. Quin and the girl had gone over. Not voluntarily, of course. Kidnapped. Snatched, Sugden yawned again. Quin was building "Leopard" for the Soviet Union by now, watched by his friendly neighbourhood KGB man. Despite wishing to maintain a frosty contempt for his present task and for those who had given him his orders, Sugden smiled to himself. Once Mrs. Quin was inside the house, a quick sandwich and a pint for him in the pub opposite the antique showroom. In the window seat, he could just about see the path up to the Quin house. Well enough, anyway. Certainly he could observe any car that parked near the house, or a pedestrian on the pavement.

20

He wondered why Quin had left his wife. Perhaps she had left him. They'd moved down to London when he began working for Plessey, and she'd come back to the Midlands after the separation because both of them were from the area and because the girl, Tricia, was enrolled at a training college in Birmingham. She'd repeated her first year twice, the file said, then failed her second year after the decree nisi, and only someone's pull high-up had prevented her from being expelled from the college. Now she'd disappeared along with her father. Another lever for the KGB to use on him, Sugden presumed. Mrs. Quin looked pleasant and capable. Greying blond hair, smartly turned out, could be taken for early forties. Quin, from the look of his picture – on the dash of the Escort – wasn't much of a catch, at least not in looks. The girl was pretty, but student-scruffy rather than making the most of herself. Almost drab, like the female of some brightly-plumaged species of bird.

She came down the path as Sugden rubbed his face and stifled another yawn. Tricia Quin, coming out of her mother's house. The closing of the door alerted him. She took no notice of the car, turned left, and began walking briskly down the hill towards the Lichfield road. Frayed denims, a long cardigan in some sludgy colour beneath a *cagoule*, untidy fair hair. Tricia Quin.

She was almost fifty or sixty yards down the hill before his hand jerked at the door handle, and he got out of the Escort. He could not believe it, though the confirmatory photograph was in his hand. He opened his mouth, fish-slow and silently, and then slammed the door behind him with an angry curse. He appeared stupid, would appear stupid, even when he took the girl in . . .

A rush of thoughts then. Quin might be in the country after all – the girl, how had she got in last night, how had Lane missed her? – comfortable thought, that. Lane's fault – where was Quin? Door opening and closing in the empty house with its For Sale notice, the one he'd suggested using but permission had been denied, too much paperwork to take it over – door closing, the girl further away down the hill, oblivious of him.

Or of the squat-featured, heavy-looking man in the grey double-breasted suit coming down the path of the empty house, a taller, thinner man running behind him. Both of them running, no more than twenty yards away from him now, and perhaps a hundred or so from the girl. KGB, so obvious he wanted to laugh, so sudden their appearance he could not move and was aware only of their numerical superiority.

"Wait a minute –" he managed to say, stepping round the Escort onto the pavement. The one in the grey suit ran with his thick arm extended, palm outwards, to fend him off like a rugby player; the thinner man dodged round the offside of Sugden's car. They were going to get past him, no doubt of it. "Wait!"

He ducked outside the extended hand, felt it heave at his shoulder, then got a hold on the arm behind it, ripping the grey sleeve of the suit immediately. A heavy fist swung at the edge of his vision and caught him on the temple. He was immediately dizzy.

The heavy man said something in Russian. Mrs. Quin was coming out of the shop, Sugden could see her over the roof of the car as the heavy man lurched him against it. The thinner man was galloping down the middle of the road, no athlete but certain to overtake the still unaware girl.

Sugden opened his mouth and bellowed her name. The heavy man struck upwards into Sugden's groin with his knee. Sugden doubled up, retching and groaning, his head turned sideways. The girl had become instantly alert, then had begun to run. The heavy man cursed, and moved away after aiming a foot at Sugden's head and connecting with his shoulder. Both men were running off. Sugden, groaning, his eyes wet with the latest wave of pain, knew he had to concentrate. They would want everything in his report.

Three hundred yards away, still just identifiable, Tricia Quin boarded a cream and blue bus as it pulled away, heading into the centre of Sutton Coldfield. The two Russians were just short of her, and the traffic lights were in the bus's favour. She was gone; they'd lost her, just as he had.

He rolled onto his back, still clutching his genitals, and listened to the tattoo of Mrs. Quin's high heels on the pavement as she ran towards him.

Patrick Hyde hurried through the rooms of the empty house, as if their last, impermanent occupants might yet be overtaken and restrained, just so long as he displayed sufficient haste. Two camp beds in one of the bedrooms, spare linen in the airing cupboard on the landing, food still in cardboard boxes, mostly tinned stuff, the refrigerator half-full, six-packs of lager, bottles of vodka. The two KGB men must have arrived before Birmingham Special Branch began its surveillance. The almost full dustbins at the side of the house suggested they had moved in almost as soon as Quin first disappeared.

Hyde snorted with self-derision and with an anger that included himself, Kenneth Aubrey, the DS, Special Branch, everyone. Quin had simply panicked, hidden himself. Or had he –? He could even be dead, and they might want the girl for some other reason . . .

Quin is alive, and well, and living somewhere in England, he reminded himself.

22

He turned to the police inspector who had followed at his heels through the house. "No sign of them now, sport?" He dropped immediately into a strengthened accent, one he had never himself possessed but which he used always to remind others of his Australian origins – because he knew it irritated them, and it served in some way to dissociate him from their incompetence. The only person secure from its mockery was Kenneth Aubrey. "A right bloody cock-up, mate. Wouldn't you say?"

The police inspector controlled his features. He disliked having to deal with someone from Intelligence rather than from what he would have considered the "proper channels", counter-intelligence. He could see no reason why Hyde, as SIS operative, should be officially functioning inside the United Kingdom, and displaying his superiority so evidently. And a bloody Aussie . . .

"You'd like to speak with Sugden now, I suppose, Mr. Hyde?" he said through thinned lips, hardly opening his teeth to emit the sounds.

Hyde scowled. "Too bloody right, Blue. Where is he?"

The inspector pointed to the lounge window, across at the Quin house. "Mrs. Quin looked after him, then he radioed in. He's still there. The doctor's taken a look at him."

"Bruised balls. He's lucky they were only playing with him. OK, let's have a word with him." The inspector made as if to precede Hyde from the room. He was taller, thicker set, in uniform. Hyde's voice and manner seemed to dismiss all of it. Hyde wagged a finger at him, bringing two points of colour to the policeman's cheekbones. "And *you* called the Branch?"

"Sugden is their man."

"You were instructed to call me – not the Branch, or the DS, or the Home Secretary or Her Majesty the Queen Mum – me. Next time, call me direct. Reverse the charges if you have to, but call me. Quin is mine." Hyde made Quin sound like part of his diet. The inspector seethed in silence, allowing Hyde to leave the room in front of him, just in case the Australian saw his eyes and their clear message. "It's a bloody cock-up!" Hyde called back over his shoulder. "Too much bloody *time* has gone by!"

Hyde banged open the front door and went down the path, the same urgency possessing his slight frame. His denims and pale windcheater over a check shirt did nothing to endear or recommend him to the inspector, who nevertheless dutifully followed him across the road and up the path to Mrs. Quin's door. Hyde rang the bell repeatedly.

"The woman's had a shock, you know," the inspector cautioned.

Hyde turned on him. "She bloody well knew we wanted her

husband and her daughter. Did she ring? No bloody fear. She almost got her precious daughter nobbled by the KGB –"

Mrs. Quin opened the door on its safety-chain. Her hair had freed itself from the restraint of lacquer, and two separate locks fell across her left eye. She brushed at them. Hyde showed her no identification, but she studied the uniformed inspector behind him, then released the chain on the door. Hyde walked past her into the cool, dim hall. Mrs. Quin caught up with him. Her mouth was trembling. The inspector closed the door softly.

"Where is he, Mrs. Quin?"

"In the lounge, lying down." Her tone was apologetic. She offered Sugden's comfort as a token of her good intentions. "Poor man."

"I'll talk to him. Then I'll want to have a word with you, Mrs. Quin."

"Mr. Hyde –" the inspector began.

Hyde turned to look at him. "Too late for that."

Hyde went into the lounge and closed the door behind him. Sugden was lying on a chaise longue, his face still pale, his tie askew, jacket draped over the arm of an easy chair. His face arranged itself into a memory of pain, through which guilt thrust itself like the outbreak of some malady.

"Mr. Hyde –" he began.

"Don't apologise, sonny, it's too late for that." Hyde pulled an armchair in front of the chaise.

"But I am sorry, Mr. Hyde. I just didn't know they were there."

"You cocked it up, son. You didn't expect the girl, you didn't expect the heavy mob – what did you expect?"

Sugden tried to sit up, to make himself feel at less of a disadvantage. Hyde waved him back, and he slumped on the chaise, his hand gently seeking his genitals. He winced. Hyde grinned mirthlessly.

"I don't know."

Hyde took out a notebook and passed it to Sugden. "These are your descriptions of the two men?" Sugden nodded. "They don't ring any bells with me. They could have been brought in for this. The KGB has trouble travelling. They didn't get the girl?" Sugden shook his head vehemently. "Neither did we. When did she arrive?"

"Mrs. Quin didn't say."

"She will. You know what it means, mm?"

"They haven't got Quin?"

"Too true they haven't. Shit, we should have guessed they didn't have him!" Hyde slapped his hands on his thighs. "Why the bloody hell did we assume they did? Too many post-Imperial hang-ups in Whitehall, sport – that's the bloody answer. Quin's gone, we're so incompetent and wet, they must have him. It's what we British

24

deserve." He saw Sugden staring at him, and grinned. The expression seemed to open his face, smooth its hard edges. It surprised Sugden as much as his words had done. "My hobby-horse. I race it around the track once in a while. Trouble is, I fell for it this time."

"You don't think much of us, do you?"

"Too right. Not a lot. You're all a lot more sophisticated than us Aussies, but it doesn't get you anywhere, especially with the KGB. Bloody Russians wouldn't last five minutes in Brisbane." Hyde stood up. "OK, sport, interrogation's over for now. I'm going to have a word with Mum. She has a lot of explaining to do."

He found Mrs. Quin and the inspector sitting in the breakfast kitchen, sipping tea from dark blue and gold cups.

"Mr. Hyde –"

"Very cosy," Hyde sneered, and the inspector coloured. Mrs. Quin looked guilty, and defiant, and Hyde was brought to admire the manner in which she stared into his eyes. She was afraid, but more for her daughter than herself.

"Tea, Mr. Hyde?" she offered.

Hyde felt pressed, even ridiculed, by the scene; by the pine furniture, the split-level cooker, the pale green kitchen units. Only he expressed urgency, was in haste.

"No time." He stood over the woman. The inspector played with his gloves on the table. "Will you check with the bulletin on Miss Quin, Inspector?" The policeman seemed reluctant to leave, but only momentarily. Hyde remained standing after he had left. "You weren't going to tell us, were you, Mrs. Quin?" She shook her head, still holding his gaze. "Why not, for Christ's sake?"

"Tricia asked me not to."

"We'd have looked after her."

"She said you couldn't. I don't know why not. She didn't explain." Her hand shook slightly as she lifted the cup to her lips. They quivered, smudging pink lipstick onto the gold rim of the cup.

"She knows where her father is, doesn't she?" Mrs. Quin nodded, minimising the betrayal. There was nothing in her eyes but concern. She cared for her daughter, it was evident, but regarding her husband she was composed, perhaps indifferent. "Did she say where?"

"No."

"Has she gone back to him now?"

"I don't know." The exchanges had achieved a more satisfying momentum which disguised the emptiness behind the answers. The woman knew little, perhaps nothing.

"Where has she gone?"

"She wasn't supposed to be going out." Mrs. Quin waved her hands limply. They were as inanimate as gloves at the ends of her plump arms. "I don't know where she is." The voice cracked, the mouth quivered.

"She came to put your mind at rest, is that it?" Mrs. Quin nodded. "And she said nothing about your husband – her father?" Mrs. Quin shook her head. Her face was averted from Hyde's eyes now. But she was concealing nothing, except perhaps inadequacies that belonged to her past. She was keeping only herself from him, not information. "She gave no clue?"

"No, Mr. Hyde. Except that he's well, and is in hiding. I think she hoped I would be pleased at the news. I tried to show I was." The confession stuck into their conversation like a fracture through skin.

"She's been with him?"

"Yes."

"Since his disappearance? She disappeared *with* him?"

"Yes, Mr. Hyde. And then she came back here. She's always bounced between us, ever since the divorce." Mrs. Quin tried to smile. "She is a trier, even if she's a failure." Assumed cynicism was an attempt to shut him out, he realised.

"Where might she be now, Mrs. Quin?"

"I have no idea whatsoever. Back with him, I suppose. But I have no idea where that might be."

Hyde breathed out noisily. He looked at the ceiling, his hands on his hips. The texture of their conversation had become thickened, clogged with personalities. There might be clues there as to the girl's character, behaviour, whereabouts, but such enquiries possessed no volition, no urgency. Hyde was impatient for action. The girl was vital now, and he and the KGB both understood that. She'd been shown to them like some tempting prize which would be awarded to the swiftest, the strongest, the most ruthless.

"Thank you, Mrs. Quin. I may be back. I just have to use your telephone –"

Mrs. Quin dismissed him with a slight motion of one hand. The other rubbed at the edge of the pine table, erasing memories. Hyde went out into the hall.

Aubrey had to know. The Deputy Director of SIS had been with the Foreign Secretary when the call from Birmingham had finally been routed through to Queen Anne's Gate. Hyde had left a message, but now Aubrey had to know the extent of their problem, and their hope – or lack of it.

He was dialling the number when the front door opened, and the inspector re-appeared. Hyde ignored him and went on dialling.

"Whoever you're reporting to," the policeman remarked with evident, hostile sarcasm, "you'd better mention the car that just

26

drove past. I'd say it contained the two men who worked Sugden over."

"What –?" The telephone was already ringing in Aubrey's office, even as Hyde examined a residual sense that he had once more blundered into, and through, a private world. Mrs. Quin hadn't deserved the way he had treated her. Yet, had he altered his manner, even though he might not have bludgeoned there would have been little gentleness, almost no sensitivity. He took the receiver from his cheek. "You've got them?"

The inspector shook his head. "Foot down and away, as soon as they saw my lads. The registration number won't be of any use either, I shouldn't wonder –"

"Shit!"

"I beg your pardon!" Aubrey's secretary demanded frostily at the other end of the line.

Ethan Clark, of the US Naval Intelligence Command (ASW/Ocean Surveillance), had been made to feel, throughout the week since he had joined the "Chessboard Counter" team in the Admiralty, very much like an executive of some parent company visiting a recently taken over small firm. He was present in both his USN and NATO capacities, but these men of the Royal Navy – of, more precisely, the Office of Naval Intelligence (Submarine Warfare) – exuded a silent, undemonstrative resentment of him. Which, he well knew, made any doubts and hesitations he had concerning the mission of HMS *Proteus* seem no more to them than American carping. The commodore and his team in this long, low room in the basement of the Old Admiralty Building in Whitehall were dry-land sailors playing a war-game, and thoroughly and blithely enjoying themselves.

Clark supposed it had its basis in a buried sense of inferiority. For years, the contracting Royal Navy had belied its great history, and now, quite suddenly, they had developed "Leopard" and installed it in a nuclear-powered fleet submarine and were engaged in mapping the "Chessboard" sonar grid in the Barents Sea. Their high summer had returned. NATO needed them as never before, and the USN wanted greedily to get its hands, and its development budgets, on the British anti-sonar system.

Nevertheless, he told himself again as he sipped coffee from a plastic cup and observed the British officers waiting for the ritual serving of afternoon tea, "Chessboard" should have waited. NATO and the Navy Department had required of the Royal Navy that they install the only operationally-functioning "Leopard" unit in a submarine, rush their sea trials, then send it racing north to the Arctic Circle. The British had responded like a child doing everything at top speed to show its willingness and its virtue. Even before they had paid Plessey the bill for what they had, and before they had ordered any more "Leopard" units. With that kind of haste, things often got smashed, plates got dropped. Boats had been lost before. It would be a great pity if "Leopard" was lost; a tragedy if anyone else found it.

The long room, with its officers seated at computer terminals in front of their screens, its maps, wires, cables, fold-away tables, was dominated by a huge edge-lit perspex screen which stood upright in the middle of the room. The perspex secreted a multitude of optic fibres which registered the input of the computers that controlled the screen. The lighting at the edges of the perspex allowed the team to use chinagraph for temporary handwork additions to the computer-fed information. At that moment, much as it had done for the last week, the screen displayed a projection of the fjordal north coast of Norway, from North Cape to Murmansk. The coast was green and brown, the sea a deepening shade of blue as it stretched northward. A fine grid of red lights, no larger than dots, was shown off the coast, as if some current in the screen were knitting, or marking a school register. Other lights moved slowly or remained stationary, units of the Red Banner Northern Fleet, ships and submarines. One or two NATO units. The Commodore's team seemed to scuttle round the base of the perspex screen as if propitiating some idol.

The room was now quiet, orderly. An hour before, *Proteus* had come up to periscope depth for one of her periodic, random but pre-determined transmissions. The transmisstion, using RABFITS (Random Bit Frequency Intelligence Transmission System) and via a satellite link, had contained every detail of the mapping work of the submarine since the previous message. This had been fed into the map-board's computers, updating the network of red spots which marked the "Chessboard" sonar grid.

Clark could not but admire, and envy, the "Leopard" equipment. He had been aboard *Proteus* as an observer during some of the sea trials, and he had also been aloft in the RAF Nimrod as the specially equipped plane tried to find the submarine. The Nimrod had been unable to locate, fix or identify the submarine, not even once, either in the Channel, the North Sea, or the north Atlantic. Not even in conjunction with the US-laid sonar carpet in the north Atlantic. No sonar trace, little and poor infra-red, nothing. It worked. Even pitted against surveillance satellites, it worked.

Perhaps, he told himself, his concern arose – like smoke, unformed but dense and obscuring – solely from the fact that when he had lunched with Kenneth Aubrey at his club at the beginning of the week, he'd learned that the man who had developed "Leopard" at

Plessey had gone missing, presumed lost to the Russians. "Leopard" was both useless and unique, if that were so.

"It's going splendidly, Captain Clark, don't you agree?" Clark snapped awake from his unseeing contemplation of the dregs in the plastic cup. Lt. Commander Copeland, the anti-submarine warfare expert on the "Chessboard Counter" team, was standing in front of him, six inches shorter and exhibiting a grin that shaded into smug mockery. The lights of the perspex map were bright behind him. "You don't seem to be too pleased," Copeland suggested with a more pronounced mockery. He waved an arm towards the glowing map. "Everyone else is feeling on top of the world."

"You're really pleased, aren't you, Copeland."

"Your people will be delighted, too, and NATO will be over the moon."

"Sure." Clark shifted his weight on the edge of the desk where he had perched.

"Really, Clark!" Copeland's exasperation was genuine. "Neither the United States nor ourselves have been able to send a ballistic missile boat, or any other sort of submarine for that matter, east of North Cape for two months, ever since the *Ohio* was first traced, shadowed, and escorted from the area." Copeland turned to study the huge map-board. "We're helpless up there until we know how big, how good, and of what kind 'Chessboard' is." He turned back to Clark. "Your Chief of Naval Operations saw that quite clearly, so did Supreme Allied Command, Atlantic. *Proteus* has the most distinguished sponsors." Again, the silent, mocking smile.

"What if we lose her? Then we've lost 'Leopard' for good."

"Lose? Lost? What do you mean? Oh, Quin, I suppose." Copeland shrugged. "If Quin is over on the other side, then 'Leopard' will be useless in a matter of months, don't you agree?" Clark nodded. "Well, then? We must neutralise 'Chessboard' now, while we have the means."

Clark looked up at the board again. A trelliswork of red dots. The carpet of active and passive sonar buoys, and other detection devices, began inside Norwegian territorial waters, less than four miles out, and extended, at present indication, perhaps fifty or more miles north into the Barents Sea. It could be a hundred miles. *Proteus* was moving between North Cape and Kirkenes like a tractor ploughing a field. The work could take weeks. Copeland was right, of course. The northern flank of NATO was imperilled by "Chessboard". The Norwegian coast was prohibited to British or American submarines, the coast of the Soviet Union rendered inaccessible to short-range attack; the Barents Sea finally transformed into a Russian lake.

"Sure. Yes, you're right, Copeland. You're right."

Copeland smiled with evident relief, and looked very young and enthusiastic. "I'm so glad you agree," he said without irony.

"Just one thing," Clark added maliciously, pointing towards the map. "Don't you think there's just too *little* Soviet naval activity up there?" The board's computer was feeding into the map display whatever the North Cape monitoring stations, the surveillance satellites, and air patrols were supplying via SACLANT's huge central computers. "Two 'Kotlin' class destroyers, one 'Sverdlov' class cruiser, two 'Romeo' submarines and one 'Quebec'. They're usually crawling all over the Barents Sea. Where are they?"

"Our information is Murmansk, old man. Perhaps they're taking things easy now they've got 'Chessboard' to do their work for them." The suggestion was in earnest.

"Maybe."

Copeland was about to reply when the door opened and a Wren wheeling a tea-trolley appeared. "Ah, tea," he exclaimed. "Excellent!"

Richard Lloyd, captain of HMS *Proteus*, was suddenly aware, on entering the cramped computer room aft of the main control room and its almost cathedral-like spaciousness, of the claustrophobia that most people imagined was the inevitable lot of the submariner. He did not experience it, merely understood what it must be like for people who never inhabited submarines; or who had served in them forty years before. The computer room was more cramped than ever, since at least half of its available space was now taken up by the "Leopard" equipment.

"Don," he said, nodding. His senior electronic counter-measures officer, Lt. Commander Hayter, had been nominated as trials officer for "Leopard" because of his existing special navigation and electronic warfare qualifications. Lt. Commander Hayter's comprehension of the equipment had relieved Lloyd from all but superficial knowledge of the effects and benefits of "Leopard". Hayter was seated in front of a computer screen, watching the pinpricks of light that emerged from its bland grey surface blankness, then slowly faded. As Lloyd watched, one pinprick brightened while two others were fading. They formed a vague triangle on the screen. Then one was gone while another emerged, glowing brighter. To the left of the screen was another, an acoustical holograph screen which displayed the buoys seemingly in three dimensions, giving them an identity, a shape. Neither Lloyd nor Hayter regarded the holograph display. There was something more obsessive about the silent, brief lights.

"Sir," Hayter acknowledged. "Welcome to the broom cupboard."

"They had submarines smaller than this room in the last war,"

30

Lloyd observed dismissively. He glanced from the screen to the holograph display, then at the accompanying print-out.

"Weird," Hayter said, as if to himself. "Really weird."

"What?"

"This feeling I have that we don't exist. Not for any practical purpose, that is. Sonar buoys, temperature transducers, hydrophones –" He pointed at the holograph as the shape of a sonar buoy formed in light. "Mile after mile of them, but we just don't exist as far as they're concerned. Like limbo. Yet I ought to feel excited, sailing east." He turned to Lloyd, grinning. "Oughtn't I, skipper?"

"Something's missing from your diet, obviously."

"Much activity?"

"Very little."

"You sound puzzled?"

"Maybe. No, not really. I suppose they're relying on this stuff –" He indicated the two screens. "They must be relying on 'Chessboard'. One or two surface vessels, a few submarines. Something moving well to the north, one of their 'Echo-II' missile boats off to take up station on the eastern seaboard of the States, no doubt. It wouldn't be much interested in us, even if it could spot us. Apart from those few items, nothing in the shop today."

"I can't say I'm sorry."

"You're not running down your pride and joy, are you?" Lloyd nodded in the direction of the main cabinet of the "Leopard" equipment.

"No. But utter reliance on an incredibly complicated system of matching sonar signals, and emission dampers and the like – it's not the same as having a big stick in your hands or a suit of armour on, is it? 'Chessboard' is the most advanced, extensive and thorough submarine detection system ever laid down. We both know that. Like tip-toeing through a minefield, or burgling the Chubb factory –" He smiled. "And here we are, same old faces and same old submarine, but now we're invisible. Mm, I think I feel excited, after all."

"How much of it have we mapped – just a guess? I won't hold you to it."

"My computers don't make rough guesses – just mistakes." Hayter typed on the computer keyboard below the screen. He waited for a few seconds before a message appeared, superimposed on the pinpricks of light, making them more ghostly and unreal than before. "See. Twelve days and a few hours more."

"That means this sonar carpet must extend at least a hundred and fifty to two hundred miles out into the Barents Sea." Lloyd's tone was one of surprise, even though he had half-expected "Chessboard" to be as impressive as he had now learned.

31

"It could be bigger. There's an assumed twelve to fourteen percent error built-in at the moment. That'll get less the more we chart." Hayter turned to Lloyd again. "I'm willing to bet that there's a similar sonar-buoy carpet being laid to stretch south and west from Novaya Zemlya. The Russians, I think, are going to close the Barents completely as far as we're concerned."

Lloyd rubbed his chin. "Could be. Not our worry, old son. Even if we end up doing trips round the Isle of Wight because there's nowhere else we can go. OK, twelve days it is. Don't let the men find out, will you?"

The intercom crackled about Lloyd's head.

"Captain to control room, please." It was the voice of his first lieutenant. Calm and urgent. Lloyd recognised the puzzled imperative in the guarded tone.

"So you think," he said, "that if ever 'Leopard' conked out or was developed by the other side, we'd see the end of NATO's submarine strike power?"

"I wouldn't be at all surprised," Hayter replied without looking at him, and not entirely without seriousness.

"Captain to control room."

Lloyd shook his head at Hayter's back, and left the computer room, passing through the open watertight door into the control room of the *Proteus*. He straightened, stretching the unaccustomed stoop from his shoulders. Artificial light was almost his natural visual medium. The control room – *his* control room – was light, almost airy after the cupboard-under-the-stairs in which Hayter spent much of his time.

Lloyd's first lieutenant, Lt. Commander John Thurston, was standing near the main bank of communications monitors, leaning over one of the operators, a headphone pressed to one ear. He looked up with something akin to relief when he saw Lloyd at his side.

"What is it, John?"

"Listen to this, sir." Thurston pressed the headphone set into Lloyd's hand. The communications petty officer twisted in his chair, watching for his captain's reactions, A brief splash of code, repeated again and again. Lloyd looked questioningly at Thurston.

"One of ours – distress code isn't it?"

"Not one of ours. The computer identified it as a quite low-priority Soviet submarine code, one we broke three months ago. Distress, yes."

"When did you start picking it up?"

"About fifteen minutes ago, sir," the petty officer replied. "It's being transmitted regularly. I fed it into the signals computer, and it came out as a distress call."

"Any ident?"

"Yes, sir," Thurston replied, acclaiming the drama he perceived in the situation by a lengthening of his saturnine face.

"Well?"

"It's a 'Delta'-class ballistic missile submarine. The full works."

"You're sure?"

"Yes, sir."

"What the hell is the matter with her, using a low-grade code? What's her trouble?"

"Massive explosion in the computer room. Most of their ECM systems have gone, and there's gas in the air-purification system. They've shut down almost everything. They're sitting on the bottom."

Lloyd screwed his face up. "They're very descriptive."

"Panic, sir. Sheer bloody panic."

"Any idea where?"

"Yes, sir."

Again, Lloyd looked puzzled. "How did we get a fix?"

"We didn't. They told us where to find them. They're screaming for help. They could begin transmitting in clear any minute now, they're so scared."

"Where are they?"

Thurston, who had evidently prepared the little scene between himself and Lloyd in minute detail, nodded towards the chart table against the aft bulkhead of the control room. Lloyd followed him across.

"Here," Thurston said. "Right here." His finger tapped the chart. He had drawn a livid red cross, dramatic and oversized, on its surface. "Tanafjord."

"What? You must have got it wrong –"

Thurston shook his head. "No, sir. They're wrong to be there, and to be using a broken code to transmit their position. But they're inside Tanafjord. They're in Norwegian waters in a ballistic missile submarine, and they're scared they're going to die!"

"My God," Lloyd breathed. He was silent for a moment, and then he said, "We'll break radio silence for this one. Run up a transmission buoy. We'd better tell the Admiralty – and the sooner the better!"

Admiral of the Red Banner Northern Fleet Dolohov paced the gantry, his footsteps and those of his aides ringing on the metal catwalk. Continually, he stared down into the well of the fleet's central Operations Room beneath Red Banner headquarters in Murmansk. Below him, the huge map table glowed with light. He had just arrived, and the warm lighting of the room, and the pin-point glows in fairy-light colours from the computer-projected map seemed to celebrate and

33

promise. It was a welcome. He paused, placed his hands on the rail of the catwalk, and turned to his aide. He might have been on the bridge of a ship.

"Sergei – status report, if you please."

The younger man smirked with pleasure, real and anticipated. "Sir. The British submarine is in this area –" He clicked his fingers, and a chart was passed to him. It was attached to a clipboard, and over the exposed fold was fixed a transparent plastic sheet. There were faint, reddish smudges on the plastic, one or two firmer images. "The infra-red satellite picked these up, sir. Very, very faint, but there. It must be the *Proteus*." He pointed out one of the brighter images. "This is the cruiser in the area. A clear image, even with the cloud cover. The faint smudges –"

"It works, then? This anti-detection equipment, it really works as well as we have been led to believe?"

The aide considered the possible implications of the question, then said, "The weather satellites promise the break-up of the cloud cover. It will improve our chances of getting a good infra-red trace."

"I didn't mean that, boy!" Dolohov snapped, his pale eyes fierce and alert. "I *understand* that it is hit-and-miss, even with our new geostationary satellite and every unit of the fleet looking for this submarine. I am *delighted* that it works, that the prize will be worth the game."

"I see, sir –" the aide said shamefacedly. "When the submarine moves closer to the Norwegian shelf, into shallower water, we may have a better trace. Not much better, but enough, sir," he added with solemn candour. Dolohov laughed.

"It is a *gamble*, Sergei, a great game!" he explained. "As long as the prize is sufficient, then one accepts the chances of losing the game." He transferred his intent gaze to the map table below. The plotters moved about it busily, yet expectant, knowing that they were as yet simply filling in time, rehearsing.

"Oh, the prize is a good one, sir. It works, only too well. We have had nothing from our sonar carpet, nothing, even though the British have been in the area for two days now."

Dolohov turned back to him, his eyes vacant, his gaze inward. The smile still hovered around his mouth. He nodded, like a very old, semi-senile man. Sergei would not have been surprised had an unregarded spittle appeared on his lips.

Then Dolohov was alert again. "Yes. Satisfactory." He looked down into the well of the huge room, at the map table. The different coloured lights. Cruisers, destroyers, the carrier *Kiev*, submarines, the special salvage vessel *Dioklas* and the submarine rescue ship *Karpaty*, all ready to sail from Pechenga and Poliarnyi, as soon as the word was given. Hours – mere hours – away from the Tanafjord and the distress signal. The thought spoiled his almost complete satisfaction. He turned to Sergei again. "If only we knew the precise moment when the *Proteus* picked up the distress call and her computers broke the code – eh, Sergei? Yes, I know when they transmitted to London, I know that. I would have liked to have known when they picked it up, though. The precise moment. What they thought, and felt, and said. Everything." He laughed. Then he spoke more softly, looking down on the map table once more. "Come, let us begin. Set course for Tanafjord, and sail into our elaborate trap. Come."

TWO:

Contact

The commodore was still closeted with a hastily assembled committee of staff officers, arguing for an investigation by *Proteus* of the distress signals from Tanafjord. In the "Chessboard Counter" room, Clark found himself a lone voice, disregarded and even derided, as he argued against any diversion of the submarine from her mission.

He could not have explained to himself the reasons for his reluctance. The cleanly-shaven, smartly-uniformed young men who surrounded him beneath the huge perspex map-board enraged him with their confidence, their boyish enthusiasm. It was their cheerful dismissal of any doubts on his part that had stung him to contempt and counter argument. He repeated himself again and again, and the baffled, kindly smiles and the frowns of dismissal greeted every statement he made. He knew it was the commodore he needed to convince, yet he once more reiterated the central thrust of his argument in a snapping, irritated tone. He justified his own stubbornness by reminding himself that he was the Navy Department's – America's – only and solely responsible representative.

"Look, you guys –" Lips twisted in derision or disdain. "You already know her type, you might even verify which boat she is. Only ten percent of their ballistic subs are out of Murmansk at any one time. If she's screaming for help, then there may be nothing left to investigate by the time *Proteus* reaches the fjord." He could see the disbelief opening on their faces, livid as blushes. It angered him. "Hell, why would she be in a fjord in shallow water with limited sea room if she was going to play rough? Use a nuke depth bomb on her – it might work out cheaper than sending in 'Leopard'."

"Really, Clark, you're quite the hysterical virgin this morning," Copeland remarked waspishly.

Clark was about to answer when the door opened. He recognised Giles Pyott as soon as he entered the room. Pyott was in army uniform, and the commodore, who entered behind Pyott, was also in uniform. A glassy, urbane, impenetrable officialdom had suddenly settled on the room, the kind of formality that the Pentagon or the Navy Department could never muster or imitate. Thank God, Clark added to his observation. Pyott, grey hair immaculate, part of his pressed, polished uniform, looked pleased and elated. Clark was again reminded of children and their haste to please or to upstage.

"Shall I tell them, Commodore, or will you?"

"Carry on, Colonel Pyott," the commodore demurred, a smile leaking into his face and warping the firm line of his lips.

"Very well." The two men had approached the group beneath the map. Pyott studied it theatrically, glanced at Clark and nodded to him, then spoke to the group of Royal Navy officers. His manner implied that Clark had left the room. "Gentlemen, it has been decided that *Proteus* be ordered to proceed, with utmost caution and all practicable speed, to the area of Tanafjord." A sigh of communal satisfaction, one or two murmurs of congratulation and pleasure; the empty compliments of sycophancy, they appeared to Clark. He was a man in a grey suit with a pocketful of unfamiliar and rather despised credit cards. Not a gentleman, they might have said of him. Worry twisted in his stomach again, and he knew he could not keep silent. "Yes, gentlemen," Pyott – who was from some faceless and important MoD/NATO committee called StratAn – continued, "the first Sea Lord and the Chiefs of Staff assign the gravest import to this intrusion into NATO territorial waters –" Again, the murmur of support. "The government of Norway, when informed, officially requested our assistance. *Proteus* will be instructed by yourselves to carry out a monitoring and surveillance action at the mouth of the Tanafjord." He smiled, at once the headmaster with his junior staff. "I leave the form of the task orders and encoding to you."

"We'll get on with it, Colonel," Pearson, the communications officer, offered, wiping his spectacles. Without them for the moment, he seemed more to suit the dark uniform and the gold cuffs. Returning them to his aquiline nose, he became clerkish again.

"Are you certain of all this, Pyott?"

It was as if Clark had cheered for an opposing team. Pyott turned a lordly glance to the American, who was as tall as he was and more muscular but who did not pose his figure in quite the same seignorial manner.

"I beg your pardon, Captain Clark?" The mention of rank was a reminder of good manners and the proper forms of address. "I don't quite catch the drift of your question." Outsider, the tone cried. Buccaneer. Pyott took in, with a raking glance that went from face to feet and back again, the civilian clothes, the muscular chest and shoulders, the tanned, square features. Clark was evidently a pretender engaged in some dubious masquerade.

"I asked if you were certain? Are their Lordships certain? Are the Chiefs of Staff certain? Is NATO certain?"

"The proper channels, the protocol, all have been observed, Captain Clark," Pyott replied frostily.

"What in hell do they think the Russians are up to in Tanafjord, with a ballistic missile boat?" Clark almost bellowed, goaded by the imperturbable arrogance and self-assurance of the army officer. Like a line of automatons, the operators in front of their screens and terminals snapped to attention in their seats. The group beneath the map seemed to move slightly away from him, as if he had begun to exude a powerful, offensive body odour. "You think they're invading Norway, starting the next war?"

"I do not know," Pyott said icily, his face chalk white. "I do not make assumptions, especially ones that might be dismissive and therefore comforting. That is why *Proteus* must do our investigating for us. Your own Navy Department has been consulted, and has agreed. Brussels is in agreement. *You* are out of step, Clark."

"*Proteus* has 'Leopard' on board. Doesn't that worry you?"

"That fact weighed heavily with everyone at the meeting, and with everyone consulted. It is to our inestimable advantage that *Proteus* is the submarine on station, so to speak –"

"Bullshit! Crap and bullshit, Pyott! You people – you want to play games, you want to *really* try out your shiny new toy. You want to walk close to the cliff. Now I understand –"

"Perhaps we could continue this conversation outside," Pyott remarked through pressed, almost unmoving lips. His face was now livid with anger. The naval officers, including the commodore, had moved away from them, sensitive of the embarrassment they knew Pyott must be experiencing.

"I wouldn't want the time of day from you, Pyott. You're an asshole. A pompous asshole, at that."

Clark brushed past Pyott, who avoided him like an experienced matador. Clark had allowed the situation to escape him. He was angry with himself, angry that it was Pyott he resented more than Pyott's suggestion concerning *Proteus*. As he prepared to slam the door of the "Chessboard Counter" room behind him, he could hear Pyott already reiterating StratAn and NATO's orders concerning *Proteus* to the assembled company. His voice was laconic, controlled, smooth as glass.

It enraged Clark, and he knew he had to talk to Kenneth Aubrey. Something in him, deep as a lust as yet unfocussed, knew that he had to stop this *adventure* with "Leopard" and *Proteus*.

He slammed the door loudly behind him.

Aubrey studied Hyde's face. It was evident the man's challenge with regard to the fact of Quin's disappearance was intended to irritate, and intended also to disguise the Australian's own new doubts.

Aubrey smoothed the last, vestigial wings of grey hair above his ears, and leaned back in his chair. Shelley, his aide, watched Hyde from the tall windows of the office in Queen Anne's Gate.

"You're not sure now, are you?" Hyde repeated.

"Don't jump to conclusions," Aubrey remarked severely. "What you saw was the girl. We know that she is unreliable, something of a failure, a drop-out. Is there any real reason to suppose that she knows where her father is? She wasn't just trying to keep her mother calm?"

"The KGB chased her to the bus stop. Those two blokes were like rape on legs."

"Perhaps Quin won't play ball with them in Moscow without having his daughter with him?" Hyde shook his head vehemently. "Your own source at the Russian embassy gave you quite clear – almost categorical – indications that a snatch squad had stayed overnight, and left again on Aeroflot the day after Quin disappeared. You believed your man then. Why not now?"

"Wait till I see him again. I was led up the garden, taken walkabout if you like. I admit that. But don't *you* go on believing there's nothing we can do. Quin dropped out of sight for his own reasons – he could have had a breakdown, for all we know – and the girl's gone back to him now, or she's on her way back. I *know* the Russians haven't got him yet, but they will have as soon as they get their hands on the girl." Hyde was patting Aubrey's desk, gently and continuously, to underline his words. He looked at Shelley when he had finished speaking, then asked, "You think they've got him?"

Shelley shrugged. Hyde, understanding his influence with Aubrey, wanted him on his side. Shelley plucked at his bottom lip with thumb and forefinger, then he said, "I don't know. There's some room for doubt, I think. It seems too good to be true, after the last few weeks –"

"I will make the assumption – because it is preferable to do so – that the appearance of the girl means that the KGB have not taken Quin to Moscow, Patrick," Aubrey said slowly. Hyde exhaled noisily and relaxed in his leather chair. "I still believe that Quin has gone east –" He held up a liver-spotted, wrinkled hand. "Until there is stronger evidence to the contrary. Therefore –" He smiled slightly, "your first task is to contact your helpful but possibly misleading friend at the Soviet embassy."

Hyde nodded. "Today's pick-up day. He's not likely to stay away after yesterday, whether he's straight or crooked."

"I suppose we might have to consider him planted, or at least re-turned?" Aubrey mused.

"The abortion was a long time ago. Perhaps he's back in favour with his bosses," Hyde suggested.

"Ask him. Then find the girl. Simply that. What about her college, for instance?"

"CID talked to some of her friends last night. Nothing."

"You will go back over the ground. And you will be careful, Patrick, if you are going to begin crossing the path of the gentlemen who were in Sutton Coldfield yesterday. You'd better draw a gun." He waited for Hyde's reaction. The Australian nodded after a lengthy pause. "Good. Don't draw attention to yourself. If your theory is correct, then they might soon begin following you as their best lead to Miss Quin."

"Anything else?"

Aubrey shook his head. "Not for the moment." Then he added, "This girl –" He tapped a file near his right hand. "Unreliable. Unconventional. Is that your impression?"

"Her Mum loves her. If she isn't just a nut-case, then she might be more difficult to find."

"I think we'd better find her, don't you? She's in danger, whether Quin is in the country or not. They want her, apparently."

"How much time is there?"

"I don't know. We have 'Leopard'. It can be manufactured in large numbers, eventually, without Quin. From that point of view, there is a great deal of time. But we are no longer alone. The girl's time, at least, would seem to be running out."

"I'll get on with it, then," Hyde said, getting up. The leather of the chair squeaked as his frame released it. "Pardon," he said with a grin. "You can talk about me when I'm gone. I'll let you know this afternoon what Comrade Vassiliev has to say." He smiled, and left the room.

Aubrey's returned smile vanished as soon as the door closed behind Hyde.

"What do you think, Peter?" he asked.

Shelley rounded Aubrey's desk to face him. Aubrey indicated the Chesterfield, and Shelley sat down, hitching his trousers to preserve their creases as he crossed his long legs. Shelley lit a cigarette, which Aubrey watched with a dry, eager concentration. He had obeyed his physician for more than a year in the matter of smoking. The occasion when the service lift at his flat had not been working for a week, and he had had to walk up three flights of stairs every evening – shortness of breath, body's fragility indicated to him like a sound blow on his shoulder. No more cigarettes, not even the occasional cigar.

"I'm afraid Patrick's right, however irritating that may be." Shelley smiled.

"We have been misled – and principally by his source of information at the Soviet embassy."

"Agreed, sir. But we all accepted Vassiliev after Hyde cleared up the matter of the abortion and the girl in the case was paid off. Vassiliev had walked into our honey-trap, we let Hyde go with him as chief contact. If Vassiliev is forged, then he's an expert job. Of course, he may just have been trying to please Hyde. The swagman's not often fooled. That's why he's so angry now. I can't say that I blame him."

Shelley exhaled, and Aubrey ostentatiously wafted the smoke away from himself by waving his hand. Shelley appeared not to notice the inconvenience to his superior.

"This incident in Sutton wasn't an elaborate charade, for our benefit?"

"I doubt that, sir."

"So do I. The problem is, this 'Leopard' business is so damned important. It really is one of those pieces of military technology the Russians haven't even begun to develop. Or so they tell me at MoD and Plessey. It would put us perhaps years ahead in the anti-submarine warfare game. I really would like to believe that they haven't got Quin. It just seems too good to be true."

"Agreed. But there is such a thing as not looking a gift horse, et cetera, sir –"

"Perhaps. Another thing that worries me – what price the safety of Comrade Vassiliev? If he fed us duff gen at their orders, then they know Hyde will be coming back now with more questions." Aubrey shook his head. "I don't like that idea."

"Bruce the Lifeguard can take care of himself."

"I hope so. Peter, get some Branch people to check around Bracknell again – the avenues we haven't explored or didn't give much credence to. Holiday rentings, cottages, that syndrome. People usually run for the hills not the city if they want to hide. I don't know why that should be."

"Very well, sir."

"And this file –" He tapped Tricia Quin's folder. "Get all the material out of it for Hyde. A list of people and leads. I have the distinct feeling that very little time is available to us, don't you?" Aubrey looked up at Shelley as the young man got to his feet.

"No comment, sir."

"Well?" Lloyd, slumped in his chair, seemed to embrace the small, neat captain's cabin of the *Proteus* as he opened his hands for an answer. Then, as if drawn by some new and sudden gravity, his hands rested on the chart on his desk. Thurston had brought the chart with him from the control room. He and Carr, the navigator, had

41

marked the course of the *Proteus* as far as Tanafjord. Thurston sat opposite Lloyd, Carr standing stockily and red-haired behind the first lieutenant, Hayter leaning against the closed door of the cabin. The air conditioning hummed like a sustained note of expectancy. "Well, John? You two? Any comment?"

Thurston cleared his throat, and in the sidelong movements of his eyes Lloyd saw that these three senior officers had conferred. They were some kind of delegation.

"No," Thurston said at last, "not now we know its position."

"Why not?" Lloyd looked up. "You two are in on this, I presume?"

Carr said, abruptly, "It makes the whole thing messy, sir. I can't understand what MoD thinks it's playing at, ordering us to the mouth of Tanafjord. It smells, sir."

"It does, sir," Hayter confirmed. "A 'Delta'-class sub in a fjord. Why? What good can it do there? It could loose any missile it wanted to from its berth in Murmansk as well as from that fjord. Why was it there in the first place? Shallow water, no sea room. Sir, we both know it's a very unlikely beginning to the next war." Hayter smiled, ingratiating his nerves with his captain.

Lloyd rubbed his face, drawing his features into a rubber mask, then releasing the flesh. It assumed a kind of challenged look. Thurston observed Lloyd's expression with a mild dismay.

"You're suggesting we disobey a highest priority instruction from the Admiralty?"

"No. Let's request confirmation. We could do that –"

"We could." Lloyd looked down at the chart again. "How many hours' sailing, rigged for silent running, taking *all* precautions?"

"A little over thirty-seven," Carr replied. Hayter looked at him in reproach, as if he had changed allegiance or betrayed a secret. "But I think we should request confirmation, skipper."

"Thirty-seven." Lloyd tapped the chart with his forefinger. "Our course alteration is minimal for the first six hours or more. We're to continue our work on 'Chessboard'. For six hours, at least, nothing's changed." He smiled. "In that time, we'll send one signal to MoD, asking for confirmation, and for a fuller definition of our mission status. Does that satisfy you trio of doubting Thomases?"

"I still don't like it," Thurston volunteered.

"You were as excited as hell when we picked up the signal from our Russian friend, John. What's changed?"

"I used to like watching boxing – it never tempted me to take it up as a hobby."

"Don, I want a full tape test and computer check run on 'Leopard' as soon as we alter course."

"You'll get it."

42

"Are we still getting signals from the Russian boat?"

Thurston nodded. "Sandy's been monitoring them since we got a reply from MoD."

Carr said, "She's broadcasting in clear now. Being careful, of course. But the power's down on the transmission. I think they're using a low-power emergency back-up set, and they're altering the frequency with pre-programmed cards. It's a bloody mess."

"Any more details?"

"No. Code-names, damage indications in some Cyrillic alphabet sequence. Can't decipher that. The letters and numerals could refer to anything."

"What other traffic?"

"Murmansk's been pouring out coded stuff –" Carr shook his head at the light in Lloyd's eyes. "We don't have it broken. Code of the day only, frequency-agile transmissions, the lot. But there's a lot of it. They're panicking all right."

"OK. Sandy, time to fetch Lt. Commander Hackett." Lloyd nodded at the cabin door, and Hayter moved out of his way as the navigator went in search of the engineering officer. When Hayter closed the door again, Lloyd said, "You don't really think MoD are wrong on this one, do you?"

Thurston pulled a melancholy face. "They aren't infallible. I think they like the idea of the game, that's all."

"We're risking this ship, and ourselves, and 'Leopard' on this wild goose chase," Hayter added with a quiet vehemence. "That doesn't seem to have struck their lordships. I think the intelligence yield from this 'monitoring action' won't be worth a candle, anyway."

"I agree with Don."

Lloyd was silent for a time, his hands over his face, the fingers slightly parted as if he were peeping child-like at them or at the chart on his desk. Then he rubbed his eyes, and shrugged himself upright in his chair.

"I'll ask for confirmation from MoD. Meanwhile, we'll rig for silent running – and I *mean* silent from now on." A grin, unexpected and gleaming, cracked the seriousness of his expression. "It isn't for real, you two. We won't be responsible for starting the next war. Nothing is going to happen to us. It's *Norwegian*, the Tanafjord. Cheer up. Just look on it as another sea trial."

Thurston was about to reply, but fell silent as they heard a knock on the cabin door. Lloyd indicated to Hayter that he should open it. The grin was still on Lloyd's face when Carr ushered Hackett into the cabin.

The wind seemed to follow Hyde into the entrance of Lancaster Gate underground station, hurrying pages of a copy of the *New Evening Standard* ahead of him, with chocolate bar wrappers. He hunched against the wind's dusty, grubby touch at his neck. He went through the barrier, and descended past the framed advertisements to the Central Line eastbound platform. A woman's legs, gigantic and advertising tights, invited him from the opposite wall. Lunchtime had swelled the numbers of passengers. Hyde lounged against the wall and observed Vassiliev further down the platform. Even here the wind moved the dust in little eddies or thin, gauzy scarves along the platform. Vassiliev wore a dark overcoat across his shoulders, over a pinstriped suit. He looked English enough despite the high Slavic cheekbones and narrow nose, yet he appeared nervous beneath the clothes and the residential veneer England had given him. Hyde was still unsure of him; whether his crime was one of omission or commission.

The train slid into the arched bunker of the platform. Hyde watched Vassiliev board it, then waited until he was the last still person on the platform, then he got into another carriage as the doors shunted together behind him. He stood watching the retreating platform as the train pulled out. Nothing. There was nothing to be learned from nothing.

He and Vassiliev left the train at Tottenham Court Road, Hyde staying twenty yards behind the Russian, closing with him as they transferred to the Northern Line and then getting into the same carriage of the first northbound train. He studied the carriage and its passengers until they pulled into Euston, then took a seat next to Vassiliev. The Russian embassy official, in making a pronounced movement away from him, squeezing himself against the window, suggested either dislike or nerves. Hyde placed his hand on Vassiliev's arm in a gesture which he knew the man – superficially confident of his heterosexuality but with sexual doubts nagging at him like toothache spoiling good looks and appetite – loathed. The arm jumped beneath his touch.

"Now, sport, you and me have some talking to do, don't we?"

Vassiliev looked out of the window. Mornington Crescent. The name slowed and materialised, like oil adopting a mould. "I – I knew you would question me," he offered.

"Too bloody right, mate! You sold me the wrong stuff, Dmitri – told me Quin was over on your side. Taken away by the bogeymen."

Vassiliev turned at the pressure on his arm and stared at Hyde. Sitting, he was slightly taller than the Australian. His face was thinly imperious for a moment – Hyde, seeing the expression, was strangely chilled – then it subsided quickly into nervousness and apology.

"I am not a member of the KGB, you know that. I am not privy to

44

the things they do. What I told you was a fact. I also heard rumours of who their objective was, I passed these on to you. I can do no more."

Vassiliev glanced away from Hyde, into the lightless tunnel.

"I don't pay you for crap, Dmitri. I don't blackmail you for rubbish. Now, what do you know?"

Vassiliev shook his arm impatiently, and Hyde released it, thrusting his hand into his pocket and slumping more theatrically in his seat, feet on the seat opposite, to the irritation – silent and frightened – of an elderly man.

"I – it is difficult to ask, I can only listen. In the staff restaurant, there is talk of what happened yesterday. I – I am, well, yes, I am almost certain that they are still looking for this Quin –" Hyde listened, every sense aware of the man in the seat next to him. Body temperature coming through the thin sleeve of his windcheater, thigh trembling slightly against Hyde's own, the faint body odour noticeable above the dusty, greasy smells of the carriage and the mothball scent from the old man. The voice, grabbing at sincerity, the breathing somehow artificially fast. The words broken by intelligence rather than emotion; thought-out hesitations. "I have not seen the two men – they were low-grade sleepers, I understand, without accreditation to the embassy –" The officialese flowing now like a broad, uninterrupted stream, but not quite because of habit. Learned, Hyde thought; but he remained silent. Quiver gone from Vassiliev's body. He believed he had acted sufficiently well. "However, there was talk about them, and about the girl – and I'm sure now it is their way of getting to the father –"

"You picked up a lot yesterday and this morning," Hyde remarked laconically.

"I am *trying*," Vassiliev pleaded, turning his face to Hyde. Mirror of helpfulness, of urgent sincerity. The eyes expressionless. "I knew what you would want. I was as surprised – shocked – as you must have been. What else can I tell you?"

Camden Town, slowing down outside the window. Hyde swiftly surveyed the passengers on the platform, those who entered their carriage. He could not believe that they would have let Vassiliev out by himself, without a minder, with such an important role to play. But he could not find his companion. What role was he playing, anyway? Why admit that Quin was still at large?

"I want more detail, more information, Dmitri. That's what you can tell me, and I want it tonight."

"I can't do that!"

Hyde stared into the Russian's face. "Yes, you can. Oh yes, you can. After all, you're my creature, I've got the arm on you. It's not the other way round, is it?" Hyde watched the face. Mouth sloping

45

downwards in admission, cheekbones colouring slightly with a sense of shame, brow perspiring in tiny silver beads – ignore, the temperature in the carriage and the overcoat explained it – the eyes quizzical, blank, then striving for the hunted look Hyde expected. Finding, losing, catching and holding it. Vassiliev was playing with him, at the orders of the London Resident or one of his senior staff. Again, he felt momentarily chilled.

"Yes, I will try," Vassiliev said mournfully.

Highgate. A moment of silence, no one getting on or off the train. Stillness. Then the doors breathing noisily as they closed again. The lights elongating, the words smudged, the darkness of the tunnel, the walls pressing close to the window. Hyde shook off the awareness of himself, the pressing vulnerability. He was being led by the nose, being set up to do their work for them.

"You're sure?" he asked, staring at his feet.

"Of what?" Vassiliev asked, momentarily confused.

"He hasn't been taken over?"

"The man Quin?"

"Yes."

"No. No, they do not have him." East Finchley. Vassiliev began to look uncomfortable, as if he had entered unexplored territory. "They think the girl will lead them to him. I am sure that is what they think." He looked pleadingly at Hyde.

"You were sure they had him three weeks ago."

"I am sure now. Then, I was wrong. There was no *talk*, then. This time, there is gossip." He was looking over Hyde's shoulder as the lighted platform slipped away behind them, then he glanced at his watch. "I must get off – I am sure. Mr. Hyde, I am sure this time!"

"OK, OK."

"Gossip, that is all I bring. You know that. You knew that when you – *found* me."

"Saved your bloody neck, sport – don't forget that."

Vassiliev blushed with dislike. "I do not forget." The train was slowing into Finchley Central. Vassiliev was eager to get up. "Where do we meet tonight, what time?"

Hyde hesitated, then: "The club. Eleven."

"Good – good. Yes, yes, I will be there –" The train had stopped, the doors had slid back. Hyde, shifting his weight, moved his feet and Vassiliev brushed past him, hopping out of the carriage. He immediately lit a cigarette, but Hyde, looking quickly up and down the carriage and the platform, did not consider it a signal. Then Vassiliev hurried into a patch of windy sunlight towards the southbound platform.

Hyde watched him disappear, then settled back in his seat, putting

46

his feet up again. The old man still smelt of mothballs. He closed his eyes. The smell of relatives from England coming out to Wollongong, bringing clothes they hadn't worn for a long time, uncertain of the Australian climate. Big bosoms – Auntie Vi, Auntie Maud, Auntie Ethel – covered by cardigans that smelt of mothballs. He with bare feet and shorts, like an urchin or a school-boy marooned in Australia. Mothballs. And the voices through his bedroom wall, conveying the magic of England, the rain and snow, the television.

Woodside Park. He bolted upright, eyes wide. His spine was cold. The childhood memories, evoked like a cloud of masking ink, faltered and retreated. He was being played. They would be one step behind, or alongside, every moment of the journey.

Aubrey had not enjoyed Ethan Clark's narrative. It was too easy, and perhaps correct, to regard it as tales out of school. He had lunched with the American, as a protégé of various senior CIA officers of long acquaintance, when Clark had first arrived in London the previous week. At numerous points, he had wanted to protest, request Clark to desist, even to leave. Gradually, however, he had become intrigued, then alarmed.

Clark described the ''Delta''-class submarine in the Tanafjord, then his voice faltered and he fell silent. Aubrey, his face gilded by weak sunshine from his office window, sat with his eyes closed and in silence. On an inward screen, he could see Quin's face, and knew that his mind had forged some obscure yet inescapable link between the man and his invention. A link of mutual danger?

"What did Giles Pyott say?" he asked at last.

"He didn't listen –"

"What did he *say*?"

Clark choked back his anger. "He said," he began slowly, "that it was none of my damn business and that everyone, including my own Navy Department, agreed with sending *Proteus* in."

"I can hear him saying it, though not quite in those words," Aubrey remarked acidly. "Everyone agrees, through to Brussels?"

"Yes."

Aubrey sat bolt upright. He appeared unconvinced, even unconcerned, then he said, "You've told me about the Russian submarine. Tell me about 'Chessboard'. That *is* important?"

"It is. 'Chessboard' could close the Barents to us unless we map it."

"And 'Leopard'. That is of inestimable value, you assess?"

"While it's unique and while the Russians don't have it, yes."

"I agree. But, what if, as we discussed the other day, Quin, its developer, is with the Russians?"

"Then the sooner we map 'Chessboard', and use 'Leopard' for

47

whatever else we want to know before the Russians develop it themselves, the better."

"Then I must tell you, Ethan, that it appears that Quin may not be with the Russians after all. How would that affect your thinking?"

Clark was silent with surprise at first, then with concentration. Clouds played shadow-games across Aubrey's carpet, across the man's head. Then he said. "It makes all the difference."

"You do believe this distress signal is genuine?"

"It – seems to be."

"I see. We know the Russians know about 'Leopard'. They must have had someone inside Plessey at some time. They were interested in acquiring Quin's services on a permanent basis. They still are. Perhaps they would like 'Leopard' instead?"

"You can't be serious?"

"I am merely speculating. Would you say that *Proteus* might be endangered by her new orders?"

"It's closer to the Soviet Union."

"Is that why you are so disturbed by all of this?" Aubrey snapped. "Or is it because you don't like Giles Pyott or the people at the Admiralty?" Aubrey's face was fierce, even contemptuous.

"Look, I came to you in good faith –"

"You came to me to moan about your lot!"

"The hell with you, Mr. Aubrey!" Clark made as if to rise.

"Sit down, Ethan!" Aubrey had turned to his desk again. His hands were calm and unmoving as they rested on its edge. "Sit down."

"Sorry –"

"Not at all. You came to me because you do feel *Proteus* might be endangered by her new mission. I did not like her sailing orders in the first place. I wanted her kept at sea undergoing trials, or in safe harbour, until the matter of Quin was resolved. I wished 'Leopard' removed from *Proteus* until such time as Quin was either recovered or known to be lost to us. I was ignored – overruled. It really isn't my field, you know." Aubrey smiled. "The trouble is, MoD is occasionally – and this is one of those occasions – filled with a few too many clots for my liking or reassurance. Giles Pyott is a clever, experienced soldier. He is also a Cavalier rather than a Roundhead. I have always seen myself in the New Model Army rather than Prince Rupert's cavalry. It always seemed much more sensibly organised, and much safer –" Clark, invited to return Aubrey's dazzling, self-deprecatory smile, did so. Apparently, he had been tested, and passed. He bore Aubrey no resentment. "My problem is that I find it hard to distinguish between death rays emitting purple light and anti-sonar systems and sonar carpets laid in the Barents Sea. However, we must turn our hand to the work that presents itself." He studied Clark. "We have one extant 'Leopard' system, in one British submarine, engaged upon a task of singular importance. We have one missing scientist. Until the one stray lamb is returned to the fold, I suggest we don't let the other one loose. Don't you?"

"What can you do?"

"I wonder. I would like to stop *Proteus* – I would like to find Quin. Ethan, I trust your judgment. I trust those intuitions that a man like Pyott would not countenance. You have worked in intelligence, he has not. We are all chronically suspicious, perhaps paranoid. However, you and I and the others like us are all we have. Perhaps all 'Leopard' has. Hm. Go back to the Admiralty, apologise to Giles Pyott – yes, please – and then keep your eyes and ears open. Ring me tonight –"

The intercom's buzz interrupted him. His secretary announced the arrival of some sandwiches and the imminence of a pot of coffee. Aubrey ordered her in. Before the door opened, Clark said swiftly, "What can you do?"

"I don't know, Ethan. Unfortunately, I shall have to do something, or else I shall begin sleeping badly at night. Ah, coffee and sandwiches – splendid!"

"We've got her."

"When?" Dolohov asked as Sergei closed the door of the Ops. Room behind him.

"Only minutes ago. The satellite's had terrible trouble with the cloud cover –"

"Show me. Admiral –" Dolohov nodded to the Ops. Room commander, then almost snatched the folded chart overlain with its sheet of developed infra-red film. Poor, pale smudges, like smeared rust or very old blood.

"The pattern's changed, as you can see." Sergei was leaning over Dolohov's shoulder. His finger tapped the sheet over the chart. "This was her three hours ago – same intermittent smudges, her mapping course, enough for us to tell she was still following the same search pattern. Then here we think there was another trace –" The smear was almost invisible. Dolohov did not move the chart closer to his face. "Then nothing for two hours, then this – then another fifty-four minutes before we got this." It was like the last ember of a dying fire. It was out of the random yet sequential pattern, and it had moved south and east of the other smears.

"You're certain?" Dolohov was looking at the rear admiral.

"We've used sonar in that area, and we got nothing. If it is a submarine, then it is the British ship."

"Excellent! It works, how well it works, mm?"

49

"Too well."

"Come, Admiral – no sour grapes. You have a computer prediction on speed and course?"

"We have one, based on the last three traces. We need at least two more to be at all accurate."

"Show me, man, show me!"

One of the rear admiral's aides scuttled into the control room. Dolohov leaned over the rail of the gantry. As he watched, the rear admiral joined him. Then a curving line appeared on the projection below, from a position far out in the Barents Sea, making south and east towards the Tanafjord. It rendezvoused with the imaginary Soviet submarine trapped in the fjord.

"In excess of thirty hours," the rear admiral murmured, "and no longer than thirty-six. That's the best we can do without another infra-red fix from the satellite. For the moment, she's disappeared again. Possibly cloud again."

"Good man," Dolohov said incongruously. He gripped the rear admiral's shoulder. The man was considerably younger than himself, bespectacled and clerkish. A computer expert, perhaps, an academic; scientist rather than sailor. Nevertheless, at that moment Dolohov felt an unaccustomed affinity with the man. "Good man." He turned to Sergei. "Call Leningrad. Whether they're at the Grechko Academy or the Frunze Naval School, I want Ardenyev and his team informed at once. They will depart for Murmansk immediately."

"Yes, sir."

Dolohov turned back to the rear admiral. "Keep up the good work. If the Red Banner Special Underwater Operations Unit does its job as well as you are doing yours, then nothing can go wrong!" He laughed throatily. "Excellent, excellent! I don't care what success the KGB has now in finding the man Quin – we will be able to present Moscow with Quin's toy. The man himself will have no value, and *we* shall enjoy the sunshine. Excellent, excellent!" His continued laughter caused one of the map table operators to look up.

The strip club was a short walk from Oxford Street, hunched in a narrow side street on the edge of Soho, as if aspiring to membership of that district, or recently expelled from it. Hyde had used it as a meeting place with Vassiliev because clubs of its type attracted the diplomats and officials of East European embassies, especially early on in their tours of duty, and even if Vassiliev had been under surveillance by his own people, such visits would have been regarded as misdemeanours rather than as suspicious or dangerous.

Hyde glanced at the membership ledger, having bribed the doorman. One or two new members that evening, but it told him nothing.

50

They might be Vassiliev's friends, or football fans or businessmen staying overnight in London. Vassiliev's friends would have ensured their membership sometime earlier, if this was an entrapment exercise. Hyde did not consider it was. They wanted him running, moving with apparent freedom. He went down the steps beneath a dim green under-sea light, the mingled odour of sweat, smoke and tawdriness coming up to meet him. The door opened to admit him – he had heard the buzzer sound from the doorman's cubicle as he began his descent.

Disco music thumped against his ears, flat, enervating, unmemorable. Strobe lights played over the heads of the audience. The tiny stage was empty, but there was a narrow bed lit by a silvery, ghostly light at the back of it. Hyde remained by the door. The large man with cropped hair wearing an out-of-style dinner jacket loomed at his shoulder. Hyde suspected he knew his profession and did not confuse him with the Vice Squad or CID. At worst, he would assume him to be Security rather than Intelligence. It did not matter. Rather, it legitimized the club, provided a governmental patron.

There were only a small number of people waiting for the next bout on the stage. Vassiliev – he saw as his eyes accustomed themselves to the peculiar, winking gloom – was in a corner, near the stage, mournfully staring into a glass. There seemed no one who had noticed, or become concerned at, his entrance. He threaded his way between the tables with their grubby cloths and expensive drinks towards Vassiliev. The Russian seemed relieved to see him. If there were other emotions, conflicting ones, then the strobe flicker hid them. Hyde settled in a chair which faced the door, and immediately a waiter appeared at his side. No girls on the floor of the club, no hostesses. A curious puritanism pervaded the place. Untouchable, flaunting, indescribably crude, silicon-enhanced, the women came and went on the stage, separate and inviolable.

Near them, the pianist resumed his seat. The drummer rolled softly, as if communicating with his drums. A bass player leaned tiredly over the neck and shoulders of his instrument. All of them appeared to be awaiting some summons to Ronnie's in Frith Street, two blocks away. Most of the girls stripped to records, anyway. Hyde ordered a beer. It came in a half-pint glass, and there was no change from his pound note. He clicked his tongue and winked at the waiter.

Hyde sipped at his drink. The trio drew attention to the stage with a peremptory call to attention that echoed Oscar Peterson, then slipped into the strait-jacket of "I'm forever blowing bubbles" as a bath was wheeled on.

"Oh, Christ – bath night again," Hyde murmured. "Ivy the Terrible." The subdued chatter of the audience tailed off into a silence that was weary rather than expectant. "Well, Dmitri?"

Vassiliev leaned towards him, eyes flicking over Hyde's shoulder towards the stage, as the pianist imitated a fanfare. Hyde could never decide whether Vassiliev's interest in the girls was genuinely naive and crude, or merely a badge of his manhood, designed to be noticed by those in his company. The KGB regarded homosexuals in only one light – as victims; malleable, male prostitutes. If Vassiliev had any hidden proclivities towards men, then he was wise to hide them.

"You were wrong," he said.

It was the one statement Hyde had not expected to hear. It generated a mass of complex doubts, questions and fears in an instant. The woman on stage was young, breasts extended to unnatural size by injection and implant, face expressionless beneath the make-up. See-through negligée, towel and loofah, bar of soap. The trio vamped the only expectancy in the now darkened room. Hyde watched the stage, picking his way towards the appropriate degree of innocent surprise. "Dmitri, what do you mean I was wrong?"

"They *have* got Quin. They have him, but they want the girl." Vassiliev's sweat gave off the pungency of the body rub he used. It clashed with his after shave, with the girl's scent, the omnipresent cigarette smoke.

"I'm not wrong," Hyde began, but Vassiliev was already nodding eagerly. Hyde felt cold.

"Yes. Look, I risked everything this afternoon. There was no more gossip. I looked in the travel ledger. I went back and checked on the people who came in. They left with a third man – the next day. They flew to Paris in a light aircraft. I have the address, the booking. Three passengers –" He reached into his pocket, but Hyde grabbed his hand – it quivered in his grip, which was slippery against Vassiliev's skin, informing Hyde that his nerves were taking him over. The girl was testing the supposed temperature of the water in the bath, letting the negligée fall open almost to the crutch. None of the audience was watching their corner of the room.

"Three? Three? What proof's that? I don't believe you, Dmitri. I don't think you know," Hyde hissed at the Russian, still gripping the man's hand near his chest. The girl had stepped – with something less than elegance – over the side of the bath. Her negligée was drooping from one shoulder, tented by one enormous breast.

"You must believe me, you must!"

"I don't, Dmitri. Now, what bloody game are you playing?" The girl was obviously going to bath with tassels on her nipples. She slid down into the supposed water. Then Vassiliev's eyes began moving, darting round the room. Hyde forced himself not to turn round. It did not mean there was someone in the room, only that there were others, either nearby or simply giving orders. Hyde gripped his thigh with his free hand, forcing the calm of angered puzzlement into his frame and face and voice. "What bloody game are you playing, mate?" The girl had divested herself of the negligée, but not the tassels. She was stroking herself with the loofah.

"No game, Mr. Hyde, no game!" Vassiliev was leaning towards him like a lover in the hot darkness, but he could not keep his eyes on Hyde's face. Escape, help, answers. He repeated the formula they had taught him. "Three men left in that plane for Paris. Yes, they want the girl, but they have Quin in Moscow – I'm certain of it."

"You don't know who the third man was. It couldn't have been Quin –" Hyde found himself engaged in an attempt to justify the suspicions he had voiced to Aubrey; as if he believed Vassiliev. The girl was on the point of engaging in intercourse with the loofah. Soon she would be dropping the soap. "No," he said, "you're lying, Dmitri. Why should they want you to lie?"

"They? What do you mean?" Too innocent.

"You weren't lying or mistaken at lunchtime. You *knew*, then. Now, you're working for them. Did they ask you how much you told me? Did they?" Hyde's face was close to Vassiliev. He could smell the man's last meal on his breath, and the brandy after dinner. Too much brandy – no, they wouldn't have allowed him more than one or two. "They knew about you all the time, but they didn't let on. Not until they realised you must have told me more than was good for me." He was shaking Vassiliev's hand, in anger and in community. The girl had dropped the soap, which did not slide across the stage. Her enormous breasts were hung over the side of the bath as she attempted to retrieve it. The trio was playing palm court music. The prissy, virginal sweetness of it assailed Hyde. "You were doing all right until you told me you thought they didn't have Quin. And you *know* it!"

"I – must go," Vassiliev said. Now the soap was back in the bath, but lost again. The girl was looking for it on her hands and knees. Snake-charmer music, and she rose to her feet, backside to the audience, buttocks proffered, swaying.

"You're going nowhere. Where are they?"

"Not here, not here!"

"You're coming in, Dmitri."

"No!"

"You have to. We'll take care of you. I can't behave as if I believe you. You're the one in danger now." Vassiliev had thought of it, but had ignored it. He shook his head, as if the idea was only a pain that would move, dissipate. The girl had the loofah again, standing up now, in profile to the room. The loofah was being energetically applied. "Come on," Hyde added.

"No! I can't leave with you, I can't!"

53

"Why not?"

"I can't!" He was pleading now. They were outside. If he emerged with Hyde, they would know Hyde had not swallowed the tale. The almost religious silence of the room was broken by hoarse cries of encouragement, underscored with what seemed like a communal giggle. The girl's body acknowledged the response to her performance.

"You can!" The gun, the gun – he'd left it at his flat, held it in his hand, almost amused, for a moment before stuffing it under a pile of shirts in a drawer. The gun –

"No, no, no –" Vassiliev was shaking his head vehemently.

"It's your only chance. Come on, the back way." Hyde got up, stood over the Russian, willing him to his feet. Vassiliev rose, and they shuffled through the tables towards the toilets. The door into the concrete, ill-lit corridor sighed shut behind them.

Vassiliev immediately turned to him. "No," he said.

"They concocted this story, right?" Vassiliev nodded, nerveless, directionless now. "Why?"

"I don't know. They told me they had known, that they had fed you the information about Quin through me, deliberately. Then yesterday happened, and while they were deciding what to do about me, we talked. I – I told them everything." A sense of shame, as sharp as a physical pain, crossed his features.

"It's all right, it's all right – was there anyone in the club?" Vassiliev shook his head. There was applause on the other side of the door. "Come on."

Hyde half-pushed Vassiliev towards the emergency exit beyond the toilet. He heaved at the bar, remembered letting in friends by similar doors in Wollongong cinemas just before the start of the main feature, then the door swung open. The windy night cried in the lightless alley. He paused momentarily, and looked at Vassiliev. Then he nodded.

They went through the door almost together, but even so the man with the gun must have been able to distinguish between them. Vassiliev cried out – Hyde hardly heard the brief plopping sound of the silenced gun before the Russian's murmured cry – then he slumped against Hyde, dragging at his clothes, smearing the front of the Australian's shirt with something dark and sticky. Then he fell back, for a moment his face green from the exit sign's light, then all of him was simply a barely distinguishable bundle of clothes on the other side of the alley. Hyde waited for the noise of footsteps above the wind's dry call, or the sound of another stone-into-water plop that would be the last sound he would ever hear.

THREE:

Intruder

The gilded French clock on the marble mantelpiece chimed twelve, a bright, pinging, musical sound. Aubrey paused in his narrative, and he and Sir Richard Cunningham, Director of the Secret Intelligence Service, listened to the sound, watching the blue-numeralled face of the clock. When the chimes had ended, Aubrey stared into his brandy balloon, aware of how out of place his employment of technological and military jargon seemed here, in the study of Cunningham's flat in Eaton Place. Books and paintings – Cunningham had a small Braque and two Picasso etchings in that room – heavy furniture, civilization. A conspiracy to belie the reality of detection systems, anti-sonar, satellites and distress signals in broken codes. Aubrey, for a moment, wished devoutly for a double agent, for the intimacies of a debriefing or an interrogation, for the clear boundary between SIS and MoD. Clark had pushed him across that border.

Cunningham had hardly spoken throughout Aubrey's recital of events, suspicions, fears. He had assiduously filled and refilled Aubrey's glass and his own, refrained from smoking a cigar, and listened, his half-closed eyes regarding his slippered feet crossed at the ankles. The book he had been reading when Lady Cunningham had shown in Aubrey lay on the occasional table at the side of his chair, the Bach to which he had been listening lay still on the turntable. His half-glasses rested on the end of his patrician nose, and his lips were set in a firm, expressionless line. Aubrey felt extremely reluctant to continue.

Then Cunningham spoke. "What, exactly, do you wish to do, Kenneth?"

"Go in there – assess the situation for myself."

"I see. You know how MoD regards us. You know how the navy regards itself. It's tricky. You've no just cause or impediment, after all."

"I realise that, Richard. However, there is a mutuality of interest that might be stressed. Quin –"

"Ah, yes. MoD will tell us that he is our proper concern, one of Her Majesty's submarines more properly their sphere of authority. They will not take kindly to you suggesting they should reverse their decision. Nor will Brussels, nor will Washington. Sure you're not simply acting the old warhorse smelling the battle afar off?"

Aubrey smiled. "I don't think so."

"Mm. Neither do I. Devilish tricky, though. I can quite well see the importance of this anti-sonar system, and of Quin, and of keeping both out of Soviet hands. But we are not the experts, we are not the military. *They* don't seem to believe there is any risk – this man Clark, the American. Trust him?"

"And his judgment."

"Mm. Knew you did." Cunningham spread his hands, wafting them in the air. "I just don't know –"

The telephone rang. Cunningham got up heavily and crossed to it. He listened, then gestured with the receiver towards Aubrey. His face was impassive.

"Yes?" It was Hyde. Aubrey listened to the voice at the other end of the line, his eyes watching Cunningham, deep in thought in his chair.

". . . they obviously didn't want the hassle of killing me – just Vassiliev out of the way. They must have known I would try to take him in if I got suspicious . . ."

"You're all right?" Cunningham looked up at the note of concern in Aubrey's voice.

"Unhurt. I said. What now?"

"You'll see Mrs. Quin tomorrow, and take a trip to the girl's college. Someone must be able at least to *guess* where she might be."

"If you say so –"

"Tomorrow, you will go armed. Good night to you, Hyde."

As Aubrey put down the receiver, Cunningham stared at him. "What is it?"

"Hyde. His contact at the Soviet embassy has just been expertly dispatched in a dark alley. Before he was eliminated, Hyde had discovered that the news of Quin's removal had been deliberately leaked, and yesterday's events in Sutton Coldfield were being hidden behind a smokescreen. The KGB were onto the poor blighter, tried to turn him, realized they'd failed, and shot him."

"Our man is all right?" Aubrey nodded. "They don't have Quin, then. I think we can be certain of it now. There is still no connection between these events and the submarine."

"I agree. Could we not argue a suspension of operations employing 'Leopard' until the Quin matter is settled?"

"We might. The first thing, I suppose, is to get you inside this 'Chessboard' matter. Once there, it will be up to you. *You* will have to find the means to persuade the minister to ask Cabinet to postpone this little adventure. I suggest you go in there for a briefing on this

'Leopard' business, sniff around, and weigh the worth of what's being done. If you can convince me, then we'll go to the minister together, and he can take it from there, if he agrees with us. Satisfied?"

Aubrey pursed his lips, studied his glass, and then nodded. "Yes, Richard. That will do nicely. I'll make an appointment for tomorrow – perhaps with Giles Pyott." His face darkened. "I'm too old for hunches and intuitions. But Clark is a clear-sighted, intelligent individual with a genuine talent for our work. I'm sorry to say it, but I think there is cause for concern, and I'm *sure* we should recall *Proteus* until we find Quin."

"Make certain, Kenneth. There are a great many sensitive corns in MoD. Tread softly."

"Mrs. Quin, you must have some idea where we can find him! I just don't believe you can't help me."

"Have you ever been divorced, or separated?"

"No."

"Your parents?"

"No."

"What happened to some of the girls you've known? Where are they now – just one of them? Tell me what she did yesterday."

"It isn't the same."

"It is, Mr. Hyde, believe me, it is. Tricia's coming here was one of her impulses. She spent her childhood making believe that my husband and I were happy when we weren't, and the last three years trying to put Humpty-Dumpty back together again." Mrs. Quin sighed, and her brow knitted into deep, thread-like lines. "I'm sorry for her – sorry for myself, too."

Hyde sat back in the chair she had shown him to when she allowed him into the lounge. Occasional traffic outside, her day off from the antique shop, the Panda car conspicuous across the street. Trees still leafless, bending and moving with the wind. The gin-hour for lonely or bored suburban housewives. She had given him tea, and seemed not to resent his behaviour of two days before.

"Jesus, Mrs. Quin, it's a bloody mess," he sighed, rubbing his hands through his hair. "Your daughter is in real danger – all right, you already know that, I'm sorry to remind you. Nevertheless, she is. So's your husband. She's with him, or still on her way back to him. The – the other people interested in your husband know that. They know we're interested –"

"Why did he have to involve her?" the woman suddenly cried, her voice and expression full of blame, even contempt. "No, that's not fair, I suppose. She involved herself. I know Tricia."

"I don't. Tell me about her."

"You mean you don't already know?" There was an arch, mocking sharp little smile, a glimpse of white teeth. Today, the hair was firmly lacquered in place, the clothes well chosen, the whole being groomed. "About the pop groups, the drugs –"

"Drugs? Soft or hard?"

"The sort you can smoke, I believe."

"Soft. Occasionally?" Mrs. Quin nodded. "OK – rock bands?"

"Not in your files?" The easy contempt. She had forgotten her alliance with the uniformed inspector, her concern for young Sugden. Neighbours had talked, asked questions, and the police were an embarrassment, a minor disgrace.

"Yes – some references. Some time ago, though?"

"She – the phrase is *slept around*, I believe. With them."

"A groupie?"

"I believe so. Am I entirely stupid to blame her college, and the kind of people they allow into them, and to teach in them, these days?" She evidently had little interest in his opinion.

"Probably," he said. "It's your privilege."

"It ended, anyway. But she never seemed to settle afterwards."

"Who – which group?"

"I don't know any of their names. I believe they were famous."

"Did she travel with them?" A nod. "When?"

"Two summers ago – all over the country, even to the Continent. And an open air festival."

"But you don't know their names?"

"Had I ever known them, I would have forced myself to forget."

"I see. Would her friends in college know anything about all this?"

"I'm sure they would have been regaled with the sordid details."

"Perhaps I should talk to them."

"It's past now – can't you leave it?" A naked plea, the face smoothed young by concern, softened.

Hyde stood up. "If there's anything, anything at all, ring this number. A man called Aubrey. You'd like him." Hyde grinned humourlessly.

"Why didn't he come himself?" The tone knife-like.

"He's too important. Thank you, Mrs. Quin." As they reached the door, he turned to her and added, "I'll get to her first, if I can. You just pray a little, mm?"

"Stop engines!"

The Soviet submarine was back. It had crossed their bows an hour earlier, fifty fathoms above them, moving away to starboard. Lloyd had ordered silent running, the engines moving them very slowly

58

ahead, because the computer identification had been of a "Victor-II"-class attack submarine, nuclear-powered and a hunter-killer. A shark had met another shark. Then the "Victor-II" had altered course again, possibly picking up faint traces of heat emission or prop noise. And she had begun looking, knowing that there was something to find.

The *Proteus* hummed with tension in the new, complete silence. Electronics murmured, those aft sonars required to keep track of the Soviet submarine, someone cleared his throat softly; Lloyd even heard the movement of Carr's sleeve across his chart as he updated the Contact Evaluation Plot at his chart table. The whisper of the hydroplane control wheels as the planesmen worked continuously to keep *Proteus* level and unmoving, constantly balancing the submarine's own attempts to alter position and depth. A juggling act. Easier on the bottom, but they weren't on the bottom.

Lloyd crossed to Thurston, who was standing behind the sonar operator monitoring the approach of the "Victor-II" and whose screen displayed the snail-trail of light that revealed the position of the Russian vessel. Below the screen, red numerals supplied the read-out of bearing and distance. The "Victor-II" was closing.

Submarines had been lost before, Lloyd reminded himself involuntarily. There was no fear and no courage, either. Vessels encountering each other in the dark, crowded sea. Collision or avoidance, attack or retreat. The "Victor-II" was following their scent – heat, prop-wash, hull-noise, the tiny skin-flakings of their passage which "Leopard" could not completely neutralise. The twin hulls that enclosed them like plasterboard walls waited to transmit any sound they might make. Closer. Bearing unaltered. Speed a cautious, stalking twelve-point-seven knots. Time to contact, five minutes.

Lloyd mouthed silently at Thurston, who nodded. The first lieutenant framed his lips to reply in the slightest whisper, after swallowing hard.

"If she doesn't find us, she might just miss us."

"By much?"

"Not much." Lloyd's hand was on the back of the sonar operator's chair. Some transmitted electricity from his captain made the rating twitch. Lloyd moved his hand. He turned to watch the two planesmen, juggling the control wheels like nervous car drivers. As if not in control of the vehicle. *Proteus* remained still, lying in the dark, waiting. Other trails of light – not new, but suddenly noticed and rendered significant by heightened nerves – on the sonar screen. Four other submarines, two destroyers and what might be the carrier *Kiev*, flagship of the Northern Fleet. She was too distant for a positive identification, and Lloyd had tended to discount her appearance in the Barents Sea. This early in the season, she was normally still refitting in Murmansk. And the "Victor-II", brighter than all of them. Contact time, four minutes fifty. Lloyd felt, despite himself, that his hands were beginning to perspire. He opened them. The control room seemed hotter. Illusion.

Bearing unaltered. Speed constant. Cancel. New red numerals appeared on the read-out panel. Speed ten knots. The "Victor-II" was slowing. Contact time three minutes twenty-eight, seven, six –

The sonar operator turned to Lloyd, his face puzzled. The "Victor-II" was stopping, contact time and distance read-outs slowing down, then settling. Stopped. Contact time two minutes thirty-one frozen. The small, cramped space of the control room hot. Thurston was perspiring, a line of beads along his hairline. Lloyd felt the sweat dampening his shirt, running chilly down his sides. The sonar operator's hair cream, a sickly smell of which he was suddenly aware. Stomach light, disturbed.

Stopped. A third of a mile away. Six hundred yards. Close enough for temperature sensors. The movement of bare forearms in the corner of his vision as the planesmen juggled the *Proteus* to stillness. The auto-suggested hum of electronics, like the buzzing of an insect seemed very difficult to discount. The "Victor II" digesting the scraps of information, her captain waiting for an answer from his computer. *Is there an enemy submarine close to us?*

Red numerals flicking off. A bare, dark green panel beneath the sonar screen with its bright blip of light. Then new numbers. Speed four knots, five, six. Contact time two minutes nineteen, eighteen, seventeen, fifteen, twelve, seven – one minute fifty-nine. Bearing unchanged.

Lloyd waited. He could hardly bear to see the "Victor-II" as it moved through the darkness towards them. One minute twenty. Speed ten knots. Distance two hundred yards, a little more, the little more eaten up even as he thought it. Eleven knots, bearing unchanged; as if they knew where *Proteus* was.

Then they listened. Two steam turbines driven by a pressurized water reactor. They would hear them, even though they were little more than idling at eleven knots.

Faces turned to the ceiling. Always that, Lloyd observed. A familiarity of orientation brought with them onto the submarine. It could be below, alongside, anywhere.

The churn of the screws. A slight, almost inaudible thrumming in their own hull. Faces tightening, the sense of fragility obvious. Louder. The illusion of a rising tremor in the eggshell of the hull. Hands sensing it where they rested damply against any part of the hull, any instrument – the planesmen juggling more violently now as the distressed water outside the hull assaulted the *Proteus* – feet feeling it, muscle-spasms in the calves. Louder.

Loudest, going on for what seemed like minutes, the planesmen failing to stop the submarine's bow from dropping, the whole vessel slipping forward into the beginnings of a dive, then arresting the movement, bringing the vessel back to stillness. Retreating noise and vibration. All around them the noise and motion had been, but Lloyd was certain the Soviet submarine had passed below them, slightly to port.

Then it was gone. Thurston mopped his brow enthusiastically, and grinned shakily at Lloyd.

"Close," he murmured.

"Too close." Then the idea came to him, and he voiced it before he considered its effect. "I think she was expecting us – I mean us, this boat and its anti-sonar."

"What?"

Lloyd looked down at the sonar operator, then at the others in the control room. He did not want to explain, not now. The idea, half-formed, frightened him, and he wanted to ignore it.

Thurston waited for his explanation, and Lloyd said, lamely, "That Russian has been following a very poor trail for an hour. As if he knew we were here."

"You're imagining it, skipper."

"As if he knew he was looking for a submarine that wouldn't show up on his sonar," Lloyd added.

"The evidence is in front of you, man. It may not be conclusive, but there is evidence there to suggest *Grishka* encountered the British submarine with its anti-sonar system working. Surely?"

"I will admit that not every trace of heat emission can be explained by temperature differences in the sea – perhaps there are identifiable traces of prop-wash and turbine activity, perhaps the faint gas traces help us –" The rear admiral looked round at his subordinates, then shrugged. "We will pinpoint the British submarine at the position signalled by the *Grishka* and await any satellite confirmation there might be."

"Excellent. She is on course. ETA?"

"On the basis of our supposition, no more than eighteen hours."

Dolohov was about to reply when the door to the control room opened, and a man in civilian clothes – very Western, Dolohov noticed, a sweater, windcheater and corduroy trousers – stood in the doorway. The man came forward into the light, and Dolohov saw that he was grinning. His hair was blown awry. Dolohov returned the smile, and waved away the junior officer accompanying the man.

"Valery – Valery, my boy!" he announced, ignoring the others in the room, embracing the newcomer, kissing him on both cheeks, a greeting that was returned by the younger man.

"Admiral – sir," the younger man acknowledged when held at arm's length by Dolohov. The rear admiral seemed surprised to discover that the civilian, in addition to having a permit of entry to his operations room, was some species of naval officer. The haircut, the acknowledgement of rank. Yet almost like a son to the admiral. A little spurt of envy flared in the rear admiral. This man was not to be treated like a schoolboy slow at his sums, apparently.

"You've come straight here?" Dolohov, even as he asked, was already drawing the younger man towards the window of the control room, already extending his free arm to direct the other's gaze. He was revealing a prized object of desire. The rear admiral bowed frostily as he was casually introduced, resenting the intimacy that had invaded his clinical, sterile control room. "Captain Valery Ardenyev, commanding the Red Banner Special Underwater Operations Unit," Dolohov explained with evident pride, almost with a proprietorial, parental tone, then ignored the rear admiral. "Down there," he said to Ardenyev. "We've marked her with a green light. A colour all to herself."

"You're sure, sir?"

"We think so. She's on course, eighteen hours away from the fjord."

Ardenyev stood looking down at the map table for some time. Dolohov, like a senior priest, allowed him silence and lack of interruption to his meditations, even though there was an impatience about his flinty features that made him appear both older, and much younger.

"The weather's worsening, sir," Ardenyev said finally. "But of course you know that." Ardenyev grinned as he brushed his hair back into place.

"It isn't that bad, Valery," Dolohov replied with a touch of acid.

"Not yet. I'll have to study the reports, and the predictions."

"You have doubts?"

"Not yet, sir. Not yet."

"We've eighteen hours, Valery."

"We have to transfer to the salvage vessel long before that, sir. By helicopter."

Dolohov gripped his arm. "Valery – it will be all right." He was instructing Ardenyev, even the weather. Commanding them both. "It will be. We'll have her." He turned to Sergei, his aide, whose position within the small group of the rear admiral's team seemed an obscure insubordination to Dolohov. "Sergei, get me an up-to-the-minute weather report for our area of interest. And get me *all* the met. predictions for the next twenty-four hours – *now*, Sergei." Then Dolohov turned back to Ardenyev as to a child he had indulged, and who now must become obedient. "It must be done, Valery. It must be done."

"If it's possible, sir, it will be. I promise you that."

The rear admiral, observing the dialogue, conceived the idea that Ardenyev was not without calculation and guile. Dolohov responded by grabbing the younger man's arm, and pressing it with gratitude and what appeared to be affection. The rear admiral recalled gossip concerning the way in which Ardenyev's career had been jealously promoted by the admiral. Some connection with Ardenyev's father, even grandfather, he had heard. For his own part, the rear admiral had risen by loyalty to the Party, and distrusted this Soviet version of what the British called the "old boy network". And he distrusted young naval officers in civilian dress with easy manners and obvious self-confidence. Elitist adventurers.

The rear admiral withdrew to the other side of the control room, to await the updated satellite surveillance information. A small hope that Dolohov was precipitate, even mistaken, he nourished in his stomach like the warmth of a drink.

The college of education was a new one, built in the grounds of a Victorian magnate's former residence in the suburb of Edgbaston. The original house, having fallen into disrepair both before and after the compulsory purchase of the grounds, had disappeared. A tower block hall of residence stood on the site, bearing the same name as the grandiose house that one of Birmingham's Ozymandiases of trade or industry had erected to his own glorification. Two or three small, supposedly exclusive housing developments encroached on the perimeters of the college campus.

Hyde parked his car outside the tower block and sat for a moment considering his forthcoming interview with Tricia Quin's flatmate, Sara Morrison. Birmingham CID had talked to her the day the Quin girl appeared and disappeared, and had described her as unhelpful. Hyde had checked with the interviewing DC, who had amplified his observation by referring to the Morrison girl as a "Lefty cow, anti-police, good background – isn't it usually the case", and wished Hyde the best of luck with her. A moment of futility as dispiriting as weariness overcame Hyde, then he got out of the car and slammed the door.

The sky was overcast, sombre with rain. The downpour that it threatened was postponed only by the strong, gusty wind that swept paper and dust and old leaves across the grass and the concrete walks

63

around the hall of residence; hurried and chafed the few figures he could see. An overriding impression of concrete and glass and greyness, a modern factory complex. He hurried up the steps into the foyer of the tower block.

A porter, uniformed and officious, emerged from a cubicle, wiping his lips. Hyde showed him the CID warrant card which avoided explanations, and asked for Tricia Quin's flat. The porter, evidently unimpressed by the length of Hyde's hair and his casual dress, begrudgingly supplied the number, and the information that Sara Morrison was in the flat at that moment. He had seen her return from a lecture half-an-hour before. Hyde went up in the lift, unamused by the mock-intellectual graffiti that decorated its walls. He gathered, however, that punk rock had achieved the status both of an art form and a political weapon.

A long corridor, blank, veneered doors. The carpet was marked and already worn, the plaster on the walls evincing settlement cracks. He knocked on the door of 405.

The girl who opened the door wore her hair in tight curls. Her face was instantly suspicious rather than intrigued or helpful. A mouth that pulled down into a scowl almost naturally, it seemed. Sallow skin, no make-up, a creased blouse and uniform denims. Her feet were bare.

"Yes?" A middle-class, south-east accent, overlain with the drawl of the fashionable urban. "What d'you want?"

"Sara Morrison?" She nodded. "Could we have a word about Tricia Quin. I believe —" the warrant card was in his hand, his shoulder against the door as she tried to shut it. "I believe she shares this flat with you."

The girl resigned herself to not being able to close the door on him.

"Past tense," she said, her eyes bright with calculation.

"Really?"

"You're Australian."

"Too right." He grinned disarmingly, but the girl did not respond.

"In Birmingham?" she mocked. "An Australian pig, in Birmingham?"

"Could be. It's not only politics that travel long distances. May I come in?"

The girl shrugged and released the door. He opened it on an untidy, cramped room with two single beds against opposite walls. A window in the end wall overlooked the campus carpark. Clothes draped over a functional chair, books spread across a small, cheap desk. Posters on the wall – Mao, Lenin, Sex Pistols, a *Playboy* centrefold with a crudely drawn moustache and glasses and even white teeth blacked out, Castro, Margaret Thatcher used as a dartboard, a Two-Tone band.

64

"What do you want?" the girl demanded belligerently as he observed the door leading off, bathroom and toilet. "She isn't here, you know." Her accent wavered between the glassy superiority of her background and undoubted money, and the urban snarl she felt he deserved.

"I suppose not. Someone would have seen her. The porter for instance?"

"Beria, you mean?"

Hyde laughed. "May I sit down?" The girl swept her clothes off the single chair, and squatted on the edge of her bed, feet drawn up beneath her, signalling indifference. Hyde sat down. The girl studied him.

"A trendy pig."

"We try, darling – we try."

"You fail – or should I have said, try and condemn?" She parted her lips in a mirthless grin, flashing her cleverness in that precise visual signal.

"A hit, I do confess. Can we talk about your erstwhile girl-friend?"

"What is there to say? She isn't here. End of story."

"Not her story. You know she's been seen. Have you seen her?" The girl shook her head, her face betraying nothing. "Sure?"

"I told your thick mate from CID that I hadn't seen her. Don't you believe me?"

"Not if I asked you for the right time. What would I get – the time in Moscow, or Peking?"

"Cuba," Sara Morrison replied without expression.

Hyde looked up at the ennobled poster of Fidel Castro. "He's a bit out of style, isn't he? Even Arthur Scargill's heard of him."

The girl applauded ironically. "Very funny – oh, too witty for words."

"Blimey, thanks, darling," he replied in his broadest accent. "Now we've both tried on backgrounds we never came from." He leaned forward in his chair. Unexpectedly, the girl flinched. He said, "This isn't France or South America, darling. Or Nazi Germany or Kampuchea or the Soviet Union. I could have you down the station, true, but your Daddy would get you out by tea-time, I should think." The girl's face wrinkled into contempt, then smoothed to indifference again, as if she had revealed too much of herself. "Always too busy at the office, was he? Chased other women? Self-made man?"

"Fuck off." The obscenity came almost primly from her lips.

"In a minute. Look, Tricia Quin is in trouble – not with us, before you harangue me again, with some people who you might think you like, but wouldn't if you met them."

After a silence, the girl said, "National security bullshit, I presume."

"Sorry darling, it's the only excuse I have."

"Why can't you fucking well leave her alone!" the girl suddenly yelled at him, her face bright-red with rage. The mood was sudden, manic in its swing.

"I *want* to. She has to be protected."

"Crap."

"Not crap. Listen to me." The girl's hands were bunched into fists in her lap, or twitched open, as if gripping some imagined weapon. There was a violence of rage and guilt and outrage in her that found the body inadequate to express such depths of feeling. "I can't help the situation in which she finds herself. Blame her father, blame national security, blame the bloody arms race if you want to – but I'm the only chance she's got. People want her because they can get to her father through her. They won't mind what they do to her to discover her father's hiding place. And before you say it – yes, I want her father, too. But I don't want to harm him, and I want to help her."

His dismissal passed like a flicker caused by dust in her eyes. Politics in place, attitudes firmly fixed, cemented. She would not tell him. Hyde saw the weapon of threat present itself, and wanted to reject it.

"I don't know where she is – and I wouldn't tell you if I did."

"For Christ's sake, girlie!" Hyde exploded. "Some of the two hundred or so Soviet diplomats with the ill-fitting suits and the poor-diet boils are looking for your girl-friend right now! When they find her, it will be a little bit of slapping about, then the closed fist, then the bucket over the head and the baseball bats, then the cigarette-ends for all I know – they won't have time to talk to her politely, some bigger bastard will be breathing down their necks for results. Even if they wanted to be nice. Your friend could tell them she was a card-carrying member of the Party and they'd pull her fingernails out until she told them what they wanted to know." He was speaking quite calmly during the last sentence, but the girl's face was white with anger and with surprised fear. There was something unselfish as well as disbelieving about her.

"You really believe all that?" she said at last. Her composure, her closed-minded prejudices, had reasserted themselves. "Christ, the perfect functionary!"

"My God, but you're stupid –"

"Tricia's been frightened out of her mind – don't you realise that?" the girl shouted at him. "Before her father disappeared, she was depressed, moody, frightened. Then she left – just like that. She hadn't slept a wink the night before. Doesn't that make *any* impression on you?"

"Was she frightened when you saw her two days ago?"

"Fuck off, clever sod."

Both of them were breathing hard. Only the wind, moaning more loudly round the building, offered a larger perspective than the cramped hothouse of the small room. The girl's face was implacable.

Hyde stood up, then crossed swiftly to her, clamping his hand over her mouth, holding her wrists in his other hand. He pushed her flat on the bed, kneeling beside her.

"You know what's coming now, darling. You've imagined it, talked about it, often enough. You're Blair Peach, love – you're a Black in Detroit, you're Steve Biko. I'm untouchable, darling. It'll be an accident." He could feel spittle on his palm, and sweat, and her eyes were wide with terror. "Everything you've ever thought about the pigs is true. Now you're going to find out."

Then he released her, moved away, sat down. The girl wiped at her mouth, rubbed her wrists. When she found her voice, she coughed out his eternal damnation.

"Sorry," he said. "You would have told me. Your eyes were already regretting your earlier bravado." His voice was calm, casual, unemotional. "We both know that. Tricia would tell them even quicker, even though it was her father."

"For God's sake –" the girl began, but there seemed nothing she could add.

"Yes. You're right again. She came here, didn't she?"

"She bloody didn't!" He knew, with an empty feeling, that it was true. The girl appeared hurt and useless. She'd have helped – lied, hidden Tricia, given her money, taken on the pigs, anything. But Tricia Quin hadn't even asked. Hyde felt sorry. Useless energy and emotion slopped around in Sara Morrison, mere ballast for a pointless journey.

"I'm sorry about that. Tell me where she might be, then?" On an impulse, he added: "Her mother mentioned she hung out with a rock band a couple of summers ago – pot, groupie-ing, the whole naughty bag. Any news on that?"

"Those dinosaurs," the girl remarked, glancing up at the Two-Tone group posturing down at her.

"Them?" he asked, looking up. The girl laughed.

"You remember a band called Heat of the Day?"

"Yes. I liked them."

"You're old enough." The girl had slipped into another skin, represented by half of the posters on the wall, and by the cassette tapes on one of the shelves, next to a huge radio with twin speakers. Something an astronaut might have used to contact the earth from deep space. The girl was now a pop music aficionado, and he someone with parental tastes. Hyde had wondered which way the retreat into shock would take her. It looked more promising than other possible routes, but it would not last long. Eventually, she would be unable to disguise from herself the threat he represented.

"I thought they disbanded."

"They did. You don't read *Melody Maker* any more, obviously."

"Nor *Rolling Stone*. My age." He invited her to smile, but she did not respond. She did not look at him now, merely at her hands in her lap. She might have been drugged, or meditating.

"They're back together – on tour. I remember Tricia was interested."

"How did she get in with them, originally?"

"The lead singer, Jon Alletson, was in school with her brother – the one who emigrated to Canada."

"Would she have gone to them by any chance, would she still be in touch with them?"

Sara's face closed into a shrunken, cunning mask. "I wouldn't know," she said, and Hyde knew the conversation was at an end. In another minute, it would be police brutality, threats of legal action. He stood up. The girl flinched.

"Thanks," he said. "Take care."

He closed the door quietly behind him, hunger nibbling at his stomach, a vague excitement sharp in his chest. Rock supergroup? Friend of her brother? Perhaps the girl knew she was being chased round and round the garden, and had gone to earth where she would be welcomed and wouldn't be looked for, amid the electronic keyboards and yelling guitars and pounding drums, the hysteria and the noise and the cannabis and the young. In that thicket, she would recognise her enemies, from either side, with ease.

It might just be –

Tedium, anger, even anxiety, were all now conspiring to overpower caution. Aubrey felt within himself a surprising violence of reaction to his hour-long tour of the "Chessboard Counter" room and operation. The broaching of *Proteus*'s diversion to the Tanafjord proved the sticking point, broke the camel's back of his discretion. Perhaps, he reasoned with himself, it was the blasé, confident, aloof manner in which the monitoring action on the stricken Russian submarine was explained that so infuriated him. But images of Quin, with their attendant fears, and the pervasive odour of a possible trap, conspired to assist the wearing of his patience. Clark, too, seemed waiting for his cue; expecting Aubrey to make some decisive move, influence events.

And the smoothly running, almost mechanical individuals in the room; the obtrusive freemasonry of serving officers. The sterile hangar of the room; his own sense of himself regarded, at best, as the man from the Pru. He could no longer keep silence, or content himself with brief, accommodating smiles and innocuous questions. The excuse that he merely sought enlightenment regarding Quin's project became transparent in its flimsiness; insupportable. Even so, the vehemence evident to himself, and to Pyott and the others, in his voice when his temper finally broke through, surprised him.

"Giles, what do you hope to gain from this monitoring action?" he snapped. He waved his hand dismissively at the huge map-board.

"Our northern security is in question here, Kenneth," Pyott replied in suprise, his nostrils narrowed to slits, the tip of his nose whitened with suppressed anger at Aubrey's tone. "Surely you can see that?"

"It is a point of view."

"Kenneth, you are not an expert −"

"No, this distress call, now. You don't suspect its genuineness?"

"Good Lord, no."

"What about you, Captain Clark?"

"Not really. I just don't think the matter's important enough to risk 'Leopard'." He looked up at the cluster of lights on the board. They seemed to have one centre, where the wavering arrow of the light indicator being operated by Pyott demonstrated *Proteus*'s position.

"Ah. Now, my immediate reaction, employing my own peculiar expertise, would be to suspect the distress call. I would need proof that it was genuine."

"We've identified the submarine concerned," the commodore explained brusquely. "We have triple checked. I don't think the matter is in doubt." He looked to Pyott for support, and received it in an emphatic shake of the head.

Aubrey was intensely aware of the opposition of the two officers. They represented an opposite pole of interests. Also, they were in some way legitimized by their uniforms. Third Murderer again, he observed to himself.

"I see. It would still be my starting point."

"What would be the object of an elaborate deception, in this case?" Pyott drawled.

" 'Leopard.' "

"Good Lord, you're surely not serious −?"

"How would you react to the recall of *Proteus* until this chap Quin is found?"

"Utter nonsense!"

"The two matters haven't the slightest connection with one another Kenneth."

"Great idea."

"Ah. You would support such a move, Captain Clark?"

"I would." Pyott looked pained by a spasm of indigestion, the commodore appeared betrayed.

"I do really think it's dangerous, risking 'Leopard' in this way without having Quin safe and sound."

"You made that point weeks ago, Kenneth. Try another record."

"Giles, the KGB have started killing, such is their interest in Quin. Am *I* to rate his importance any lower – or that of his project?" Aubrey pointed up at the map, then indicated the rest of the room and its occupants. "Who else is looking into this distress call?"

"It's our show."

"Your work here is important, even if I consider it precipitate. But this present adventure – Giles, what can you possibly gain?"

Aubrey saw the answer in Pyott's eyes before the man spoke.

"Kenneth, I am at liberty to inform you – you, too, Clark – that this present adventure, as you term it, has a highest category security tag on it."

"For a distress call?"

"For *Proteus*'s mission," Pyott explained quietly and fiercely. Aubrey guessed at the nature of the mission, and was appalled. It was what he had suspected he might hear, if he needled Pyott sufficiently, and what he had wished devoutly not to hear. "The mission has been code-named –"

"You mean it's another, and extreme, *sea trial* for the 'Leopard' system, Giles?"

"Why, yes," Pyott admitted, somewhat deflated.

"What in hell –?"

"Excuse me, Captain Clark. Giles, you mean that approval has been given to sail *Proteus* almost into Soviet home waters, merely to prove the efficacy of the anti-sonar system?"

"That's it precisely."

"My God, Giles, it's lunacy. Playing games. You have put the system, the submarine, her crew, at risk, just to score extra marks in the examination. It is nonsense, and furthermore, dangerous nonsense!" He studied Pyott's face, which was colouring with anger, and then the commodore. An identical, undented confidence.

"What is *Proteus*'s ETA in the Tanafjord?"

Pyott smiled thinly. "I see no harm in telling you, Kenneth. Disregarding changes of course and speed, we estimate sixteen to eighteen hours. Some time early tomorrow morning, GMT."

"Giles, what intelligence do you have from the Norwegians?"

"They've backed off, fortunately."

"Aerial surveillance?"

"We have some confirmation – infra-red, naturally. We've more or less pinpointed the Russian boat."

"It *is* just an excuse, isn't it, Giles?"

Pyott shrugged, expansively; self-deprecation and dismissal featured jointly in the gesture of his shoulders and hands.

"It is an important – crucial – NATO exercise. A sea trial, as I explained. It cannot be described as an *excuse*."

Aubrey paused for a moment, then he said quietly and distinctly: "Giles – Giles, I am deeply sorry about this, but I must act." His throat seemed tight, and he coughed to clear it before adding, "Everything I have seen today, every instinct in my body, tells me to act." In his turn, he shrugged; a smaller, more apologetic movement. "There is no justifiable reason for this mission which outweighs its inherent risks to men, boat, or security. I have no other choice."

"You'll never obtain authority to override StratAn, MoD *and* NATO."

"I do not need to. This intelligence mission is on the point of going critical. I shall, therefore, invoke an ETNA order. I shall apply to the foreign secretary to make *Proteus*'s mission an SIS operation, and then I shall cancel it and recall the submarine."

Pyott was almost visibly shaking with fury. When Aubrey finished speaking, the silence of the huge room pressed in upon the tight group beneath the map; silence lapping against them like waves.

"Be damned to you, Aubrey," Pyott said at last. "I'll oppose you every inch of the way."

Aubrey regarded him for a moment. There was nothing conciliatory he could say, no palliative he even wished to offer. He said, "It should not take long. I expect to return later this afternoon with the appropriate authority – authority to stop this foolish school prefects' prank!"

FOUR:

Closing

"Kenneth – I'm with the minister now."

"Yes, Richard." Cunningham had called him on a scrambled line direct from the Foreign Office.

"Your request for special status – the ETNA order –"

Aubrey grasped at Cunningham's hesitation. 'C' would have talked to one of the ministers of state, and undoubtedly to the Foreign Secretary directly after lunch. As a Permanent Under-Secretary, the director of the intelligence service could command such immediate access, as might Aubrey himself, whose civil service rank was Deputy Under-Secretary. However, Cunningham had chosen to represent Aubrey's case himself, and alone. It appeared he had failed to convince the politicians.

"Yes, Richard?" Aubrey repeated, prompting his superior.

"The Secretary of State has agreed to your request. The Admiralty has been informed of the decision. 'Chessboard Counter' is, as of three-fifteen this afternoon, an SIS intelligence operation."

Aubrey's sigh of relief must have been audible to Cunningham. "Thank you, Richard," he said. He wanted to know more, disliked having been kept waiting upon events. "I'm sure you were most persuasive."

"I think we might say that the moment was opportune," Cunningham drawled. Aubrey understood. The Secretary of State, for his own reasons, had perceived and employed a means of impressing his authority upon another ministry. "Your authorisation will be waiting for you here. I suggest you come over right away."

They knew, and they resented him. Each and every one of the "Chessboard Counter" team, with the exception of Ethan Clark, met his entry to the underground room with silence and a carved hostility of expression. One tight group stood beneath the map-board, Pyott and the commodore were at the latter's desk, standing as if posed for some official portrait which recaptured the aloofness and distance of ancestral oils; the communications and computer operators had their

72

backs to him not so much in gainful employment, more in some communal snub.

Aubrey went immediately to the desk, shedding his dark overcoat, taking off his hat. Man from the Pru, he reminded himself, and the image amused rather than belittled him.

"Gentlemen – I'm sorry."

"We're not simply going to lie down under this –" Pyott began, waving Aubrey's written authorisation, but Aubrey raised his hand. At the edge of his vision, Clark was moving towards them, triumphantly.

"I'm sorry gentlemen, the time for discussion is past. I regret having usurped your authority, but 'Chessboard Counter' is now my responsibility. And I expect your cooperation." His voice was heavy with interrogation. The commodore appeared, strangely, more reluctant than Pyott. It was the soldier who finally spoke. Clark hovered a few yards away.

"Very well, Aubrey, you shall have our cooperation. The damage you have done today to NATO's security, and to the good relations between the various intelligence branches, is something that will only emerge with time." He paused, his lips smirking. "I shall make every effort to see that this matter is fully and properly investigated."

"I expect nothing less, Giles. When the time is right." Aubrey smiled; challenge and sadness in the expression. Then he turned to Clark. "Captain Clark, our first priority –" His voice invited the American into conference with himself and the two senior officers, "is to recall the *Proteus*."

"That, I'm afraid, is impossible," the commodore remarked bluntly. Aubrey realised he had been mistaken. The posed and still expressions had not expressed resentment, not in Pyott and the commodore. Rather, the closed, secret blankness of card players. They did not consider themselves beaten.

"Why, pray?" Aubrey asked frostily.

"*Proteus* is observing the strictest radio silence until the mission is completed and she has returned to a position off North Cape. Only then will she transmit, and be able to receive."

"Sorry, Kenneth," Pyott added. "I omitted to tell you before. It's quite true what the commodore says – no communications facility exists between ourselves and *Proteus*."

Inwardly, Aubrey was furious, but his face retained an icy control. "I see," he said. "Impossible?"

"Not quite," Clark remarked quietly at Aubrey's shoulder. The old man looked round and up into the American's face. It was gleaming with satisfaction, with the sense of outwitting the two senior British officers. Clark was working out his private grudge.

73

"Go on," Aubrey prompted.

"*Proteus* has pre-determined listening out times. She could be reached then. With a hydrophonic buoy."

"Dropped from an aircraft, you mean?"

"Yes. One of your Nimrods. Highest priority code, continuous frequency-agile transmission. An unbroken, one-time code. Just tell *Proteus* to get the hell out."

The commodore appeared deflated. Pyott was merely angry, but he kept silent.

"I want to look at the state of play," Aubrey said with gusto, as if he had come into an inheritance and was about to be shown over the property. "Ethan, come along. Giles –?"

Pyott shrugged, and followed. The group of young officers beneath the huge map-board dispersed a little. They sensed that Aubrey had won. They had been betrayed by the American who had opened the judas-gate into the castle. The enemy was amongst them; they had been routed.

Aubrey looked up, then turned to Clark and Pyott: "Well? Where is she?"

"About here." Clark flashed on the light-indicator's arrow. A cluster of lights surrounded it, very bright like falling meteors.

"Those lights are all Soviet vessels, I take it?" Aubrey asked in a quiet voice.

"Right."

"Explain them to me."

Now the arrow dabbed at each of the lights, as Clark talked.

"These positions haven't been updated for three hours – we have another hour before the satellite comes over the horizon and we can pick up transmission of the current picture. This is the carrier *Kiev*, the pride of the fleet. She's changed course three times, the last one took her from here to here –" Southwards. "She *was* heading west. These two are 'Kashin'-class destroyers, they left Pechenga yesterday. These three are ELINT vessels, probably spy-ships rigged as trawlers, but they're not with fishing fleets – they've changed course, here to here –" Southwards and eastwards. "This, according to some very bad satellite photography yesterday is a rescue ship, the *Karpaty*. She left Murmansk a couple of days ago. Why she's in the area, I wouldn't know. It may not even be her, could be another ELINT vessel, but a big one. And these are the submarines –" The arrow dabbed now at spot after spot of light. "Hunter-killers, every one."

"Thank you, Captain Clark." Aubrey turned to Pyott and the commodore, who had now joined them. Behind them, the junior officers formed a knot of silent supporters. "Is it because I am a mere layman that these Soviet naval dispositions frighten me, make me

74

leap to one conclusion, and only one?" He paused, but there was no murmur of reply. He continued: "Gentlemen, it would seem obvious to me that the Soviets have at least surmised that *Proteus* is in the area and making for Tanafjord. This activity is not directed towards the rescue of the crippled submarine. What is intended I do not propose to guess. If anything happens to *Proteus*, I am now required to accept responsibility. If I can prevent it, nothing untoward will happen. Clark, come with me. We apparently require the cooperation of the Chief of Air staff. Commodore, a secure line, if you please."

"Thank God for sanity," Clark whispered. Aubrey turned on him.

"Ethan, it may already be too late. It is now simply a matter of deciding tenses, from what you have shown me. *Proteus* is walking into – *has* walked into – a trap. Pray that the present tense still applies!"

A bright yellow TR7. It was an easy car in which to be tailed, and the two men in the Ford Granada had stuck to him from Edgbaston through the centre of Birmingham – even in the afternoon traffic – and out onto the M6 motorway. Standing in the doorway of the café near the college, the *Melody Maker* tucked under his arm, one hand disguising the burping indigestion that the sausage and chips had given him, he had seen the car parked across the street from his own. It had U-turned and followed him. He had never lost sight of it in his mirror, and they had never lost sight of him.

Thus he passed his turn-off eight miles further back towards Birmingham, and now the signs indicated the next service area. He signalled, and pulled off the M6, up the slope into the car park. He got out of the car without glancing at the Granada sliding into an empty place twenty yards from him, and went into the foyer of the building. He slipped into the toilet, walked the length of it, and exited through the second door, leading out again to the carpark from the side of the building. He approached the corner slowly, peering round it. One of the two men was standing by the Granada, the other was nowhere to be seen. Presumably, he had followed Hyde into the service station.

Hyde waited impatiently. If the second man didn't move almost at once, he would have to go back into the toilet and attempt to shake them later. And now impatience was a nagging toothache. The man by the Granada was smoking, and picking at his teeth with the hand that held the cigarette. Come on, come on –

The man patted his stomach, which was ample, resting over the lip of his waistband. He hesitated, then he drifted towards the shop at the front of the building, moving with angering slowness out of Hyde's line of vision.

Hyde began running then. He reached the TR7, jerked open the door, and slid into the low seat. He had left the keys in the ignition. He started the engine, and squealed in reverse out of his parking space, swinging the car towards the carpark's exit. In the wing mirror, for a moment, the running figure of the fatter man, then the other emerging from the building behind him, yelling. Then he was down the slope and into the entry lane. He pulled out in front of a heavy lorry, and stamped on the accelerator. The next exit from the M6 was two miles away. He would lose them there, then double back to his intended destination. The speedometer registered ninety. He was still breathing hard, but he was grinning.

Hyde turned the TR7 into the most convenient carpark for Hall 5 of the National Exhibition Centre. The fountain in the middle of the artificial lake in front of the huge hotel complex looked cold and stiff, like dead, blowing grass. It had taken him almost an hour to back-track the twelve miles or so to the NEC site. He had not been followed through the suburbs of Coventry, back towards the airport. They might – just might – have assumed that he was heading east, towards the M1.

Streamers bearing slogans. A queue had formed already, sleeping bags were in evidence, denim like a uniform or prison garb, combat jackets blazoned with insignia, out-of-style long hair worn by many. The audience, or part of it at least, for Heat of the Day's concert at the NEC, kick-off at eight o'clock. It was now almost five. Edwin Shirley's trucks were already unloading the sound and light equipment. Policemen.

Hyde showed his CID warrant card, and was allowed through the cordon. He immediately picked out Fat Mary, one of the formerly much-publicised road crew. Many of the faces seemed half-familiar from television documentaries when Heat of the Day were on their pinnacle. They had come back like lost disciples.

"Excuse me – "

"Piss off," the fat girl replied.

"Police, darling." He tiredly waved the warrant card.

"Nobody's carrying."

"I'm not interested. Are the band here?"

"Two hours yet. Want some autographs?" She watched two of the road crew carrying a huge mirror, and bellowed, "For Christ's sake, haven't you got all the mirrors up yet?"

"No autographs. Tell me – is Tricia Quin with them?"

A flicker, like a wasp sting, at the corner of her mouth, then the sullen look returned. "Who?"

"Tricia Quin. She was with you on the Europe tour two years ago. Her brother knew Jon."

"Oh, yes. I remember. No, haven't seen her. It's not *all* the same as before, you know."

"I don't suppose it is. She's not with them, then?" The fat girl shook her head. Her pendulous breasts distorted the claim on her T-shirt that she had attended the University of California. "Perhaps I'll stick around. Collect a few autographs."

"Or a few smokers."

"Who knows, Fat Mary." The girl seemed pleased at the use of her name, the recollection of a former, half-celebrity status. "Keep it in your pocket, not in your mouth. See you." The girl scowled after him.

Tricia Quin, unless he was mistaken – no, he wasn't – was with the band. Two hours seemed an intolerable length of time.

The one-time code message was lengthy, and even the computer's rendering of it into plain seemed to occupy far more time than was usually the case. Even so, when KGB Resident Petrunin possessed the plain-language text, irritation immediately replaced impatience. He felt hampered by his instructions from Moscow Centre at the same time that he wished, fervently, to comply with those orders.

He left the code room in the embassy basement and took the lift to his office. *At any cost – immediately. The girl.* It was almost demeaning that an unavoidable test of competence and loyalty should have as its object an immature girl unable to cope with growing up. And it was infuriating that superior officers as eminent as the Deputy Chairman responsible for the KGB's 2nd Chief Directorate should indulge in some vulgar, glory-seeking race against the Red Banner Northern Fleet to see who could first acquire "Leopard" for the Soviet Union. All those old men belonged to the same class, the same era. *Dolohov appears confident the submarine is sailing into his trap. You have little time.* The girl, the girl –

He locked the door of his office behind him, and flung the high-security document case onto one of the armchairs. He thrust his hands into his pockets, and stood at the window. Lowering clouds, pulled across the sky by a fierce wind. Trees bending.

Damn those clowns in Birmingham, losing Hyde. Correction. Letting Hyde lose them. Hyde was the key, even more so than the girl. And he was at one further remove from Quin, and that was another cause of anger at the unfairness of the task set him. Hyde must know something, must have discovered some clue as to the girl's whereabouts, otherwise he would not have bothered to shake the tail.

What did he know?

The girl student, the mother? Either of them? Something popping into his head as he was driving out of Birmingham? Tamas Petrunin grinned. It was impossible to know. Interesting to speculate. It was what he enjoyed. Guesswork. He rubbed his hands together, and turned his back to the window where the wind rustled tinnily outside the double glazing. Birmingham. He couldn't send anyone to see the girl Morrison, nor the mother. Not so soon after Hyde. And it might not be necessary.

Birmingham. When did he spot the tail car? Petrunin opened the wad of newspapers on his desk. Normally, they would be sent down to junior staff for analysis, but Petrunin often liked to glance through the provincial newspapers for evidence of KGB activity, actual or potential. The *Birmingham Post*. A rather stuffy, empty paper. He flicked through the pages. Nothing. The *Evening Mail*. Nothing. Hyde would not expect to find the girl at a football match.

Then where? Where would he expect to find the girl? Be Hyde, he instructed himself. Talking to the mother and the friend, then suddenly there is something to cling to, some chance of finding the girl. And the need to shake the surveillance he had discovered – *clowns*.

Where?

He returned to the newspapers. The girl now. What did he know about her? He crossed with rapid, bustling steps to a large filing cabinet against the far wall of the office, wood-veneered so that its function did not obtrude upon the room. He opened one drawer and removed the file on Quin's daughter. A narrow, shadowy file. He carried it back to his desk, dumping most of the newspapers on the carpet, leaving open the two Birmingham dailies. Where would Hyde expect to meet the girl?

Movements in Birmingham: he scanned the digest in the file. Clubs, pubs, cinemas, one or two exhibitions, concerts, visits to her mother. Dull stuff.

Social habits: clubs, pubs, cinemas. *Sexual behaviour*: Petrunin scanned the itemised digest. For the last two years, one or two casual, short-lived relationships within the college, a very brief affair with one of her lecturers, then a teacher she met while on teaching practice. Hyde had had Birmingham detectives question all these people. No one had seen her recently. When she ended an affair, she never revisited the scene of the crime. Petrunin savoured the epithet, then grew angry at the truism it contained. It was true that the girl never went back.

Alletson? Oh, the pop singer. The big affair, travelling with the pop group from place to place. Her parents had been worried by that, from all accounts. Soft drugs, promiscuity. A nightmare in Sutton Coldfield. Again, Petrunin grinned. Even Alletson had failed to make any lasting impression upon the girl. A pity.

Psychological Profile: a fine example to us all, he told himself. He skimmed through it. He already knew the girl, as well as she could be

78

known at second hand, and even though her background and past history prompted him to indulge in stereotypes to account for her – she so easily fitted Western and Soviet myths about modern youth and permissive societies – he was certain that there was nothing in the Profile to explain why Hyde had charged off in his little yellow car.

He slapped the file back on his desk. He knew it almost by heart, it had been the merest illusion to assume that the answer would spring from its flimsy sheets. Had she been his own daughter – as he supposed she could have been, in age at least – he would have no real clue as to her whereabouts. As KGB Resident, he could not walk around in her head with ease or certainty. Hyde's head bore more similarity to his own.

Where?

The newspapers. He put the file to one side. Football, cinemas, factories on strike, a Royal visit proposed for later in the year – the appropriateness of the blank crossword – share prices . . .

He folded the morning paper to one side, and returned to the tabloid evening newspaper from the previous day. Grinning beauty queen, footballer with arms raised gladiatorially. Cinemas, clubs, discos, concerts.

The print began to blur. He knew he was not going to find it. Picture of a queue of people, sleeping bags, combat jackets, long hair. He wasn't going to find it. Pop concert at the National Exhibition Centre. Headline to the picture caption, "Who are we all waiting for?"

He flicked over the page, then the next page, before what he thought he had not bothered to read entered his consciousness and immediately caused his heart to thud and his hand to tremble. He creased the pages of the paper turning back to the picture and its caption. Other, smaller pictures underneath, of course. The heroes of yesterday. Heat of the Day. Alletson, the girl's lover. Long hair and soft, almost feminine features. The NEC, Birmingham, concert tonight.

He laughed aloud, congratulating himself. Accident, luck, good fortune, chance never disturbed him. He had placed himself in the way of it. Hyde had stumbled across this in the same kind of way. Something the Morrison girl said, or the mother, or two years ago merely popping into his head.

Whether the girl would be there or not, Hyde would. That was a certainty, and perhaps the only one. In which case, Tamas Petrunin would also be there. He looked at his watch. After five-thirty. He calculated. Just time, if they could get out of the centre of London without delay, to the M1. Just time –

*　　*　　*

"Is that extra signals traffic co-ordinated?"

"Sir," Sergei answered. The young aide swallowed a mouthful of bread before he answered Dolohov. Then, finding it stuck in his throat, he washed it down with tea. One corner of the Ops. Room control centre had become a preserve, marked off by invisible fences – authority, nerves, tension – from the normal staff. Around a metal chart table, Dolohov, Sergei and Ardenyev sat drinking tea and eating bread and cheese. There was something spartan and disregarded about the food and drink with which Dolohov kept them supplied, as if the three of them were engaged in the field, kept going by survival rations. Sergei began slowly to understand the feverish, self-indulgent manner in which the admiral regarded the operation. The admiral was an old man. He had selected this capture of the British submarine as some kind of suitable valediction to his long and distinguished career. Hence he attended to every detail of it himself, however small and insignificant.

"Just in case," Dolohov explained to Ardenyev, the young man nodding in a half-impatient, half-attentive manner, "in case she receives any signals, or monitors our signals, we'll appear to be making every covert effort to reach, and rescue, our own submarine." He smiled, the mouth opening like a slack pouch in the leathery skin.

"I understand, sir," Ardenyev supplied.

"You're impressed by the British equipment, Valery?"

Ardenyev paused. Sergei felt he was calculating the degree of flattery his answer should contain. "Very. We must have it, sir."

"Yes, yes – but, its effectiveness? It exceeds our expectations, mm?"

"Yes, sir."

"She'll keep on course?" Dolohov asked suddenly.

"I – think so, sir." Ardenyev seemed struck by the idea, as if he had not considered it before. "I think so. She's committed, now, under orders."

"Our activity won't discourage her?"

"I doubt that. The captain of the *Proteus* would have the authority to abort – I just don't think he will. As long as 'Leopard' functions, he'll enjoy the cat-and-mouse of it."

"Exactly my reading of the man – of the situation." Dolohov looked at his watch. "She appears to be maintaining course and speed. We have five hours, or less. Success or failure." Sergei could hear the admiral's breathing. Hoarse gulps of air, as if the sterile atmosphere of the control room offered something more necessary than oxygen. "You'd better get off to Pechenga to join your men, Valery."

Ardenyev immediately stood up, an automaton galvanised by the order. Sergei felt the man was simply supplying an impression of instant action such as Dolohov would expect, had waited for.

"Wish me luck, sir."

Dolohov stood up and embraced the young man. "I do, Valery – I wish you luck. Bring me back the British submarine, eh?" He clamped Ardenyev's forearms again with his liver-spotted hands. Ardenyev felt a strength of desperation in the embrace. And of old age refusing to admit the growing dark. He felt sorry, and irritated. He felt himself no more than Dolohov's creature. Later, it would be different, but now it was unpleasant. He would be glad to be aboard the chopper, being flown to the port of Pechenga. "The weather won't prevent you?" It was a command, and a doubt.

Ardenyev shook his head, smiling. "Not if I can help it."

"Report in when you arrive – then wait for my order to transfer to the *Karpaty*."

"Of course, sir."

When he had left the room, Dolohov went on staring at the door which had closed behind him. From the concentration on his face, Sergei understood that the old man was attempting to ignore the voice of one of the rear admiral's team who was reading off the updated weather report from a met satellite for the Tanafjord area. To Sergei, it sounded bad.

Almost as soon as it lifted clear of the main runway at RAF Kinloss on the Moray Firth in Scotland, the Nimrod surveillance aircraft turned north-eastwards, out over the Firth, and was lost in the low cloud. A blue flare beneath the wings, the flashing red light on her belly, the two faint stars at wingtips, and then nothing except the scudding cloud across the cold grey water, and the driving, slanting rain.

It had taken less than two hours to authorize a Nimrod to pursue the *Proteus*, carrying, in addition to her anti-submarine electronics, the encoded instruction to the submarine to return to base with all possible speed. The time was two minutes after six in the evening.

It was almost dark when they arrived. A luxury coach pulled up at one of the rear entrances to Hall 5, and Hyde, standing with the uniformed superintendent responsible for security and order at the rock concert, watched as Heat of the Day descended from it and slipped into the open door to their dressing rooms. Arrogance, self-assurance, denim-masked wealth. Hyde absorbed these impressions even as he studied the figures he did not recognise; managers, road managers, publicity, secretaries. The girl had not been with Alletson, and Hyde's immediate and uncontrollable reaction was one of

81

intense disappointment. After the hours in the carpark and on the platforms of Birmingham International station and inside and outside Hall 5 – all with no sign of the KGB or the Ford Granada, but the more intensely wearing for that – there was an immediate impression of wasted time, of time run out. Of stupidity, too.

But she was there. Denims and a dark donkey jacket too big for her – was it her, certainly the jacket was too big for the present wearer? – slipping out of the coach without pause, walking with and then ahead of the two other women. The white globe of a face for a moment as she looked round, then she was through the lighted door and gone.

"Was she there?" the superintendent asked. His manner was not unfriendly, not unhelpful. Hyde had been scrupulously deferential and polite.

"I don't know." He felt a tightness in his chest. Was it her? Furtive, certainly furtive. Alletson had paused, allowed himself to be recognised, taken the limelight. Declaring he was alone, there was no girl. "I think so."

"The one with the too-big coat?"

"I think so."

"OK. You'd better go and find out. Want one of my chaps to go with you?"

"No. I'll be enough to panic her by myself."

"Suit yourself."

"Thanks for your help."

Hyde crossed the tarmac, rounded the coach, and showed his warrant card to the PC on duty at the door. The superintendent was apprised of Hyde's real capacity, but it was unnecessary for anyone else to know. "Where are the dressing rooms?"

"Down the corridor, turn left. You'll see another bloke dressed just like me. And the press, and the bouncers and the hangers-on. Can't miss it."

"Not your scene, this?"

"I'd rather be at the Villa, yobs and all."

"They playing at home tonight?"

"Too bloody true."

"Shame."

Hyde followed the corridor, and turned the corner into a crowd of pressmen and cameramen, carefully orchestrated outside the closed dressing room doors. Heat of the Day were back in business. Interest had to be stoked, and kept alight. Hyde pushed through the crowd towards the policeman on the door of one of the rooms. He waved his warrant card.

"Which one is Alletson in?"

"Who?"

"The short bloke with the wavy hair."

"Uh – that one," the PC supplied, indicating the other door, outside which two bulky men in denims and leather jackets stood, arms folded. Hyde wondered who, precisely, they were guarding. A press or publicity secretary was informing the cameramen that they would be allowed to take their pictures just before the band went onstage. Her announcement was greeted with a chorus of groans. Hyde showed his warrant card to one of the band's security men, who seemed to loom over him.

"Who do you want?" The question was wrong, and revealing. Again, Hyde felt his chest tighten with anticipation. The girl was in there.

"I'm not after his autograph."

"So, what do you want?" Both of them seemed uncertain what to do.

"Just a security check. And I want to talk to Jon about after the concert. Getting away."

"I'll ask him."

"Don't bother. I'll talk to him." He made to reach for the door handle. A large hand closed over his own, and he looked up into a face adopting aggression reluctantly, uncertainly. "Don't be stupid," Hyde said. "It might be big trouble – *will* be big trouble." The two men glanced at one another, then his hand was released.

"Easy, eh?"

"I'll take it easy – don't upset the artiste, right?" Hyde opened the door without knocking. The girl turned in her chair, alert, nervous, instantly aware of what he was and why he was there. Alletson was lying on a camp bed, and the keyboard player, Whiteman, was scribbling with a pencil on stave paper.

"Who the hell are you?" he asked. Alletson's voice provided a more nervous, knowing undertone.

"Trish – what is it?"

The girl simply stared at Hyde as he shut the door behind him. Whiteman, oblivious to the other two and their anxiety, added, "Piss off, we're busy." He glanced contemptuously at the warrant card. "Autographs later," he sneered.

"Miss Patricia Quin, I presume?" Hyde asked. The girl said nothing. Her face, however, was voluble with confession. Alletson got up lithely and stood in front of her.

"What do you want?" he asked.

"The lady in the case."

Alletson took the warrant card, inspected it, then thrust it back into Hyde's hand. "Harassment?" he asked.

83

"This isn't about smokes or shots, Jon-boy," Hyde drawled. "It isn't really any of your business. You get on rehearsing or composing or something." Whiteman was standing now, just behind Alletson. Long blond hair, his frame bulkier with good living than two years before. He looked healthier.

"Why don't you piss off?"

"Why did they let you in?" Alletson demanded.

"They'd have been silly not to."

"What sort of copper are you?" Whiteman was a Londoner. "You're a bloody Aussie by the sound of it."

"Too true, Blue. I'm the sort that wants to help her. Can I talk to her?"

"Not unless she wants to."

"Stop it, Jon. It won't do any good." Tricia Quin pushed to Alletson's side, and held his arm. "Who are you?"

"My name's Hyde."

"I didn't think it would be Jekyll – he was the goody, wasn't he?" Whiteman sneered.

"He was. Look, Miss Quin, I'll talk to you with your friends here, if you wish, as long as they can keep their mouths shut." He looked steadily at Alletson and Whiteman, then continued. "You are in danger, Miss Quin. It's stopped being a game. You know there are people after you?"

"You are."

"No, not me. Not even my side."

"What's he talking about, Trish?"

"What do you mean?"

"The men in Sutton, at your mother's house?" She nodded, fear flickering in her pale eyes. Cleverness, too. "That wasn't us. Our bloke got kicked in the balls trying to look after you. You need protection – mine. Will you come back with me?"

She shook her head. "No, I won't. I'm safe here."

"I can't risk that, Miss Quin. We want you and your father safe. You could lead the KGB right to him." She was shaking her head violently now. Her fair hair flopped about her pale, small face. She looked vulnerable, afraid but determined.

As if her shaking head was some signal, Alletson stepped up to him and aimed his knee at Hyde's groin. Hyde bucked backwards and the blow struck his thigh. Off-balance as he was, Alletson pushed him against a tall metal locker. Hyde, watching Tricia Quin move towards the door, jarred his head and shoulder against the locker, then slumped into the corner of the dressing room.

"Trish!" Alletson called, but the girl was already out of the door. Two hopeful flash-bulbs exploded. Hyde got shakily to his feet.

"You stupid buggers!" Hyde snapped, rubbing his shoulder. "She's a menace to herself at the moment, as well as to her father. Christ — you stupid buggers!" He opened the door, and yelled to the PC on duty. "Which way did the girl go?" Someone laughed.

"Towards the hall."

"Who is she?" someone asked.

"It'll be pot," someone else answered. "Poor bitch."

Hyde forced his way through the press, jabbed uncomfortably more than once by the lens of a camera, then he was running. At the far end of the corridor, the door into the hall was open. He rubbed his thigh as he ran, his resentment against Alletson growing not because of the pain but because of the girl. Stupid bugger, silly bitch, he chanted to himself, grinding his teeth at the opportunity that had been spoiled. He had had the girl safe, for a moment. It was only a matter of getting her to his car, getting her to Aubrey — *shit!*

In the hall, lighting gantries were being pulleyed up to the ceiling, mirrors were being positioned for the light-show that the band used, and the roadies were still working furiously to rig and test the amplification equipment. Two grubby girls passed him without a glance, pushing one of Whiteman's electronic keyboards. Up the ramp and onto the stage. He was standing just below the stage. Lights, mirrors, amplifiers, instruments — and Tricia Quin picking her way delicately like a cat through the maze of boxes and wires. She must have taken the other turn in the corridor to enter onto the stage itself.

She saw him. Part of her slow and delicate passage across the stage was due to her continual backward glances. She began to move more quickly, upstage towards the far side. Even as he moved, she disappeared into the wings. He pushed past the girls with the keyboard, and ran as quickly as he was able through the maze of cables and boxes — someone yelled at him — and then he was in the semi-darkness of the wings. He paused, listening. Above his heartbeat and breathing, footsteps. Running. He blundered forward again, sensing rationality disappearing and panic encroaching. He suddenly knew that the KGB were out there, and that she was running towards them. He shook his head, cannoning off a wall as he rounded a bend in the corridor.

Lights again. The foyer and main corridor connecting Hall 5 with its companions and with the railway station. A handful of people moving slowly, and one slight figure running. He did not call after her, merely pursued her, his feet pounding, his blood beating in his ears. He felt a sickness of self-recrimination, an anticipation of disaster.

A tunnel of lights down which she fled, a small dark shape. The scene wobbled in his vision. He seemed no nearer to her. The station concourse was at the end of the wide tunnel. She was almost there, sixty or seventy yards away.

Someone turning, moving with her, after her. She was oblivious to whoever it was, didn't even look round for him as she reached the concourse. He began running, impelled by the certainty of disaster now. Someone had recognised her – other men, two of them in overcoats, just come in from the cold of the carpark outside the station, moving to intercept her.

He reached the concourse. The girl had disappeared. Two men had pushed into the small queue for tickets, one of them arguing. He hadn't imagined it. They were stereotypes. The girl must have gone down onto the platform. Two of them, three – where was the other one, the one who had turned in the tunnel, recognised her?

Petrunin. Hyde could not believe it. Standing beneath the announcement board, impatiently watching his men create the wrong kind of disturbance, then turning to the platform ticket machine and banging it because it appeared jammed or empty. No, girl, no girl –

Petrunin, London Resident. KG-bloody-B. Where the hell was the girl? Petrunin. The clever bugger must have worked it out. Tickets being issued, the small queue silenced by embarrassment. Petrunin almost hopping from foot to foot. Train announcement, the next train arriving, Petrunin turning his head from side to side as if regretting something or because he had lost something – and seeing him. Knowing him not so much by his face as by his colour and heaving chest and wary, tense posture.

Hyde ran at the barrier, Petrunin moved to cut him off, slowly drifting, so it seemed, on a collision course. The next train arriving, for Birmingham – special train? He saw the dark, frightened face of the ticket collector, then he vaulted the turnstile, almost stumbling on the far side, hearing the noise of the train. He ran headlong down the flight of steps to the platform, round the corner, skidded, righted himself, flung open the glass doors.

She was almost alone on the platform. He saw her immediately. And she saw him. Policemen, too. Clattering footsteps behind him, but it was all right. Policemen. All round them, policemen. He hadn't lost her. He called to her as she stood looking at him. The nose of the train covered his words as it slowed, then came to a stop.

One of Petrunin's men grabbed him from behind. He turned, lashed out to try to prevent a second man passing him, heading towards the girl. Then they seemed to be drowning in bodies as the special train from Euston debouched hundreds of rock fans onto the platform, every one one of them intent on reaching the exit first. Noise assailed Hyde, and perfume. He was brushed aside, the only certainty the hand holding his collar. He raised his fist, but the crowd trapped it against his chest, pinning it there as in a sling. Petrunin's man had his arm above the heads of the crowd. He was waving a rubber cosh. He struck slowly down. The movement was awkward because he was being relentlessly pushed back towards the exit. Hyde lost sight of the girl, of Petrunin who seemed to have retreated back up the steps, and of the cosh which struck him across the neck and shoulder, numbing him after the spurt of fire through his head. Then the Russian's hand was gone from his collar and he stumbled forward, flung sideways to his knees, then onto his chest. Feet pressed on his back, compressing his lungs. People began surging over him. He was drowning for a moment, then he could not breathe, and then it was dark.

FIVE:

Cripple

"Sir, why the hell is the *Kiev* in the area? There's no major Soviet exercise on, and she couldn't possibly be any help in rescuing those poor dead buggers in the crippled boat – so why do they need an aircraft carrier? What's her game?"

"I don't know, John."

"And the course changes – sir, we remained rigged for silent running for too long. If we'd had the magnetic and acoustic sensors working, and gone to active sonar, we'd have known sooner she was closing on us."

"I know that, John. I know we're the quarry."

"Sir, what in hell are we doing here?"

"Playing MoD's games for them, John. Undergoing our final examination."

"What?"

"I mean it. In this sea-trial, the danger's all the better for MoD for being real."

"Bastards. Sir, we're being gathered into a net. The net is in the Tanafjord, and we're being driven towards it."

"Agreed."

"What do they want?"

"I should have thought that was obvious. What they want is called 'Leopard'. As to what they'll do, you guess."

"What do *we* do?"

"ETA Norwegian territorial waters?"

"Two hours plus some minutes."

"Then we'll run for shelter. We might just get away with it, inside Norwegian waters. We'll hide, John. Hide."

"Ethan, has the Nimrod's position been updated?"

"She's here, Mr. Aubrey, as of five minutes ago."

Aubrey stared up at the huge map-board. The cluster of lights glowed with what he could easily imagine was malevolence. A single white light had been introduced to the board to represent the *Proteus*. Aubrey periodically wished it had not been done. The white dot was

88

in a ring of coloured lights representing the Soviet naval vessels in the immediate area. Far to the south and west of that cluster, a second white light shone like a misplaced or falling star over the fjordal coastline of western Norway, perhaps a hundred miles south of the Arctic Circle.

"Not enough, not far enough," Aubrey murmured. The dot seemed hardly to have moved since the aircraft's previous signal.

"You can't know that, Mr. Aubrey."

"Don't offer me morsels of comfort, Ethan!" Aubrey snapped, turning to the American. Heads turned, and then returned to screens and read-outs. Aubrey had subdued the "Chessboard Counter" team by cajolement and command, and by exploiting their sense of failure. The map-board had completed their change in function as it increasingly betrayed *Proteus*'s danger. They were now a rescue team, busy and helpless.

"Sorry."

Pyott and the commodore had sought another place of residence. Vanquished, they had left the field to Aubrey. Rather, he saw them as children running away from the broken window, the smashed greenhouse.

"My apologies. What's the Nimrod's ETA?"

"A little more than an hour to Hammerfest, then maybe another twenty minutes to the Tanafjord."

Aubrey looked at his watch. "Eight-fifteen. Can we do it, Ethan?"

Clark rubbed his chin. To Aubrey, he looked absurdly young, and much too unworried to be a repository of authoritative answers. And he was tall enough to make Aubrey physically uncomfortable.

"Maybe. Then *Proteus* has to get the hell out."

"Why hasn't Lloyd aborted on his own initiative?"

"Maybe he wants to. Maybe he's running for the coast and keeping his fingers crossed. Who knows?"

"My *God*, what an impossible situation!" Aubrey's face darkened after the quick rage had passed. He leaned confidentially towards the American. "Ethan, I'm worried about Quin. I haven't heard from Hyde. He was at the NEC in Birmingham, some sort of pop concert. He thought – no, he was certain – the girl was with this group. She knows them, once travelled with them." Aubrey's face was drained of colour and expression now. "It is very hard to contemplate, Ethan, but I feel myself staring at the loss of the *Proteus* and of the man responsible for the development of 'Leopard'. It is not a comfortable prospect."

Clark recognized, and admitted to himself, Aubrey's age. Yet he respected the man's intellect and his expertise. Aubrey might, appallingly, be correct in his diagnosis.

"Maybe," was all he could find to say.

"I think we have to consider the possibility that what is happening up there –" he waved a hand at the top of the map-board " – is deliberate." He paused, but Clark said nothing. "We have no proof that there is a Soviet submarine in distress. It has stopped transmitting, and still no Russian vessel has gone in after it. But a great many Russian ships are concentrating in the area we know contains *Proteus*. If they *find* her – and they may be attempting to do just that – then we will have surrendered an almost priceless military advantage to them. If we lose Quin, too, then we will place ourselves in an abject position indeed."

Aubrey tapped at the surface of the commodore's desk, which he had had moved to a position beneath the map-board. As if the gesture was a summons, the telephone rang.

"Shelley, sir."

"Yes, Peter?"

"I've just been informed of a routine surveillance report from the DS team at the Russian embassy –"

"Yes, Peter?" Aubrey found it difficult to catch his breath.

"They think Petrunin left the embassy unofficially around five-thirty this evening."

"Where was he going?"

"I've checked that, sir. His numberplate was spotted heading north, I'm afraid, on the M1."

"Damn!" Aubrey's lips quivered with anger. "Thank you, Peter. You'd better inform Birmingham Special Branch. Get them over to that concert at the NEC – quickly!"

Aubrey put down the telephone.

"I guess I see what you mean," Clark said slowly. "Without even really noticing, we're down to the wire."

"I think we are. The KGB Resident wouldn't charge off unofficially without good cause or strong suspicion. Hyde couldn't have lost his trail. Damn that girl and her father!" He returned his attention to the map. The dot of the Nimrod was crossing the Arctic Circle. *Proteus* was surrounded. The *Kiev* was steaming at full speed to the Tanafjord, and the rescue ship *Karpaty* was on station. There really was no escaping the conclusion, and little chance of avoiding disaster. Aubrey felt very tired, entirely incompetent. "I think we have already lost, Ethan. This may be the view from the canvas, from the loser's corner."

"I hope to God you're wrong about that."

"I don't think I am."

The interference crackled in front of Ardenyev's voice, masking it and giving it, to Dolohov's ears, a peculiarly unreal quality, as if the man were fading, becoming ethereal. Then Dolohov raised his voice, not to be heard but to remove the strange, uninvited perception; the whisper of failure.

"Get aboard the helicopters, Valery! You must transfer to the *Karpaty* now!"

"Sir, I'd really like you to have a word with one of the pilots —" Ardenyev's voice seemed more distant still, the storm smearing his words mockingly.

"No! It is too late for words! The traces are piling up. We're almost there." Dolohov looked round at Sergei, who stood obediently and silently at his elbow as he hunched over the table in front of the telephone amplifier. To Sergei, it seemed that the admiral was losing control, was dangerously elated by events, by the slipping, chasing minutes that passed and the sightings or partial and unconfirmable reports of the British submarine that kept coming in. The old man was racking them up like a score, mere multiplication stimulating his confidence and his arrogance. "We have them, Valery, in the palm of our hand. They're *ours*!"

"Sir, you don't seem to understand. It's a question of whether they can put us down on the deck of the rescue ship —"

"Don't argue with me, boy!" Dolohov thundered, his fist beating a counterpoint to his words on the surface of the table. "You have your orders – the pilots have their orders. You will board the helicopters at once and set course for the rescue ship. Understand?" There was a gap, then, of space and silence in which the storm hissed. "Do you hear me?"

"Yes, sir. Very good, sir. Your orders will be carried out, to the best of my abilities."

Dolohov was suddenly, manically expansive and generous. "Good boy, good boy. Good luck and good hunting. Over and out." The old man flicked off the telephone amplifier and stood up. He moved with some of the robotic jerkiness of arthritis battled and temporarily overcome; or the driven, muscular awkwardness of someone possessed of an unquenchable desire. He slapped his hand on Sergei's shoulder and the young man hoped that his smile did not appear too artificial. Dolohov looked at him, however, with eyes that had little perception in them. Not glazed or dulled, rather fierce and inward-looking. "The end-game, Sergei – the end-game," he murmured in a strange, ugly, caressing voice.

The rear admiral was punctilious, almost smirking, full of a bustle that had previously been absent. "Final positions, Admiral," he offered, indicating the computer print-out sheets in his hand.

"Good, good – come, let me see." He took the rear admiral's arm, ushering him to the window, clutching the sheets with his other hand. Sergei realised that the rear admiral had cast aside all doubts and reservations; whether from self-interest or because he had contracted the admiral's current illness, Sergei could not decide. Probably both. "Where?" They were at the window.

"There," the rear admiral proclaimed, histrionically waving his hand down towards the map-table. "*Kiev, Karpaty* on station waiting for Ardenyev, *Grishka* and the other submarines – see? There, there, there, there, there –" The finger jabbed out at each of the lights below. "The other units of the fleet in back-up positions, or sailing on deception courses." He looked at Dolohov. "It's up to them now. They have their orders. All they need is a positive ident on the British submarine."

Dolohov's face possessed a beatific expression. His eyes were almost closed. Sergei, embarrassed and disturbed, realized that it was a moment of love. The cold, stern, paternal admiral was unrecognizable. Sergei did not know, however, what it was that Dolohov embraced – this challenge, the drama of the moment, the prize, or the winning of the game. Perhaps even the game itself?

"Good, good," the old man murmured again. Then, suddenly, his eyes opened and all his attention was concentrated on the voice of one of the officers behind him in the control room.

"Submarine unit *Frunze* reports a magnetic contact –"

Dolohov was across the room and at the officer's shoulder with the speed and physical grace of a younger man. "Where?" he demanded. "What range?" Then, before the man could answer: "Can they lock on to her course?"

The communications officer listened to his headphones after repeating Dolohov's questions, and the old man could see his head begin to shake. "No, sir – they've lost it. Could have been sea temperature –"

"Rubbish. It was a *magnetic* contact, not infra-red! It was *them*, you idiot!" He turned to the rear admiral. "Order all submarine units to converge on the *Frunze* at once!"

"Admiral, is that –?"

"Do it."

"Very well, Admiral."

Dolohov walked aimlessly yet intently back to the window. He appeared to have little interest in the glowing map below him. The situation had been ingested in its entirety or – here Sergei corrected himself – perhaps it had always been in his head. Sergei half-listened to the rear admiral issuing a stream of orders, half-watched Dolohov, principally being aware of himself as an unimportant cipher, something like a parcel left in one corner of the room.

92

Then: "Submarine unit *Grishka* reports another magnetic trace –"

"Magnetic trace fading, Captain."
"Thermal trace fading, Captain."
"Planesman – ten degrees down, level at eight hundred feet."
"Sir."
"Steer twelve degrees to starboard."
"Sir."
There was silence in the control room of the *Grishka*. The bow sonars were blank and silent, their sensors absorbed or deflected by the British anti-sonar equipment. The infra-red trace was decaying, was already almost non-existent, illusory. The magnetic anomaly detection equipment was already inducing a frustrated hunching of the shoulders in its operator. The advanced, delicate, heat-sensitive "nose" was sniffing cold ocean water without trace of the British submarine. Every trail was cold, or growing cold.
"Steer fifteen degrees to port."
"Sir."
Guesswork, the captain of the *Grishka* admitted. A blind dog with a cold in its nose seeking an elusive scent. No prop wash even, not a trace of the trail she ought to be leaving in the sea from her movement and her turning propeller. They had picked that up once before, then lost it again.
"Nine knots."
"Sir."
Silence.
"Weak magnetic trace, sir. Bearing green four-oh, range six thousand."
"We're almost on top of her – don't lose it. Steer starboard thirty."
"Starboard thirty, sir."
"No thermal trace, sir."
"Magnetic trace fading again, sir."
"Stand by, torpedo room. Any sign of prop wash?"
"Negative, sir."
"Steer starboard five, speed ten knots."
"Magnetic trace lost, sir."
"Damn!"

"Steer port four-five."
"Port four-five it is, sir."
There was silence then in the control room of the *Proteus*. Whispered orders, like the rustling voices of old men, lacking authority. The sonars which, in their passive mode, were difficult for any enemy

to detect with his electronic sensors, registered the movements of the Russian submarine; demonstrating the proximity of the hunter.

"Computer ident, Number One?"

"A 'Victor-II' class submarine, sir. Our friend is back."

"Range and bearing?"

"Moving away, sir. Speed approximately nine knots, range eight thousand, bearing green one-seven-oh. She's passing behind us."

"Other activity, John?"

" 'Kashin' class destroyer, range eleven thousand. 'Alpha' class attack submarine, range fourteen thousand, bearing red six-five, and closing. *Kiev* at range sixteen thousand, and increasing. The submarine rescue ship is holding station, sir."

"Coffee, sir?"

"What – oh, thanks, chief. ETA Norwegian waters, John?"

"At present course and speed, eleven minutes, sir."

"Speed fourteen knots."

"Prop wash, sir?"

"Correction – twelve knots."

"Twelve knots it is, sir."

"Steer port ten."

The transmissions from the *Grishka* and the other Red Banner units were being received via the aircraft carrier *Kiev*. Dolohov had ordered the abandonment of coded signals in favour of high-speed, frequency-agile transmissions in plain language. Transferred to tape and slowed down, Dolohov then heard them broadcast in the control room. The voices, and the silences between the words, seemed equally to agitate and excite him. Sergei observed his admiral closely, worriedly. He felt like a youthful relative watching a grandparent growing senile before his eyes.

Dolohov's shoulders were hunched as he stared down into the well of the operations room, watching the moving, dancing lights and the flickering, single light that represented the British submarine. It flickered on and off as if there were an electrical fault in the board.

Sergei guessed that Dolohov had begun to entertain doubts; or rather, the doubts he had formerly crushed beneath the heel of certainty had now sprung up again like weeds. It was more than an hour since the first contact signal had been received from the submarine *Frunze*. Since then, the *Grishka* and two other units had reported traces on more than one occasion – *Grishka* three times – but the British submarine still eluded them. Dolohov had been able to ignore his doubts for hours, even days; but now, watching the cat-and-invisible-mouse game on the board below him, he had begun to disbelieve in success. Or so Sergei suspected.

94

The old man was talking to himself. His voice, in the silence from the loudspeaker, was audible throughout the room.

"Can it be done, can it be done?" He repeated it again and again, a murmured plea or a voiced fear. "Can it? Can it?" The shorter phrase became more final, more full of doubt. "Can it? Can it?" The old man was entirely unaware that he was speaking audibly, and Sergei felt a hot flush of shame invade his features. To be associated with this old man, muttering to himself in this moment of crisis like a geriatric in a hospital, was embarrassing, insulting. Others were listening, everyone in the room –

Then the voice of the monitoring officer on the *Kiev* silenced Dolohov, smearing across his words, erasing them. The admiral's shoulders picked up, his head inclined like a bird's as he listened.

"Submarine unit *Grishka* reports lost contact – "

Dolohov's shoulders slumped again. It was evident he thought he had lost the game.

"The 'Victor-II' is turning to starboard, sir."

"Damn. John, insert our track and that of the 'Victor-II' onto the display screen."

"Track memory is on, sir. Submarine bearing red one-six-eight, range nineteen thousand."

"Do we still have that layer of warmer water below us?"

"Yes, sir."

"Right. Let's make it much more difficult for them. Take us down through it."

"Aye, aye, sir."

Lloyd sensed the dipping of the *Proteus*'s bow. The Russian submarine was on their tail again. They were still three minutes out into international waters, and the "Victor-II" was closing rapidly. Even though he doubted now that an imagined political line on a chart would have any beneficial effect on their circumstances, Lloyd knew of no other move he could make. The display screen traced their track over the seabed, and that of the Russian. A swifter-moving, hazy line of light was dead astern of them now that the Russian captain had altered course.

"Information on the 'Victor-II' becoming unreliable, sir."

"I can see that. The warmer layer's causing ghosting and refracting. Are we through it yet?"

"Yes, sir."

"Level at eighty fathoms, cox'n."

"Eighty fathoms, sir."

"Is that the coast at the edge of the screen, John?"

"No, sir." Thurston was at his side, staring down at the screen. The image of the Russian submarine was faint. The warmer layer of sea water through which they had descended would be confusing the Russian's sensors, hiding the *Proteus*. "It's a small plateau. Our depth makes it look like a mountain."

" 'Victor-II' now bearing green one-seven-oh, range fourteen thousand, and she's in a shallow dive, sir."

Thurston looked into Lloyd's face. "We didn't fool her. She's back with us," he whispered.

"The computer confirms course and bearing, sir."

Lloyd hesitated for only a moment. Then a tight determination clamped on his features. He had accepted the evidence of his sonars and his computers.

"John," he said in a steady voice audible to everyone in the control room, "call the crew to Alert Readiness. The time for playing games with this Russian is over. He's after us, all right."

"Aye, aye, sir."

"Negative contact on magnetic, Captain."

"Maintain present course for one minute, then hard starboard – mark."

"Marked, Captain. One minute."

"Negative contact, sir."

Always the negative. The Russian captain sensed the *Grishka* around him, slipping through the blind darkness of the sea. He sensed the crew closed up to Action Stations, as they had been for more than half an hour on this occasion alone; and three other times he had spoken to the torpedo room, readying them, and calling his men to Action Stations. It could not go on for much longer, he would have to relax them. He was wearing them down. He sensed, especially, the torpedo crew room and the wire-guided, wake-homing torpedoes, one with reduced warhead and the second with the special MIRV warhead, the "Catherine Wheel". Once he ordered their launch, one expert crewman would guide them to their target, relying solely on his own skills. His man was good enough, and the torpedoes would do their job. Yet everything – *everything* – depended on tiny, delicate sensors in the bow of the boat; magnetic sensors, thermal sensors. Somewhere ahead – or below or beside or above or behind – there was a magnetic lump of metal which was emitting heat and which could not be entirely damped and rendered invisible. The British submarine was leaving faint traces, flakings of her skin, faint noises of her breathing. Somewhere in the ocean, those traces lay waiting for him to discover them.

"Coming hard round, Captain."

"Planesman – hold her steady."

"Sir."

Somewhere, out there in the dark, lay the *Proteus*.

"Sir, the 'Victor-II' is coming hard round –"
"I have her. Engine room – plus fifty revolutions."
"Plus fifty, sir."

"Heat trace confirmed and growing stronger, Captain."
"Ten degree quarter – sixty second rate."
The captain of the *Grishka* leaned against the periscope housing. The range of the British submarine was still too great, and though the trace was strengthening it was still elusive. The game might continue for hours yet. He sensed the pressure on him not to fail, but more importantly he was aware of the growing, slightly desperate need for action in himself and his crew. His loyalty was, therefore, to the stifled, tense atmosphere of his control room.

"Torpedo room," he said distinctly, pausing until everyone was alert with attention to his voice, despite their own tasks. "Torpedo room, load manual guidance torpedo, set it for a screw-pattern search. Set maximum range and wait for my order."

There was relief, palpable as cold, fresh air, in the set of every man's shoulders and on every face that he could see. He kept a sudden assault of doubt from his own features.

"Heat trace strengthening, Captain."
"Magnetic trace positive, Captain."
"Sonars negative, Captain."
"Range and bearing?"
"Bearing unchanged, sir. Range thirteen thousand, and decreasing. We're overhauling her, sir."

"Very well." He paused. The low-warhead torpedo was in the tube. He had four of them, and four multiple-warhead "Catherine Wheel" torpedoes. Could he risk the first one at that range? "Torpedo room – fire One! Keep calling."

"Tube One away, sir, and running. Sensor on, lights green. Negative readout."

The Russian captain looked at his first lieutenant standing at the depth indicator panel. He shrugged expressively.

"Torpedo sensors have made contact, Captain."

The wake-homing torpedo began its search immediately it was launched. The wire that connected it with the *Grishka* transmitted to its tiny computer the instructions of the experienced operator in the torpedo room. Its guidance control was tested, and responded, then the speed of the torpedo was altered a number of times in quick succession. On each occasion, the torpedo responded immediately and precisely.

The torpedo crossed the traces of the *Proteus*'s wake one thousand metres from the *Grishka*. Its corkscrewing movement through the sea, which enabled it to search in three rather than in two dimensions, took it across the wake well astern of the British submarine's position. There was, however, sufficient trace of the wake remaining for the torpedo to register it.

The torpedo nosed on through the dark water until it reached the conclusion of its next one thousand metre run, then it began retracing its course, back towards the wake. Once it crossed the wake for the second time, and its sensors registered either a stronger or a weaker trace, then it would be instructed to turn to port or starboard, and to run down the submarine's track until it made contact. Once its path was chosen, and the wake's direction established, contact was unavoidable.

The torpedo crossed the wake and turned to port almost immediately with a flick as lithe as that of some hunting sea creature. Its corkscrewing track evened out as it began tracing its way down the wake of the British submarine.

"Contact continuous, Captain."

"Excellent – keep calling." The captain of the *Grishka* grinned at his first lieutenant.

"Lock on indicated . . . three thousand five hundred metres of run completed, sir . . . four thousand metres completed . . . heat sensor responding and locked on . . . command override on, sir . . . proximity fuse armed and *on*, sir . . . seven thousand metres of run completed . . . TV camera on, light on –"

"Come on, come on," the Russian captain murmured. Too long, too long, he told himself. Should have waited, she's out of range.

"Seven and one half thousand metres of run completed, sir . . . eight thousand metres of run completed."

"Positive contact, sir!"

"Cox'n hard astern!"

"Hard astern, sir."

"Contact identified as a torpedo, sir!"

On the tiny television monitor in the *Grishka*, receiving pictures from the camera in the nose of the torpedo, there was nothing more than a weakly illuminated rush of grey water, almost like a heavy, dull curtain being continually whisked aside. Then there was a blur of darker water, then the grey, whale-like shape of the *Proteus* as the

British submarine began her turn. The torpedo seemed to dip towards the submarine, strangely hesitant, and the proximity fuse detonated the reduced warhead. The television screen at which the captain of the *Grishka* stared went blank, making him wince as if the flash of the explosion had been visible and had startled, even blinded him.

"Target acquired, Captain! Hit, hit, hit!"

"We've got her?"

"Direct hit, Captain!"

There was cheering, which he immediately silenced.

"Torpedo room, load Two. Multiple warhead torpedo, set range at nine thousand. Manual guidance, direct search track."

"Tube Two ready, Captain."

"Fire Two!"

"Planesman, check that roll!"

"– can't hold the turn –"

"Emergency lights – cancel –"

"Can't hold the trim, sir!"

"Trim responding, sir."

"Engines down one-fifty revolutions."

"The dampers aren't controlling the oscillation, sir."

"All stations – immediate damage report." Lloyd wiped a hand across his forehead, his eyes riveted on the forearms of the two planesmen as they struggled to right the trim of the *Proteus*. The muscles flexed and strained, veins standing out, the tattoo of an anchor and chain livid on one of the arms. The whole submarine was oscillating wildly, like a bicycle out of control, a child in the saddle, feet unable to reach the pedals. The lights had come back on. His arm felt nerveless and weak as his thoughts churned like his stomach, over and over, and fused into a circuit. The Russians had fired on them, fired on them . . . Thurston crossed the vibrating control room towards him and lurched against the periscope housing, where he clung unsteadily. "Christ, John – they fired on us!"

Thurston's face confirmed the inadmissible. Enemy action.

"Chief engineer, sir," Lloyd heard over the control room speaker.

"Yes, Chief?"

"Initial damage report suggests external impact, sir. Pressure hull OK, outer plates and aft ballast tanks ruptured. Planes and rudders misaligned, but responding, sir. The vibration we're experiencing is linked to our revs, so there must be prop damage. Or maybe it's the shaft. Or both. The main shaft bearings are heating up."

"Can we still remain under way, Chief?"

"I think so, sir. We'll have to try various rev settings to find an optimum for remaining under way with least vibration and some degree of control. We may be lucky, if the bearings don't get too hot. They're in the orange now, sir."

"Very well, Chief. In your hands."

"Aye, aye, sir."

The multiple-warhead torpedo tracked down the wake of the *Proteus*, following the range and bearing instructions fed into its tiny computer. It, too, was armed with a proximity fuse. The Red Navy's experts had concluded that a reduced warhead, although capable of damaging the *Proteus*, might not have sufficient stopping-power to render the British nuclear submarine immobile, which condition was essential to the success of the operation. Therefore, an experimental multiple-warhead, code-named "Catherine Wheel", had been hurried through its last stages of development and its laboratory and sea trials, to fulfil the preliminary work of the reduced-warhead torpedo that would cripple, but not ensnare, the *Proteus*.

The TV camera switched on at an instruction from the torpedo room operator, and the light came on at the same moment. On the tiny screen, the Russian captain watched the swirling rush of water, and thought he detected the bubbles and general disturbance of the *Proteus*'s wake. He tensed himself, almost as if he had been riding the torpedo like a horse, then the grey-black, whale-backed shape of the submarine emerged from the darkness of the sea. He imagined – saw? – the damage to the rudder and the hydroplanes, and bent his head and cocked it to one side in order to perceive the outline of the stern more easily. Then the warhead detonated, and to his intense disappointment the TV screen went blank. Memory continued the succession of images.

He had seen the "Catherine Wheel" in operation on an old sub during trials. The film had been poor, grainy and cut-about, but the images had been stark, vivid, deadly. When the separate warheads split from the body of the torpedo, they would whirl and spin and weave outwards in a net-like circle. Some of them carried small explosive charges, some barbed hooks of super-strengthened steel, some suction caps or magnets. Twelve in all, each of them trailed a length of toughened steel cable, whipped into a frenzy of whirling movement by the spinning-top effect of the small war-heads. Two, three, four or more of these would make contact with the hull and rudder and hydroplanes of the *Proteus* and, as the submarine moved forward under power, the trailing, whipping steel cables would slash at the hull, be dragged with it, and would fasten and entangle the propellers, twisting tighter and tighter like strangling cords.

It would take no more than seconds, and little more than a minute

100

to halt the submarine, her propeller bound and made immovable by the entangled steel cables.

He closed his eyes, seeing the drama on an inward screen, himself seated in the darkness of the briefing room as the film was shown. He did not hear, did not need to hear the exultant cry from the torpedo room, nor the cheering in his control room. He awoke when his first lieutenant shook his elbow, startling him. The young man was grinning.

"Direct hit, sir. Another direct hit!" he bubbled.

"Good," the captain said slowly. "Well done, everyone." He stood upright. Already, the British submarine would be slowing, her crew terrified by the vibration as the cables tightened against the revolutions of the propeller, strangling it. "Very well. Send up an aerial buoy. Transmit the following message, Lieutenant. Message begins TOLSTOY, followed by target impact co-ordinates. Message ends. Direct to Murmansk, code priority nine."

"Yes, sir!"

"Retrieve the aerial buoy as soon as the transmission ends."

"It's no good, sir," Lloyd heard the voice of the chief engineer saying, "that second impact has either damaged the prop even further, or we're entangled in something." Lloyd was shuddering with the vibration, and the noise of the protesting propeller and shaft was threatening to burst his skull. It was impossible to stand it for much longer. The submarine was slowing, the prop grinding more and more slowly. The Russians had done something, caught them in a net or some similar trap, choking them.

"Very well, Chief." He could not utter the words clearly, only in an old man's quaver because of the shudder in the hull which was worsening with every passing second. He shouted his orders above the noises. They were in a biscuit tin, and someone was beating on the lid with an iron bar. "First Lieutenant." Thurston nodded, holding onto the depth indicator panel, his legs as unreliable as those of a drunk. "John. I want a reading of the bottom as soon as we're over that plateau. If we find a flat bit, set her down!"

"Aye, aye, sir!"

The tension in the control room, even though it remained filled and shaken by the increasing vibration, dispelled for a moment. He'd done what they expected of him, demanded of him. The two planesmen struggled with increasing difficulty, veins proud like small blue snakes on their skin, muscles tight and cramped with the strain. They had to slow down, stop.

"Captain to all crew!" he yelled into his microphone, which jiggled in his hand. "Prepare for bottoming and maintain for silent running!'' Silence. A bad joke. The protest of the propeller, the shaft, the bearings drummed in his head.

"Lieutenant, come about and set up another sweep pattern two thousand metres to the east. Sensor control – no relaxation. We *can't* have lost her! She's here somewhere. Keep looking."

"Well done, John." Lloyd tried to lighten the sudden, sombre silence. "Light as a feather." No one smiled. The tension in the control room tightened again like a thong around his temples. The din had ceased, the torture of the prop and shaft was over. Yet the silence itself pressed down on them like a great noise. "All non-essential services off. Stand down non-operational crew and safety men. Get the galley to lay on some food."

"Hayter to Captain."

"Yes, Don?"

"The 'Victor-II' is still sniffing around, but I think she's lost us for the moment."

"Good news, Don."

The lights blinked off, to be replaced by the emergency lighting. The submarine seemed to become quieter, less alive, around him. They were more than twenty fathoms down on a ledge jutting out from the Norwegian coast, and the Russians would now be looking for them, more determined than ever.

PART TWO

SEARCH AND RESCUE

SIX:

Lost

Part of him, immediately he left the warmth of the headquarters building, wanted to respond to the driving sleet and the howling wind and the lights of the port of Pechenga gleaming fitfully like small, brave candles in the white-curtained darkness. He wanted the weather not to be critical, merely something to be endured, even enjoyed. Instead, there was the immediate sense of danger, as if a palpable, armed enemy was closing at his back. He turned up the collar of his heavy jacket, and crossed the gleaming concrete, slippery already, to the waiting car.

His driver was a *michman* – petty officer – from Pechenga base security, and he saluted despite the fact that Ardenyev was not in uniform. His face was cold and washed-out and expressionless in the purpling light of the lamps. Ardenyev had the strange and unsettling impression of death. Then the driver opened the rear door of the Zil staff car, and the momentary feeling evaporated.

The car wound swiftly down from the hump of higher ground on which the Red Banner Fleet's headquarters in Pechenga stood, towards the port and the naval helicopter base. Lights out in the roads, the glare of the arc-lamps from the repair yards, the few commercial and pleasure streets sodium-lit and neon-garish, like the stilled arms of light from a lighthouse.

Ardenyev was disturbed by Dolohov's manic desire for success. The admiral had never been careless of risks before. This adventure with the British submarine obsessed him. He knew the details of the met reports as well as anyone, and yet he ignored them. Ardenyev had, on his own authority, delayed his departure for the rescue ship out in the darkness of the Barents because of the worsening conditions. Delayed, that is, until further postponement would have meant running behind the schedule of the operation; and that he was not prepared to do. Instead, he nursed his conviction that Dolohov was unjustified in ordering them out.

It was cold in the back of the staff car despite the powerful, dusty-smelling heater. Ardenyev rubbed his hands together to warm them. Then the staff car slid under the canopy of white light of the helicopter base and the driver wound down the window to present his pass to the naval guard at the gate. The guard took one swift look at Ardenyev, the cold air blanching his face from the open window, more out of curiosity than to identify him. Then the heavy wire-mesh gates swung open, and the driver wound up the window as they pulled forward. The car turned left, and they were passing hangars and repair shops where warmer light gleamed through open doors. Then a patch of darkness, then the sleet rushing at the windscreen again. Through it, Ardenyev could see the two helicopters, red lights winking at tail and belly. Two MiL-2 light transport helicopters, the only naval helicopters in current service small enough to land on the seemingly fragile, circular helicopter pad of the rescue ship *Karpaty*.

The car stopped almost in the shadow of one of the small helicopters. Snub-nosed, insect-like, frail. Ardenyev thanked the driver abstractedly, and got out of the car. The sudden wind and cold sleet did not drive out the unwelcome, crowding impressions that seemed to have taken possession of his imagination, leading into the rational part of his mind, polluting clear thought. The Zil staff car pulled away behind him.

"You changed your mind then, skipper – decided to come?" came a voice from the door of the MiL. A grinning, cold-pinched face, blown fair hair above a dark naval jersey. Senior Lieutenant Andrei Orlov, Ardenyev's second-in-command and leader of Blue section of the special operations unit. Ardenyev summoned a wave he hoped was optimistic, then looked up at the sky, wrinkling his face.

"The pilot's moaning about the weather, skipper," Orlov added. "It's just having to turn out in this muck, I reckon."

Orlov took Ardenyev's arm, and he swung up into the hollow, ribbed interior of the helicopter. The door slammed shut behind him. Someone groaned with the cold. Young faces, five others besides Orlov. Blue section. Ardenyev nodded at them, business-like. Then he clambered through into the helicopter's cabin. The pilot nodded to him. His face was disgruntled.

"Get your clearance – we're on our way," Ardenyev told him, "just as soon as I get aboard your pal's chopper. Take care." Already, the inertia of the mission had affected him, sweeping him along like a current growing stronger each moment. An easy and familiar adrenalin invested his body. His mind was clear now. He clambered back into the passenger compartment. "OK, you lot?" Each man nodded. Most of them grinned, nerves flickering like small electric shocks in their faces and arms. "Good. See you on the *Karpaty*. Open the door, Andrei."

The door slid back, and Ardenyev dropped lightly to the ground. He

106

crossed the patch of wet, slippery concrete to the next pad, and the door of the second MiL opened with a screech. The senior *michman* who was his deputy leader in Red section hauled him aboard, wiping sleet from his jacket even as he slammed the door shut behind Ardenyev.

"Thought you weren't coming, sir," he offered. His face was bony and angular beneath the cropped hair. Viktor Teplov.

"Thanks Viktor. Lieutenant Orlov thought just the same." He looked round at the other five men, grinning. One or two older faces. Red section was the senior team in the unit. The faces were as they should be. A couple of good youngsters, too. "Everyone keeping warm?"

"With difficulty, sir," Teplov answered.

"Let's get going, then." He clambered through to the passenger seat beside the pilot. "Very well, Lieutenant, shall we proceed?" he said as he strapped himself into the seat.

"You're going to be very lucky, Captain, to get down onto the *Karpaty*. The weather out there is worse than this."

"I have implicit faith in your skills, Lieutenant." He gestured towards the windscreen of the helicopter where two huge wiper blades and the de-icing equipment struggled with the sleet. "Shall we go? I take it you're cleared for take-off?"

"We are. We've been waiting an hour, fully cleared."

"What's the matter, Lieutenant?"

"I've told my superiors – I've told anyone who will listen."

"Told them what?"

"The wind is force four plus. What if we can't get down, just can't make it?"

"The *Kiev*, I suppose. Why?"

"Let's hope it's not too bad for the *Kiev*, then. The range of this chopper means that once we get out there, we haven't enough fuel to get back. You should be in a MiL-8, one of the big boys, all of you. They shouldn't have assigned this –"

"Shouldn't have assigned you, you mean? Two small, light helicopters were requested. The rescue ship contains all our equipment. The *Kiev*'s no good to us. MiL-8s can't land on the *Karpaty*. Now, we can go?"

"All right. Just wanted you to know."

"I'm grateful."

The pilot lieutenant cleared with the tower. Ardenyev settled himself more comfortably in his narrow seat. The two Isotov turbo-shafts began to whine, and above his head the rotor blades quickened, cutting through the sleet, swirling until they were transformed into a shimmering dish. The lieutenant altered the angle of the rotor blades, the engine pitch changed to a higher note, and the helicopter moved off its chocks. The pilot paused, checking his instruments, the wheels of the MiL were just in contact with the ground. The pilot's knuckle was white on the stick.

"The wind," the pilot observed gloomily.

"Yes."

The MiL lifted, with seeming reluctance, from the patch of concrete. The sleet whirled round them in the downdraught. A fist of wind swung at them, made contact, knocked them sideways. The pilot shuffled his feet on the rudder bar, juggled the stick and they steadied, drifted, steadied again, and rose above the lights of the helicopter base. A white dish beneath them, darkness above.

"See what I mean?" the pilot offered. "We're right on the edge of possible flying conditions." The wind buffeted them. It seemed a physical strain on the pilot to maintain course. It had seemed a struggle to alter the stick and head the MiL out to sea, as if the helicopter was some reluctant, untamed animal.

"Yes, I see," Ardenyev replied thoughtfully. "Is our fellow traveller with us?"

The pilot looked in his mirror, then spoke into his throat-mike. The other pilot's voice was a pinched, unreal sound.

"He's there."

A shudder ran through the fuselage, as if it had received a powerful blow, some direct hit with a weapon.

Hyde opened his eyes. For a moment, Shelley's features were unfamiliar. Then he recognised Aubrey's aide, and attempted to sit up. Pain shot through his ribs, and his back, and he groaned. Hands pushed him back down on the hard bed. He could feel the thin, hard, uncomfortable blanket beneath his fingers, and he wiggled his toes, eyes very tightly shut for a moment until he opened them in relief.

"You're all right," Shelley said. "God knows how, but you're just bruised pretty badly."

His neck and shoulder ached more than his back and ribs. "One of them hit me," he complained.

"We assumed that was the case. It's why you've been out so long."

"How long?"

"Almost four hours."

"Christ." He covered his face with his hands, as if the light hurt him or he was ashamed. "Jesus, my head."

"I caught the end of the concert. Mine feels much the same."

"Very funny."

"Who was it – Petrunin?"

Hyde's eyes snapped open. "How did you know?"

"Routine surveillance report on the embassy. Unauthorised trip north by the Resident. It had to be you and the girl."

"I saw him." Hyde saw Shelley motioning towards another part of the narrow, cream-painted room. A door closed. Shelley's face appeared above his own again, and then he was being helped to sit up. Shelley proffered a mug of tea. Hyde sipped the sweet, scalding liquid, hands clasped round the mug as if to warm them. "I almost had her." They were alone in the room now. "I'm all right?"

Shelley nodded. "You're all right — just a bit crook."

"I feel it. The girl panicked. She's like something high on LSD. Seems to think they're coming out of the woodwork for her."

"She's right."

"That bloody rock band. They got in the way."

"Where do you think she is? Do you think they've got her?"

"I don't know. She could be anywhere." Hyde concentrated. "I got the impression Petrunin had gone back off the platform — the bloke who clobbered me was being pushed towards the steps — the girl was down the other end of the platform. One of them went after her. He might have made it."

"By the time I got here, they'd all disappeared. No one saw the girl."

"Shit."

"I know."

"What does Aubrey want us to do?"

"He's otherwise occupied. He's taken control of the submarine business. He seems to think it's in a hell of a mess."

"He's got the set now, then. It's all a bloody mess."

"Where is she, Patrick? If she isn't at the embassy or one of their safe houses? I've got everything I can screened. They won't be able to get her out — I hope. If they want to, that is. But if she's free, where is she?"

"Why not Heat of the Day? It's where she ran for help and cover in the first place? She might have nowhere else to go."

"The group?"

"Yes."

'Where are they?"

Hyde groaned as he swung his legs off the bed and sat up. He touched his ribs gingerly. "Are they sure nothing's broken?"

"Quite sure."

"Free Trade Hall, Manchester, is their next venue. Where they're staying tonight, I've no idea. Maybe here?"

Shelley shook his head. "Not here. Some country hotel in Cheshire. I'm having it checked out."

"You won't find the girl. She won't stick her neck out again. They could even have hidden her somewhere. She'll go to ground for the duration if the Branch trample all over the garden in their big boots."

"You can't do it by yourself."

Hyde rubbed his neck and shoulder, groaning softly. Then he looked into Shelley's face. "I'll accept discreet cover, but nothing more. The girl doesn't believe me as it is. If I go in mob-handed, she'll never tell us where Dad is. You can see that, can't you?"

"Aubrey wouldn't like it."

"He might. The girl is frightened. She knows one mob is after her, one mob and me on my own. Give me until tomorrow night, and if I can find her and talk to her, she might come in. I won't lose her again."

"Petrunin won't let go of you."

"All right. But the girl's more important. It won't be any good arresting a rock band and sweating the lot of them. She has to be coaxed. She's near panic. Her father must be a mistrusting bastard. She's neurotic about us."

Shelley paced the room, one hand rubbing his chin, the other thrust into the pocket of his overcoat. He glanced at Hyde from time to time. Indecision blossomed on his face. Eventually, he said: "I don't know – I just don't know."

"Look, you work on the assumption that Petrunin has her, and I'll work on the assumption he hasn't. Get back to London and mobilize the troops. I'll go up to Manchester, and sit on my arse and wait. Get me cover, *discreet* cover, from the Branch up there, and then let me try to get to the girl. If she isn't in Manchester, and they won't tell me where she is, then you can take over. OK?"

"All right," Shelley said after another lengthy pause. "All right. We'll do it your way, for the moment."

"At least I'm a familiar face."

"You won't be if you get knocked about any more." He glanced at the telephone on a folding table, next to a black medical bag. "I'll try to talk to Aubrey, though. I want him to be fully informed."

It was a tableau of activity, a frozen still-life of tension, fear close to panic, routine and emergency procedures. In other parts of the submarine, men lay in their bunks or sat on the floor. No one moved unless movement was unavoidable and essential to the survival of the *Proteus*. In the control room, men stood or sat as their functions dictated, and when they moved – which was rarely, and with Lloyd's express permission – it was with an exaggerated, burglar-like stealth. All unnecessary electrics had been switched off, and the control room was made eerie by the emergency lighting. Only Lloyd stalked the control room like a hunter, like an escapee.

110

The sonars, in passive mode, their screens illuminating the faces of their operators from beneath, making arms and chins and cheeks blue or green or red, a ghastly imitation of disco strobe-lights, revealed the *Proteus*'s danger. Under the cloak of "Leopard" the submarine lay on the ledge almost fifty fathoms down, while Soviet submarines moved back and forth around, below and above them like prowling sharks outside a diver's cage. As Lloyd watched over the shoulder of one of the sonar operators, a bright trail on the screen slid slowly to the port like the hand of a clock, mere hundreds of yards from their position. Noise – any noise – would be like blood to that shark, and bring the others.

Lloyd left the screen and stood beneath one of the emergency lights. Once more, he scanned the damage report that his chief engineer had compiled in silence and semi-darkness. They had not dared send a diver outside the hull, outside the cloak of the anti-sonar. Much of it was guesswork, or deduced from the instruments and the computer. The damage was relatively slight, but almost totally disabling. Thurston and the chief engineer had guessed at a low-charge torpedo – wake-homing, as they had known in those last seconds before it struck – which had damaged the propeller blades and the port aft hydroplane. It left the *Proteus* with no effective propulsion, and little ability to maintain course and depth. She needed repairs before she could go anywhere. And in that conclusion, Lloyd perceived the Russian objective.

He was calm. It was partly an act for the benefit of the crew, and yet it was genuine, too. He had not known he would react in this way, in harm's way. It had little to do with the fact that the pressure hull remained undamaged, or with the invisibility bestowed by "Leopard". It was, simply, him. He had no inclination to curse MoD or to blame himself for not aborting the mission hours earlier. The past, even as recently as two hours before, was dead to him. The Russians did not know where they were and, eventually, help must come – diplomatic, military, civilian, mechanical, political.

Thurston left the navigator and Hayter, who was taking a much needed break from monitoring the functioning of "Leopard", and crossed the control room. In his hand he had a notebook and pen. He held it up to Lloyd.

Thurston had written: *What do we do?* Lloyd merely shook his head. Thurston was puzzled, then scribbled furiously on a fresh sheet of the notebook: *We have to tell someone*. Lloyd took a pen from his breast pocket, and borrowed Thurston's notebook. He scribbled: *And tell them where we are?* Thurston – Lloyd could not help being amused by the pantomime they were enacting – wrote: *Must be Nimrod in area by now*. *We can't transmit. Too risky*. Lloyd scribbled.

They want "Leopard" — but how? Thurston wrote.
Salvage?

They couldn't, Thurston began writing, then his hand trailed off to the edge of the sheet. Savagely, he crossed out what he had written. Defiantly, he wrote: *Have to find us first.* Lloyd patted his shoulder, then wrote: *Only a few days.*

The sudden noise was deafening, literally terrifying to every man in the control room. It was more than two seconds before the rating at the code-signals console cut the amplification with a hand that dabbed out, as if electrified, at the switch. He stared at Lloyd guiltily, afraid, his youthful face behind his ginger beard blushing. Lloyd tiptoed across to him, his whole body shaking with reaction. The chatter of a high-speed coded signal, incoming. The rating removed his headphones, offering them like a propitiation to Lloyd, something to avert his wrath. Lloyd pressed him, firmly but not unkindly, on the shoulder, and held the headphones to one ear. He nodded, as if deciphering the signal for himself, or hearing an instruction in plain language. The rating flicked switches, and waited. His screen remained blank. Lloyd watched it, looking into a mirror, a crystal ball. Thurston arrived behind him, his breath ragged and only now slowing down. Lloyd felt the tension in the control room of the shrilling chatter of the signal, and the awareness of the Russians beyond the hull, and the knowledge that the signal was continuing. It crawled on his skin like St. Elmo's Fire, or a disturbed nest of ants.

The screen displayed a line of white print. A message buoy. Thurston nudged Lloyd, and mouthed *Nimrod*, and Lloyd nodded. The code identification then appeared, deciphered. *MoD*, then the placing of the security level of the instructions. *ETNA*. Lloyd looked startled. A civilian override by the intelligence service. The comprehension of their danger by some outside authority made him feel weak. They had known, had tried —

The message unreeled on the screen, line by line, then began to repeat itself. *Abort the mission, return to home waters immediate. ETNA. ETNA. Acknowledge, code 6F, soonest. Compliance immediate —*

Compliance impossible. Someone had known, someone in SIS or the Directorate of Security or the CIA, or the Norwegians, the Germans, the Dutch — someone somewhere had known, or suspected, and had tried to warn them, recall them. The knowledge was like a debilitating illness.

There was a Nimrod in the area, on-station. It would, perhaps, wait for an acknowledgement. It would, doubtless, remain on-station to monitor Soviet naval activity. Such would be its orders. It was up there, somewhere.

Signal, Lloyd wrote on Thurston's pad. The rating watched the screen.

112

The message began repeating for the third time. Lloyd reached out, flicked a switch angrily, and the screen darkened. The rating's shoulders hunched as if against a blow from behind.

You can't, Thurston had written by the time Lloyd looked back at the pad. The two men stared at one another, their faces seeming agonised in the dimness of the emergency lights.

Lloyd crossed the control room. Four trails of light, not one of them more than a mile-and-a-half from the ledge on which they lay. Four hunter-killer submarines, waiting for the blood that would spur them, fix the position of *Proteus*. That blood might be any noise, even the sonar shadow of the aerial buoy they would have to send to the surface to contact the Nimrod.

You can't.

Lloyd realized he still had Thurston's pad in his hand. He dare not, in his anger, tear out the sheet or throw down the pad. It would not make a detectable noise. Yet he did not dare.

In how many rooms had he waited, on how many occasions? Clocks. How many clocks? So many of them with large, plain faces and a red sweeping second hand. Arms that clicked onto the next minute. Clocks. The persistence of memory. Even now, there was no clarity to his thoughts, no cleanness. Only the many other occasions on which he had endured the same, endless waiting.

Aubrey sighed. He had not been aware of the number of clocks in the underground room until all the protocol had been observed and Brussels and Washington and MoD had agreed to his assumption of complete authority over the safe return of the *Proteus*. Furious telephone and signal activity, followed by a post-coital lassitude, restlessness. Waiting for the Nimrod's report, waiting then for the first safe occasion when the submarine could send an aerial buoy to the surface and answer their peremptory summons home. Until a certain time had passed – the remainder of that night, perhaps the next day, too – they could make no assumptions. Nor would they be able to prevent dread from flourishing like a noxious weed in each of their minds.

Aubrey knew it, understood the Soviet scheme in its entirety. Daring, almost foolhardy, reckless, extreme. But possible of fulfilment. "Leopard" as the prize. Clark, too, he knew agreed with his insight. He had not asked the American; he had asked no one. He stared at the cup of coffee in his hand, and found its surface grey. His watch peeped like a rising, ominous sun over the curve of his wrist, from beneath his shirt-cuff. He ignored it.

He had never been interested in seconds, in the sweep of the quick hand. Blister or burn operations that relied on that kind of exactitude had never been his forte. Yet he had waited longer, and more often. Back rooms of empty buildings near the Wall, with the rats scampering behind the skirting-board and the peeling wallpaper; or beneath the slowly revolving ceiling-fans, in hotel rooms with geckos chasing insects up the walls or places where, with the fan less effective against even hotter nights, crickets chorused outside; or with windows fugged by the warmth of wood-burning stoves, and wooden walls; and so many embassy basements and signals rooms, and so many rooms like this, in London and a dozen other cities. Memory's persistence, its retained vivacity, wearied and oppressed him.

Shelley's telephone call was, perhaps, the worst moment; the small, personal act of spite or neglect amid a more general ruin. Of course Hyde was correct – he must reach the girl himself, if they were not only to possess her, but to possess her confidence also. Manchester. Aubrey was doubtful that the girl had returned to the pop group; and at the same moment wondered whether his disdain toward their kind of music made him think that. He could not, he found, identify in any way with a modern girl of twenty-plus. An alien species. And Shelley's background was probably wrong. Hyde might know more than either of them.

With great reluctance, Aubrey looked at the clock on the wall opposite his chair. Another minute clicked away. Twelve twenty-four. Another six minutes, with good fortune and communications, before the Nimrod transmitted a status report on Soviet naval activity in the area of the Tanafjord.

And, despite the weariness of the waiting, he felt no desire to receive that report.

"No trace of them? After almost three hours, no trace of them?" Dolohov raged at the rear admiral, who blanched with a suppressed indignation of his own, and the sense of humiliation at once more being berated in front of junior officers, his own and those who had come with Dolohov. "It is not good enough, Admiral. It is very bad. We *knew* it would come to this, we knew it! They found her, crippled her so they say, and now they have lost her. It is not good enough!"

"I – can only repeat, sir, that everyone, every unit on station, is using every means to locate the submarine. We have reduced the search area to a matter of fifty or so square miles of the seabed. The British submarine is inside that square. It is only a matter of time."

Dolohov stared through the window of the control room, down at the map table. A cluster of glowing lights, now merely the decoration for a fir-tree. He dismissed the childhood image, but he could no longer believe in the symbolic importance of those lights. They were strung together for no reason. The rear admiral's voice seemed to whine in his ear, and his own breath whistled in and out of the spaces under his ribcage.

114

"They could stay down there for weeks, unless the hull has been damaged, which evidently it has not." As he spoke, his exhalations clouded a little circle of glass in front of his face, as if he were attempting to obscure the signals of temporary failure that glowed below him. "It will be wearying for them, but not uncomfortable or dangerous, while we listen for the whispers of their breathing, the sound of their feet." He turned on the rear admiral. "We should not have lost contact when the submarine was hit. *Grishka's* captain should not have lost contact."

"Admiral, he had poor target acquisition, just a trace of the submarine's wake. The torpedo had to be launched, or held, and he made his decision. I – I happen to think he made the right decision."

"You do?" Dolohov's face was bleak with contempt and affront. Then it altered; not softened, but it became more introspective. His voice was softer when he continued. "Perhaps. Perhaps. If they don't find her soon, then we shall pass from the realm of action into that of diplomacy, achieve an international situation. She is in Norwegian waters, and they will attempt to rescue her. Already, they have made contact. You have no idea what that message contained?"

The rear admiral shook his head. "A one-time code. We would need all their computer cards, and then know which one."

"Very well. It was probably a recall signal. What of the aircraft?"

"A British Nimrod. It will be watching us."

"You see my point, Admiral? Once they understand what we are doing, they will attempt to intervene. There will be evidence, photographs, computer print-outs. It will all serve to complicate matters."

"Yes, sir."

"Temperature sensors, sonar, infra-red – all useless." Dolohov rubbed his chin, staring at the ceiling above his head. In a quiet voice, he said, "Likelihood. Likelihood. If there was some element of *choice* open to the British captain – eh?" He turned to the rear admiral. "If he was able to decide, at least to some extent, his final location, where would it be? A ledge, a cleft, a depression? Feed into the computers every detail of every chart and every sounding we have of your fifty square miles. If necessary, we can send down divers – *before* Ardenyev's team are let loose. Or we can use submersibles with searchlights –" Dolohov was elated again. He controlled, he contributed, he conceived. "Yes, yes. We must be prepared." Then, seeing that the rear admiral had not moved, he motioned him away. "Get on with, it, man, get on with it!"

Twelve twenty-nine. Clark had joined him, together with Copeland, one of the less reluctant members of the "Chessboard Counter" team. He had requested a conversation with Eastoe, the pilot and captain of the Nimrod. The high-speed, frequency-agile transmissions would delay question and answer but not prevent it. When Eastoe spoke, his words would be recorded on the Nimrod, speeded up to a spitting blur of sound transmitted on frequencies that changed more than a hundred times a second, re-recorded in MoD, slowed and amplified for Aubrey. Then his words would take the same few seconds to reach Eastoe in comprehensible form.

"What's she doing now, Ethan?" he asked suddenly. "*Proteus*, I mean?"

"Getting the hell out, if her captain's got any sense," Clark replied gloomily.

"You really think they're onto her, don't you?" Copeland challenged Clark. Clark nodded, his face saturnine with experience, even prescience. "I can't believe that –" Copeland turned to Aubrey and added: "Nor should you, sir. 'Leopard' is undetectable, and they'll have taken no action against her."

"Ah," Aubrey said. "Would they not?" Copeland shook his head vigorously. "I wish I shared your faith, young man."

The communications officer approached them. "Transmission time, Mr. Aubrey." He was punctiliously polite, but there was little respect. As if Aubrey had somehow, by some underhand trick, succeeded to the commodore's job and salary and pension.

"Thank you – we'll come over."

Aubrey ushered Clark and Copeland towards the communications console with its banks of switches and reels of tape. Almost as they arrived, a red light blinked on, and a tape began to whirl at near impossible speed. A spit of noise like static.

"The Nimrod's transmitting," Copeland explained off-handedly.

"Thank you."

The communications console operator typed on the bank of switches like a competent secretary. Another tape began to turn, slowly. After more than a minute-and-a-half it stopped and the operator rewound it. Aubrey was aware of other people gathered behind him, much as men might have gathered around a radio for the cricket scoreboard.

Eastoe's voice, a man Aubrey did not know. Nevertheless, informed of the ETNA order and aware of its significance, Eastoe addressed his words to Aubrey.

Call sign. Identification. Then: "We have concluded a square search of the area, dropping patterns of sonar buoys while surveying the area by means of infra-red and radar. There is a great deal of Soviet naval activity, surface and sub-surface –" Clark scribbled the co-ordinates, even though they were already being fed into the map's computer. "We have identified by sonar at least four hunter-killer submarines in the immediate area, and the VTOL carrier *Kiev* and the rescue ship ident is confirmed. There are other surface units of the Northern Fleet engaged in what appear to be sonar searches of the area. Infra-red and radar is also being extensively and intensively used by all surface and sub-surface vessels –"

"They're looking for her," Clark remarked unnecessarily.

"We conclude an intensive search of a very small area of the seabed, especially inshore. Two Tupolev 'Bear'-Cs function exactly similar to our own, are also on station in the immediate area. All units are aware of us, we conclude. Over."

Aubrey glanced around at Clark, then at Copeland.

"You can speak to Squadron Leader Eastoe now," Copeland informed him.

"I realise that, young man. I am merely considering my reply." Aubrey remarked frostily. He paused. The open channel hummed in the silence.

"Squadron Leader," he began without introduction, "you evidently have no trace of the *Proteus*. Is it your opinion, your considered opinion, that the submarine has received your message and is acting upon it? Over."

The fast tape whirled, and again there was the little asthmatic cough of sound. Then the humming silence again, into which Pyott's drawl dropped theatrically, startling Aubrey.

"Not quite as easy as you thought, Kenneth?"

Aubrey did not turn round. Pyott had entered the room without his noticing. Aubrey sensed a lofty acquiescence in his tone.

"Ah, Giles," he said, "I'm afraid things don't look awfully sunny, just at the moment." Aubrey's own voice was similarly affected, announcing the draw, the honourable compromise. Pyott pushed past Clark and arrived at his shoulder.

"Have they got her?" he asked. Genuine guilt, concern.

"We don't know. I've asked the captain of the Nimrod to make a guess."

Tape whirl, then the slow tape, then Eastoe's unemotional voice.

"My guess is she's on the bottom, not moving." A pause, then, as Eastoe realised that Aubrey could not comment immediately, he continued: "The submarines and surface ships are concentrating in a very, very small area. Either they've lost contact altogether, or they have a pretty good idea where they'll find her. Over."

Immediately, Aubrey said, "In your estimation, is the *Proteus* damaged?"

"You're not serious, Kenneth?" Pyott asked while they waited for Eastoe's reply.

Aubrey looked at him. "The possibility has to be considered. If they are searching a very small area, it may be because they suspect, even know, she can't move out of that area."

"God," Pyott breathed, and his face was slack and grey, much older.

His mouth was slightly open, and he looked very unintelligent.

"I don't think we could raise Him on this set," Clark observed, having overheard Pyott's admission of negligence, culpability. Pyott glanced at the American malevolently. Clark raised his hands, palms outwards. "OK, I'm not crowing, Pyott." Giles Pyott nodded.

Then Eastoe's voice, as naturally, it seemed, as if he was in the room with them. "It's possible, sir." Aubrey's astuteness had won Eastoe's respect, at least for the moment. "The search appears to be concentrated well inshore, but it isn't being extended outside a certain radius. They're refining the search all the time, they're not widening it. I think she's in there somewhere. Over."

Aubrey looked at Clark. "Could they have damaged her, Ethan?"

"It's possible."

"How?"

Clark considered the problem. "Wire-guided torpedo, maybe. If they got a temperature trace – " Hidden fear now made itself apparent on his face. "Wake-homing – yes." He shook his head. Copeland's face was lengthened with realization, complicity in fear. Clark cleared his throat. "If they got some kind of heat trace, and then used a wake-homing torpedo, maybe with a proximity fuse, then the torpedo would follow the *Proteus*'s wake like a hound. Yes, it could be done."

"Do we accept that it has been done, and act accordingly?"

"I – guess so," Clark replied.

"No," Copeland said softly.

"What action, Kenneth?" Pyott asked.

"Diplomatic, of course, through the Norwegians. And practical. What other vessels do we have in the area?"

"Not much – and far away. Maybe the closest is a day's sailing from the Tanafjord."

"I see. I wouldn't like to escalate NATO activity in the area, anyway, with the present Soviet concentration of vessels." He paused. "I shall instruct Eastoe to monitor and report continuously. It would seem that, at the moment, the Red Banner Fleet cannot find our elusive submarine. That situation may not exist for much longer. There is a rescue ship in the area – Eastoe must monitor its activities with particular care. Meanwhile, gentlemen, we must consider all possible scenarios for the prevention of the loss of the 'Leopard' equipment to the Russians. Even at the expense of the *Proteus* herself."

Aubrey turned back to the communications console. It was a few seconds before his audience realised the implications of his statement and the uproar prevented him from completing his instructions to Eastoe and the Nimrod.

The sand dunes on the northern side of the airfield at Kinloss appeared momentarily through the lashing rain, and then vanished again. Tendrils of low cloud were pulled and dragged like bundles of worn grey cloth across the higher ground. Glimpses of hills and mountains were just discernible between the heavier squalls. Three RAF Nimrods gleamed in the rain, their nose sections shielded under protective covers, and the only colour in the scene was the brilliant red of a lone Hawk trainer. All four aircraft were lifeless, abandoned like exhibits in some open-air museum.

The controller watched, from the fuggy warmth of the control tower, a khaki-coloured crew bus returning across the concrete, its lights fuzzily globed by the rain, its whole appearance hunched, its roof shining like a snail's shell. Beyond it, two red anti-collision lights winked rhythmically, and a fourth Nimrod was just discernible. A fuel bowser edged cautiously away from it. Because of his headset, the scene had no sound for the controller, not even that of the incessant rain beating on the control tower roof and windows.

"Kinloss tower – Kestrel One-six requesting taxi clearance."

"Roger, Kestrel One-six. You're cleared to the holding point, runway Zero Eight."

Take-off conditions were bordering on the critical. A decision taken on the station would have resulted in the Nimrod's flight being cancelled. The controller disliked the interference of civilians with all the habitual ferocity of the long-serving officer. Eastoe was over the Barents Sea, waiting for this relief Nimrod. This crew were going to take off in distinctly risky conditions at the order of the same civilian, a little old man from the intelligence service. The controller had not been present at the crew's briefing, and the station commander had not seen fit to inform him either of Eastoe's mission or of the origin of their orders from Whitehall. That small resentment flickered through the controller's mind like one of the anti-collision lights out there in the murk.

If he kept quite still, he could line up the nearest Nimrod's fin with a joint in the concrete. He could see the shudders through the airframe as the wind buffeted it. Someone in a nice warm Whitehall office – *ah, tea Miss Smithers, excellent, is it still raining outside?* – giving easy orders with his mouth full of digestive biscuit and risking other people's lives –

The Nimrod Kestrel One-six was almost invisible now, tail-on to him, its winking red lights accompanied by white strobe lights. They alone announced its presence and movement.

"Kestrel One-six – Kinloss tower. You have your clearance."

"Affirmative."

"Roger. One-six. You are cleared for a left-hand turn out above five hundred feet."

The lighting board showed all the lights on the taxiway and the runway to be on. A telephone near him blinked its light, and the duty corporal picked it up, interrupting his making out of the movements slip. The controller lifted one headphone, and caught the information that Flying Officer Harris was sick and would not be reporting for the first shift the next day. He replaced the headphone.

"Kestrel One-six ready to line up."

"Kestrel One-six, you are cleared to line up, runway Zero Eight, for immediate take off. Wind zero-two-zero, gusting thirty-two."

"Roger, Kinloss tower. Kestrel One-six rolling."

The controller picked up his binoculars, and stared into the gloom. At first, there were only the pinpricks of the lights, then a slate-grey and white moving shape began sliding down the corridor of high-intensity lights, the shape resolving itself into the familiar outline of the Nimrod. He imagined the pilot's struggle to hold the aircraft steady against the fierce cross-wind.

The nose wheel began to lift from the runway. The four huge Spey engines began acting like hoses, blasting sheets of water up from the runway beneath them. Fog flickered across the wings as the change in pressure condensed the water vapour. The Nimrod began to disappear almost immediately.

"Kestrel One-six, I'm aborting."

"Roger –"

Too late, he thought, too late.

"I can't hold her – I'm off the left of the runway –"

The controller could see only one indication of the whereabouts and the danger of the Nimrod. The spray of water thrown up had changed colour, dyed with brown earth as the aircraft ploughed across the field alongside the runway.

"The port leg's giving way!"

"No!"

Then there was a silence that seemed interminable, he and the corporal staring frozenly at one another, until he managed to clear his throat and speak.

"Kestrel One-six, do you read, Kestrel One-six."

No flame, no explosion, nothing. The corporal's finger touched the emergency button. He could hear the alarm through his headphones.

"Kestrel One-six –"

A bloom of orange through the rain and murk, like a distant bonfire or a beacon. The windows rattled with the explosion, which he heard dully. Irrelevantly, yet with intense hostility, he heard the voice he had earlier imagined. *Sorry to hear that, Miss Smithers. All dead, I suppose. Is there any more tea?*

It had been so easy, and so pointless. The dull orange glow enlarged and brightened.

SEVEN:

Found

The helicopter dropped through the murk, and there were no longer rags of cloud and a sensation of unreality. The night was empty, blacker than the cloud, and the wind squalled around the cramped cabin with a demented shrieking that Ardenyev simply could not accustom himself to accept or ignore. Only the momentary absence of the snow and sleet reduced the unnerving reality of the wind's strength and velocity, because he could no longer see the wind as a visible, flying whiteness against the dark.

Then he spotted the *Karpaty*, below and to port of them. Blazing with light like a North Sea oil platform, yet tiny and insubstantial, her lights revealing the pinprick flecks of wave-crests against the black sea. Beyond *Karpaty*, outlined like an incomplete puzzle-drawing by her navigation lights, was the bulk of the *Kiev*. Even at her greater distance, she seemed more secure, more a haven than the rescue ship.

The second MiL emerged beside them, dropping into view, an eggshell of faint light.

"Express One to *Karpaty* – Express One to *Karpaty*, over."

The pilot's voice in his headphones startled Ardenyev with the immediacy of their attempt to land on the rescue ship's helipad. He strained his eyes forward, but could not even see the illuminated, circular platform. The *Karpaty* was a blur of lights seen through the still-running tears that streamed across the cockpit canopy and the windscreen of the MiL. The rescue ship was tiny, and they seemed to be making no visible progress towards it.

"*Karpaty* to Express One. We read you, and have you on radar. Range eight point five kilometres. Over."

"Weather conditions, *Karpaty*?"

"Winds oh-five-oh, thirty-five knots, gusting to forty-five. Sea state five to six, waves varying ten to twenty feet. What are your intentions? Over."

The pilot looked across at Ardenyev. He seemed satisfied by the glum, strained silence he observed. Ardenyev considered the shadow of the *Kiev* beyond the lights of the rescue ship. And rejected them.

121

"Well?" the pilot asked.

"Can you get down?"

"It's on the edge. I don't recommend trying –"

"Express Two to Express One, over."

"Go ahead, Express Two."

"Are we going down?"

"I don't like it."

"We can make it. I'll go in first, if you like. Over."

"You haven't got all night," Ardenyev remarked, looking at his watch. They were running perhaps thirty minutes behind schedule already. A diversion to the *Kiev*, and then a sea transfer back to the *Karpaty* would delay them by perhaps as much as two hours. Dolohov would find that delay unacceptable. The *Proteus* might be located at any moment, and Ardenyev had no wish to be still airborne when that happened. "We're late."

"I fly this crate, not you, Captain. My judgment is all that counts, and my judgment tells me to divert to the carrier." The pilot was calm, irritated with his passenger but unafraid. He assumed his authority would carry the day.

"Hold on, Express One – I'll set down first. When *Karpaty* has filled my tanks, I'll get out of your way." The other pilot sounded to Ardenyev to be less afraid, yet he wondered whether his own pilot might not be right.

"Express Two – I suggest we divert to *Kiev*."

"I'm not putting my bollocks on the chopping-block with Dolohov, Andrei, even if you're prepared to. Just watch my technique!"

Ardenyev's pilot's face was tight with anger, resentment, and something deeper which might have been self-contempt. Ardenyev watched, in a new mood of satisfaction, as the second MiL surged ahead and below them, towards the *Karpaty*. His pilot was playing safe, they would get down now. It meant only that Orlov and Blue Section would be kitting out by the time they arrived, and amused at their superiority.

The second MiL banked, looking uncertain for a moment below them, as if turning towards the surface of the black ocean itself rather than to the Christmas tree of the ship. Then it appeared to steady and level, and began to nervously, cautiously approach the stern of the rescue ship. The helipad was now a white-lit dish, no bigger than a dinner plate from their altitude. The radio chatter between the pilot and the ship flicked back and forth in his headset, suggesting routine, orderliness, expertise.

Ardenyev's pilot brought his MiL almost to the hover, as if they were drifting with the wind's assistance, feather-like. Yet when Ardenyev glanced across at him, the man's knuckles were white. It

122

did not indicate mental or emotional strain, merely made Ardenyev aware of the turbulence outside; its heaving against the fragile canopy of the helicopter. The pressure to move them, overturn them, crush them, was like a great depth of seawater. Once the image made contact with reality, a circuit was formed that alarmed him. The slow-motion below was fraught, dangerous now.

The fly-like MiL drifted towards the helipad. Ardenyev could see tiny figures on the deck, and their bent shapes, their clinging to rails and surfaces, indicated the force of the wind. Its volume seemed to increase outside.

The deck of the rescue ship heaved, and the light seemed to spill like liquid over the ship's side and onto the surface of the water. The whitecaps opened like teeth in a huge black jaw. The sight of the water's distress and power was sudden, making the rescue ship fragile and the helicopter approaching it more insect-like than ever. It was a fly hovering above a motorway, awaiting an encounter with a windscreen.

The helicopter flicked away, much like a gull caught by a gust of wind, and the pilot's voice was high-pitched, his relieved laughter unreal and forced.

"Mishka, get away from there! We'll divert to the *Kiev* and winch them down. You'll never be able to use auto-hover, the deck's pitching too much."

"Don't worry, Grandad," the voice of Orlov's pilot came back. "Just a temporary hitch. Watch this."

The words now seemed to Ardenyev to have an empty bravado which he despised and which frightened him. Yet the rescue ship seemed to have settled again, the whitecapped waves to have subsided, slipping back into the shadows beneath the deck of the *Karpaty*. The MiL began to sidle towards the helipad again. Tiny figures crouched, as if at its approach, ready to secure the helicopter the moment its wheels touched.

The pilot instructed the *Karpaty*'s captain that he would switch to auto-hover just above the deck, which would allow the helicopter to automatically move with the pitching of the ship, so that the deck would always remain at the same level beneath the MiL. Ardenyev saw his own pilot shaking his head.

"What's wrong?"

"What?"

"I said, what's wrong? You're shaking your head."

"The deck's pitching and rolling too much, and I think he's out of the limits for auto-hover and height hold." The pilot shrugged. "Perhaps it isn't from where he is. I don't know." He glanced at Ardenyev as if daring him to comment, or inviting personal insult.

"If there's any real danger, order him to divert – or I will."

Creeping whiteness appeared at the edges of their canopy, like some cataract or a detached retina beginning to float. The sleet had returned. Ardenyev's pilot increased the beat of the wipers, and they watched, oblivious of everything else, even of attempting to interfere, as the MiL below them banked, levelled, sidled forward, moved above the white dish of the helipad. There was a long moment of stillness, accompanied by the breathy whispering of Ardenyev's pilot: "Go on, go on, my son, go on, go on –"

The noise irritated and disturbed Ardenyev. The MiL was above the deck now, and lowering towards it. Stillness. A white-knuckled hand at the corner of his eye, whiteness creeping around the canopy, flying between them and the garishly-lit scene below. The navigation lights of the carrier, outlining a huge, safe bulk, in the distance. Ardenyev held his breath. They were going to make it. When they, too, had landed, Orlov would study his face; there'd better be no trace left of anxiety or doubt, or the young man would burst out laughing –

Dropping slowly like a spider coming down its thread; very slowly. Ardenyev could see himself, years before, watching such a spider in his bedroom, coming slowly down its thread, confident, small, agile, an acrobat. And slowly he had begun to blow upwards, making the spider swing, making it uncertain, vulnerable, that tiny creature who had abseiled from the ceiling with such arrogance. It had crawled, scuttling upside-down, back up its rope of thread, then dropped again with slightly more caution. Blow again. He had blown again.

The MiL hopped away from the deck as if electrocuted. Then it began to drop slowly, more slowly than before, towards the deck as it once more became level. The glimpse of the whitecaps vanished into the night.

The spider had scuttled away, dropped again, but its weight now could not deaden or steady the swing of the thread to which it clung. It had been descending from the lampshade, like a small black god climbing out of the sub. Swinging, unable to control the motion.

Ardenyev's hand touched his throat, feeling for the transmitter switch of his microphone. The spider was swinging across the ceiling above his bed, interestingly, helplessly. The helicopter shifted in a grumble of the wind, and the deck of the *Karpaty* shifted, too. Pitching towards the MiL, which hopped out of its way, then moved back down, drawn by magnetism, it seemed. The deck steadied. The spider swung across the ceiling, flying the landscape of cracks and damp patches, swinging to almost touch the shadows in the corners of the room. And nearing his face all the time as fear or instinct or helplessness made it pay out more of the rope of thread.

Six feet. Stillness now. White knuckles, his own fingers dead as he

124

fumbled with the microphone, tried to think what to say, why he was going to speak. Appalled and fascinated. Five feet, four –

The spider just above his face. Cheeks puffed out, he waited to catch it at the optimum moment, blow it across the bedroom, perhaps at his younger brother's bed and his sleeping form. Cupping his hands round his mouth to direct the breath when he expelled it.

Three feet, two –

"Auto-hover – come on, come on –"

A foot, then two feet, three, four – the deck of the *Karpaty* pitched again, the lights spilling across the angry sea. Five feet – spin, flick, twist upside-down, turning like a top. The MiL staggered with the blow of the helipad, and then the repeated punching of the wind. The spider flew through the air, into shadow, its rope of thread loose, wafting in the air's current he had disturbed.

The MiL hung upside-down for a second or more, then drove back towards the port side of the ship, breaking its rotors then its back on the side of the *Karpaty*, just forward of the helipad. A billow of flame, incandescent and paling the ship's lights, a tiny figure struck like a match falling into the sea, the MiL's wreckage pursuing him into the whitecaps. Flame flickered over the wild water for a second, then the MiL was doused like a torch – and gone.

Ardenyev came to himself, yelling into his microphone that the pilot should abandon his attempt and divert to the carrier. His words were clipped, orderly, syntactically correct, but he was hoarsely yelling them at the top of his voice. He must have begun shouting even before the MiL crashed.

"Shut up, shut up –!"

Ardenyev's mouth remained open, his throat dry and raw. There was nothing. On the pitching deck of the rescue ship, fire-extinguishers were playing over spilled fuel that travelled like lava along the deck and down the side of the ship. Slowly, the flames flickered and disappeared.

"My God," Ardenyev breathed finally. Teplov was at his shoulder.

"All right, sir?"

"No, Viktor, it is not all right," he said in a small voice. "Tell the team that Blue Section have crashed and that we are diverting to the *Kiev*."

"Sir." Teplov offered nothing more in reply. Ardenyev was aware of his departure to the passenger compartment. Ardenyev looked at the pilot.

There was a silence in which each man registered the other's pain, and guilt, then the pilot cleared his throat and spoke into his microphone.

"Express One to *Kiev* – permission to land."

"Permission granted." An older voice, senior. A commiseration of rank. The same voice went on to supply wind velocity and the effect of the sea and wind on the pitch of the *Kiev*'s deck. As he acknowledged, the pilot continually shook his head. Then he looked at Ardenyev.

"I was right – for fuck's sake, I was right!"

"We can get down?" The pilot nodded. "Christ –"

"Express One to *Kiev* – message received. We're on our way."

Ardenyev sat in a misery of grief as the MiL increased speed and the *Karpaty* slipped beneath its belly. He was appalled at the deaths of Orlov and the others, *his* men, *his* people, *his* responsibility. And he was shaken and anguished at the ease with which it had happened and with which he had allowed it to happen. Distance, slowness, lights – it had all become innocuous, something for spectators, cardboard danger. He had meant to issue the order to divert, but he had not. He had not believed it would happen. A child stepping from a pavement, behind a milk-float, crushed like an eggshell by the car it had not seen. But the distance between the front gate and the road is so small, it cannot signify danger –

He wiped savagely at his eyes. Through the blur as he blinked, the shadowy bulk of the *Kiev* drew closer, then lights sprang out on her starboard after-deck. The superstructure bulked beyond these lights. Tiny pinprick men moved on the deck, bent and huddled to display the ominous force of the wind. Ardenyev wiped his eyes again. The pilot and the carrier were in constant contact, as if instruction and counter-instruction, speed, distance, altitude, pitch, wind velocity would all render the collision of the two objects safe.

Ardenyev felt Orlov and the others in the burning MiL go away and his own fear for himself emerge, invading his stomach and chest and consciousness. The floor of the cabin under his feet was thin, so thin he could sense the buffeting air streaming beneath it, and anticipate the deck of the *Kiev* rushing up to meet them.

The MiL drifted towards the *Kiev*, so like Express Two just before it collided with the *Karpaty*. The deck did not, to Ardenyev's comprehension, enlarge with proximity. It was a grey strip, angled across the substance of the carrier, all the lower decks between them and the sea.

The pilot turned to him. "You'll winch down while the chopper's on auto-hover."

"Can't you land?" There was a strange relief amid the surprise.

"Yes – but I'm not risking it with you lot on board. You'll winch down. OK?"

Ardenyev nodded. "We haven't got a winchman on board."

"Can you do it?"

126

"Yes."

"Get back there and get on with it. I'll clear it with the bridge."

Ardenyev paused for a moment, and then forced himself out of his seat and climbed over it into the passenger compartment. The imperatives of Dolohov's orders were insinuating themselves again, until he saw the blank, automaton faces of his team. Stunned into emptiness of mind, except where their own fears peered over their shoulders or crawled like indigestion in their stomachs. A sharp pain of fear, a bilious taste in their throats.

"Viktor, we're winching down. Get the door open." Teplov looked up at him, acknowledging the necessity of the snapped order, resenting it, too. The offices for the dead, their mates, their importance to the operation; all clear in Teplov's eyes. Then he got up and went aft, unlocking the door and sliding it open. The wind howled amongst them as if Teplov had admitted an enemy already triumphing. "Get ready – one at a time." The helicopter lurched, one man getting to his feet was flung back against the fuselage, and his face revealed no pain, only a concentration of fear.

Ardenyev lifted him to his feet and shuffled him to the door. They clung to the straps, watching the lighted deck beneath them edge closer, shifting as the sea willed. The young man looked into Ardenyev's face, and seemed to discover something he could trust there. A habit of obedience, it might have been. He allowed Ardenyev to slip the winch harness beneath his arms, and to guide him to the open door. His hair was blown back from his white forehead, and his hands gripped the edges of the doorway. Ardenyev placed his hand against his back, and nodded to Teplov. The motor of the winch started up, and the man sat down, dangling his legs over the deck. He looked up as it swung away from the chopper, and then suddenly the MiL was moving with the deck, perhaps thirty or forty feet above it, swaying as in a breeze by virtue of the auto-hover matching its movements to the pitch of the carrier's deck.

"Right, off you go." Ardenyev held the man's shoulders for a moment, and then propelled him through the doorway. He spun on the wire for a moment, then straightened and dropped slowly and smoothly towards the deck. Uniformed and oilskinned men waited in the downdraught, arms reaching up to him. His legs were held, he was lowered like a child or cat from a tree, then Teplov was recalling the winch harness. Ardenyev looked at him, and nodded. "Next."

Shadrin, the explosives expert, was at his shoulder in a moment, grinning. "Let's get out of this bloody tin box, skipper," he said. There was a shadow in his eyes, but Ardenyev was thankful for the man's attempt at normality. A small re-establishment of cameraderie, teamwork. Sinkingly, Ardenyev realised that when he got them

127

safely aboard the carrier, he had to rebuild them in his own image; an image in which he felt uncomfortable, even treacherous, at that moment.

He strapped the harness around Shadrin, and slapped him on the shoulder. As Shadrin sat down, then dropped out of the MiL, Ardenyev recollected broiling flames and ignited, spilled fuel and a spider, and prayed that they would locate the British submarine soon. Very soon.

Aerial buoy, Lloyd scribbled on his pad. It rested on the chart table, beneath a dim emergency light. The temperature of the control room seemed higher, and could not be entirely discounted as illusion, which he knew it to be. Silence was humming in his ears.

We can't, Thurston scrawled in ugly, misshapen capitals, and added two exclamation marks for additional emphasis.

You were right – we must.

Lloyd and his first lieutenant stared at one another. The pads between them on the chart table were like scraps of food each of them envied the other. Thurston was now confirmed in Lloyd's original opinion that they must do nothing more than sit and wait out the vessels that searched for them. Lloyd – his calm eroded by the dead, limping passage of time, the slowness of clocks, and the sense that the forces mobilised against them could not indefinitely go on seeking and not finding – had now succumbed to the desire for action.

There was an RAF Nimrod above them – twenty, thirty, forty thousand feet it did not matter – on station, not knowing where they were, what condition they were in. MoD had to be told they needed rescuing, otherwise the Russians would inevitably get to them first. Lloyd was utterly convinced that the Russians wanted "Leopard". He could not envisage how they intended obtaining it, or conceive the recklessness that must have led them to this course of action, but he understood their objective. MoD had to be told; there was no time to be lost.

He scribbled again on a fresh sheet of the pad. *It's an order.* A helpless, obedient malevolence crossed Thurston's features for a moment, then it was gone. His face was blank of all expression as he nodded his acquiescence.

They crossed silently to the bank of sonar screens. Two only in closest proximity, the other submarines farther off, nudging their sensors into other corners of the box in which they had contained the *Proteus*. Lloyd read off distance and bearing. Both of the nearest submarines were, for the moment, moving away from the ledge on which they rested. Lloyd glanced at Thurston, and whispered: "Now."

Thurston moved away, and Lloyd found the control room crew, almost every one of them, and Carr the navigator, looking in his direction. He nodded meaningfully, miming the sending up of the aerial buoy. Thurston, at the encoding console, gave the thumbs up – temperature of the control room suddenly jumping – and his hands played over the bank of switches which would release and direct the aerial buoy to the surface. Its journey would take it perhaps a whole minute. Depth figures unreeled on a tiny display unit near Thurston's hand.

Breathing. Ragged, stifled, louder. The control room was full of nervous men trying to control their breathing. Lloyd, his arm draped around the periscope in the centre of the control room, felt hotter, less sure, supremely aware of the aerial buoy bobbing up through the layers of water to the surface.

A small object, a tiny pinprick. Capable of receiving and bouncing back a sonar signal. Something solid that betrayed their location. A flare they had sent up – we're over here, can't you see us?

Lloyd clamped down on the thought, and crossed to Thurston. He gestured for the first lieutenant's pad and then wrote quickly, in block letters, the message he wished encoded and transmitted to the Nimrod. Thurston nodded reluctantly when he read it, and turned in his chair. The console operator beside him began typing at the keyboard, and the code-of-the-day card was automatically fed in. The operator added the transmission instructions – high-speed, frequency-agile. Lloyd watched the depth figures unreeling near Thurston's elbow. The aerial buoy was still twenty fathoms from the surface, almost twenty seconds still to run until it bobbed up into the waves.

Sweating, now. Cold sweat, surprising in the heat of the control room. Lloyd tried to control it, to calm his body. Ten fathoms. Nine –

Someone clearing his throat, the noise of someone else scratching the cotton of his shirt. Six fathoms, five, four. Almost a minute since they had released the aerial buoy. Three fathoms.

Lloyd broke away from the encoding console and crossed to the passive sonars. Pinpricks, distances, bearings. Still moving away. One moving back, one moving back –

Bearing green nine-five, almost amidships, range two thousand yards. Speed eleven point two five knots. Lloyd looked over his shoulder. Thurston saw him, raised his thumb. The aerial buoy was transmitting the message, a split-second blurt of sound, repeated and repeated. They would have to repeat at least fifty times to be anywhere near certain their message had been picked up by the Nimrod. Ten seconds, no more.

Speed twelve point three knots, bearing unchanged, range closing.

Lloyd stared in disbelief. Twelve point seven knots and rising. Dead amidships, a Russian submarine. The buoy, or the message, untranslatable but audible to the Russians, had pinpointed them. Lloyd waggled his hand at Thurston, and the first lieutenant ceased the transmission and began recalling the aerial buoy.

Thirteen point six knots. Closing.

Lloyd crossed to Thurston, and indicated in savage mime that he must release the buoy, a chopping motion of his hand, again and again. Thurston paused for a moment, then his hands flickered over the console's keyboard. The figures near his knuckles on the digital read-out slowed, then stopped. The buoy was gone, up to the surface again where it would be swept away from their position by the current. Lloyd wiped his forehead with his handkerchief in undisguised relief, not even beginning to think that they had now only the back-up aerial buoy.

He hurried back to the sonars. Speed fifteen point nine knots, bearing unchanged, closing amidships. Range little more than a thousand yards. He realised he had been standing mopping his brow for almost a minute after they released the buoy. Speed fifteen point seven, fifteen point five.

He sighed audibly, a ragged sound from an old man's asthmatic chest. Speed fourteen knots and dropping, bearing green eight-four. Change of course, uncertainty setting in, scent lost.

Scent lost.

The Russian navy had sea-bed maps they could feed into their computers, superimposing them on their sonars and infra-red. It couldn't last for much longer. "Leopard" would be defeated by likelihood and by the concentration of vessels in their immediate area.

It couldn't last long. Lloyd felt weary, and depressed. It was hard to believe that the Nimrod had heard them, knew where they were and what had happened. No one knew. No one at all.

The decoded message from the *Proteus* unrolled on the screen of the Nimrod's display unit with the kind of stutter given to the pages of a book when they are riffled quickly. Group Captain Eastoe bent over the shoulder of his communications officer, and sensed the man's shoulder adopt the quiver of excitement that was evident in his own body. Like an audience of two, they were experiencing the same emotions, the gamut of surprise, shock, satisfaction, hope, and anxiety that the words had little apparent power to evoke.

When the message began repeating on the screen, Eastoe straightened and rubbed his cheeks with his hands. He yawned, surprising himself, then realised it was a ploy of the mind to gain time; time for consideration. *Proteus* on the seabed, position unknown, immobilised by a reduced warhead torpedo, surrounded by Russian vessels, surface and sub-surface. It did not bear consideration.

"Inform MoD immediately – Flash, code of the day. Poor sods."

"Skipper –" A voice behind him, the Nav/Attack officer in his niche in the fuselage of the Nimrod.

Eastoe crossed to him. Beyond the man's head the porthole-type window revealed the late slow grey dawn beginning outside; only at their altitude, and above the cloud cover. Below them, the *Kiev* and the other surface vessels would be moving through darkness still, and beneath them *Proteus* lay in the permanent darkness of the seabed, where hunter-killers attempted to sniff her out.

"What is it, Bob?"

"Something's happening down there, on the rescue ship."

"You mean in connection with last night's little party?"

"*Karpaty* is changing course, moving closer to the *Kiev*."

"I wonder why. You think one of those two choppers crashed on landing, mm?"

"Yes, skipper, surface wind would have made a landing very dicey. There was that quick infra-red reading, and I'm almost sure only one chopper eventually moved off in the direction of the carrier."

"Then what did they deliver, or try to deliver, to the rescue ship?" Eastoe considered, staring out of the tiny window, down at the roof of the cloud cover, lightening in its greyness, but thick and solid as the roof of a forest. Eastoe felt a detachment he did not enjoy, and which somehow interfered with his thinking. Being on-station, just watching, for so many hours had deadened the reality of what they could only see by means of radar and sonar and infra-red. Detachment; making thought and decision unimportant, without urgency. "Some sort of team? Experts? People important enough to be ferried out in this weather, anyway. Now you think they're going to transfer to the rescue ship?"

"I do."

"OK, Bob, I'll tell Aubrey. Leave it up to him. We'll be off-duty in a couple of hours, anyway. Someone else's problem, then."

Eastoe went forward again, into the cockpit of the Nimrod.

"Anything, skipper?"

"Signal from *Proteus*," Eastoe replied glumly.

"Bad?"

"She's been hit, Terry."

"Christ – they're all right?"

"At the moment. But she can't move."

"He was taking a chance, sending up a buoy."

"Wouldn't you want someone to know?" Eastoe paused. "Now

131

who the hell was in those two Russian choppers, and why do they need to get aboard the *Karpaty* so desperately?"

"Skipper –?"

"Doesn't matter. It's Aubrey's problem, not ours." Eastoe got out of his seat again. "Call up Bardufoss – tell them we're off-watch in an hour, and we'll need to refuel. Meanwhile, I'll tell Mr. Aubrey straight away. He might need time to think."

"You saw what happened last night, Captain Ardenyev. I can't guarantee any greater degree of success this morning." The captain of the carrier *Kiev* studied his hands, folded together on the table in his cabin. To Ardenyev he appeared carved, unyielding, even unsympathetic. Yet he was right. A helicopter transfer to the *Karpaty* could not be risked. He even wondered whether his team, Red Section, would board another helicopter. When they reached the *Karpaty* by whatever means, Ardenyev was uncertain of their reaction. The scorched plates, the damaged, twisted rail – he'd seen them through binoculars from the bridge as the grey, pallid light filtered through the heavy cloud – would be too potent, too evident a reminder of their mates, their rivals.

"Then it will have to be by launch, sir."

The captain of the carrier looked up. "I'm not unsympathetic, Captain. I am as concerned for the success of this operation as you are. Which is why I must minimise the risks with regard to your – depleted forces."

Dolohov had signalled the carrier during the night, when he had been informed of the MiL's crash and the loss of Blue Section. His message had been terse, steely, anxious. It had not been humane. He had asked, principally, whether the mission could now be completed. He had not expected a reply in the negative, and Ardenyev had not given him such an answer. Instead, he had assured the admiral that the *Proteus* could still be boarded by Red Section working alone, as soon as they found her.

For Ardenyev, it seemed the only answer he could give, the only possible outcome of his mission. His team wasn't ready, perhaps it never would be. He could only attempt to purge them of fear and shock and grief through action. Desperation might prove effective.

"I understand, sir. I'll assemble my men on the boat deck immediately."

"Very good, Captain. And good luck."

"Sir."

Ten minutes later, Ardenyev was forced to admit that Teplov had done his best with them, and the older men – Shadrin, Petrov and Nikitin – would do, but the two younger members of the team,

132

Vanilov and Kuzin, were unnaturally pale; cold so that they shivered beneath their immersion suits. It was really their mates who had died, all the younger ones. They seemed hunched and aged, standing amid the others in the companion-way to the aft starboard boat-deck. The movement of the carrier in the waves, slow and sliding and almost rhythmical, seemed to unsettle them even though they were experienced sailors.

"Very well," Ardenyev said, "as soon as we've transferred to *Karpaty*, I'll want a very thorough equipment check. It could take hours, I'll want it done in one. If a signal is picked up from that sub again, we'll be going straight down to her. OK?"

He scrutinised them in turn, not especially selecting the two younger men, but with his eyes upon each face until there was a nod of acquiescence. In one or two gestures, there seemed almost to be a quiet enthusiasm. Not from Vanilov or Kuzin, perhaps, but from Teplov and Shadrin certainly. It would have to do.

He turned to the watertight door, and swung the handle. The wind seemed to howl through the slight gap he had opened. He pushed against a resistance as heavy as a human body, and they were assailed by flying spray. They were below the flight deck, on a narrow, railed ledge on the starboard side of the carrier where two of the ship's four big launches were positioned on their davits. A sailor waved them forward, towards the launch allocated to them and which had been manned in readiness. White-faced, white-handed sailors fussed around the davits, ready to swing the launch out over the water and lower it into the waves.

"Come on, come on," Ardenyev said, hurrying them aboard, clapping each of them on the shoulder as they passed him, climbing the ladder into the launch. Ardenyev followed them, then leapt down again onto the boat-deck as one sailor lost his footing as the deck pitched. He grabbed the man's arm and hoisted him to his feet. He grinned at the sailor, who nodded his thanks. Ardenyev understood how everything except the activities of the moment had gone a long distance from him, and prayed that their mission would begin soon and would have the same numbing, enclosing effect on Red Section. He climbed the ladder again, ducked through the doorway, and joined the officer in charge of the launch, a junior lieutenant, in the wheelhouse.

Karpaty lay a matter of a few hundred yards to starboard of the carrier. In daylight, however gloomy and unreal, the sea raged. Ardenyev was chilled already through his suit from the wash of icy water onto the boat-deck.

"Captain," the young officer acknowledged.

"Lieutenant. We're ready?"

"As we'll ever be. I don't think we ought to make the attempt, Captain – to put it bluntly."

"Forget your thoughts, Lieutenant. We're going. Give the orders."

The junior lieutenant appeared reluctant, disliking his own junior status and the obedience it required him to express. He nodded, stiff-lipped, and spoke into his microphone, adjusting the headphones and the speaker to comfort, or as an expression of disagreement. The launch shifted on its blocks, then began to swing free, moving out over the boat-deck as the davits swung it away from the hull of the carrier. The launch oscillated alarmingly on its davit wires, demonstrating its frailty. Then they began to slide down the side of the *Kiev* the fifty feet or more to the water. The hull of the carrier moved in Ardenyev's vision. It was almost easier to imagine that they were the still point, and that the carrier moved with the wind and swell.

Rivets, rust, sea-life, spillage marking the plates of the hull. Then a grey sheen acquired by distance, then rivets and rust again. A constant chatter of instruction and comment from the lieutenant into his headset, then a shudder as the sea leapt up to meet them. The windscreen of the launch obscured by water for a moment, the hull of the *Kiev* splashed white and grey before the swell let them hang over a trough. The lieutenant spoke rapidly, and the rate of descent increased. Then they were wallowing, and the davit wires came free, and the engine of the launch coughed into life, just as the next peak of the swell broke over the bow and side of the craft, obscuring everything. The screw whined as it was lifted out of the water for an instant, then a trough released them, and the lieutenant ordered full speed and a change of course, towards the rescue ship *Karpaty*.

They butted and rose and dipped their passage across the few hundred yards of sea towards the *Karpaty*. Movement, however violent and uncertain, deadened thought, promised action. The coxswain's hands were white like those of the helicopter pilot the previous night, holding the vessel to her course. Everything was immediate, physical or sensuous.

It took fifteen minutes to make the crossing. Then *Karpaty* was above them, rusty-plated, grey, grubby with use, expressing a kind of toughness that comforted. Less than half the height above them of the carrier, nevertheless the rescue ship was one of the biggest of its type in the fleet. The scorched, blackened plates came into view, the sea working at them as if to scour off the evidence of disaster. The twisted rail, buckled plates at the stern, the damaged helipad, one edge broken as cleanly away as the snapped edge of a biscuit or a dinner plate. Simply missing.

The launch bucked and rode in the swell. The lieutenant was

134

chattering into his microphone. Ardenyev heard the voice of the tiny, black-clothed, gleaming figure on the port side amidships, beneath the archway of the rescue ship's central gantry, where the cargo deck was located. The boom swung across, and a specially rigged harness was slowly lowered towards them. Teplov appeared, as if by some instinct, at Ardenyev's elbow.

"You first this time, sir," he said. "Just in case."

Ardenyev was about to reply when the lieutenant broke in.

"I have the captain of *Karpaty*, sir. He'd like you aboard without delay. Apparently, one of the submarines has picked up a trace and he's been ordered to alter position."

Teplov grinned. "Come on, sir – get moving."

Patrick Hyde studied the façade of the Free Trade Hall in Manchester. He was sheltering from the rain in a shop doorway in Peter Street, almost directly opposite the home of the Hallé Orchestra, which now displayed, like some unbecomingly young dress on an ageing aunt, the banners and streamers and posters that bellowed the appearance that evening of Heat of the Day. The KGB man on the opposite pavement appeared uninterested in the announcement as he walked down the serpentine, bunching queue of people that stretched almost as far as the Midland Hotel. Hyde did not know whether the man had been detailed to look for the girl or for himself, but he kept the collar of his raincoat turned up and his cap pulled down over his eyes. If one of them was in the immediate vicinity, then he would not be alone.

Two. The other one was coming along the pavement on Hyde's side of Peter Street, walking slowly, conspicuous because he carried no umbrella. Umbrellas handicapped surveillance. There were a couple of young, denimed Special Branch officers in the queue for the rock concert, and plain-clothes police in cars parked at the junction with Watson Street and in the square at the other end of Peter Street. A presence inside the Free Trade Hall, too.

Hyde had spoken to Aubrey – the second KGB man he recognized was drawing level with the doorway in which he sheltered – at the Admiralty and persuaded him that Petrunin and the others should not be approached. Most of them were "unofficials", agents not attached to the Soviet Embassy or to trade missions or cultural organizations. They could not be certain how many there were. Removing Petrunin would be a false security. Free, Petrunin was a focal point. Hyde turned to the window. Transistor radios, stereo equipment, TV sets. The KGB man paused, but his inspection of Hyde was cursory, and he moved on. Petrunin running free would never be far from the action, and those under his control would gather round him, magnetized by his rank. They needed Petrunin and the few they knew from the files in order to identify the others.

Hyde moved out of the doorway. The KGB man inspecting the queue was returning to the main entrance of the Free Trade Hall, the second man was crossing Peter Street to meet him. Hyde nor the police had seen any sign of Petrunin during the morning.

Aubrey had been very clear about the risks, and the responsibility. It rested with Hyde. The girl must be found that day, that night, otherwise alternative methods would have to be employed. The girl would be taken in, regardless, and persuaded to cooperate. Hyde had one chance. Shelley's enquiries at the country hotel where Heat of the Day had stayed the night had proved fruitless. The girl had gone to earth. Shelley was inclined to the opinion that she had abandoned Alletson and the band. Hyde disagreed. There was nowhere else for her to run. Evidently, she was staying clear of her father, desperate not to lead anyone to him.

The two KGB men strolled together towards Watson Street. An Austin Allegro drew level with them, and they bent to the window as it opened, becoming instantly engaged in a voluble conversation with the driver of the car. Then the lights changed, and the green Austin turned into Peter Street. As it passed him, Hyde saw that the driver was Petrunin. There was no one else in the car, which drew in and parked in the square. Petrunin did not get out.

Hyde felt hunger expand as a sharp, griping pain in his stomach. Nerves were making him hungry. He had probably another seven or eight hours to wait. This time, he would not go in until the band was on stage.

He crossed Peter Street to speak to the Special Branch men in the queue. If he was going to wait that long, no one was going in before him.

Aubrey, Clark and Pyott had become, with the passage of the night and morning, an uneasy, indecisive cabal inside the organization of the underground room and the parameters of the rescue operation.

"Kinloss have another Nimrod standing by, with a fresh crew," Pyott argued. "They can be on-station in two or three hours. They won't resent the job, they won't be tired."

Aubrey shook his head. "Get them to contact Eastoe at Bardufoss. He and his crew must go back on-station immediately. I cannot afford to have that area unsighted for that long – no, not even with satellite surveillance. The cloud cover is making things difficult. Eastoe will have to go down to sea level if necessary. I must have *eyes* there, Giles."

"They'll be dog-weary, Mr. Aubrey," Clark offered.

"I have slept for three hours in the last twenty-four, Ethan. We

136

must all make sacrifices." Clark grinned at the waspish remark. "Very well, when the relief Nimrod is on-station, Eastoe and his crew will be recalled – for the moment. Let us discuss ways and means to preserve the security of 'Leopard'. That is our real priority."

"We're to take it you have abandoned any notion of destroying the *Proteus*?" Pyott asked with a mocking lightness.

"That was never my intention – you misconstrued. We may have to expose *Proteus*, however, by ordering Lloyd to destroy the 'Leopard' equipment."

Pyott nodded. "We may have to. We can, however, run it extremely fine. No need as yet. I'm not sure you'd get Lloyd to do it, anyway."

"He would disobey a direct order?" Aubrey asked in surprise.

"For the sake of his vessel and his crew, he would be entitled to do so."

"Very well, Giles. What can we do – before *tomorrow*, when the first NATO vessel arrives in the area? We must do something."

"Diplomacy?"

Aubrey snorted in derision. "I'm afraid the Foreign Office is running its head against a brick wall of denials. The Soviet ambassador has denied all knowledge of the matter. Soviet vessels are engaged in bad-weather exercises in the Barents Sea. He confirmed that, apparently, with Red Banner Fleet headquarters in Murmansk. It will take too long, I'm afraid, to unstick this matter through the proper channels." Aubrey looked drawn, thinner, older. He had slept in a cramped, cupboard-like room off the main operations room, on a thin, hard bed that seemed to imprison him. It had not improved his temper, or his patience. He wondered at his frenetic desire for action, and at the inertia of events which seeemed to be bearing him with them like a great tide. Yet he could not retreat into the dim, cool, shadowed walks of military sang-froid as Pyott did. "It will take too long," he repeated. "Far too long."

"And tomorrow never comes," Clark remarked. "By tomorrow, they may have a fix on *Proteus*, and then you'll find – what'll you find?" He looked at Aubrey. Clark in shirtsleeves and without his tie seemed more American; less sophisticated, stronger. Perhaps a hard-boiled newspaper editor, or a policeman. Yes, without the formality imposed by his suit, he looked more like Patrick Hyde; of the same type or species.

"What will we find, Ethan?"

"My guess is a salvage operation – if they can pinpoint the sub."

"You're serious, aren't you?" Clark nodded. "Why so certain?"

"There's no other way. They have to salvage *Proteus* if they're to save 'Leopard'. At least, I think so."

137

"And Lloyd may not destroy 'Leopard' now, if we order him to do so – I agree with Giles there. Then we are on the horns of a dilemma, gentlemen."

"Kenneth, we're left relying on 'Leopard' itself. At the moment, it protects *Proteus* and itself. It must continue to do so for at least another twenty-four hours."

"The rescue ship from Tromsø will take longer than that," Aubrey remarked gloomily, staring at his liver-spotted hand caressing the edge of the commodore's desk. "All we will have in the area tomorrow is one American submarine and a Norwegian 'Oslo'-class frigate. The day after, more, I agree. But, too late. We have to have surface ships engaged in any rescue operation, a counter to the Soviet concentration. They will, hopefully, go away when we arrive. I did not want to escalate our presence, but there is no alternative. We have nothing there *now*, that is our problem." His hand slapped the wood of the desk.

"Sorry to be the bad-news boy," Clark said, "but you're ignoring the latest movements of the rescue ship the Soviets have on-station, and those helicopters that arrived last night."

"Yes?" Aubrey snapped impatiently. Then: "Sorry – go on."

"The boarding party?" Pyott queried, and Clark nodded.

"Damnation! What do we *do*? Tell me that. What do we do?"

"Send Eastoe down on the deck to look over the rescue ship and the immediate area – and continue our orisons, I should think," Pyott drawled. Aubrey looked venemously at him, and Pyott blushed slightly with the memory of his culpability. "Sorry," he said softly.

"It's escaping from us," Aubrey sighed. "I feel it. It is too far ahead of us to be overtaken."

Lloyd paused for a moment at the door of the computer room, aft of the control room. Don Hayter's summons – a rating tapping his captain on the arm, beckoning him theatrically – had been peremptory and urgent, and Lloyd's sense of bodily temperature had leapt. Yet he could not bring himself to move through the door, not for a moment. The rating's face had been worried, pale and disturbed in the red lighting. It had seemed, immediately and without embroidery by Lloyd's jumpy imagination, to indicate disaster. Then Hayter saw him, and urgently waved him in. Hayter was bent over one of the "Leopard" screens. The noise he was making tapping a pencil against his teeth shocked Lloyd.

Hayter grabbed Lloyd's arm as he reached the panel, and tapped at the screen with the pencil, underlining the computer-print words the screen displayed. He tapped again and again at one phrase.

FAULT NOT IDENTIFIED.

Then he looked up at Lloyd, who concentrated on reading the rest of the computer's assessment of the situation.

"Leopard" had developed a fault.

"What is it?" Lloyd asked, then repeated his question in a whisper that was not clogged with phlegm. "What is it?"

Hayter shrugged. "It's been happening for four minutes now. We've checked –" He nodded at the rating who had brought Lloyd to the computer room, and the sub-lieutenant who was Hayter's second-in-command. "– everything, so has the computer."

"What – what is the fault doing? What effect is it having?" Lloyd almost wanted to smile at the exaggerated seriousness of Hayter's expression. Lugubrious.

"It's blinking. On, off, on, off. Sometimes, they can see us, sometimes they can't."

"*What?*"

"Whatever the malfunction is, it's intermittent."

"And now – at this moment?"

"Invisible. A moment before you came in, it came back on, full strength, fully operational. Before that, for eleven seconds, nothing, nothing at all."

"Christ."

The sub-lieutenant, Lloyd now perceived, was removing the front panel of the main container housing the "Leopard" equipment, a metal box little bigger or taller than a large filing cabinet.

"We're going to have to do a manual, if the computer can't tell us."

"How long?"

"No idea."

"Could it have happened when we were attacked – the damage to the prop and hydroplanes?"

"Possible. The sensors and dampers at the stern could have been damaged. If they have been – and the fault's outside – then we can't do a bloody thing down here without divers."

"Complete failure?" Hayter nodded. "What about the back-up system?"

Hayter's face became more lugubrious than ever; not a painted clown's downturned mouth but a human expression of concern and fear. His fingers played over the keyboard beneath the display screen, and the message vanished. Then he typed in a new set of instructions, and the response from the computer was almost instantaneous.

MALFUNCTION.

Hayter opened his palms in a gesture of helplessness.

"The back-up system won't cut in."

"It doesn't work at all?"

"At the last check, it worked. Now, it doesn't. I don't understand it.

Immediately after the attack, we checked everything through on the computer. It registered no malfunction in either the main or back-up systems. Then we start winking at the Russians, and the computer doesn't know why. At the same moment, the back-up system is u/s. We'll do our best – that's all I can tell you."

The message vanished from the screen before Lloyd had finished reading it. More words came spilling across the screen, line after line in block letters.

MALFUNCTION IN MAIN SYSTEM.   UNIDENTIFIED

"Is it –?"

Hayter nodded. "It's gone again. 'Leopard' isn't working. Anyone who cares to look in our direction can see a British submarine lying on her belly."

Lloyd looked at his watch. The second hand crept across the face like a red spider's leg, ugly, jerking, uncoordinated. Eight, nine, ten, eleven –

"Longer this time," Hayter murmured.

Twelve, thirteen, fourteen –

"Come on, come on, –" Lloyd heard himself saying a long way below his mind. "Come on –"

Sixteen, seventeen –

There were four submarines within a radius of six miles of the *Proteus*. He had been studying the sonars just before he was summoned by Hayter.

Twenty-one, two, three, twenty-four, almost half a minute –

"I think she's gone," Hayter whispered, flicking switches on the console in an almost demented fashion. The movements of his hands appeared in all the more frenzied because of the expressionless lines and planes in which his face seemed to have coalesced. The message on the screen blinked out, then returned with a status report on the back-up system.

MALFUNCTION.

Thirty-two, three, four –

Lloyd could not remove his gaze from the second hand of his watch. Hayter's hands still played across the banks of switches as he attempted to coax life back into "Leopard", or to rouse its back-up system. Complete failure.

MALFUNCTION.

The word seemed to wink on and off the screen at a touch of a key or switch; as if the whole system had failed in each of its thousands of parts and circuits and microprocessors and transistors and coils.

Forty-two. Lloyd knew he ought to be in the control room, knew that they would be picking up changes of course and bearing, changes of speed. Forty-four.

The word vanished from the screen. A status report replaced it. Hayter sighed, perspiration standing out on his forehead, which he wiped with the back of his hand. He grinned shakily.

"We're back in business – for the time being," he said.

"Everything's working?"

"As normal. The main system. Back-up's still dead."

"Get working on the back-up system." Then Lloyd almost ran from the room, down the companion-way to the control room, anticipating what he would see on the sonar screens.

"Skipper, I'm getting a reading from one of our sonar buoys – it's *Proteus*."

"What? Bob, are you certain?"

"Skipper – I picked up a trace. It disappeared after about ten seconds, so I assumed it was a shoal of fish or something of the sort, or a false reading. Then, a couple of minutes later, the same reading on the same bearing, for almost a minute. Now it's gone again."

"What's happening?"

"Could be a malfunction in their equipment?"

"I don't know. Have you got a fix on her position?"

"Not the first time. The second time she came in on two of the buoys. Yes, I've got her."

"Well done. Where is she?"

"What looks like a ledge. Shall I bring the chart through?"

"No. Not until I've decided what message to send to MoD. Have the Russians picked her up?"

"I don't know. Perhaps not –"

"You hope. Keep looking. The moment anything moves closer to *Proteus*'s position, let me know. You're *sure* it's her?"

"What else could it be? I don't understand 'Leopard', even after the briefing, but I know what it's supposed to do. We couldn't see her, now we can. Correction, we *did* see her."

"OK, OK, I believe you. Pass her position to John and tell him to stand by to transmit a Flash signal to Aubrey."

"I'm already standing by, skipper."

"Good. We'll take her down for a look-see first."

Eastoe turned to his co-pilot, and nodded. The cloud cover beneath the nose and wings of the Nimrod gleamed with sunlight, innocent; yet it extended downwards almost to sea level and it was moved by gale-force winds. Their calm was illusory, achieved only by altitude.

"Give me a bearing on the carrier," Eastoe requested into his microphone. Almost immediately, the navigator supplied the coordinates and the course change that would take them over the *Kiev*.

Eastoe dipped the Nimrod's nose towards the clouds. Sunlight, the dense, smoothed roof of the cloud-forest, then a creeping greyness, the first rags and twigs of mist, the darkening of the flight-deck, then the cloud rushing past, swallowing them as they moved into it. The co-pilot switched on the wipers, and water streamed away from their furious beat. Eastoe felt the tremor of the winds through the control column as he watched the altimeter unwind. Down through twenty thousand feet, nineteen, eighteen.

Turbulence buffeted the Nimrod as the aircraft dropped towards the sea. Eastoe sensed for a brief moment the fragility of the airframe around him, imagined the last moments of the Nimrod that had crashed on take-off, remembered the pilot and the crew who had died, and then they broke through the lowest fringes of the cloud, into squalling rain and a headwind. He levelled the Nimrod no more than a hundred and fifty feet above the whitecapped water. The carrier was a fuzzy, bulky shape through the rain, less than a mile ahead of them.

In his headphones, the senior Nav/Attack officer began calling out the readings from his screens and sensors, describing the movements of the surface and sub-surface vessels during the time they were descending. The carrier seemed to leap towards them like a huge stone across the stormy water.

The subs were altering, or had altered, course, and all were closing on the same bearing. The carrier appeared to be lumbering onto a new course. All units closing on the fixed position of the *Proteus*. They'd found her. Maybe foxed for the moment, but they had her now.

Eastoe throttled back the four Rolls-Royce engines, and the Nimrod appeared merely to float above the deck of the *Kiev*. No activity, launches stowed on both the port and starboard boat-decks – the co-pilot calling out confirmation of what Eastoe had seen for himself

and then the rescue ship was ahead as the *Kiev* passed out of sight beneath them. The *Karpaty* was making slow headway and, as Bob called out her course, Eastoe realized that the rescue ship was on a heading that would take her over the *Proteus*.

He realized, too, the significance of the rescue ship. He throttled back once more, and they drifted towards the *Karpaty*.

"See it?" he said.

"Yes, skipper. They're trying to launch a boat from the starboard side, looks like."

The Nimrod crept towards the rescue ship. Tiny figures, moving with what seemed hopeless and defeated slowness around the starboard launch on its davits. Eastoe strained forward in his seat. The co-pilot increased the beat of the wipers. Shiny, oil-skinned crewmen – no, not all of them, surely?

142

"What in hell –?"

"Divers."

"*Divers*! Shit and hell!"

The Nimrod floated over the dipping bow of the *Karpaty*. A chaos of water flung up over her deck, the surge of an animal as the wave released her into the next trough. Men in shiny, tight-fitting suits, face-masked, oxygen cylinders on their backs. They were pinpricks, tiny matchstick men, but they were divers, climbing into the launch.

"How far is she from the *Proteus*?"

"Less than a mile," he heard the navigator reply as the nose of the aircraft blotted out the scene directly below them.

"I'm going round for another look and some more pictures," Eastoe said, "and then we'd better send Aubrey the bad news – they're going down to the *Proteus*, for God's sake!"

EIGHT:

Seizure

Aubrey stared at the note he had scribbled, the small, neat handwriting suddenly expressive of powerlessness, and realized that they had lost. "Leopard" had malfunctioned, betraying the position of the *Proteus* to the Russian submarines in the immediate area. The rescue ship *Karpaty* was preparing to launch a small boat on which were a team of divers. They had received photographic proof of that over the wireprint. Opposite his note, Clark had scrawled in his strangely confident, large hand *RB Spec Ops Unit – Ardenyev*. Aubrey presumed it was no more than an informed guess, and it had no significance. The identity of the divers did not matter, only that they existed and were less than a mile from the reported position of the British submarine.

It was dark outside now. Perhaps not quite. A drizzling, gusty dusk. Aubrey had taken a short afternoon walk in St. James's Park, but he had been unable to shake off the claustrophobic, tense gravity of the underground room beneath the Admiralty, and had soon returned to it.

Lost. Found by others. The Russians evidently intended that *Proteus* should be salvaged, perhaps even boarded, and the "Leopard" equipment inspected before it was presumably returned, together with the submarine and her crew. An accident, not quite an international incident, no real cause for alarm, no ultimate harm done. He could hear the platitudes unroll in the days ahead, perceive the diplomatic games that would be played. He knew the Russians would take *Proteus* to one of their closest ports – Pechenga, Poliarnyi, even Murmansk – and there they would effect apologetic repairs, even allowing the American consul from Leningrad or a nominated member of the British embassy staff from Moscow to talk to the crew, make the noises of protest, send their London ambassador to call on the foreign secretary and the PM, heap assurance upon assurance that it was an accident, that all would be well, that this indicated the willingness for peace of the Soviet Union – *look, we are even repairing your submarine, send experts to inspect our work, why are you so suspicious, so belligerent, you will have your submarine back as good as new –*

The diplomatic support for the operation sprang fully-envisaged

144

into Aubrey's awareness, like a childhood or youthful moment of extreme humiliation that haunted him still in old age. It did not matter that it was all a blatant lie; it would work. It would give them enough time to photograph, X-ray, dismantle "Leopard", and learn its secrets.

And, at the same time, they might obtain its designer, Quin, who would help them to build more. In the moment of the loss of "Leopard", Aubrey feared for Hyde's failure and the girl's capture.

"What do we do, Kenneth?" Pyott asked at his shoulder. The channel to Eastoe in the Nimrod was still open, the tapes waiting for his orders. Aubrey waved a hand feebly, and the operator cut the communications link.

Aubrey looked up into Pyott's face, turning slightly in his chair. "I do not know, Giles – I really do not know."

"You have to order Lloyd to destroy 'Leopard' – I mean literally smash it and grind the pieces into powder," Ethan Clark remarked, his face pale and determined. "It's the only way. The guy must know by now that's what they're after, and how close they are to getting it. He has to get rid of 'Leopard'."

"Just like that? I seem to remember the *Pueblo* made a monumental cock-up of a similar procedure some years ago," Pyott observed haughtily. "It won't be easy. 'Leopard' isn't in a throwaway wrapper, Clark."

"You British," Clark sneered. "Man, you're so good at inertia, you make me sick."

"There has to be something else we can do – besides which, 'Leopard' is working again."

"For the moment."

"Gentlemen," Aubrey said heavily, wearily, "let's not squabble amongst ourselves. Ethan, is there anything else we can do?"

"You're not able to rescue *Proteus*, Mr. Aubrey."

"Then perhaps we should warn her what to expect."

Aubrey got up from the chair at the communications console, and crossed the room to the map-board. He seemed, even to himself, to be shrunken and purposeless beneath it. *Proteus* – white light – had been repositioned, closer inshore, and the updated courses and positions of the carrier, the rescue ship, the destroyers and the submarines created a dense mass of light around one thin neck of the Norwegian coast. The sight depressed Aubrey, even as it galvanized him to an action of desperation. He had lost the game, therefore he must damage and make worthless the prize.

"Encode the following," he called across the room, "and transmit it to Eastoe at once, for relay to *Proteus*. Mission aborted, destroy, repeat destroy 'Leopard'. Priority most absolute. Append my signature."

145

Every man in the room listened to him in silence, and the silence continued after he had finished speaking. A heavy, final silence punctuated only by the clicking of the keys of the encoding machine.

Ardenyev watched Vanilov's feet begin to slip, saw the white face surmounted by the facemask and half-obscured by the bobbing mouthpiece of his breathing apparatus, and felt the wave surge round his own ankles and calves. His hands gripped the rail of the launch, but Vanilov's grabbed for a handhold like clumsy artificial claws he had not learned to operate. Ardenyev reached out and gripped the younger man's elbow, almost as if he were about to twist Vanilov's arm painfully behind his back. He pulled the frightened, off-balanced man to him, hugged him upright, then pushed at his back and buttocks until Vanilov was over the rail of the launch and into it, a look of fearful gratitude on his face. They were all in.

The sea flung itself against the *Karpaty* more ferociously than had been apparent on the carrier, as if encouraged by its success in making the rescue ship bob and duck and sway in the water. Amidships, where they were boarding the launch that would then be swung out on its davits, the sea boiled across the deck as each succeeding wave caught them in the trough behind its predecessor. Ardenyev watched a grey, white-fringed, boiling wall of water rise level with and above the deck, and tightened his grip on the launch's rail and widened his stance. Teplov offered his hand, and Ardenyev shook his head.

"Get below!" he yelled.

The wave smashed against the side of the hull, then flung its broken peak across the deck, drenching Ardenyev. He was deafened and blinded by the water, and he thought the thin, inhuman noise he heard distantly was merely illusion. When he opened his eyes again, there was one yellow-oilskinned figure less than before, gathered around the boat station – and other men were looking blankly and fixedly towards the ship's side. Ardenyev realized, as he shivered and tried to control his chattering teeth, the fragility of their enterprise, even its lunacy; resented to the point of hatred an old man ensconced in the non-climatic, antiseptic surroundings of the Red Banner headquarters in Murmansk. He wanted to open his mouth and yell his anger as the *Karpaty* wallowed her way into the trough behind the wave that had killed one of her crew.

He swung himself up and over the rail, and hurried into the shelter of the launch's cabin, seeking the determination to order the officer in command of the frail little boat to issue his own orders for the launching of the vessel. A tiny yellow blob for a second, out there in the water –?

Ardenyev shook his head, clearing the last of the water from his face and eyes with his hands. The air tanks were heavy on his back. He'd insisted – despite the discomfort and the loss of agility – that they don their full equipment, everything except flippers, in the comparative calm of the *Karpaty*, while the ratings of the rescue ship struggled to load their special equipment into the launch.

The lieutenant in command of the launch watched him, immediately he entered the cabin, with a thin-lipped, colourless expression. His face reflected Ardenyev's thoughts, with its sense of the threadbare rationality of Dolohov's scheme that now made the old man seem mad. Dolohov appeared to have cobbled this operation together in a fit of lunacy.

"Gone again, sir," the *michman* on the launch's sonar called out, and the lieutenant appeared to take this as a final condemnation of what they were doing, the last bitter irony of forces he could hardly comprehend but which controlled him.

Ardenyev crossed the cabin to the sonar. "Show me," he said.

The *michman* indicated a line across the screen with his finger, as if slicing the perspex surface of the sonar. "That bearing," he said. "Range six hundred."

Six hundred metres from them, the British submarine lay on a ledge, less than fifty fathoms down. The invisible Norwegian coast had thrust out a hand, a fingertip, to aid her. Her anti-sonar was flicking on and off like a signalling torch.

"That's it – let's go."

Teplov's head appeared at the door at the rear of the cabin.

"It's all in good shape, sir."

"What about the men?" Teplov paused for a moment, then he nodded slowly. "Good," Ardenyev added. "Make sure everything's secure. Tell them to hang on tight, and be ready to move fast when I give the order." Teplov nodded again, and his head then disappeared as the door closed.

The launch lurched off its blocks, swung fragilely outwards above the deck and then the grey water – they were in another trough between great waves – and the winches with their tiny, yellow-garbed figures working furiously at them, trundled them downwards towards the water. Speed seemed to lend stability and cancel the force of the wind, even still the water as it rushed up towards them. The rusty plates again of the hull, the thin wires above them, then the launch's keel smacking into the water, screw churning, its whine in air disappearing and its power failing to move the launch. Ardenyev grabbed a handhold and braced himself as the launch was lifted towards the grey-white peak of the next wave. It teetered there for a moment, deck awash, windows blind and running with water, the coxswain spinning the wheel feverishly and without apparent effect, then it began falling.

Ardenyev heard someone cry out just after he registered a metallic, screeching slither from beyond the closed door at his back, then he was aware only of the ugly, frightening sensation of being swallowed by a huge, grey-fleshed, open mouth. Then they were in a trough and the rudder and the screw began taking effect and the boat moved with some of its own volition rather than that of the sea. A sense of stability returned to his legs and feet, the illusion of a firm surface, a level world.

The warble of the sonar again, then, as if hearing were just returning.

"She's there again, sir!" the *michman* called out.

"Has she changed position?" Ardenyev asked.

The *michman* calculated swiftly. "No, sir. Bearing now red one-five, range five-seven-eight."

"Helmsman – port one-five."

"Port one-five, sir."

Teplov's face, white and drained and old, appeared at the door again.

"Sir, it's Petrov – his leg. The hose broke loose, sir, wrapped itself around his leg – think it's broken, sir."

"God," Ardenyev breathed, closing his eyes. Six of them now. Dolohov was a fucking lunatic –

"Will you come, sir?"

"It should have been stowed properly!" Ardenyev yelled in his enraged frustration.

The launch teetered, then the bow fell drunkenly down and forward, the noise of the screw disappearing, sinking into the throb of the labouring engine. Six of them had to get themselves, their sleds, hoses and canisters, welding equipment and communications over the side of the launch, below the surface, down to the *Proteus*. There should have been thirteen of them. Impossible now.

"I'll come," he said, suddenly weary and cold.

"One minute ten seconds, eleven, twelve, thirteen –" Lloyd whispered, the lowering of his voice an act of mockery, pointless. "Sixteen, seventeen – twenty."

Hayter and the sub-lieutenant were examining the mass of wiring and circuitry and microprocessors inside the main metal cabinet housing "Leopard". Hayter and the sub-lieutenant were checking the efficiency of each component manually, with multi-meters. The rating was removing the panelling of the second box, kneeling like a safecracker against the metal.

148

Hayter looked up desperately, shaking his head. "It's no good, sir. We could be doing this for hours yet. Unless it switches itself back on, we're finished. It's no good pretending we're not. Everything here appears to be working, dammit!"

"Get to work on the back-up system, will you?" One minute forty-two seconds. It wasn't going to come on again.

"You know where that's housed. We can't work in there with the space and freedom we've got here. It'll take even longer –"

"Christ, Don – what are you going to do, then?"

"I don't *know*, sir!"

One minute fifty-nine, two minutes of visibility on any and every sonar screen in the area. On the *Kiev*, the rescue ship, the subs, the destroyer, the aircraft overhead. Everyone could see them.

The subs were holding off, not coming in for the kill. But then, they wanted 'Leopard', not blood. And they were jamming every radio frequency they could. *Proteus* couldn't talk or receive. In a corner, beaten, defenceless –

Two minutes ten. Hayter was back at his orisons in front of the exposed innards of 'Leopard', kneeling in what might have been a prayer of desperation. If he could get it functioning again, if it would only switch itself back on, then he would risk the ship by moving her, limping off into another dark corner. At least he'd try to play hide-and-seek with them as long as he could, if only 'Leopard' would work.

Hayter looked at him again, shaking his head. Two minutes twenty-four. It wasn't going to work.

Carr, the navigator, appeared at the door of the cabin. "Sir, sonar's picked up a very small vessel moving away from the rescue ship." As if there had been a public admission of failure, Carr spoke in his normal tone, normal volume. "Ship's launch, we think."

"What does the First Lieutenant think?"

"Divers, sir. Some attempt to inspect our damage."

"Very well." Two minutes fifty. It wasn't going to come on, now. Now it was too late. The rescue ship was less than half-a-mile away. They'd fixed her position by now. Lloyd looked with helpless vehemence at the exposed, purposeless interior of the "Leopard" cabinets. "Tell the First Lieutenant I'm on my way." Carr disappeared. There was no attempt to modify the noise of his footsteps now. It was an admission of defeat, a surrender. "Keep me informed, Don – for Christ's sake keep on trying!"

As he headed for the control room, the image of the opened, useless cabinets remained with him, like a sudden, shocking glimpse of a body undergoing surgery. Hideously expensive, sophisticated almost beyond comprehension, impossible to repair. So much junk –

A team of divers. A threat that somehow diminished even as it presented itself. Perhaps a dozen men, outside the twin hulls of the *Proteus*. His own crew numbered one hundred.

The control room reasserted Lloyd's sense of authority, supplying also a fugitive sense of security. They were almost fifty fathoms down. He must consider moving the *Proteus*, when the critical moment arrived. Thurston looked up from one of the sonar screens, and Lloyd unexpectedly grinned at him.

"Sorry, skipper – nothing. Just the howl of the jamming."

"Make a guess – did *Proteus* pick up Aubrey's order?" Eastoe demanded.

"Doubtful. Almost impossible."

"So Lloyd doesn't know he must destroy the equipment?"

"Don't you think he's done so, skipper? She's been on sonar for over four minutes now."

"That could be the malfunction. Can we contact MoD?"

"No."

"OK everybody. I'm taking her down again, for a look-see. It's almost dark down there. Keep your eyes wide open. Cameras ready. We might as well get any gen we can."

Hyde looked at his watch. A minute before eight. He got out of the unmarked police car parked in Watson Street, then looked back in at the Special Branch inspector before closing the door.

"Half-an-hour. Just keep clear of the place for half an hour, OK?"

"You're taking an unnecessary risk, Mr. Hyde," the policeman offered without inflection. "Yours is a face they know. They'll pick you up on your way in, and bingo –"

"Maybe. And if your lot go in, the girl will panic and either run off or refuse to talk when we've got her. Sorry, sport, we have to take the risk." He looked at his watch again. "Thirty minutes from now, you can come running blowing whistles, anything you like. But not till I've talked to the girl."

"Have it your own way."

"I will. Look –" Hyde felt a sudden need for reassurance, a desire to ameliorate the police resentment of him. "The girl's almost paranoid about us. *We're* the enemy, not the Russians. Christ knows how she came by that idea, but it's what she believes. I have to *talk* her out."

"OK. You've got thirty minutes."

Hyde shut the car door softly. It was almost dark, and the shadows were black pools between the street lamps. Shop windows lighted, and a few pedestrians scuttling ahead of the wind. According to reports, there was one man at the back of the Free Trade Hall – but only one. Hyde thrust his hands into his pockets, and began slouching up the narrow street leading to the rear of the concert hall.

The cars were parked and empty, the street lamps betrayed no pedestrians or loiterers. The weak strains of a country-and-western song came from a slightly open upstairs window of a flat above a shop. The pervasive odour of fish and chips fluttered on the wind, then was gone. It made Hyde feel hungry. He felt small, and alone.

Dim, unlit shop windows. Dust in his eyes. Bookshop, sex shop, barber's. Then Hyde saw him, on the other side of the street, no more than a shadow that moved, perhaps a bored man shifting his weight on tired, aching feet. Hyde stopped, staring into the unlit window of a tiny record shop. Garish LP covers, posters, price cuts daubed in white. The language English but the place no longer Manchester. Some foreign place where he was outnumbered, known, sought. He shivered. If he passed the man, presumably his presence would be noted and reported. They would conclude it was him, even if he hadn't been recognized. On the other hand, if he removed the man from the board, his failure to contact Petrunin – still reported to be sitting in his car in the square – might similarly prove Hyde's presence in the area.

The man had emerged from the doorway of a baker's shop, and was standing on the pavement. As Hyde turned slowly to face him, it was evident that the man was staring directly at him, aware of who he was. Hyde, hands still in the pockets of his corduroy trousers, shoulders hunched, feet apart, was helpless. A Volvo was awkwardly parked, pulled right up bumper-to-bumper against the rear of a Ford Escort directly in front of him. Between him and the man across the street.

One hand of the bulky figure in a raincoat and a hat was moving towards his face, as if to feed himself the tiny R/T set. They hadn't picked up any transmissions all afternoon, Hyde thought, and had discounted R/T. In a moment, two or three paces of time, Petrunin would know that Hyde was about to enter the Free Trade Hall. The hand was moving, Hyde's foot was on the Volvo's bumper, his left foot on the bonnet of the car, the man's hand stopped moving – Hyde could almost see the finger press the transceiver button – one step on the bonnet, then down half-way across the street. The man was surprised, the hand moved away from his face, his other hand fumbled in his raincoat, two strides, one more, collision –

The man staggered back into the darkened doorway of the shop. Old mosaiced threshold, the man's mouth opening in a groan as the ornate, polished brass door-knocker thrust into his back. Hyde, one hand scrabbling at his side, reached for the transceiver in the Russian's hand, and punched at the face that had opened in pain. The

Russian's head ducked to one side as if he had avoided the blow, but the knees were going, and the body sagged. Hyde felt the hand surrender the transceiver, and hit the Russian again, behind the ear. Then he lowered him in his arms on to the mosaic of the threshold. The Russian was breathing as if asleep, on the verge of snoring.

Hyde dropped the transceiver, and was about to grind it beneath his shoe. Then he picked it up and put it into the pocket of his windcheater. If Petrunin tried to contact the man in the doorway, then at least he would know; know, too, that he would have only minutes after that.

He hurried now, shaking from the brief violence, the surge of adrenalin.

There were double gates at the rear of the hall. A uniformed constable opened a small judas-door to him, and closed it behind him. Hyde debated for a moment whether to tell the young policeman of the Russian in the doorway, or the others that might come looking for him, then decided against so doing.

The Edwin Shirley trucks were drawn up in convoy, as if the Free Trade Hall were some cargo terminal. Hyde skirted them, searching in the almost complete darkness for the rear entrance that the Special Branch inspector had pointed out on a plan of the building. He climbed three steps, his hand resting for a moment on a cold metal railing, then tried the door. It had been left unlocked by one of the plainclothes detectives who had been inside the building all day. Hyde went in and closed the door behind him. A lighted passage in need of a fresh coat of cream paint. Dark brown doors. Cramped, uncomfortable, draughty, strip-lighting the only modernism. There was no one in the corridor.

Heat of the Day – Hyde paused to listen, Alletson's high, clear voice riding over keyboards and guitar, part of the suite of pieces "No Way Back" – could be heard mutedly but plainly. He would have to hurry. Normally the band followed the suite with a keyboard display by Whiteman, the other four leaving the stage to him. He had only a few minutes, he realized, becoming aware at the same moment of the small transceiver in his pocket. He opened a dressing-room door. The room was empty and in darkness.

The second room was locked and he saw, looking down, that there was a light on, gleaming beneath the door. Then it went out. He fished for the stiff little rectangle of mica in his back pocket, and inserted it in the door jamb. He paused, listening. The noise of an opening window?

Alletson's voice silent, the slow keyboard section of the suite, building to the ensemble climax. Three, four minutes. A window opening?

He sprang the Yale lock and opened the door. In the light that entered the room from the corridor, he could see a small, slim figure at the dressing-room window, balanced on the sill. He crossed the room in three strides, knocking over a chair, hearing the slight, rustling twang of a guitar he had disturbed, then he had his arms around the figure, keeping his head back from the fingernails that instantly sought his face. He pulled Tricia Quin back into the room, clamping one hand over her mouth, pressing her against him with his other arm. Her body wriggled in his embrace, small, slippery. She backheeled his shins, and he winced with pain but did not let go. He felt the door behind him, raised his elbow, found the light switch, and held her against him after the light came on, but more gently. Eventually, he turned her head so that she could see his face. She stopped wriggling and struggling for a moment, then tried to tear away from him.

"Listen to me," he whispered, "just listen to me without struggling, will you?' His voice was almost petulant rather than threatening, and its tone struck her. Her eyes widened, and he took his hand from her mouth carefully. "OK, will you listen? You'd have broken your bloody neck if you'd jumped from that window."

"We're on the ground floor," she remarked in a superior tone. "What do you want?" She pulled down her T-shirt – a pointing hand in white, black background, the legend *Keep your eyes on the face, sonny* – and then tugged her cardigan straight on her narrow shoulders. She looked vulnerable, intelligent, arrogant, and somehow old-fashioned, out of date. A flower-child who had wandered into the wrong decade. "Well, what do you want? Or was it all for a quick feel in the dark?"

Hyde studied his hands, then looked up. Slowly, slowly, he instructed himself. In his broadest Strine he drawled, "I like 'em with bigger tits, girlie."

Her face narrowed in anger, then she seemed more puzzled than anything else. "You're very persistent, aren't you?"

"And you're very elusive." He stepped forward, hands raised in a signal of harmlessness, and righted the chair he had knocked over. He sat down. "Give me five minutes of your time – just listen to me. I'll try to make you an offer you can't refuse."

"You don't have anything with which to trade, do you?"

"Maybe not. Sit down, anyway."

Tricia Quin slumped untidily, sullenly into a sagging armchair. "All right. Talk."

"I know your mates will be back in a couple of minutes – they're almost finished with 'No Way Back' –" The girl's eyes narrowed with cunning. "So, I'll be brief. There are Russian agents – no don't sneer

153

and don't laugh and don't get clever – outside. The real McCoy. They're interested in contacting your father, and they're sure you know where he is."

"They're just like you."

"No." Hyde bit down on his rising temper. The band murmured beyond the door, close to the climax of the suite. Perhaps no more than a minute. "At this moment, there are a hundred lives at risk under the Barents Sea because of your dad."

"What?"

"The submarine, girlie. Shit, the little old submarine with your old man's wonderful piece of machinery on board, the one everyone wants to know all about." Hyde's voice was scornful, carefully modulated. The band sounded louder, closer to the finish. "Only it isn't working so bloody well at the moment. The Russians have damaged our side's submarine, and your father's bloody expensive equipment isn't working properly. Keeps going on and off like Radio Caroline in the old days."

"I – what am I supposed to do about it?" She was attempting to regain her composure, and she was listening to the sounds from beyond the door.

"Let me talk to your dad – tell him what's what." The girl was already shaking her head. "A telephone number – *you* ring him, I won't watch." Tricia Quin examined the offer for its concealed booby-trap. "No trick," Hyde added.

Alletson walked into their intent silence. Whiteman's tumultuous keyboard playing could be heard through the open door. Alletson's tight-curled hair was wet with perspiration, his damp shirt open to the waist.

"What the hell do you want?" he asked.

"What's up, Jon?" Hyde heard someone in the corridor ask. The lead guitarist, Howarth, pushed into the room carrying two cans of lager. "Who's he?"

"The *secret agent* I told you about." Tricia Quin explained with laden sarcasm. "The *spy*."

"What's he want – you?"

"If you're coming in, close the bloody door," Hyde said lightly, "there's a bloody draught."

Howarth closed the door, and leant against it, still holding the cans of lager. He studied the guitar lying near Hyde's feet with a silent malevolence. Hyde turned on his chair and looked up at Alletson.

"Jon-boy," he said, "tell her to piss off, tell her you don't love her any more, tell her she's a bloody nuisance who could ruin the tour – tell her anything, but persuade her to come with me."

"Why should I do that? She's afraid of you."

"You should see the other side, mate. They frighten me." Alletson grinned despite himself. "See, I'm not such a bad bloke after all." He stopped smiling. "I've told her why I have to find her father –"

"You're probably lying." she remarked.

Hyde turned back to her. "I'm not as it happens. Your father's bloody marvellous invention has dropped a hundred blokes in the shit! Now, will you call him and let me tell *him*?"

It was evident the girl was on the point of shaking her head, when Alletson said quietly, "Why not, Trish?" She stared at him, at first in disbelief then with a narrow, bright vehemence, sharp as a knife. "Look, Trish," Alletson persisted, "go and call him; we'll keep James Bondi –" Hyde laughed aloud "– here while you do it. *Ask* your father if he wants to talk to Don Bradman."

The girl screwed up her face in concentration. She looked very young, indecisive; an air of failure, inability, lack of capacity emanated from her. She irritated Hyde as he watched her.

"All right," she said finally, resenting Alletson for making the suggestion, the capitulation, in the first place. Hyde also noticed that in a more obscure way she accepted the role forced upon her. Perhaps she was tired of running, tired of keeping her father's secrets. Alletson had made a decision for her that she could not entirely resent. "Make sure he stays here," she added. Hyde controlled his sudden fear, and made no effort to follow her. She pushed past Howarth, and closed the door behind her.

Hyde studied Alletson. The man was nervous of him now, had accepted that he could do no more to protect Tricia Quin.

"Sorry – about last night," Alletson said eventually.

Hyde shrugged. "I don't blame you, mate," he said, raised palms facing outwards. "Pax. I will help her," he added.

"I told you, Jon, we ought to dump her –" Howarth began but Alletson turned on him.

"Piss off. For old times' sake. It was for old times' sake."

"How's the tour going so far?" Hyde asked pleasantly, wondering whether Tricia Quin had taken the opportunity to bolt again. He did not think she had, but the closed door at Howarth's back troubled him.

"You're interested?" Howarth asked in disbelief.

"I'm old enough to remember your first album."

"Thanks."

"Why is she running?" Alletson asked, looking almost guilty.

"Her father's paranoid about security. She's caught the infection."

"It is all real, then?"

Hyde nodded. "Oh, yes. Silly, but real. The Russians want her dad, or her, or both, because he's invented a purple deathray which will give world dominion to whoever possesses its deadly secret. I'm Flash Gordon, no less."

"That's about what we thought," Alletson admitted, grinning in a puzzled way. Then he looked at his watch. "We're back on. You – you'll take care of her?" Hyde nodded.

Alletson and Howarth left the room, Howarth picking up the acoustic guitar lying on the floor near Hyde's feet before he went. Then Tricia Quin was standing in the open doorway as Whiteman's final keyboard crescendo echoed down the corridor. Her face was white. She looked guilty and afraid.

"OK?"

She nodded. "Yes. Yes, he's very tired. He'll talk to you, but only to you. I think he's got a gun." Her last words were a warning, and an attempt to excuse her own and her father's capitulation. "He's been worried about me."

"He's still safe?"

"Yes."

"Where?"

"I'll tell you when we've left here."

"Luggage?" She shook her head. "Let's go, then." She looked up sharply at the tone of his voice. Hyde had remembered the KGB irregular lying unconscious in a windy shop doorway on mosaic tiles. He hadn't reported in –

His hand patted the pocket of his windcheater in which he had placed the tiny transceiver. As if he had triggered it, it began bleeping. Tricia Quin's face blanched, her hand flew to her mouth. Hyde cursed.

"It's one of their radios," he explained, getting up quickly. His chair clattered over, and she began to back into the corner of the room, as if he had threatened her with violence. The transceiver continued to bleep, its volume seeming to increase. Her eyes darted between Hyde's face and the door she had left defencelessly open. "Come on, let's get moving!" She was opening her mouth, all capitulation forgotten, betrayal seeping into her features. Hyde bellowed at her. "It's no time to change your mind, you stupid, mixed-up cow! Shift your bloody arse!" She reached for her jacket.

He grabbed her arm and propelled her towards the door. The corridor was empty. At the back of his mind, Hyde could see the Russians fitfully on a dim screen; wondering, worrying, beginning to move, guessing, *knowing* –

He could hand her over now to the police, to the Branch, and she would be safe. If he did, they'd spend days trying to find out where Quin was hiding. She'd be in catatonic suspicion, comatosed with her secret. If he went with her, alone –

156

"You're hurting –" she said meekly as he bundled her down the corridor through the door. He released her arm, and paused to listen, holding his hand in front of her face, indicating silence. He could hear her ragged breathing, like the last ineffectual plucking of his mother's lungs at the hot Sydney air in the darkened room. The day she died.

"Shut up!" he whispered fiercely.

"Sorry –"

He strained to hear. Nothing. The dim music from inside, the murmur of a radio in one of the trucks, traffic muted in the distance.

"Come on." He propelled her down the steps, reached for her hand – she allowed him to hold it, it was inanimate and cold in his grip – and they moved swiftly across the yard. The transceiver in his pocket became silent. Moving; fearful, angry, *quick*, closing in –

The same police constable was on the gate, and he acknowledged their appearance with a nod. He did not seem surprised to see the girl.

"Everything all right, sir?"

Tricia Quin seemed reassured by the manner of his addressing Hyde.

"I think so, constable." Nothing in the narrow, dimly-lit street, but he could not see the baker's shop from the gate. They could be there already. Petrunin might already be out of his car, his minions much closer than that. There was little point in the constable being involved. "Nip inside, constable. Now I've got her, we can start sniffing them out."

"Very good, sir. I'll just report in."

"When you get inside." He realized he was still holding the girl's hand, and he squeezed it. "Come on. My car's only round the corner." Probably with someone very unfriendly sitting in it, he added to himself.

A curious but not unfamiliar elation seized him. His chest seemed expanded with some lighter-than-air gas like helium, and his head was very clear. One of his Vick moments, as he had once described them. Everything clear, cold, sharp. The TR7 was behind the Midland Hotel, in the old railway station that had become, without redecoration or conversion, a huge car park. He jiggled her arm, and they began running up the narrow street, away from the rear of the Free Trade Hall and the baker's doorway. Sensuous information flooded in, his brain sifting it swiftly, unerringly.

Light from around the corner – Peter Street. Their footsteps, the girl's padding lighter in flat, crêpe-soled shoes, the rubbing of her arm against her borrowed, too-big jacket, the spillage of music – Brahms – from an upstairs window, the splash of one foot in a puddle, the gun cold and noticeable in the small of his back, thrust into his waistband.

The emptiness of the end of the street, no shadow against the lights of Peter Street. He was grateful.

The Midland Hotel was across the bright, traffic-filled street. It was a moment before Hyde remembered that Petrunin's car was parked in the square in front of the hotel.

"OK?" he asked the girl. She was gulping air, but she nodded and tried to smile shakily. "Keep going, then, shall we?"

Pavement. Pedestrian crossing. Normality. Red man, traffic swooping past them and round into the square or into Oxford Street or Moseley Street. Central Library, Midland Hotel. Forget it, don't turn your head, stop searching for them. You either fully pretend or not at all –

Red man. Green man, traffic stopping. Walk. He tugged at her hand. One pace, two, you can hurry a little here, people always do on zebra crossings.

They were almost across the street before he heard the first shout, the answering call, and sensed the acceleration of the pursuit. On the pavement, he turned. A man waved to him, as if to call him back over a matter of a dropped book or wallet, or an unpaid bill. He stepped off the opposite pavement. Petrunin himself. He'd been the closest, most experienced, sharpest mind. He'd guessed, and just strolled round the square from his car, and seen them emerge. Petrunin, who knew him, knew the girl's face, no mistake –

"Is that one of them?" the girl asked, as if facing some extremely difficult task of recollection or recognition.

"That's him." Petrunin was almost smiling. Green man still. Two others, running out into Peter Street from the rear of the Free Trade Hall. Not the man in the doorway, two others who had found him and come running. "Ready?" Hyde asked.

"Yes." Her hand trembled in his.

Red man. Petrunin, three paces onto the zebra crossing, paused so that the others could catch up with him. The sound of an impatient horn, then the blare of another and revving engines. Petrunin skipped back onto the opposite pavement.

"Now!"

They raced down the shadowy side-street alongside the bulk of the Midland Hotel. The illuminated façade of the old railway station was ahead of them, the car park barrier like a border to be crossed into a safe country. Hyde pulled at the girl's arm, urging her on, sensing that she was flagging.

The squeal of brakes behind them, the bellow of a car horn. Petrunin wasn't waiting for the green light. They ran together across the road, up the slope to the barrier. A black face was behind the glass of the booth. Hyde looked behind him. All three men were across

Peter Street and running towards them. Hyde inwardly cursed the bravado of his isolation with the girl. There were police in the square, in Peter Street, Watson Street, in the Free Trade Hall, and he had chosen to run with the girl, making Manchester as alien and dangerous as Prague or Warsaw or Moscow. He slapped notes and change onto the counter of the booth, together with his ticket.

He swallowed saliva, said "I'm in a hurry. Keep the change. Open the barrier when I drive out – yellow TR7. Got it?" Then his hand was in his pocket and he was waving the shorthand of the CID warrant card. The Indian nodded.

Hyde ran on, the girl ahead of him now, but slowing because there seemed no safety amid the cars under the cracked, glassless station roof.

"Where?" she said.

"Over there," he said, pointing.

One or two weak lights revealed the massed, hunched, beetle-like shells of car bonnets and roofs. The girl stared around her wildly. Hyde glanced back. Petrunin and the other two had slowed their pace, almost strolling past the barrier, confident but wary, imitating legitimacy. Seconds between them. Hyde ran out onto the platform with the girl. Dully gleaming, crustaceous cars; silence. The wind soughing thinly in the shell of the station. The three Russians were past the barrier and had paused on the threshold of the station itself. Hyde ducked down, pulling the girl into a crouch, and began weaving awkwardly between parked cars.

He paused, listened, then moved on. They came to the edge of the platform, and he dropped down. He reached up and the girl surrendered to his grasp on her waist. He lifted her down. A row of cars, one of them yellow.

"Mr. Hyde?"

He thought for the moment it was the girl speaking, because of the light, interrogative tone. But it was Petrunin – accent and authority seeping into Hyde's awareness just behind the words. He gestured to the girl to remain silent, and they moved, crouching, along the rear bumpers of cars until they were leaning against the TR7. He heard the girl's ragged breathing again, but not like his mother's now; too alive for that, too much wanting to live. Hyde fished the car keys from his pocket and reached up to unlock the door.

"Mr. Hyde?" Then whispered instructions above the girl's breathing, the shuffle of footsteps as the three men spread out. Petrunin was confident. He hadn't left anyone at the barrier. "Mr. Hyde." A sharper tone, impatient.

Hyde eased open the door of the TR7, and indicated that the girl should climb in. They'd be looking for the yellow car. He crept round to the driver's door, unlocked it, clambered into the low hard seat. He eased the door shut on the footsteps that were coming closer. Steel-tipped heels to the heavy shoes. He slipped the key into the ignition, and pulled out the choke. He looked at Tricia Quin. Hair damp on her forehead, face pale, cheeks quivering.

"Which way?"

"North," she said, hugging herself as if to keep warm; trying to retreat from her danger.

Hyde breathed in deeply, then turned the key. Cough, chatter of the ignition, cough, firing of the engine, drowning a surprised and delighted cry from up on the platform. He thrust the gears into reverse, screeched out of his parking place, heaving on the wheel. The TR7 skidded, almost stalled, and then the car was bucking over the uneven ground.

He reached the end of the platform, and swung the car left, across the hard-packed earth where the tracks had once been, until he mounted the platform ramp at the other side of the station. He had heard no gunfire, nothing after that shout of discovery. The engine whined, the tyres screeched as he roared along the platform, then turned again onto what had been the concourse, heading for the entrance.

One man, stepping out from behind a car, gun levelled. Hesitation, a slight turning of his head – a cry of protest from Petrunin? Then the TR7 was almost on top of him, a spit of flame from the shadowy bulk of the man before he flicked aside like a matador, between two cars. The bullet's path was a groove in the thin metal of the roof, directly above Hyde's head. He screeched the car round and through the entrance to the station, and the barrier was going up, very slowly. Another man was entering the booth alongside the barrier – barrier going up, making a chopping motion as it reached the peak of its swing, beginning to descend almost immediately. The TR7 raced beneath it, bounced over cobbles, and squealed into the road behind the Midland Hotel.

"North," Hyde said loudly when his breath returned and the hotel's bulk was between them and the station. His palms were damp on the steering wheel, and he was perspiring freely. "North."

"Come on, come on!" Ardenyev yelled, his voice already hoarse from its combat with the wind and the sea, his gloved hands seemingly frozen and incapable as he attempted, with Teplov and Nikitin, to drag the largest of the sleds across the deck of the launch to its side.

The trough made them wallow as the helmsman steadied the launch. The young lieutenant watched them through the cabin window, his head flickering back and forth like a tennis spectator, towards them then towards the next peak, looming ahead of them.

"One more, sir!" Teplov bellowed back at him, even though they were not more then three or four feet apart on either side of the sled and its mound of cylinders. Shadrin and Vanilov and Kuzin were already submerged, safe under the water, with the second sled and the welding and cutting gear. Their ten minutes had already begun. There should have been four sleds, more communications equipment, more everything. Petrov was lying on a bunk, his leg broken and splinted in an inflatable plastic bag. Groaning and useless.

The sled tilted on the side of the launch as the next wave reared up in the darkness and opened its jaws. Teplov glanced over his shoulder. Regret was useless, too. Ardenyev strained like someone demented or terrified as Nikitin, attached by a line, flipped over the side of the launch into the water, mask and mouth-piece in place, his ten minutes already beginning. One thought re-emerged from the panic of Ardenyev's mind. Unless they could get onto the *Proteus* within the ten minutes, then they would have to spend hours coming back to the surface to avoid the bends, and no launch would be able to pick them up with ease – perhaps not at all – in this sea and at night. It was a one-way journey.

Nikitin's barely discernible bobbing head was accompanied by a raised hand, and then he swam close to the side of the launch. Ardenyev felt the dead weight of the sled pull towards Nikitin, and saw Teplov's face grey with strain. He yelled at the senior *michman*, who nodded, and went over the side. The wave loomed over the launch, flecked, old, immense. Two black-capped heads bobbed in the water. Slowly, almost out of his control, the sled dipped into the water and sank immediately. Teplov and Nikitin struck down after it.

Then the water, even as he turned his head to look and thought of time once more, lifted him and threw him across the deck of the launch. He glimpsed the lieutenant's appalled face, the rearing nose of the launch, then he was headfirst into the water, spun and tumbled like a leaf or twig in a stream's torrent, whirled down as he fitted his mouthpiece by instinct. His legs were above his head, just discernible; then blackness, and orientation returning. There were lights below him, two pale blobs like the eyes of a deep-ocean fish. He breathed as calmly as he could, then struck down towards the lights.

He tapped Teplov on the shoulder, and signalled with upraised thumb. Teplov's relief sounded withdrawn and almost mechanical through his throat-mike. Teplov slid further back against Nikitin on the seat of the sled, and Ardenyev swung himself into the saddle, holding onto the steering column. Directly in front of him, the tiny sonar screen was switched on, and the bright spot of the British submarine lay below and thirty degrees to port.

161

"Shadrin?" Ardenyev enquired into his microphone. All formality, all wasted words and energy and air disappeared beneath the surface.

"Skipper?"

"Got her fixed?"

"Yes, skipper."

"Let's go."

Ardenyev dipped the nose of the sled – a light, frail craft now that it was in its own element, not being manhandled across a sloping, slippery deck – towards the ledge on which the *Proteus* lay, not two hundred yards from them. The headlights of the sled picked out the winking, vanishing shoals of fish before they glanced across the silted ledge. Blackness beyond the ledge, but the lights turning the ledge itself almost sand-coloured, almost alive and three-dimensional. The cold seeped through the immersion suit, began to ring in his head like the absence of oxygen. Teplov clung to him, and Nikitin to Teplov. Without Petrov, Ardenyev had decided that the two main sleds would suffice. He hadn't been thinking clearly on the launch, only swiftly, rapping out orders and decisions as if keeping a mounting, insidious sense of failure, of utter futility, at bay with the sound of his voice and the fence of quick thought.

Grey, white numerals, then the blackness of the sea behind. Ardenyev, feeling Teplov's tap on his shoulder in response to what they both had seen, turned the sled slowly in a sweeping curve. He circled slightly above the British submarine like a gull in the wind, and watched as the headlights of Shadrin's sled slipped like a caress across the midships section of the submarine, then up and around her sail.

They'd found her. He looked at his watch. Seven minutes remaining. He pushed the nose of the sled down towards the *Proteus*.

"There she is skipper!"

"Infra-red cameras?"

"Cameras running, skipper."

"Can you see them, Terry?"

"No – wait – *there*?"

"What the hell is that?"

"Looks like a sled. It's going, going over the side. They'll get caught by the wave, no, one of them has – he's going over!"

"All fall down. Can we communicate with MoD yet?"

"No, skipper."

"Then you'd better send the pictures over the wire straight away. Even Aubrey ought to be able to work this one out!"

162

"I'm sorry, Mr. Aubrey, it could take hours to analyse these pictures." Clark was holding irritation in check, his apology an exercise in calming his breathing and no more.

"There's no way we can communicate with the Nimrod?"

"I'm sorry, sir," Copeland replied lugubriously, shaking his head, folding down his lower lip to complete the mask of apology. "The jamming makes that impossible. Eastoe must have sent these by way of a substitute – and without sub-titles."

"I am in no mood for cheap remarks, young man!" Aubrey snapped wearily.

"Sorry, sir."

Aubrey turned back to Clark. "How many men, would you say?"

They were still clustered round the wireprint machine, and the grainy reproductions of the infra-red photographs that the Nimrod had transmitted, torn off the machine as each frame appeared, were in every hand, or lay scattered on the bench near the machine. The whole room seemed crowded, like boys urging on two unwilling combatants, around Aubrey and Clark.

"This sled?"

"What do you mean, *this* sled?" Aubrey wanted, demanded information, answers to his question upon which he could base a decision. The desire to make a decision, to act, pressed upon him like a manhole-cover which would mask a trap. Failure, complete and abject and humiliating, stared up at him like a nightmare into which he was falling.

"I mean there may be more than one sled. It looks like two, it's a two-man sled all right. Could be three –?" Clark was examining the photograph with a magnifying-glass. It seemed old-fashioned, inappropriate to the advanced technology that was their pressing concern. "Leopard" lying like junk on the floor of the Barents Sea.

"That equipment, then?" Aubrey asked snappily, using his own magnifying-glass, making nothing of the shapes and bulky outlines of the underwater equipment that was strapped and secured on the back of the sled. Yes, he could see it was a two-man sled, there were two men, perhaps one of the grainy dots was another head bobbing in the water –? "You say this man Ardenyev would be in command here?"

"That equipment – welding or cutting gear, oxygen, who knows? And yes, I guess it would be Valery Ardenyev."

Clark was grinning.

"You've met him, then."

"We've been – *observers*, at the same oceanographic conferences, sure."

"What is his field of expertise?"

"Red Banner Special Operations – rescue, salvage, demolition, offence, defence, – you name it, they can do it."

"The launch, Ethan – how many of these sleds could it hold?"

"No more than two, three – why?"

"The numbers involved, my dear fellow." Aubrey was expansive again, confident. Clark was amazed at the brittle, transitory nature of the old man's emotions, whether optimistic or pessimistic. When he encountered the next obstacle, he would fall back into a trough of doubt and anxiety. "Can I assume that they would not attempt salvage – or anything more *intrusive* – with so few people?"

"You might do. Inspection? Maybe."

"Come, Ethan. Give me a best guess. Is this likely to be an inspection?"

"They'll have little time down there, at that depth. Just enough time, maybe."

"Then we have some time available ourselves?"

"To do what?" Clark turned on Aubrey angrily as it seemed self-satisfaction was the object, the sole purpose, of his questions. Feel good, put your mind to rest – and then you don't need to do any more. He almost voiced his thoughts.

"I don't know. We are prevented from making any moves other than diplomatic and political, until tomorrow or the following day. Have we that much time?"

"I don't know. Let's hope Eastoe goes down for another set of pictures when these divers return to the surface. Then we'll know it was only an inspection."

Aubrey's face darkened. He wondered what madcap idea had sprung into Clark's mind, and whether, because he was younger and of the same experience and background, he might not have perceived something of what was in the man Ardenyev's mind. He did not, however, ask Clark his meaning.

"Norway must make another protest about this incursion into her territorial waters," he said, and even to himself it sounded both too little and too late. He avoided looking at Clark as he pushed his way out of the circle of people around them, towards the telephones.

The *Proteus*'s stern lay bathed in the headlights of the two sleds, parked side by side on the ledge. The silt which they and the submarine had disturbed had settled. There was a wide ugly furrow the *Proteus* had gouged before she finally stopped. Beyond it, the damaged stern was grey, twisted, scorched metal, flayed by the coils of steel the MIRV torpedo had released. Ardenyev saw, as he picked his way fly-like in the illumination of the lights, that the fifteen-blade propeller had been thrown out of alignment, or dragged so it became

164

embroiled with the whipping tendrils of steel cable, and that three of the phosphor-bronze, boot-shaped blades had been sheared off. One or two of the others were distorted, but intact. Without the MIRV torpedo, the damage wreaked by the low-warhead hit would not have been sufficient to stop the submarine.

Teplov's shoulder nudged against his as they clung to the port aft hydroplane. A steel cable twisted away from them like a great grey snake slithering towards the silt beneath the submarine. The hydroplane was buckled and torn beneath their hands and flippers, and its skin of metal had begun to unpeel like the layers of an onion, having been damaged and then subjected to the pressure of the water before the *Proteus* slowed and halted. In front of them, the bulk of the submarine retreated into the darkness. Buckled plates, damaged ballast tanks, but there was no evidence that the pressure hull had been ruptured.

"They made a bloody good job of it," Teplov's voice croaked in his earpiece. Ardenyev nodded.

The rudders were misaligned, too, but not badly.

"We can patch it – she'll have to be towed. We don't have time to repair the prop."

It was Teplov's turn to nod. His eyes seemed to be grinning behind his facemask.

"What next?"

"Let's move amidships. Signal the others to start making a din in –" He looked at his watch, "one minute." Ardenyev pushed away from the damaged hydroplane. His watch informed him that four minutes had already passed for himself, and perhaps five for Shadrin, Vanilov and Kuzin. No time to waste. He had six minutes to get aboard. Teplov behind him instructed the others, his voice tinny in the earpiece as Ardenyev glided like a black fish along the whale-like back of the *Proteus*. Each man knew his job; they had performed a hundred time trials in the deep tanks at the Frunze Naval School, and off-shore in the same depth and sea conditions as now pertained. Ardenyev's hands touched the two canisters strapped to his chest, smaller imitations of the two air tanks on his back.

They'd rehearsed it on submerged mock-ups, on the old "Whiskey"-class boat they'd commissioned for practice. After the first month's training the ten minutes had always been sufficient, even with the adrenalin running lower than now. But Ardenyev could not help remembering one severe case of the bends he had suffered by going through the mock-up's escape chamber too quickly, which had incapacitated him, and he could not forget the first full sea trial which had included the use of the MIRV torpedo. The steel cables had ripped open the hull of the old submarine they were using, killing its crew. He and his two teams had been in the launch, waiting to go down, when the wreckage and the released air and the oil had come to the surface.

The great fin-like sail of the *Proteus* loomed out of the darkness. His lamp played on it. Below it, the officers and control room of the submarine. And "Leopard", his target. He hovered, and Teplov joined him. Ardenyev gave him the thumbs-up signal, and the senior *michman* swam down to the base of the sail, his shape becoming indistinct, the light of his lamp feeble, winking on and off, it seemed, as he moved away and sought his own objective. Teplov would begin communicating in morse on the hull of the *Proteus*, offering apology and assistance and reassurance in the name of the Red Banner Fleet, distracting the officers of the submarine and retarding suspicion and activity.

Ardenyev kicked on, moving more swiftly now, dipping down to touch the hull once with his fingertips, then moving off again as soon as he sensed the vibration. The other four were using cutting gear and making as much noise as they could at the stern, a further distraction. Now, everything – the whole operation and its success – depended upon himself. The knowledge satisfied him as he urged his body through the water. He could just make out the forward hydroplanes. A shoal of fish, brief as a torch-signal, were caught in the light of his lamp. He glanced again at his watch. Four minutes fifty since he had reached bottom. Three-and-a-half minutes to decompress slowly enough not to be incapacitated. He kicked on more urgently, gliding over the hull, his lamp playing upon it now with an almost frenzied movement, sweeping back and forth like a small searchlight. The diagram of the submarine was vivid in his mind, as if he possessed vision that allowed him to see beneath the skin of the double hull. He was passing over the officers' wardroom and the crew's quarters beneath them, towards the torpedo room. He reminded himself that the submarine would be silent, alert. He would be making noises almost next door to the wardroom, which would contain the off-duty officers, sitting in silence, nervous of moving. Would they be sufficiently distracted by the tapping, by the noises from the stern thrumming through the hull?

His lamp washed across the hull, then swung back. He had found his objective, the forward escape hatch above the torpedo room. Even here, the British had made it easier for him. A Royal Navy fleet submarine had gone down in the North Sea two years before. The crew had died because the air purification system had suddenly failed, and the rescuers had taken too long to cut their way into the hull. Since that disaster, it had been specified that all nuclear submarines, as well as all the older diesel subs in the Royal Navy, be fitted with two-way hatches that could be opened without difficulty from the outside. The Red Navy had known that when it began to plan the abduction of "Leopard".

He gripped the wheel of the flood control valve and began to twist it, wrenching at it violently, then turning it more easily. He looked at his watch. He had been under for six minutes, some of the others for seven. He had already lost them half a minute. It increased decompression time by the same amount. He began turning the wheel more rapidly. He could not account for the strange loss of time. How much time had he wasted looking at the damage, almost enjoying it, satisfied at the helplessness of the huge submarine? That must have been when he lost the forty seconds he was now behind schedule.

"Viktor?" he whispered into his mouthpiece.

"Sir?"

"How is it?"

"They're demanding to know what we're doing, and how their submarine was damaged?"

"Have you asked to come aboard?"

"Yes, sir. They've refused a liaison officer. I'm giving them the fictitious damage report now."

"I'm going in."

"Good luck, sir."

Ardenyev lifted the hatch slowly, sensing its great weight even under water. A rush of bubbles enveloped him. He would have made a noise already that might have been heard. They'd rehearsed that, too. The other distracting noises had been sufficient to mask his entry – but were they now, when it mattered? He dropped slowly into the chamber, and pulled the hatch down on himself. Then the submarine lurched forward, and his head banged in surreal slow-motion against the side of the compartment. His lamp's light wobbled on the walls around him. He was in a cylinder like the inside of an artillery shell which felt as if it was being slid into the breech of a gun.

The *Proteus* was moving, wriggling like an animal trying to rid itself of fleas. He pressed feet and back against the walls of the cylinder, simply hanging on because the buoyancy within the flooded chamber allowed him no weight, no steadiness. He could imagine, vividly, the control room where the decision has been taken; imagine, also, the hull of the submarine. Teplov might have been flung off – what about the others, the flail of cutting gear, the roll of tanks, the whip of the steel cables around the prop. He could sense the grinding as the submarine's prop struggled to turn against the restraint of the cables, his teeth grinding in his head, his whole head aching with the vibration. They must stop, must –

A glimpse of his watch. Seven minutes and ten, eleven seconds.

Then the lamp banged against his arm painfully. He squeezed himself flatter, taller, bigger, holding himself still. Welding gear, cutting torches, tanks, the whip of cables. He sensed like a medium that one of them, perhaps more, would be dead or injured. All of them were running out of time. Time. That was the calculation; they knew it in the *Proteus*. Twenty fathoms equalled ten minutes' working time, then the excess nitrogen in the blood slowed the body, hampered the mind, began to kill. He was killing them now –

The scraping, the cries of metal as the crippled submarine dipped time and again to the bottom of the ledge, dragging her belly across silt and mud and rock, the grating, thrumming noise and vibration of the captive prop as it tried to turn, the smaller vibration – almost normality – of the small docking propeller being used. It seemed endless, unbearable.

He turned in the chamber, banged against the wall of the cylinder, gripped the lower hatch venting wheel, turned again, banged, was thrown off, his lamp flickering wildly against the flooded metal of his prison, gripped again, braced himself – the vibration and movement slowing now? – and turned a third time. The water began to seep slowly from the hatch into the torpedo room. Three-and-a-half minutes. He had practised the number of turns to allow the pressure to alter at the necessary rate, the precise amount of water to release per second, perhaps two hundred times. But not when it really mattered. He remained gripping the wheel of the lower hatch, the light of his lamp playing on his watch.

Ten, eleven, twelve seconds. Almost eight minutes of time gone, and another three minutes fifteen before the water had drained away and he had safely depressurized. A total of more than eleven minutes. And where were they? Had they hung on? Were they alive?

Slowing, vibration bearable. Scraping on its belly, lurching to starboard, a cry of rent metal, the main prop not being used, docking prop dying away. The *Proteus* was stopping again. He had waited too long. He should have acted earlier, when the noise and vibration were at their height. Now water dripped onto the empty torpedo room floor in the sudden silence as men's hearing returned. Thirty-seven seconds, thirty-eight, nine, forty –

Silence. He stood upright in the chamber. The water was at shoulder-height. He ducked back beneath its surface. Fifty-five seconds. He couldn't wait, *had* to wait. Perhaps the great bulk of the submarine had rolled on one or more of them? Teplov? Nikitin? The others? If they were alive, could they find the *Proteus* again in time in the forest of silt that must now obscure her? They would swim through an unending, almost solid grey curtain of silt, looking for the submarine that was their only hope. It was already too late to begin

168

slowly ascending to the surface. Now he was safely decompressing, no one could enter the torpedo room escape chamber until he had left it. If any of them were still alive. He thought of the whip of a loosened steel cable across an immersion-suited body –

One minute twenty seconds. He was crouching against the floor of the chamber as the water drained slowly into the torpedo room below. Not a trickle, not a drip, but a slow, steady fall, noisy. The wardroom next door, normality returning, things being righted again, objects picked up from the floor, bruises rubbed, hearing returning, awareness of surroundings increasing. *What's that noise? Sprung a leak? Better go and take a look* –

Ardenyev was on his own. He remembered the helicopter going down in flames, then Petrov's broken leg, then the hellish noise and vibration of the *Proteus*. Dolohov, he was able to consider distinctly, might have killed every member of the Special Underwater Operations Unit, *his* unit. For a box of tricks to make a submarine invisible.

Two minutes five. The compartment was less than half full of water. He was squatting in a retreating tide, as he might have done at Tallinn or Odessa as a child, watching the mysterious, fascinating water rush away from him, leaving the froth of foam around him and the stretch of newly exposed wet sand in which shells sat up in little hollows. Two minutes twenty.

Noise, they must hear the noise, no they won't, they're too dis-orientated, they'll be listening for water, the dangerous water of a leak, a buckled or damaged plate, they'll hear it –

Two minutes thirty-two. Fifty-eight seconds remaining. He pulled at the hatch, and it swung up, emptying the chamber in an instant. His hands had been locked on the wheel, turning it slowly though the forebrain had decided to wait. The pressure of imagination as to what might have happened outside the submarine was greater than any other, pressing down and in on him like the ocean. He dropped through the hatch into the torpedo room, the water already draining away, leaving the cold, clinical place merely damp. Instantly, he felt dizzy, and sick. Too soon, too soon, he told himself. He had never tried to get through decompression at this depth in less than two minutes fifty. He'd been prepared to cope with the dizziness and sickness, the blood pounding in his head, that would have assailed him only half-a-minute early. This was worse, much worse. He staggered against the bulkhead, his vision unable to focus, his surroundings wobbling like a room in a nightmare. The noise in his ears was a hard pounding, beneath which he could almost hear the accelerating blood rushing with a dry whisper. His heart ached. Pain in his head, making thought impossible. His hands were clutched round the two canisters on his chest as if holding some talisman or icon of profound significance and efficacy. His legs were weak, and when he tried to move he lurched forward, almost spilling onto his face like a baby trying to walk for the first time.

He leaned against the bulkhead then, dragging in great lungfuls of the mixture in his air tanks, trying desperately to right his vision, and to focus on the door into the torpedo room. It was closed, but its outline shimmered, and threatened to dissolve. It was no barrier. Around him lay the sleek shapes of the torpedoes. Cold, clinical place, the floor already almost dry, except for the puddle that still lingered at his feet from his immersion suit. He tried to look at his watch, could not focus, strained and blinked and stretched his eyes, pressing the face of the watch almost against his facemask. Three minutes fifty, almost four minutes. He could have – should have – waited. He was further behind now. He snapped the lock on the weighted belt around his waist. It thudded to the floor.

He looked up. Close the hatch, close the hatch. Moving as if still under water, with diver's weighted feet and restraining suit, he reached up and closed the hatch, turning the handle with aching, frosty, weak limbs. If they were alive – he felt tears which were no longer simply another symptom of decompression prick helplessly behind his eyes – then now they could open the outer hatch.

Door opening. Refocus. Slowly refocus. He had been about to focus on the port and starboard air purifiers on either side of the torpedo room when the door began opening. But it still ran like a rain-filled window-pane, the image distorted. A figure that might have been reflected in a fairground mirror came through the door, stopped, yelled something indistinct above the rush and ache in his ears, then came towards him.

Quick, quick, useless instincts prompted. He pushed away from the bulkhead. He could make out the port purifier clearly, then it dissolved behind rain again for a moment, then his vision cleared. He could hear the words, the question and challenge shouted. Another figure came through the open bulkhead door. Two of them. Ardenyev moved through a thicker element than air, and hands grabbed him from behind, causing him to stagger near one of the torpedoes. Slowly, aquatically, he tried to turn and lash out. His other hand cradled one of the two canisters on his chest, and the young face seemed riveted by his hand and what it held. Ardenyev could distinguish expression on the face now – knowledge, realization. The young man enclosed him in a bear-hug, but Ardenyev heaved at the thin, light arms, pushing the man away by his very bulk.

He bent, opening the inspection plate; then his hand was pulled away, and another, larger hand clamped on his own as it held the first canister. The second canister was torn from its strap and rolled across the floor, beneath one of the torpedo trestles. All three of them watched it roll. The two British officers feared it might be a bomb after all.

Ardenyev chopped out with the lamp attached still to his wrist, catching the smaller officer on the side of the head, knocking him aside. He flipped over one of the torpedoes, and subsided to the floor, a vague redness staining the side of his face. Then Ardenyev was hit in the stomach and he doubled up. Another blow against the side of his facemask, then he lunged upwards with his upper torso, catching his attacker in the chest with his head. A soft exhalation of air, the man staggering backwards –

He turned, twisted the canister in both hands, releasing the incapacitating gas, then jammed the canister into the air purifier, closing the inspection plate immediately. Then he was punched in the small of the back, just below his air tanks, then hands were round his shoulders and face, and his mask was coming off. He felt the mouthpiece ripped out of his mouth, and he inhaled the warm, sterile air of the submarine. He staggered across the torpedo room, still held by the second man, lurching against the trestles, his eyes searching the floor for the second canister, oblivious even of the need to re-insert his mouthpiece before the gas passed the length of the submarine down the air ducts and returned to them in the torpedo room.

He dropped to one knee in a feint, then heaved with his shoulders. The second man, the heavier, bearded officer, rolled up and over his neck and shoulders, falling in front of him, winded by the metal floor of the room. Ardenyev scrabbled under a torpedo trestle, his fingers closing over its damp coldness, gripping it. He got to his feet, clutched the canister to his chest, which was heaving with effort, and staggered clumsily across the torpedo room in his flippers, to the starboard air purifier.

Other men were coming in now. He opened the inspection plate, twisted the canister, and jammed it into the purifier, closing the plate after it. He was grabbed, then. The room was full of noise, an alarm sounded somewhere, while he tried to jam his mouthpiece back into his mouth. They wanted to stop him. It was as if the hands that reached for him had only that one minor object, to prevent him regaining the safety of the air mixture in his tanks while the gas moved swiftly through the submarine. He felt himself hit, but his attention could not be spared for his torso, arms and legs, kidneys, stomach, chest. He went on trying to force the mouthpiece back into place.

One breath, two, three, doubling over on the floor, not resisting now, hoping they would assume he was beaten, even unconscious.

Someone turned him over; he saw through slitted lids a hand reach for the mouthpiece and mask again – the mask askew, obscuring much of the scene – then the hand lunged past him, a body toppled down beside him, subsiding with a peculiar, slow-motion grace, mimicking death. He opened his eyes now, knowing he had nothing to fear. Others fell like skittles, ninepins, but in the same seeming slow-motion.

Ardenyev closed his eyes. He alone was conscious on board the British submarine. There was no hurry, no hurry at all. They would be out for an hour, perhaps longer. There were no noises from the escape chamber, and therefore there was no hurry whatsoever. He had captured the *Proteus* and "Leopard", and he was entirely alone. A sad, even vile heroism. He surrendered to the exhaustion that assailed him, as if he, too, had inhaled the incapacitating gas.

NINE:

Retrieval

From their identification papers, Ardenyev knew them to be Thurston, the first lieutenant of the submarine, and Hayter, the officer responsible for "Leopard". Because of their importance, he had allowed them to remain with Lloyd in the control room of the *Proteus* after the remaining officers and ratings had been confined to the wardroom and crew quarters "for security reasons".

Ardenyev had watched Lloyd come round, come to an almost instant wakefulness, and he had immediately warmed to the man and granted him his respect and his wariness. Lloyd would now sabotage "Leopard" in a moment, if he could. Ardenyev stood before the captain of the submarine and his two senior officers at attention, like a junior officer presenting his compliments. It was part of the charade he was now required to play.

"As I was saying, captain," he began again, having been interrupted by an expletive from Thurston, "we very much apologize for the manner in which we were required to board your vessel. However, it is lucky that we did. Your purification system had developed a fault that would almost certainly have proved fatal had we not arrived." He said it without a flicker of amusement or self-mockery. The truth did not matter.

His men, his team were missing, presumed dead. Vanilov, brokenly, had told him he had seen Kuzin catch a whipping, freed tendril of steel cable across his back, and he had seen him flung away into the dark, his body tumbled and twisted in a way that would have been impossible had it been unbroken. Nikitin had fallen beneath the weight of the *Proteus*, forgetting in surprise to loosen his hold on the cutting gear. Stabs of blue flame had come from the cutting-pipes as the silt had boiled round, and swallowed, Nikitin. Shadrin he had not seen at all. Teplov and Vanilov alone had clung to the submarine, been dragged through the water and the boiling mist of silt and mud, rested dazed and exhausted and were slowly being poisoned by nitrogen in the blood until Teplov had crawled back to the stern and found Vanilov and boarded the *Proteus* through the aft escape hatch, into the electric motor room. They had waited in the slowly-draining compartment for five minutes, until it was safe to emerge into the submarine. Dizziness and exhaustion, yes, but not the bends. Teplov had put the neutralizing agent through the aft purifiers, and then come seeking his commanding officer.

Ardenyev felt his left cheek adopt a tic, the last, fading tremors of weariness and shock. These men in front of him had killed three of his men, indirectly killed Blue Section. The knowledge that he would have done precisely the same, threatened as they had felt they were, intruded upon his anger, dimming it. Lloyd, the captain, was watching him carefully, weighing him, the expression on his face like a suspicion that they had met before, or always been intended to meet.

"Fucking piracy, that's what it is," Thurston offered into the silence, and Hayter rumbled his agreement. "How do you explain the guns if you're here to help us?"

Ardenyev smiled innocently. "We understand your concern with security. We would not wish to be blamed for any –*mistakes* you might make, any damage you might cause to sensitive equipment. It is merely a precaution."

"Locking up my crew is just another precaution, I presume?" Lloyd asked sardonically, sitting in a relaxed manner in one of the sonar operators' chairs, which he swung to and fro slowly, almost as if he intended mesmerizing the Russian. A relaxed, diffident, confident child. Ardenyev was pricked by his seeming indifference to the fate of Nikitin and the others.

"Captain, I would understand, even expect, some reaction such as that of Commander Thurston translated into action, either from one of your officers, or some of your men. That would only complicate an already complicated situation. We are here to *help* you –" Here, sincerity seeped into his voice in a measured, precise dose. "– because it is our fault that you are in this situation."

"You admit it, then?"

"What else can we do? The captain and officers of the submarine *Grishka* will be severely disciplined for their provocative action."

"This is unreal –!" Thurston exploded.

"Not at all – is it, captain?" Ardenyev said with a smirk. "It will be the agreed version of events."

"How do you explain the cuts and bruises on two of my officers?" Lloyd enquired. "The air purifiers struck them, I suppose?"

"Falling to the deck, I suppose," Ardenyev replied, "overcome by the lack of oxygen. I came aboard when your signals from inside stopped – you tapped out one word, HELP, before that happened. You don't remember?"

Lloyd shook his head. "No, I don't. Oxygen starvation plays tricks with the memory, obviously."

Ardenyev sighed with pleasure. "I see we understand each other, captain."

"What happens now?"

"From the damage report, there will be some repairs, to your buoyancy and to your hydroplanes. Then you will be towed back to Pechenga, our nearest naval base, for sufficient repairs to allow you to return to Faslane under your own power." He spread his hands innocently in front of him. "It is the least we can do, apart from the sincerest diplomatic apologies, of course. It will take little more than a day or two before you are on your way home." He beamed.

"If your mission is so humanitarian, why is your petty officer carrying a Kalashnikov with the safety-catch in the 'Off' position?" Thurston remarked sourly.

"Security." Ardenyev sighed again. He was tiring of the charade. It was not important. Everyone knew the truth. "Now, I will have to contact the rescue ship *Karpaty* and arrange for divers and equipment to be sent down to us."

"I'm sure you're reasonably familiar with our communications?" Lloyd remarked with forced lightness, as if his situation had come home to him in a more bitter, starker way.

"Thank you, yes." Ardenyev's hand released the butt of the Makarov pistol thrust into the belt of his immersion suit. He tousled his hair in an attempt to retain the mocking, false lightness of his conversation with the British officers. He wanted to clamber back into the fiction of a terrible accident, a life-saving boarding-party, apologetic repairs in Pechenga, as into a child's tree-house. But he could not. Whipping steel cables, boiling flame from a crashed helicopter, accompanied him vividly to the communications console.

As if admitting that the fiction could not be sustained, he drew the Makarov and motioned the three British officers to the far side of the control room before he seated himself in front of the console.

"These pictures were taken forty minutes after the previous set," Aubrey remarked. "You are telling me, Captain Clark" – The excessive politeness seemed designed to stave off any admission of disaster – "that since no divers have resurfaced, they must be on board *Proteus?*"

"Right."

"Why?"

"They couldn't stay down more than ten minutes at that depth. Then they'd come back up slowly, but by now they'd be back on board the launch. Sure, the launch has returned to take station on the port beam of *Karpaty*" – Here Clark nodded in Copeland's direction – "but as far as I can make out, they're loading heavy cutting gear from the rescue ship. And these men on deck. More divers. In full rig, not scuba gear. They're going

175

down. Therefore, you can bet Ardenyev's men are on board."

"But why and how would Lloyd have allowed him on board?" Aubrey asked in exasperation. He was baffled and plagued by the murky high-resolution and light-intensified photographs transmitted from the Nimrod. Clark seemed to be reading tea leaves. The whole matter seemed like a fairy tale.

"He wouldn't need to –"

"The escape hatches," Copeland blurted out. "After *Phaeton* went down a couple of years ago, all the hatches had to open two-way. They'd know that, dammit!"

"Exactly," Clark said drily. "Ardenyev would have let himself in."

"Eastoe reports a change in position of *Proteus*."

"Lloyd trying to get rid of his guests," Clark commented acidly. "Someone's in there, you can bet on it."

"Then none of our messages got through?" Aubrey asked forlornly. " 'Leopard' will not have been destroyed."

"I'm afraid not."

"Clark – what will they do now, for heaven's sake?" Aubrey's eye rested on Giles Pyott's expressionless face with a glance of pure malevolence. Pyott's implacability refuted the accusation of the gaze. Clark cleared his throat, breaking the tension between the soldier and the intelligence agent. Aubrey shrugged.

"Raise her – depending on the damage, or simply take what they want down there. The situation's complicated by the fact that 'Leopard' isn't operational at present. I guess they'll raise her and tow her into port."

"What?" Pyott asked in disbelief. "That would be piracy. The international repercussions would be – enormous."

"You'd declare war?" Clark asked ironically.

"Don't be stupid."

"Then the shit hitting the fan will have been worth it. What will you do? All of you. You won't go to war, *we* won't go to war on your behalf, you won't tell anyone because it's all too embarrassing – so nothing will happen. 'Leopard' will belong to both sides or to none. That'll be the only outcome."

"What can we *do*, Clark?" Aubrey demanded with the impatient emphasis of a frustrated child on a wet day. He was almost shaking with rage and frustration.

"You've been outboxed, Mr. Aubrey."

"Don't be so damned American," Pyott drawled. "So insufferably smug and patronizing."

"Sorry, Colonel Pyott," Clark apologized. He could not mask his grin completely, even though he sensed the gravity of the situation as completely as anyone else in the room beneath the Admiralty. It was so – so *caricatured*, this panic in the dovecote. The new shiny toy was missing.

176

There was an absence of concern for the crew of the *Proteus* that Clark resented on their behalf, even in Aubrey. He also felt, and admitted, a sneaking admiration for the man he felt must have masterminded the boarding of the submarine, Valery Ardenyev. He could remember the man's face and build now, and he could entirely believe in the Russian's ability to successfully surprise and overcome a crew of over one hundred.

Everything depended upon the degree to which *Proteus* was damaged. The nearest NATO units were twenty hours' sailing from the present position of the submarine, except for certain small Norwegian units which the government in Oslo would not deploy in the Barents Sea. They could watch, by radar, sonar and aircraft, but they could not intervene. If it took more than twenty hours to raise and tow the *Proteus*, then the full five acts of the disaster might not be performed. Unless Ardenyev and his men simply unplugged "Leopard" and took it away with them. Clark was inclined to doubt this. The Russians would preserve, at some effort, the bland, apologetic face they had begun to present via the Soviet ambassador in London.

"Can we rescue it – them?" Aubrey asked. "Can we get out of the elephant trap that has been dug for us?" he insisted, worrying at the insuperable problem as at a bone. There had to be some hope within the situation, surely?

"Rescue?" Copeland blurted in disbelief.

"I can't see how," Clark said more carefully as Aubrey glared at the young Royal Navy officer. The map-board loomed over them all, all its lights gleaming and unmoving, except for the plotted course of the Nimrod on-station as it was updated every few minutes. A fly buzzing above the scene, a carrion bird over a kill.

"I don't see why they need to raise the sub," Pyott said. "They're interested in only one thing, surely?"

"Ardenyev's done maybe a half-dozen of these rescues on Russian boats in his career. Board and raise operations. He's an expert at it. They needed him to get on board, sure – but they maybe want his expertise at raising boats, too."

"I must talk to 'C' at once," Aubrey remarked. "Our talking is pointless at the moment. We must establish what the Soviet authorities intend."

Clark shrugged, unoffended that Aubrey doubted his prognosis. His respect for Aubrey had seemed to waver during the past twenty-four hours, like a light revealed and obscured by the movement of clouds. Yet the American, despite the clarity of his own mind, realized he still expected a solution to occur to Aubrey; even a successful solution.

Aubrey made no distinction of security between himself and the "Chessboard Counter" team, and used one of the battery of telephones in the underground room. Cunningham, he knew, was with the Foreign Secretary, having been summoned to a second meeting with the Soviet ambassador. He heard Cunningham at the other end of the line within half a minute of placing the call to the Foreign Office.

"Yes, Kenneth? What news?" Cunningham sounded breathless. Aubrey supposed it stemmed from events rather than exertion.

"Expert opinion – " Aubrey could not suppress an involuntary glance towards Clark and the tight-knit group around and beneath the map-board – "has it here that the Russians may have boarded *Proteus*."

"Good God, that's outrageous!"

"The ambassador hasn't confirmed as much?"

"He's talking of rescue, of course – but not of boarding. Not directly. Not as yet, that is."

"How does he explain the incident?"

There was a chilly chuckle in Cunningham's voice, the laugh of a man succeeding, just, in appreciating a joke against himself. "The captain of the Russian submarine suffered a nervous breakdown. He ordered the firing of the torpedo in question before he could be relieved of his command by the usual heroic young officer, loyal to the Party and the cause of world peace."

"That is perhaps the unkindest cut of all, that they can get away with such a ridiculous tale, knowing we can do nothing to refute it. And nothing to rescue our submarine."

"The Foreign Secretary has informed the PM, Kenneth. She's monitoring the situation. Every effort is being made to pressurize the Soviet Union into leaving the area and leaving *Proteus* to us."

"And –?"

"Very little. They insist, *absolutely insist*, on making amends. For the lunacy of one of their naval officers, as the ambassador put it."

"Washington?"

"The President is gravely concerned –"

"And will do nothing?"

"Is prepared to accept the Russian story at face value, for the sake of international tension, despite what his military advisers tell him. I don't think he quite grasps the importance of 'Leopard'."

"I see. We are getting nowhere?"

"Nowhere. What of this man Quin?"

"Nothing. The girl is the key. I'm waiting for a report from Hyde."

"Would it help if we recovered him, at least?"

"We might then destroy 'Leopard', I suppose."

"The PM will not risk the lives of the crew," Cunningham warned sternly. "The Foreign Secretary and I were informed of that in the most unequivocal manner."

"I meant only that we could attempt sabotage, or Lloyd could if Quin was in our hands again."

"Quite. You don't think 'Leopard' had been damaged by Lloyd or his crew?"

"It is possible, but I think unlikely. None of our signals reached the *Proteus*."

"Very well. Kenneth, I think you'd better come over here at once. You may have to brief the Foreign Secretary before he sees the PM again. Leave Pyott in command there."

"Very well. In fifteen minutes."

Aubrey replaced the receiver. The room was quiet with failure. Clark watched him steadily, some of the younger men regarded him with hope. Pyott appeared resigned. It was, he admitted, a complete and utter intelligence disaster – precisely the kind he could not tolerate or accept.

"Giles," he called, and then thought: Where the devil is Hyde?

Quin beckoned like a light at the end of a dark tunnel. A false, beguiling gleam, perhaps, but he had no other point of reference or hope.

Hyde wished he could call Aubrey from the row of telephones with their huge plastic hair-dryer hoods that he could see through the glass doors of the cafeteria. He was afraid, however, of leaving the girl for a moment. He was afraid of letting her out of his sight for any length of time, however short, and afraid, too, that she was beginning to regret her earlier decision. And he was also wary, treading delicately on the fragile, thin-ice crust of the trust she meagrely afforded him, of reminding her that there were other, more faceless, more powerful people behind him. The kind of people her father had fled from originally.

The telephones remained at the edge of his eyesight, in the centre of cognition, as he sipped his coffee and watched her eagerly devouring a plate of thin, overcooked steak and mushrooms and chips. For himself, beans on toast had been as much as he could eat. Tension wore at him, devouring appetite as well as energy. Quin was somewhere in the north of England – the girl had said nothing more than that, and he refrained from pumping her further for fear of recreating the drama of obsessive suspicion in her mind. He behaved, as far as he was able, as a driver who was giving her a lift north. The adrenalin refused to slow in his veins. He was nervous of pursuit – though he had seen no evidence of it – and he was suffering the stimulant effects of their escape from Petrunin.

"How's the tour going?" he asked conversationally.

She looked at him, a forkful of chips poised at her lips, which were shiny with eating. Her face was amused, and somehow obscurely contemptuous.

179

"I didn't have time to notice."

Hyde shrugged. "I thought you might have heard. I hope they do well."

"You expect me to believe that's all that's on your mind – the profits of an over-thirties rock band?" she sneered, chewing on the mouthful of chips, already slicing again at the thin steak. The cafeteria of the motorway service station was early-hours quiet around them. One or two lorry drivers wading through mountainous plates of food, a carload of caravanners avoiding the traffic of the day by travelling by night, smuggling their way to their holiday destination, the two waitresses leaning at the cash register, grumbling. Just south of Lancaster. Hyde hoped that Quin was somewhere in the Lake District. The sooner he got to him, the better.

He shrugged. "No, I don't think you're that stupid. Just filling in time, trying to lull you into a false sense of security." He grinned in what he hoped was an unsuspicious, engaging manner.

She studied him narrowly. Her plate was empty. "You're odd," she said eventually. "And too bloody clever by half. Don't pull the dumb ocker stunt with me."

She was still in control of their situation, leading him by the hand to her father, only because her father had agreed. She would tell him nothing until the last minute, to retain control.

"Thank you. Tell me, why did your father up and away like that? He wasn't really frightened of us, was he?"

She screwed her face up in thought, then released the skin into clear, youthful planes and curves again. With a bit of make-up, Hyde thought, she wouldn't look bad. They all wear a sneer these days.

"He was frightened of them – people like the ones tonight," she said. "And he didn't believe people like *you* –" An old and easy emphasis lay on the words like a mist. *Pigs, Fascists, cops, the fuzz.* The necessary vocabulary of her age and her education. The silence after the emphatic last word was strained, and she looked down, suddenly younger, more easily embarrassed.

"I see," he said. "We would have looked after him, you know."

"No you wouldn't!" she snapped, looking up again. "They watched him all the time. *Your* people took time off for meals, and the pub, and to go for a piss – *they* didn't! They were there all the time. Dad said there were a *hundred* times he could have been kidnapped while your lot weren't there or weren't looking!" She was leaning forward, whispering intently, a breathy shout. "You wouldn't have taken care of him – he took care of himself."

"I agree we're not as efficient as the KGB," Hyde said evenly. "But he wasn't in any real danger." Immediately, he was sorry he had uttered the words. The girl's features were rich in contempt, and he had no business defending the DS. Quin had been right, in a way. The KGB might have lifted him, any time. "Sorry," he added. "No doubt he was right. Sloppy buggers, some of them." Her face relaxed. "But he's safe now?" Her eyes narrowed, and he added: "Do you want coffee?" She shook her head.

"You?"

"No." He hesitated, then said, "Look, you have to trust me. No, I don't mean because you realize I'm trying to save you and your old man from the baddies – you have to believe I can do it. I'm not tooling around Britain waiting for you to make up your mind."

She thought for a moment, then said, "You'll have to turn off the motorway at the exit for Kendal." She watched his face, and he suppressed any sign of satisfaction.

It was the importance of it, he decided. That explained her almost fanatical care for her father. She was the key, even to herself. Importantly useful for the first time in her parents' lives. Crucial to her father's safety. She clung to her role as much as she clung to her father. "Ready? Let's go, then."

The man near the telephone booth in the car park watched them approach the yellow TR7, get in, and drive off down the slip-road to the M6. There was just time for the brief telephone call to Petrunin before they set off in pursuit. Once clear of Manchester and onto the motorway, Hyde had not driven at more than sixty or sixty-five. If he kept to that speed, there would be enough time to catch him before the next exit. He dialled the number, then pressed the coin into the box. Petrunin's voice sounded hollow and distant.

"I may have some trouble getting away. A slight delay. Keep me informed."

"Trouble?"

"No. I must, however, be careful leaving Manchester. I am known by sight. Don't lose them."

The man left the booth, and ran across the car park to the hired Rover and its two occupants. They were less than a minute behind the yellow TR7.

Lloyd was still angry. The effort to keep his appearance calm, to portray acquiescence to the inevitable, seemed only to make the hidden anger grow, like a damped fire. His father, encouraging the first fire of the autumn by holding the opened copy of *The Times* across the fireplace in the morning room. He smiled inwardly, and the memory calmed him. His stomach and chest felt less tight and hot. It was worse, of course, when the Russian was there – even when Thurston with his impotent raging and coarse vocabulary was in the same room.

There was nothing he could do. With his crew confined to their quarters and one guard on the bulkhead door, and his officers similarly confined to the wardroom, three men had held them captive until a relief, augmented guard had arrived from the rescue ship and the damage repair team with their heavy equipment had begun their work on the stern of the *Proteus*. Ardenyev forced one to admire him, and that rankled like a raging, worsening toothache. The effort of three weary, strained men to drag unconscious bodies through the submarine to monitor the essential, life-supporting systems, to inspect "Leopard", and only then to call for help, surprised him. Enraged him afresh, also.

There was a knock at his cabin door. Presumably the guard.

"Yes?"

Ardenyev was looking tired, yet there was some artificial brightness about his eyes. He was obviously keeping going on stimulants. Lloyd tried to adopt a lofty expression, feeling himself at a disadvantage just because he was lying on his bunk. Yet he could not get up without some admission of subordination. He remained where he lay, hands clasped round his head, eyes on the ceiling.

"Ah, captain. I am about to make an inspection of repairs. I am informed that they are proceeding satisfactorily."

"Very well, Captain Ardenyev. So kind of you to inform me."

"Yes, that is irony. I detect it," Ardenyev replied pleasantly. "I learned much of my English in America, as a student. Their use of irony is much broader, of course, than the English – I beg your pardon, the British."

"You cocky bastard. What the hell are you doing with my ship?"

"Repairing her, captain." Ardenyev seemed disappointed that Lloyd had descended to mere insult. "I am sorry for much of what has happened. I am also sorry that you killed three members of my team. I think that your score is higher than mine at the moment, don't you?"

Lloyd was about to reply angrily, and then he simply shrugged. "Yes. You haven't – ?"

"One body, yes. The youngest man. But that is usually the way, is it not? The others? No doubt they will be awarded posthumous medals. If I deliver your submarine to Pechenga."

"What happened to the fraternal greetings bullshit?"

"For public consumption, captain. That is what our ambassador will be telling your foreign secretary, over and over again. I'm sorry, but your inconvenience will be short-lived and as comfortable as possible. My interest in the affair ends when we dock. Now, if you will excuse me – "

Lloyd returned his gaze to the ceiling, and Ardenyev went out, closing the door behind him. The guard outside Lloyd's door was stony-faced, and his Kalashnikov was held across his chest, stubby metal butt resting lightly against one hip. Ardenyev nodded to him, and passed into the control room. His own team should have been there, he reminded himself, then wished to quash the reminder immediately. The pills, damned pills, juicing up the emotions, making pain easy and evident and tears prick while they kept you awake –

They would have a steering crew brought down from the rescue ship once the repairs were complete. Under his command, they would raise the submarine in preparation for towing to Pechenga. Teplov looked up from monitoring the life-support systems, and merely nodded to him. Vanilov was slumped in a chair, his head on his arms next to a passive sonar screen. Teplov was evidently letting him rest.

Ardenyev went out of the control room and into the tunnel which passed through the reactor housing to the aft section of the *Proteus*. He ignored the windows into the reactor chamber, and passed into the manoeuvring room above the huge diesel generators. Empty. Then the turbine room, similarly empty. The silence of the submarine was evident in the huge aft section, despite the banging and scraping, setting his teeth on edge, that thrummed in the hull; the noises of the repairs under way. Empty, silent, to the imagination beginning to smell musty with disuse. He passed through the bulkhead door into the room housing the electric motors, where the aft escape hatch was located. His replenished tanks waited for him on the floor by the ladder up to the hatch.

He checked the air supply, then strapped the tanks onto his back. He adjusted his facemask, and fitted the mouthpiece. He breathed rapidly, re-checking the air supply. Then he climbed the ladder and opened the hatch. He closed it behind him, and turned the sea-cock to flood the chamber. Water rushed down the walls, covering his feet in a moment, mounting to his ankles and knees swiftly.

When the chamber was flooded and the pressure equalized with the depth and weight of water outside, he reached up and turned the wheel of the outside hatch. He pushed it open, and kicked upwards, drifting out into the sudden blind darkness of the sea, his eyes drawn by pinpricks of white light and the flashes of blue light at the stern of the submarine. He turned, swimming down the grey back of the submarine where streaks of turning, swirling small fish glided and winked in the passing light of his lamp. Slowly, he made out the tiny figures working on the damaged stern, outlined and silhouetted by the flare of their cutting and welding gear and by the arc lamps clamped to the hull.

He crouched on the hull of the *Proteus*, next to the underwater salvage chief from the *Karpaty*, a man he had trained with for the past three months, Lev Balan. Beyond them, the hydroplanes and the rudder were being patched. The force of the seawater against their damaged, thin steel skins as the *Proteus* moved on after being hit by both torpedoes had begun stripping the metal away from the ribbed skeleton of steel beneath. The effect, Ardenyev thought, was like exposing the struts and

183

skeleton of an old biplane, where canvas had been stretched over a wooden frame, and doped. Or one of his old model aeroplanes, the ones that worked on a tightened elastic band. The repairs were crude, but sufficient to prevent further damage, and to make the minimal necessary use of rudder and hydroplanes now possible. The propeller would not be needed, but the evidence of the MIRV torpedo's steel serpents was being removed twenty fathoms down rather than in the submarine pen at Pechenga. The hull around the propeller and even forward of the rudder and hydroplanes was scarred and pocked and buckled by the effect of the whiplash action of the flailing steel cables as they were tightened and enmeshed by the turning of the propeller.

As Ardenyev watched, one length of cable, freed from the prop, drifted down through the light from the arc lamps in slow motion, sliding into the murk beneath the submarine. A slow cloud of silt boiled up, then settled.

"How much longer, Lev?"

"Two, three hours. In another hour we should be able to start attaching the tow lines." Lev Balan was facing him. Within the helmet of the diving suit, his face was vivid with enjoyment and satisfaction. Airlines snaked away behind him, down to the huge portable tanks of air mixture that rested on the ledge near the submarine. "We'll have to come in for a rest before that. Temperature's not comfortable, and my men are tired."

"OK – you make the decision. Is the docking prop damaged?" Balan shook his head. "What about the ballast tanks?"

"When we get her up to towing depth, we might have to adjust the bags. We've repaired one of the tanks, but the others can't be done down here – not if we're sticking to your timetable!" Despite the distortion of the throat-mike, Balan's voice was strong, full of inflection and expression, as if he had learned to adapt his vocal chords to the limitations of underwater communication.

"OK. Keep up the good work."

"Sorry about your boys."

Ardenyev shrugged helplessly. "Don't they call it operational necessity?"

"Some shits do."

"I'll get the galley operating ready for your men."

Ardenyev registered the drama around him once more. Now that his eyes had adapted completely, the arc lamps threw a glow around the scene, so that figures appeared caught in shafting sunlight, the minute sea life like motes and insects in summer air. He patted Balan on the shoulder, and kicked away back towards the hatch. As he travelled just above the hull with an easy motion of his legs and flippers, a curious sensation of ownership made itself apparent. As if the submarine were, in some part, his own, his prize; and some kind of repayment for the deaths of Kuzin, Nikitin and Shadrin.

When he dropped through the inner hatch again, he passed through the compartments of the huge submarine as a prospective purchaser might have strolled through the rooms of a house that had taken his fancy.

Teplov was waiting for him in the control room. Vanilov was sheepishly awake, and seated at the communications console.

"Message from Murmansk. The admiral wants to talk to you, sir," Teplov informed him. Obscure anger crossed Ardenyev's features.

"Weather and sea state up top?"

"It's no better," Teplov answered, "and then again, it's no worse. Forecast is for a slight increase in wind speed and a consequent slight worsening of sea state. The skipper of the *Karpaty* is still in favour of waiting the storm out."

"He doesn't have the choice, Viktor. In three hours' time, we'll be on our way home. Very well, let's talk to Murmansk, and endure the admiral's congratulations."

The feeling of possession and ownership had dissipated. The congratulations of the old man in Murmansk would be empty, meaningless. It wasn't about that, not at all. Not praise, not medals, not promotion. Just about the art of the possible, the art of making possible. And he'd done it, and Dolohov's words would make no difference, and would not bring back the dead.

"I see. Thank you, Giles. I'll tell the minister."

Aubrey put down the telephone, nodded to the Foreign Secretary's Private Secretary, and was ushered into the minister's high ceilinged office. Long gold curtains were drawn against the late night, and lamps glowed in the corners of the room and on the secretary of state's huge mahogany desk. It was a room familiar, yet still evocative, to Aubrey. The Private Secretary, who had been annoyed that Aubrey had paused to take the call from Pyott, and who had also informed him that His Excellency the Soviet ambassador was waiting in another room – protocol first, last and all the time, Aubrey had remarked to himself, hiding his smile – closed the double doors behind him.

Her Majesty's Secretary of State for Foreign and Commonwealth Affairs rose and came forward to take Aubrey's hand. In his features, almost hidden by his tiredness and the strain imposed by events which brought him unpleasantly into collision with the covert realities of the intelligence service, was the omnipresent memory that he had been a junior boy at Aubrey's public school and, though titled and wealthy, had had to fag for the son of a verger who had come from a cathedral preparatory school on a music scholarship. It was as if the politician expected Aubrey, at any moment and with the full effect of surprise, to remind him of the distant past, in company and with the object of humiliation.

"Kenneth. You were delayed?"

"I'm sorry, minister. I had to take a telephone call from Colonel Pyott. The Nimrod has been picking up signals from the *Proteus*, as have North Cape Monitoring." The minister looked immediately relieved, and Aubrey was sorry he had chosen an optimistic syntax for what he wished to convey. "Russian signals, I'm afraid," he hurried on. "We can't break the code, but it is evident that the Soviets are in command of the submarine."

"Damnation!" Cunningham offered from the depth of the chesterfield on which he was sitting. The Foreign Secretary's face dropped into lines of misery.

"The PM must be informed at once," he said, returning to his desk. "Find yourself a seat, Kenneth." He waved a hand loosely, and Aubrey perched himself on a Louis Quinze armchair, intricately carved, hideously patterned. Cunningham looked at Aubrey, and shook his head. The Foreign Secretary picked up one of the battery of telephones on his desk, then hesitated before dialling the number. "Is there anything you can suggest, Kenneth? Anything at all?" He put down the receiver, as if to display optimism.

"Minister – I'm sorry that this incident has had to spill over into legitimate diplomacy. I can only recommend that all diplomatic efforts be maintained. There is nothing else we can do. We must press for details, of course, and demand that one our people in Moscow is in Pechenga when the *Proteus* docks. He must be allowed immediate access, and there must be every attempt to preserve – by complaint, fuss, bother, noise, whatever you will – to preserve the security of 'Leopard'." Aubrey spread his hands on his knees.

"Pechenga?"

"The nearest naval base. Murmansk if you prefer – or wherever?"

"One of your people?"

Cunningham did not reply, but looked towards Aubrey.

"If you wish, minister," Aubrey answered. "But I would prefer someone rather senior on the embassy staff, and someone *legitimate*."

"Very well. I'll put that in motion.'

"I think, however," Aubrey pursued, "that the Russians will delay the travel permits, and that sort of thing, so that by the time our people are on the scene, they will have done whatever they wish and be waving *Proteus* goodbye from the quayside."

"I'm inclined to agree," Cunningham murmured.

"Then there is absolutely nothing we can do!" the Foreign Secretary fumed, slapping his hand repeatedly on the surface of his desk. He looked towards Aubrey as if he were to blame for the situation. Aubrey's features were impassive. "This really is not the way to play the game. The Russians have disobeyed every rule of international behaviour. It really is not good enough." There was a peculiarly old-fashioned inflection to the voice, to accompany the outdated sentiments.

"They are inclined to do that," Aubrey observed mockingly and received a warning glance from Cunningham. "I agree, minister. Obviously, the Kremlin has fully involved itself with, and sanctioned, this covert operation. Because they have done so, they place us at a considerable disadvantage. It is, indeed, a mixing of the legitimate and the covert which is both improper and very difficult to counter. And it has worked. This sort of mixed marriage usually flops badly – like the Bay of Pigs. The Russians seem to have more success than we do."

"You imply that any remedy is strictly the concern of the intelligence service?"

"I have no answer."

"The PM will give her blessing to *any* counter-operation, I'm quite sure of that. Our hands are tied, as you say. We do not even wish to become involved. Our people are in no danger, they will be released within the next couple of days. Our submarine will be repaired. Only 'Leopard' will no longer be our property. Therefore, if you can prevent the loss of 'Leopard', do so. But it must be – and the PM would wish me to stress this, even at the same time as she gives you her blessing – *it must be* an intelligence operation. It will be disowned, it must not endanger the crew of the submarine or any non-intelligence personnel, and it must be done immediately." The Foreign Secretary smiled glumly, though there was a snuff-pinch of pleasure in his gloom because he considered he must have discomforted Aubrey. "Is there anything, anything at all?"

Aubrey cleared his throat. "NATO naval units are too far from the area to intercept. The Soviet government wish to apologize to us by repairing the damage they have inflicted. I have one agent-in-place in the Pechenga district. He is a grocer. I do not have a satellite-mounted laser beam whereby I can secretly and silently destroy half of the Red Banner Fleet – therefore, minister, I am inclined to conclude that there is very little I can effectively do to secure the secrecy of 'Leopard' and the remainder of the sensitive equipment aboard HMS *Proteus*."

"Very well," the secretary of state said tightly, "I will inform the PM of the state of play, and recommend that we have only the diplomatic alternative." Again, he picked up the receiver and placed it to his ear.

"Unless," Aubrey began, amazed at his empty temerity and observing his own words as if spoken by another; and that other a pompous ass without sincerity or resolution. "Unless we can get one man into the naval dockyard at Pechenga or wherever, with a brief to destroy the 'Leopard' equipment before the Soviets have time to inspect it."

187

Aubrey was intensely aware of the eager, then disbelieving gazes of Cunningham and the Foreign Secretary. But, he told himself, attempting to justify what some obscure part of his mind or imagination had prompted him to utter, the whole capture of *Proteus* was the work of little more than one man, in the final analysis. Why not the reverse, then? The question echoed in his mind, but no answer appeared. Not so much as the first whisper of an answer. He asked himself a second, perhaps more pressing question.

Where the blazes was Hyde, and where the devil was Quin?

Kendal was asleep and windy. At one set of traffic lights, a board advertising ice cream outside a newsagent's shop, where the lights were on within as the proprietor marked up the morning editions for delivery, blew over in a gust, noisily startling the girl who was dozing in the passenger seat. Hyde had watched her face in repose from time to time since they left the M6. Her lips pouted, still greasy from her meal, and her features were pale, small and colourless. Obscurely, he felt responsible for her. She had passed from being the object of a search, the key to a security problem, into a chrysalis stage where she was almost a person, with human rights and human demands upon his time and energies. She hovered, waiting to be born into his emotional world. He did not welcome the change. It complicated matters. It was a pity he seemed to understand her. It would have been easier had she been a replica of her Left-wing, feminist friend Sara, whom he could have comfortably disliked.

He had paused on the outskirts of Kendal and waited, but no cars approached in his mirror or passed him. He relaxed until they passed through Staveley and turned west on the main Windermere road. Headlights followed him out of the village, keeping behind him for almost two miles before turning off down a narrow track. He discovered himself sweating with relief the instant the headlights disappeared. Like a cat being woken by a tension in its owner, the girl stirred and sat up.

"Anything wrong?"

"Nothing. Go back to sleep."

"I'm not tired any more."

"Great. Pity you can't drive."

The girl subsided into a sullen silence. There were people on the streets of Windermere, standing at bus stops, walking with bent heads beneath black hoods of umbrellas in the misty drizzle that clung to the town. The roof of a train gleamed darkly in the lights of the station, which lay below the main road.

By the time they were on the outskirts of Windermere again, the dog-leg of the long ribbon of the lake lay to their left, its further shore tree-clad, wreathed with a chill mist, its steep sides buttressing the low cloud that was just turning from black to grey. It was a slow, wintry, unwelcome dawn as they crossed Trout Beck, heading for Ambleside.

"I reckon Wordsworth lived in Croydon and made it all up," he remarked. "He never said it was always pissing with rain while he was having his visions of nature."

"You have no soul," the girl replied lightly. She seemed to warm herself at humour as at a small fire. He looked at her. She glanced away.

"It's all right," he offered, "I'm not about to pull the car into the side and take advantage of you."

The girl did not reply. A tinge of colour in her cheeks, but no other reaction. He glanced at her from time to time, but she continued to gaze out of the side window, watching the far shore of Windermere slide past, the cramped, heavy firs crowding down to the water like a herd or an army, then giving way to damp, grassy outcrops, almost colourless under the low cloud cover. The land climbed away on his side of the car above the tree-line to bare-sided, long-backed hills, scalily wet and monstrously slumbering. Ambleside was shiny in its hollow between the hills and the grey water.

He pulled into a lay-by overlooking the northern end of the lake, just south of the town, and turned to the girl.

"Where to now, sweetheart? I've driven as far as Ambleside on trust, now where?"

She got out of the car without replying, and walked to the edge of the lay-by. Hyde followed her. She turned and looked up at him. She appeared to be entertaining another bout of distrust, even fear of him. She shook her head, and looked away towards the perspective of the long lake stretching away south. Water and sky merged no more than a couple of miles from them into a non-existence. Hyde found the scene extraordinarily depressing. He touched her shoulder, but she shook his hand away.

"You *have* to trust me," he said.

"I know!" she almost wailed, so that he wondered whether she might not be psychologically disturbed. She certainly seemed neurotically suspicious. "I – can't . . ."

Anger welled up in him. Stupid little bitch. He bellowed at her: "You're wasting my bloody time, girlie! I don't know what's the bloody matter with you, or what the hell the world could have done to make you act like this – but I'm interested in what happens to a hundred blokes at the bottom of the sea relying on your old man's invention!"

In the silence that followed, he heard the water lapping gently out of sight below the verge of the lay-by, some water bird calling, the hum of a generator from somewhere behind them, the noise of the chain-saw from the trees on the far shore, and her quiet sobbing. Then she spoke without turning to him.

189

"You're a bloody shit, you are." Then, as if intending to be both more precise and younger, she added, "A bully."

"Sorry." He began to consider that Mrs. Quin was the strongest member of the family, and felt a preconceived anxiety about the girl's father, and his similarity to his daughter. He found her, at that moment at least, too helpless to be a sympathetic figure.

"It's a cottage, off the road between Ambleside and Coniston. Less than half an hour in the car. I'm ready to take you there now."

The noise of the car startled him, appearing round a bend in the road that had masked its noise until it was almost upon them. His reaction was instinctive, but it revealed also the stretched state of his nerves. Before he assimilated the Renault and its trailing white-and-brown caravan and the two mild faces behind the windscreen, the pistol was in his hand, and beginning to move up and out into a straight-arm firing position. A moment later, it was behind his back again, being thrust back into the waistband of his corduroy trousers. But not before the girl, at least, had witnessed the tiny incident. She appeared terrified, hands picking around her face like pale bats.

"Don't be bloody stupid," he told her, his hands shaking as he thrust them into his pockets, an inward voice cursing his jumpiness. "What do you think it is, a bloody game?"

She hurried past him towards the car.

"What's the time?"

"Eight-thirty."

"The blip's stopped moving and the signal strength is growing. Listen."

"All right, turn it down. That means the car's stopped somewhere, less than a couple of miles up the road."

"Great. Stop at the next phone box, and we can call Petrunin."

"And sit around all day waiting for him to get out of Manchester, I suppose? Marvellous!"

"Don't grumble. With a bit of luck we've got Hyde, the girl, and her father. Ah, there's a phone box. Pull off the road."

"Yes?" Ardenyev prevented an anticipatory grin from appearing on his lips, until Lev Balan nodded and rubbed his hand through his thick dark hair with tiredness and relief. "Great!" Ardenyev hugged Balan, laughing, feeling the man's helmet digging painfully into his ribs as Balan held it under his arm. "Great! We can go?"

"Any time you like. My boys are knackered, by the way – not that it'll worry you." Balan's answering grin was like a weather crack opening in seamed grey rock. Only then did Ardenyev really look at him, and fully perceive the man's weariness.

190

"Sorry. Tell them – tell them when we get back to Pechenga, we'll have the biggest piss-up they've ever seen. On me!"

"You've done it now. You're on."

"Tow lines, too?" Ardenyev asked eagerly, surprised at his own child-like enthusiasm. Again, Balan nodded, his cigarette now pressed between his lips, in the corner of his mouth. He looked dishevelled, unkempt, and rather disreputable. Insubordinate, too. "Great. What about buoyancy?"

"We've got the bags on. Just sufficient to keep you at snorkel depth for towing. Any fine adjustments we'll make when you take her up. Then we'll do some more fine-tuning in the outer basin at Pechenga, before you dock. Assuming you can drive this bloody thing, of course!"

Ardenyev indicated the skeleton crew of Soviet ratings in the control room. "All volunteers," he said wryly. "They can drive it, I'm quite sure."

"Just in case, I'm on my way back outside – to watch the disaster from there. Good luck."

"And you. See you in Pechenga. Take care."

Balan walked wearily back through the aft section of the *Proteus* to the stern escape chamber. He strapped his auxiliary air tank to his back, requiring it until he could be recoupled to the hoses outside, and climbed through the lower hatch. He flooded the chamber, and opened the upper hatch, climbed the ladder and floated out into the darkness. His legs felt heavy, not merely because of his boots but because of the surpassing weariness that had invested itself in every part of his body. He waddled slowly and clumsily down the whale's back of the submarine, arms waving like some celluloid ghoul, or as if in imitation of one of the cosmonauts space-walking. He was bone-weary, he decided. Another half-hour's working and one of them might have made some small, fatal mistake. Any one of the cables, the jagged edges, the cutters could have injured or killed any of them.

Another underwater cosmonaut, looking ridiculous in a way that never failed to amuse Balan, came towards him from the upright, aircraft's tailplane of the rudder, almost staggering with the resistance of the heavy air hoses. The two men patted each other and clung together like the automatons on a musical box, then Balan turned his back and the hoses were fitted. A moment of breath-holding, then the rush of the air mixture, putting pressure on his ears and face, then the auxiliary tank was in his hands. He looked at it, grinned, and heaved it over the side of the submarine. It floated away down into the darkness.

Balan inspected his work once more. The stern of the *Proteus*, in the hard light of the lamps, was a mess, but it was a mess of which he felt justifiably proud. The rudder and the hydroplanes had been patched with a skin of metal, or their plates twisted back into shape and form by

191

use of the hammer, the rivet-gun, the welding and cutting torches. Scarred, twisted, cracked metal, blackened and buckled. The propeller had not been repaired, merely cleared of the entangling, choking seaweed of the steel cables from the MIRV torpedo. Balan thought the shaft might be out of true, but that was Pechenga's worry not his. Then, masking the operation scars along the side of the hull, where the ballast tanks had been ruptured and the outer hull of the *Proteus* damaged, a lazily flapping, transparent growth idled in the currents moving across the ledge, like the attachment of a giant, translucent jellyfish to the submarine. Buoyancy bags, ready to be inflated when Ardenyev gave the order to blow tanks, they would serve in place of the unrepaired ballast tanks at the stern of the submarine, giving it a workable approximation to its normal buoyancy control.

Balan was proud of what amounted to almost ten hours' work on the British submarine. The work had been as dispassionately carried out as always by himself and his team. Unlike Ardenyev, there was no pleasure at the meaning of the task and its completion. It was merely a job well done, a task completed successfully. The nature of the submarine, its nationality, had no meaning for Balan.

He spoke into his headset. "Right, you lot, clear away. Our gallant, heroic captain is going to take this tub to the top, and I don't want anyone hurt in the process!"

"I heard that," Ardenyev said in his ear, slightly more distant than the laughter that soughed in his helmet from some of his team. "I've been in contact with *Kiev* and *Karpaty*. Ready when you are."

"OK. I'm clearing the slaves from the hull now. I'll get back to you."

Balan took hold of his air hoses in one hand, checking that they did not snag anywhere and trailed away across the ledge to the pumps and the generator. Then he turned clumsily but surely, and began climbing down the light steel ladder that leant against the port hydroplane, attached by small magnets. He lowered his air lines gingerly to one side of him as he climbed tiredly down to the surface of the ledge. The crewman who had attached his lines came after him. They were the last to descend, and when they stood together at the bottom of the ladder, Balan and the other diver hefted the ladder between them, and they trudged through the restless, distressed silt to where the arc lamps had been re-sited near the generators and the sleds on which they had brought down their equipment. The small group of diving-suited figures who composed his team was gathered like nervous spectators beneath the bloom of the lights. Balan joined them, dropping the ladder onto one of the sleds and securing it before he spoke again to Ardenyev.

"OK, chief – you can make your attempt on the world rate of ascent record now. We're safely out of the way!"

"Thanks, Lev. Don't forget our piss-up in Pechenga – if you're not all too tired, that is!"

There was a murmur of protest and abuse at the remark. Balan was almost prepared to admit his tiredness, but there were certain fictions that had to be preserved, whatever the cost; one of them being the indestructibility, the immortality of salvage men.

"We won't forget. You just bring your wallet." The banter was required, expected, all of them were recruiting-poster figures, without separate identity, without reality. Living their own fictions; heroes. Silly, silly –

"I will. OK, here we go."

Balan studied the submarine, partly in shadow now, the light of the arc lamps casting deep gloomy patches over their repair work, rendering it somehow shabby and inadequate. The *Proteus* looked half-built, half-destroyed. He did not attend to Ardenyev's orders, still coming through the headset, presumably for his benefit, until he heard "Blow tanks!" and the submarine – after a moment in which nothing seemed to happen – shifted under the discharge of sea water from her ballast tanks, and then the jellyfish bags began to bloom and roll and fold and inflate. Balan felt the new currents of the submarine's movement and the discharged water. They could feel the hull grinding against the ledge through their boots; the stern of the submarine seemed to be lifting slightly higher than the bow. It would need adjustment. The bow itself was in darkness, where the tow-lines were attached. They'd have to be inspected, too.

Someone cheered in his headset, making him wince. One of the younger men, he supposed. There were sighs of pleasure and relief, though, like a persistent breeze; noises that were their right.

The *Proteus*, still a little bow-heavy, drifted up and away from them, out of the boiling cloud of silt, becoming a great shadow overhead, just beyond the arc lamps, then a dimmer shape, then almost nothing as it ascended the twenty fathoms to the surface. The bags round its stern – like nappies, he thought. Around its bum.

"Come on, you lot. The volume on those bags is going to have to be changed for a starter! Don't waste time, get organized!"

Theatrically, the arc lamps began flicking off, leaving them in a sudden darkness, where their helmet lamps and hand-lamps glowed like aquatic fireflies. Above them, as they began climbing onto their sleds, the *Proteus* stopped at snorkel depth and waited for them.

"Well done, Hyde – excellent work, excellent!" Aubrey was effusive, his tiredness gone in a moment, if only briefly. Hyde had Quin, beyond all reasonable expectation, and at this critical moment. Their first real piece of luck – a change of luck? They needed it. "Well done. Bring him directly to London. You'd better let me arrange for a helicopter from the Cumbria force to pick you up. I want Quin here as soon as possible – What? What do you mean?''

Hyde's voice had dropped to barely more than a whisper, something conspiratorial. Aubrey swivelled in his seat as if in response to its tone, turning his back on the underground room and its occupants. Pyott and Clark, attentive to his enthusiasm at the call that had been put through, now remained some yards away. Clark was making some point about the *Proteus*, his finger tracing across a large-scale cutaway plan of the submarine which Aubrey had had brought down from the second floor of the Admiralty.

"Back-up's here," he heard Clark saying. "Right out of the way –" Then he was attending to Hyde's quiet voice.

"He's in a bad way, Mr Aubrey. Out in the garden now, blowing his nose a lot and upsetting his daughter. Can you hear me all right?"

"Yes, Hyde, yes," Aubrey replied impatiently. "What do you mean, *a bad way?*"

"One of those who can't take isolation, even if he is a loner," Hyde replied flatly, without sympathy. "He's been up here for weeks, almost a week on his own. And when the two of them were here together, I reckon they just wore each other down with mutual nerves. Quin's a neurotic bloke, anyway."

"Spare me the psychology, Hyde."

"You have to understand him," Hyde said in exasperation. "He doesn't want to come back, he's scared stiff of his own shadow, he doesn't seem to care about the *Proteus* – all our fault, apparently."

"That, at least, is true."

"I've spent hours talking to him. I can't get through to him. He'll come back because he's scared not to, and because he thinks the opposition may have followed us here –"

"Have they?"

"No. But now we've found him, he thinks it'll all start up again, and he wants to hide. I don't want him scared off by a helicopter. He'll come back with me, or not at all."

"What about the girl?"

"She's the one who's just about persuaded him to trust me. *I* have to deliver him somewhere safe."

"I didn't mean that. What will you do with her?"

"She'll stay here. Either that, or I'll put her on a train."

"I haven't time to waste, Hyde. Is he fit to work?"

"No."

"Then he'll have to work in an unfit state. Very well. Drive back to Manchester. You and he can fly down from there. I'll arrange it. *You* can hold his hand."

"Yes, Mr. Aubrey."

"And – once again, well done. Keep him happy, promise him anything – but he must be here this evening, and ready to work!"

Aubrey put down the receiver, and stood up, the purposefulness of his movements keeping doubt at bay. He had dozed lightly and fitfully on the narrow camp bed in the adjoining cupboard-like room without windows. The darkness had seemed close and foetid, and the light and noise under the door had drawn him back into the underground operations room. Cold water had restored a semblance of wakefulness, and Hyde's message had completed the work of reinvigoration.

"Well?" Giles Pyott asked, turning from the chart pinned to a board, resting on an easel. "What news?"

"Hyde has found Quin."

"Thank God! Where is he?"

"Lake District – near Coniston Water, I gather."

"He's been there all the time?"

"Apparently. Rented a cottage through an agency."

"Can he get here today?" Clark asked more purposefully.

"He can. Hyde says that the man is in a state close to nervous exhaustion." Aubrey shrugged his shoulders. "I don't know how that complicates matters. Better have a doctor to look at him, I suppose. It really is too bad –"

"Hell, can he *work*?"

"Whether or not, he will work." He indicated the drawing of the *Proteus*. "He has to do something about this, after all. Doesn't he?"

It was almost three before Quin was finally ready to depart. His luggage, which consisted of one small suitcase and an overcoat, had been a means of delaying his departure. He had driven Hyde to the edge of rage again and again, and then capitulated, afraid of the Australian in a more immediate way than of the other figures and dangers that crowded his imagination. Aubrey had telephoned the cottage at noon, and had been frustrated and angered at the further delay. After that, Hyde had handled Quin like unstable explosive; cajolement and masked threat had eventually subdued him.

He stood now at the door of the whitewashed cottage, hesitant while Hyde carried the suitcase to the TR7. Tricia Quin was at his side like a crutch, touching his arm, trying to smile him into complacency. In some obscure and unexpected way, she had strengthened during the day, adopting much of Hyde's attitude and many of his arguments. It was as if she had adopted the plight of the *Proteus* as a charitable cause worthy of contribution; or perhaps she sensed her father needed help, that the greatest danger to his health lay in his present solitary surroundings. Hyde wondered what Quin would have made of the Outback, even the

195

dead centre of Australia. The unnerving silence *was* audible there. The Lake District hummed and buzzed with life, by comparison.

He looked away from Quin and his daughter, towards the stretch of water that was The Tarns, and then at the road and the land falling away, down from Black Fell behind him through the firs towards Coniston Water two miles away. The land pressed in upon the cottage, and Hyde admitted a claustrophobic isolation so different from the Australian hinterland. Perhaps it wasn't surprising Quin couldn't take it after all, staying in that cottage and its garden for a week without seeing another soul after his daughter left. They'd quarrelled about her going to see her mother, apparently. That might have set him off, created his sense of abandonment amid danger.

Hyde shrugged, and opened the boot. The weather was windier now, moving the low cloud but breaking it up, too. Gleams, fitful and unoptimistic, of blue sky; a hazy light through the clouds. It had, at least, stopped drizzling.

The bullet whined away off the yellow boot before the noise of the gunshot reached him. He stared at his hand. The bullet had furrowed across the back of it, exposing the flesh. An open-lipped graze which still had not begun to hurt, matching the furrowed scar on the boot lid. He looked stupidly around him.

A second shot then, chipping pebble-dash from the wall of the cottage two feet or so from Quin's head. His frightened, agape features, the girl's quicker, more alert panic, her hands dragging at her father's arm, the shrouded hills, the distant dark trees – he took in each distinct impression in the moment that he heard the heavy report of the rifle, and then the pain in his hand began, prompting him like a signal. He began running for the door of the cottage.

PART THREE

PLUMBER

TEN:

Rescue?

"What are they waiting for? Why don't they *do* something?" Quin's voice was plaintive, fearful; yet the words sounded strangely irritated, as if the men outside had disappointed him.

"You've seen the bloody cowboy films, haven't you?" Hyde replied, almost snarling, weary of Quin's unabated nerves. "The lynch-mob always waits for dark." The man seemed to possess an infinite capacity to remain on edge, and his emotions rubbed against Hyde's attempts to evolve a solution to their situation like sandpaper against skin.

"Why *are* they waiting?" Tricia Quin asked in a studiedly calm tone, sitting near him on the floor beneath the cottage window.

Hyde turned to her. "Petrunin can't be here yet."

"Who?"

"The bloke who chased us – the big cheese. He's got a face everyone will have a copy of. Must be hard to get out of Manchester. They'll be waiting for orders."

"How many of them do you think there are?"

Hyde watched Quin as he listened to the girl. The man was sitting in a slumped, self-pitying posture with his back against the wall, near the settee with its stained stretch covers. Hyde disliked Quin intensely. The man got on his nerves. He was a pain in the backside. He was going to be useless to Aubrey, even if he delivered him.

"Two, maybe three."

"You don't think they might try something before dark?"

"Why? They'll assume I'm armed, they know I'm a professional, just like them. They're not going to volunteer to get their balls blown off. Your dad's here, and he isn't going anywhere."

She studied her father, then looked away from him.

"What about your people? This man Aubrey?"

"When we don't turn up in Manchester, he'll worry. He knows where we are."

"Will he worry in time?"

"That what I'm worrying about." He smiled, and studied her face. "How are you?"

"I'm all right." She avoided looking at her father.

"What are you going to do?" Quin asked.

"For Christ's sake, stop moaning!"

"It's your fault – you brought them here! This is just what I tried to avoid – what I came here to get away from," Quin persisted. Hyde perceived deep and genuine and abiding fears, disguising themselves in self-pity. He could almost feel sorry for Quin; might have done so, had their situation at that moment been less acute. And had Quin's voice had been less insistent, less whining. "I knew I couldn't be adequately protected, that no one took my fears seriously. And now look what's happened – they're out there, the very people I tried to avoid. And *you* – you brought them here. You've as good as handed me to them on a plate!"

"All right. So they stuck a bleeper under the car. Sorry."

"That won't do us any good."

"Shut up! It's *your* bloody fault we're all stuck here."

"Leave him alone," Tricia Quin pleaded softly.

"All right. Look, once it's dark, I can try to get to a telephone that hasn't had its wires cut. But I'm not walking out there just at the moment. He'll have to sit it out, just like us."

"As long as nothing happens to him."

"It won't. Petrunin's in a corner himself. It's a stalemate. Nothing's going to happen to Dad – unless I break his bloody neck for him!"

Quin scowled like a child sulking. Hyde looked at his watch. Just after three. Patience, patience, he instructed himself. Aubrey has got to catch on soon.

He wondered, without letting the thought tinge the bland expression on his features, whether Petrunin's orders might not have changed because of the capture of the submarine by the Russians. The death of Quin, rather than his capture, might be a satisfactory conclusion to the operation.

It was hard to discard the thought, once he had admitted it. It was unlikely, but possible. Of his own death, he did not think. That, he had considered almost as he closed the cottage door behind him after he had run from the car, would be inevitable whether Petrunin wanted Quin alive or dead. He looked at his hand, wrapped in his handkerchief. His gun made an uncomfortable, pressing lump against the small of his back. It was not entirely a stalemate, it merely gave that impression. Petrunin wanted Quin badly. Petrunin was finished in the UK anyway, after this. When he went, he'd want Quin with him. As soon as it was dark, he'd come for him.

"Ethan, it is not an old man's vanity, or sense of hurt pride – or even senility. I am asking a serious question. Could someone get into

200

Pechenga and destroy 'Leopard' before the Russians can examine or dismantle it?''

''You're crazy, Mr. Aubrey. In twenty-four hours the Russians will have that submarine turned around and on her way. There's no time to do anything.''

''I'm not sure about that.'' Aubrey looked up from the narrow camp bed where he sat perched like a tired, dishevelled prisoner under the hard strip-lighting of the cupboard-like room. Clark leaned against the door, dressed like a golfer in sweater and slacks. Clark's increasing informality of dress during the past days had been a badge of defeat and of defeatism. Aubrey felt tired, directionless; yet at the same time he was possessed by the quick seductive glamour of a counter-operation. ''I'm not sure about that,'' he repeated.

''You don't even know it's Pechenga,'' Clark persisted.

''Satellite and Nimrod suggest it might be. There are signs of what might be preparations for *Proteus*'s arrival at Pechenga, but not at Murmansk.'' Aubrey rubbed his hands together in a washing motion. To Clark the activity suggested a pretended, mocking humility. The room was coffin-like, stale and dead, and pressed in on him uncomfortably.

''Maybe. Look, these quick-burn operations always look good on paper. Our intelligence is *nil*, Mr. Aubrey, and there's no time or capacity for back-up. Face facts – the Russians have *Proteus* on their ground, on their terms. They'll give her back.''

''I realize that,'' Aubrey snapped, ''but I am not prepared simply to wait until she is handed back like a toy that no longer works.''

''Listen, Mr. Aubrey,'' Clark began angrily, turning from the door, which he had been facing as Aubrey spoke, as if to hide the expression on his face, ''I can't give you what you want. I don't know enough about 'Leopard' to be able to tell you how to destroy it effectively without blowing up the damn boat, too! The Russians may have their superman in Ardenyev, but don't put the role onto me. I can't help you.''

''Someone at Plessey, then,'' Aubrey murmured disparagingly.

''You need Quin.''

''I realize that. If I get you Quin, can you do the job?''

''What?''

''I said – if I get you Quin, will you do the job? *Can* you do the job?''

''Job?''

''Don't be dense, dear boy. You would have to do it. You are familiar with the whole operation, you are familiar with the equipment, you are in naval intelligence, you have a great deal of field experience. Who else would I consider sending?''

''One man?''

201

"One particular man, yes."

"And all I have to do is get into Pechenga, board the *Proteus*, destroy the equipment, and get out again with no one any the wiser?" Clark raised his hands in the air. "You've really flipped, Mr. Aubrey. It can't be done."

"It must be attempted."

"I'm not on your staff."

"I'm sure I can arrange your temporary assignment."

"There's no time."

"We must *try!*"

"So where's Quin? Your house of cards falls down without him."

Aubrey's face became saturnine. "I don't know. Hyde should have arrived at Manchester airport by now. He has not done so."

"Then he's in trouble."

"You think so?"

Clark paced the tiny cubicle. "You've spent all your time dreaming up this crazy scheme instead of worrying about realities. Your guy has to be in trouble, and you haven't even given him a thought!"

Aubrey's face registered an expression of rage, directed at Clark. Then, in admission, his look turned inwards. He had been taking an afternoon nap of the intellect. Clark was perfectly correct. He had ignored Hyde, and Hyde must now be in trouble. He clenched his fists in his lap, then got up and opened the door.

"OS map of the Coniston Water area!" he shouted into the underground room, directing the order at every one of its occupants. Pyott looked up, startled, and then reached for a telephone. "Quickly!" He slammed the door and looked steadily at Clark. "You are right. I have been foolishly, dangerously remiss. But if we get Quin here, we shall talk again. You are not off the hook, Ethan!"

"Neither are your guy and Quin."

The *Proteus* reached a moment of equilibrium after her seeming rush from snorkel depth to the surface, and then the motion of the waves began to affect her. Ardenyev watched as the hatch above them slid back. Water dripped on him and Lloyd and the armed guard, and then the platform of the bridge was raised electronically until their heads rose above the fin of the submarine. The *Proteus* rolled gently in the swell of the outer harbour of Pechenga, the adjusted buoyancy bags at the stern maintaining her at the correct depth but impairing her stability.

Ardenyev smiled, and waved an arm towards the low shoreline.

"Welcome to the Soviet Union, Commander Lloyd."

Rain whipped into their faces, and fuzzy lights glowed through the dark late afternoon. Low submarine pens lay ahead of them, beyond

202

the harbour wall with its guard towers and its anti-submarine net. The rain was chilly, mingled with sleet which numbed the side of Lloyd's face as he studied the scene with the hunched shoulders of a prisoner. The rescue ship *Karpaty* made cautious headway, still towing the *Proteus*. He turned to look back aft of the sail. Huge jellyfish bags surrounded the stern of the submarine like splints on a damaged limb. He could make out, through the white-edged spray and the driving rain, the scars and the rough repairs that had been affected beneath the surface by the rescue team. The bow of the *Proteus* was still angled slightly below the horizontal because of the crudity of measurement employed in inflating the bags. A bow-wave surged along the forward deck as Lloyd turned his gaze back towards Pechenga. The *Karpaty* had passed through the gap in the harbour wall where the net had been swung electronically away to allow her access, and *Proteus* was slipping, in an almost lurching, ungainly fashion between the towers on the wall. Lloyd could see faces looking from the towers; they all seemed to be grinning, and an arm waved. The sight created a sense of humiliation in him.

Ardenyev was speaking.

"I'm sorry – you were saying?" he said, indulging his sense of defeat and self-blame. He had made mistakes, fatal ones for "Leopard". Because the situation was so unreal, and its consequences dangerous only for a lump of inoperable equipment in the bowels of his vessel, his mind was more keenly aware of errors of judgment and tactics. He should not have been so slow in realizing their danger, he should not have settled on the bottom. There seemed no limit to the catalogue of blame.

"I intrude upon your self-examination?" Ardenyev asked lightly. "But there is no danger. No cause for alarm."

"That's the most unreal thing of all, isn't it?" Lloyd replied.

Ardenyev ignored the reply. "As I was saying, we will have the submarine docked in two or three hours. Of course, we will not delay you more than is necessary. Your reactor will not be run down, you will be docked in a wet dock – we can manage the repairs quite adequately without a dry dock – and you will be ready to sail in no more than forty-eight hours. That I promise you."

"You would be able to make such a promise, of course," Lloyd replied acidly, "since the damage to my ship was quite precisely calculated, no doubt."

"I'm sorry –?"

"Forget it. It was all an accident, a most unfortunate accident."

"Of course."

The swell was hardly discernible inside the harbour wall. Lloyd was uncomfortably aware, however, of the forward motion of the submarine and of the other vessels in the harbour basin. Pechenga was unsubstantial still, masked by the murk and the flying rain and sleet and remained as unreal as the satellite pictures he had seen of it and of dozens of other Soviet naval ports, but the big ships were real, uncomfortably so. Two "Kara"- class cruisers at anchor, one half-repainted. Three or four destroyers, like a display of toys, small and grey and bristling with aerials and radar dishes and guns. Frigates, a big helicopter cruiser, two intelligence ships festooned with electronic detection and surveillance equipment. A submarine support ship, minesweepers, ocean tugs, tankers. The sight, the numbers, overawed him, ridiculing Portsmouth, Plymouth, Faslane, every naval port and dockyard in the UK. It was like going back into the past, except for the threatening, evident modernity of these vessels, to some great review of the fleet at Spithead between the two world wars, or before the Great War. The harbour at Pechenga, a satellite port for Murmansk, daunted Lloyd. He felt completely and utterly entrapped.

The submarine pens, mere nest-holes in the concrete at this distance, winked with lights ahead of the *Karpaty*. One of those small black holes would swallow his vessel, contain it until people like this Russian on his bridge said they could leave, gave them permission. He shrugged hopelessly.

"You're impressed?" Ardenyev asked.

"As long as they're not all cardboard mock-ups, yes."

"They're not." Lloyd looked at Ardenyev. The man seemed unenthusiastic about the conversation he had begun.

"So familiar as to be boring?" he asked.

"What? Oh, this. I was just thinking what a dull town Pechenga is."

"I see."

"I doubt it." They slid beneath the lee of a cruiser. Crewmen leaned over the rails, looking down at the British submarine, waving their caps, yelling indistinguishable words and greetings. Ardenyev watched them as he might have observed the behaviour of monkeys at a zoo. "The brothels are quite dreadful," he continued. "All right for conscripts, but not for the likes of you and me. A good job you will not be allowed ashore. The casualty rate would be staggering. Quite unacceptable to the Admiralty."

"You seem to have run out of steam," Lloyd remarked.

"What? Oh, perhaps." Ardenyev brushed a hand through his wet hair, and assayed a tired grin. His waving arms indicated the whole bulk of the *Proteus*. "It's over for me. The dull time after excitement. I am feeling sorry for myself. Forgive my bad manners."

They were slowing now. *Karpaty* seemed to lag, and they began to overtake her in a snail-like pursuit, until the *Proteus* herself came to a stop. Tiny figures emerged from the forward hatch and scuttled along the slippery, gleaming deck, casting off the tow-lines swiftly and expertly. A hard-lit submarine pen gaped before them. *Proteus* began to edge towards the open gates of the pen on her intact docking propeller, the "egg-beater" located forward of the main propeller and retracted when not in use. Lloyd shuddered.

"As soon as we dock, I must leave you to make my report," Ardenyev murmured. Lloyd ignored him, watching his vessel slide forward into the maw of the submarine pen. Down the line of pens, men had stopped work to watch. The sterns of Soviet submarines were visible through the open gates of other pens, but Lloyd, after one quick, self-conscious glance, returned his gaze to the bow of the *Proteus*. She stopped again, and men scrambled over the deck, attaching the hawsers whereby she could be winched into the pen. An order was given, the deck was cleared again, and then the winches picked up the slack, measured the bulk of the submarine and began to pull her forward.

Each moment was marked by a further surrender to circumstances. Lloyd felt an emotional pain that was as acute as a physical injury. The hull of the *Proteus* seemed marked like a ruler, measuring off her entry into the pen. Hard lights gleamed in the roof. The pen contained the torpedo tubes, the forward hatch, the forward hydroplanes, then the fin itself. *Proteus* was half-swallowed.

There was cheering from the dockyard workers lining the concrete walks on either side of the water, which sickened and enraged him. Lloyd could see the first teams of men with the props that would support the hull, eager to begin berthing the *Proteus*.

Then Ardenyev's hand was on his shoulder, and he was shouting above the echo of the cheering bouncing back from steel and concrete.

"I'm sorry, my friend! You have lost!"

Lloyd shook his head, not to deny but to admit defeat. *Proteus* was slowing as orders were passed from the officer in charge of the docking procedure to the winch operators. Even the motion of his vessel was out of his control. He felt utterly humiliated. Strangely, there was an air of dejection about Ardenyev, too, amid the coarse cheers and their magnified, inhuman echoes.

A mist was beginning to rise in the dusk. The wind had dropped to an occasional breeze which stirred the tendrils and shrouds of grey. The landscape was subsiding into darkness, the hills already no more than smudges, the trees merely dark, crayon shadings. Hyde saw the mist as a final irony. It cloaked Petrunin now, not any attempt on his part to reach a telephone. Petrunin had arrived too early, just before six, announcing his presence with a deadline for Hyde's surrender. Yet in another sense he was belated. Hyde had already, slowly and reluctantly and with an inward fury, decided he could not leave the girl and her father exposed to capture, and there was no way the three of them could get safely away from the cottage. He had to make the difficult, even repellent assumption that they would be safer, if only because they would be alive and unharmed, in surrender than resistance. Hope springs eternal was a difficult, and unavoidable, consolation. He had admitted to himself that they were successfully trapped even before Petrunin reiterated that simple message through a loud-hailer.

Quin had rendered himself useless, like some piece of electrical equipment that possessed a safety circuit. He had switched himself off like a kettle boiling too long. He was slumped where he had sat for hours, staring at his lap, sulking in silence. Even his danger no longer pricked him to complaint. The girl, moving only occasionally to check on her father's condition, had remained near Hyde. Their conversation had been desultory. Hyde had hardly bothered to alleviate the girl's fears, possessed by his own self-recriminations. The bug on the car, the bloody bug –

Then Petrunin was talking again. "Why not attempt to reach a telephone, Mr. Hyde?" his magnified, mechanical voice queried from behind a knoll a hundred yards or more from the cottage. Hyde was certain he could hear soft laughter from one of the others. "This mist should hide your movements quite successfully." Again the accompanying, sycophantic laughter, coarser now? Hyde could not be certain he was not mocking himself, imagining the amusement. Petrunin was enjoying himself. Was he covering an approach, distracting them? "The problem is, your friends would not be safe while you were away. Can the girl use a gun? Can her father?"

"Fuck off," Hyde replied with a whispered intensity. The girl touched his arm, making him start.

"Give me the gun. Why don't you try to get out?"

"I gave that idea up hours ago, girlie. We're right in the shit, and bloody Lenin out there knows it."

"Won't your people be looking for us?"

"I bloody hope so! But, he knows that, too. He won't wait much longer now."

"Your time is up," Petrunin announced, as if on cue. Hyde grinned mirthlessly. "Please show yourselves at the door. Throw your gun out first, please. We have night-sights. No movements you make will be missed, I assure you."

"The trouble with bloody desk men when they get in the field is they're so bloody gabby." He looked at the shadowy outline of Quin across the room, then at the girl. His hand was clenched around the butt of the Heckler & Koch pistol, and it would take one movement to smash the window and open fire. Useless to try; but in another, more febrile way, satisfying to do so. Bang, bang, he recited to himself, pointing the gun into the room as if taking aim. Bloody bang, bang. And these two would be dead, or wounded. "Nowhere to go, nothing to do," he announced aloud.

"You can't —" the girl began.

"I'm bored with sitting on my bum," he said. "Besides, when the shooting starts, someone else always gets hurt. It's in the rules. Petrunin knows I won't risk your father or you, and *I* know I won't. Shitty, but true. Now, we have no chance. Later, who knows?" He stood up to one side of the window. It was open at the top, and he raised his voice to a shout. "All right, Trotsky — we're coming out. We've both seen this bloody film before!"

"No cavalry, I'm afraid. Only Apaches," Petrunin called back through the loud-hailer. Hyde tossed his head.

"I'll open the door and chuck my gun out. Then Mr. Quin will come out first."

"Very well. Please do not delay."

Quin was sitting upright now, and seemed to have sidled towards one corner of the room. His white, featureless face seemed to accuse Hyde in the room's dusk. Hyde bumped the edge of the table as he moved towards him.

"No —" Quin said feebly, putting his hands up in front of him, warding off Hyde like an evil presence.

"Sorry, mate. We don't have any choice. They're not going to do *you* any harm now, are they?" He reached down and pulled Quin roughly to his feet, embracing him as the man struggled half-heartedly. There was a mutuality of hatred and blame between them. Hyde sensed it in the tremble of Quin's arms.

He studied Quin's face. The man appeared as if he had been confined in some prison, with no hope of release or escape, for a long time. The prison had been his own mind, of his own making. No, Hyde corrected himself. The KGB had done that, created the stifling sense of the trap closing on him. And perhaps the DS, and even SIS and himself, should have been quicker, smarter, more thorough.

"We may have a chance if we go out now," he said in a soothing, allaying voice. "In here, we have none. You get hurt, Tricia gets hurt. I'm sorry, mate, but it's our only chance."

"I don't *want* to —!" Quin almost wailed. "They'll take me with them. It's not you they want, it's me!"

"I know that. For God's sake, I'm trying to help you!"

"I can't spend the rest of my life in Russia, heaven help me!"

"Better Red than dead," Hyde offered, his shallow sympathy exhausted. Quin's fear and reluctance were now no more than irritants, slowing reaction, muddying thought. Quin would just have to accept his situation. Hyde no longer had time or energy to expend on his psychological condition.

"Now, as the patient said to the dentist as he grabbed his balls, 'we're not going to hurt each other, are we?'. Just wait until I give you the word, then walk slowly out of the door. OK?" Quin slumped in resignation against Hyde. Hyde's mockery was expressed, incongruously, in a comforting tone of voice. "A nice little plane ride across the Channel, then another ride to Moscow. You might even like it there. They'll like *you*, anyway." He gripped Quin's arms as the man's body protested at his envisaged future. "Nothing bad's going to happen. Just do as they say."

He took Quin by one arm to the door, and opened it, keeping the scientist out of sight. He threw his gun in a high arc towards the knoll, away from his car so that it was easily visible.

"Excellent!" Petrunin confirmed. "No other little toys?"

"I left my bloody death-ray in the car!"

"Very well. Come out, one at a time. Mr. Quin to lead."

"Right, off you go. Just walk straight towards the knoll. Don't deviate, and don't run."

Quin moaned. Immediately, the girl was at his side, holding his other arm. She shouted through the door.

"My father's not well. We're coming out together." Without hesitation, she guided Quin through the open door. Hyde stood framed in the doorway for a moment, then he moved out into the dusk, his feet crunching on the gravel in front of the cottage. He raised his arms in the air, studying the knoll, waiting for the first head to appear. Unreality seized him, and he wanted to laugh. Captured by the KGB, in England! It was laughable, a joke for Queen Anne's Gate for years to come. Perhaps they'd use his urn on Aubrey's mantelpiece to knock their pipes out while they giggled at the story of his demise. As Aubrey would have said, *It really was too bad* –

Petrunin came down the slope of the grassy knoll towards them, a second man following him, carrying a rifle. Quin and Tricia stopped, awaiting him. A third man moved out of the shadow beneath a stand of firs towards Hyde, his rifle bearing on its target. Hyde felt weak, and sick. Petrunin stopped to examine Quin as carefully and as unemotionally as he might have done a consignment that had been delivered to his door. He ignored the girl. The third man had reached Hyde, studied him warily, and then moved in to touch-search him. When he had finished, he spoke to Petrunin.

"He's clean."

208

"Good." Petrunin approached Hyde. He was smiling with confidence and success. He was a bigger, taller man than the Australian, and this increased his confidence almost to a swagger. He paused before Hyde, hands on hips, appraising him.

"I know I don't look like much," Hyde offered, "but it's the public spending cuts. They're going in for smaller spies."

"Aubrey's man, of course? Mm, I don't think you are the cheerful colonial idiot you pretend. Not that it matters. Thank you for leading us to Mr. Quin."

"Not my pleasure."

"Quite. Very well," he said, addressing his two companions, "let us not waste time." He looked at Hyde. "Just a wound, I think," he said with surgical precision and lack of concern. "This incident is already too – significant. We mustn't create an international event from it." He stepped aside. "We don't want him going anywhere. Both legs, I think."

"No –!" the girl shouted, but one of the riflemen knocked her down, swiping the barrel of his gun sideways into her ribs. Hyde remained quite still, tensing himself to accept the pain. He lowered his hands to his sides. The marksman stepped forward – the third man had moved away, Petrunin was still appraising him with an intent curiosity – and raised the gun to his shoulder. Hyde felt the tremble begin in his left leg, and could not control it. Knee, shin, thigh, calf, foot, ankle –

His imagination made the skin on his legs crawl. Hyde tried to concentrate on only one of his legs, letting awareness of the other one become numb. The blood rushed in his ears like a howl of protest.

Then the helicopter. Loud enough at once in the silence to be apparent even to Hyde. Petrunin glanced up at the cool evening sky, then his head whipped round as he located the source of the noise. Red lights beneath a shadowy belly, the racket of the rotors yelling down into the hollow in which the cottage lay.

Hyde's thoughts came out of shock, out of their mesmerized concentration on his still quivering left leg, and prompted him towards Quin and the girl, who were huddled together. The girl was on her feet but almost doubled over with pain and fright. Then a pain wracked him, and he fell to his knees, groaning as if he had been shot. His whole body was trembling, and he could not move, merely grip his stomach and retch drily again and again.

The noise of the helicopter beat down on him, and he heard a voice through a loud-hailer, yelling the same kind of authoritative noises over and over. The helicopter's down-draught distressed his hair, inflated his windcheater, but he could not straighten up. He waited for the sound of firing, but there was none.

Eventually, he rolled over onto his side. He saw scattering figures running, and Quin and his daughter clinging together. Then he heard shots. One of the marksmen – he saw with a fierce delight that it was the one who had been ordered to maim him – crumpled near Quin and Tricia. Other figures moved into, merged with, the trees, and were gone. The police helicopter settled heavily onto the grass below the knoll, comfortingly large, noisily business-like. It was over.

The girl was kneeling over him, one hand pressed against her ribs.

"All right?"

He nodded. "Just scared stiff. You?"

"Bruised."

"How's your father?"

"Mr. Hyde?" A shadow loomed over them. A policeman in denims and a combat jacket.

"Yes."

"Are you hurt?"

"Only my manly pride." Hyde stretched and sat up. He rubbed his hand almost without thinking through the girl's hair. She did not seem to resent his touch.

"We're to get you on a plane at Manchester as soon as we can," the police officer informed him.

"Right. What about my car?"

"One of my men will drive it down."

"I want to see my mother," Tricia Quin announced.

"Your father's to go straight to London, Miss. Mr. Aubrey's instructions," he added by way of explanation to Hyde. "He'll want to see you, no doubt, at the same time."

"Get us to Manchester," Hyde replied. "We'll see, then."

"I'm not going to London."

"OK, OK," Hyde conceded. "I'll take you to see Mummy as soon as we've got your dear old dad on the plane. All right?" The girl nodded firmly. "Christ, why you spend your time worrying so much about them, I don't know!" He looked up at the police officer. "Caught 'em?"

"I doubt it. We haven't the time to waste. Leave that up to the Cumbria constabulary. Come on – let's get moving."

Hyde stood up. The girl immediately held his arm to steady him, unnecessarily.

"You're all bloody solicitation, Tricia," Hyde observed. "No wonder you get hurt all the time. People aren't worth it." She saw that he was looking at her father as he spoke, and a wince of pain crossed her face. Misinterpreting the expression, he added: "Your ribs OK?"

"Yes!" she snapped, and walked away from him. Hyde watched her go, and shrugged. Relief returned in a rush of emotions, and he exhaled noisily. It was over. The cavalry had arrived, with a loud-hailer instead of a bugle. But they had arrived –

They allowed Quin five hours' sleep, under light sedation, before Aubrey had him woken. The doctor had examined him as soon as he had arrived at the Admiralty, and had pronounced him unfit for strain or effort, mental or physical. Aubrey had thanked the doctor and dismissed him. He pondered whether Quin should be prescribed stimulants, and then reluctantly decided against this course. Aubrey suspected drugs, except in their interrogational usefulness. He wanted Quin completely and reliably rational. Quin was the lynch-pin of the scheme that was increasingly obsessing him. It had prevented him from taking any sleep himself, it had made him impatient of Quin's rest and impatient during his first conversation with the man, so much so that Ethan Clark had intruded upon their conversation and eventually commandeered it. Aubrey, seething at Quin's weariness, his retreat from reality, his reluctance to consider the plight of his own invention, had left the Admiralty to walk for half an hour on Horse Guards, but the military statues and the nobility of the buildings had made him flee to the more agreeable atmosphere of St James's Park.

The park, across which people hurried at the beginning of a bright, windy day, offered him little solace. From the bridge, he could see, in an almost gilded white clarity, Buckingham Palace in one direction, Whitehall in the other. If he followed the path from the bridge, it would bring him to Birdcage Walk and Queen Anne's Gate and his own office. Shelley would bring him coffee and soothing information of other parts of the world; not Pechenga, not the place on that blown-up aerial photograph propped on an easel. The parade of government officials and office workers passing him composed a race to which he did not belong. His office was barred to him until this business was resolved.

He skirted the lake, back towards Whitehall. The sun was gilding the roofs, providing an unremarked beauty. Aubrey was profoundly doubtful whether Quin would be of the least use to them. He seemed a poor specimen, physically, emotionally. He certainly seemed inadequate to the role in which Aubrey wished to cast him.

One man, who is a grocer. A Harrier jet. The AWACS Nimrod at Farnborough which was used to give *Proteus* her sea trials with the "Leopard" equipment. Eastoe and his crew, returned by now to RAF Kinloss, no more than two hours away by aircraft from Farnborough. And Clark.

And Quin. Miserable, whining, ungrateful, uncaring Quin. Aubrey clenched his hat more firmly, savagely in his hand, mis-shaping its brim with the rage he felt against Quin. It could work, but only with Quin. With Quin as he was, it was doomed.

Pyott and Clark were alone in what had once been the "Chessboard Counter" operations room. Aubrey had stood-down all RN personnel, who would be briefed to run what had become, in his mind, a rescue rather than a destruction operation. He intended that "Leopard" should be repaired and that *Proteus* make her escape, under cover of its anti-sonar, from Pechenga. The scheme seemed utterly unworkable to Clark and Pyott, and it had seemed so to him in the windy light of the park, between the gilded buildings. In this underground room, precisely because Quin had obviously been allowed to rest by Clark, it seemed only a little less ridiculous. An old man's fancy. He had code-named it "Plumber".

Clark's face expressed disappointment, beneath the surface of superiority. He had been proven right; Quin was a broken reed. Yet Clark evidently wished it had been otherwise. There was an undisguised disappointment on Pyott's handsome face as he stood with Clark in what had the appearance of a protective hedge of easels supporting mounted photographs and charts. The bric-à-brac of an operation that would never be allowed to run. The board would never be set up for it, the timetable never decided, the communications and the back-up never arranged. It was already dead.

The knowledge made Aubrey furious.

"I'm sorry, Mr. Aubrey," Clark began, "but that guy's in no condition to cross the street. He's in bad shape, psychologically."

Pyott fiddled with his moustache, as if caricaturing his uniform and rank. "I'm afraid so, Kenneth. Nerves shot to bits, willingness to help nil. Bloody little man –"

"What are these?" Aubrey asked, pointing at the easels in turn. "Did we order these?"

"I did," Pyott admitted, "before we had a good chat with our friend Quin."

"Is this *Proteus*?" Aubrey had stopped in front of one of the grainy, enlarged monochrome pictures. A harbour, the slim, knife-like shape of vessels seen from the air.

"Yes." Clark sounded suddenly revived. He joined Aubrey, Pyott coming to the old man's other shoulder. Aubrey felt hemmed in by younger bone and muscle. "The quality's poor. Satellite picture in poor conditions. Getting dark down there, and the cloud cover obscured most of the shots. This is the inner harbour at Pechenga. That's her." His long, thick finger dabbed towards the top edge of the picture.

"What damage has she sustained?"

"Hard to tell. Look through this." Clark handed Aubrey a magnifying glass, and the old man bent to the photograph, moving the lens slowly over the scene, which threatened at any moment to dissolve into a collection of grey, black and white dots. "Those look like buoyancy bags at the stern. Must have been a low-warhead torpedo, maybe two. She's not under power, she's being towed by the rescue ship ahead of her."

Aubrey surrendered the magnifying glass. "How long?" he asked.

Clark shook his head. "Impossible to guess. One day, two. I don't know. No one could tell you from this shot, not even with computer enhancement."

"Show me where on the chart of Pechenga."

The three of them moved, in a tight little wedge, to another easel. Their voices were echoing drily in the empty room. There was a marble, sepulchral atmosphere about it. The huge map-board in the middle of the floor registered, frozen like something unfinished but preserved in ice, the conditions and dispositions at the time the *Proteus* was boarded. Even the dot of the relief Nimrod was frozen on station above the coast of Norway. The board had not been allowed to continue revealing the extent of their defeat.

"Here," Clark said. "These are the submarine pens."

"Well? Well? Is it only Quin we are worried about? *I* will take responsibility for him. We have discussed this operation for most of the night. Is there more than Quin to hold us back?"

"You never give up, do you?" Clark said.

"Would *you* drop out?"

"No."

"Giles?"

"Too risky – no, I'm not sounding like a granny just for the sake of it. Quin is crucial. If Clark can't get the right information, at the *precise* split-second he requires it, then everything could be lost – including Clark." Pyott shook his head, held his features in a gloomy, saturnine cast, to emphasize his words.

Aubrey was exasperated. He had *seen* the *Proteus* now. He had to act.

"You've talked to MoD Air?"

"There's no problem there. A Harrier could get Clark across Finland and into the Pechenga area – yes. You have the authority to send it. The AWACS Nimrod that was rigged up especially for sea trials with *Proteus* is on stand-by at Farnborough. They could accommodate yourself and Quin. Eastoe and his crew are on stand-by to be flown down from Kinloss to Farnborough." Pyott's face now changed to an expression of exasperation; he was angry with Quin for wasting his time and his organizational talents.

"Communications?"

213

"Yes, we can do that. Between the Nimrod and Clark, with a range of a hundred miles, speaking in a whisper."

Aubrey had passed to the cutaway chart of the submarine. A multitude of hand-written labels had been appended, explaining and exposing each minute section and piece of equipment and function of the *Proteus*. Aubrey, by studying it, would know as much about the most secret of the Royal Navy's submarines in an hour as the Russians would know by the time *Proteus* sailed again from Pechenga.

"Damn," he said softly as the realization sprung itself upon him like a bad dream. "Jamming or interception? Location?"

"Can be overcome," Pyott admitted reluctantly. His enthusiasm had dimmed again, with his own realization. His eyes had strayed towards the door of the room where Aubrey had slept and which now contained a sedated Quin.

"Your equipment, Clark?"

"Portable – just. I could make it, with an infinite amount of luck, without drowning under the weight of what I need – *would need*, Mr. Aubrey. It can't be done without Quin. I can't learn enough in time. He has to be there – in range of my transmitter – all the time, and able to talk me through whatever I find." He jabbed a finger at one section of the hull of the *Proteus*. "Hell, the back-up system's *here*! Not to mention that this stern section, where some of the sensors are, has been damaged by one, maybe two, torpedoes. I can't go climbing over the hull spot-welding alongside Russian dockyard workers! It's crazy."

"If it can't be done, you will abort 'Plumber' and destroy the 'Leopard' equipment with the maximum efficiency," Aubrey said in a tight, controlled voice. "But perhaps it can be done."

"What will you do with Quin? Twist his arm, Kenneth? Threaten to fling him out of the Nimrod if he doesn't answer Clark's questions correctly and without hesitation? I'm afraid that Clark and I agree on this occasion. It would be a complex, expensive, dangerous and ultimately wasteful operation. If Clark must go in, let him go in simply to destroy 'Leopard'. Someone other than Quin could point him in the right direction there."

Aubrey was plucking at his bottom lip, staring at the chart of the submarine, its workings and innards exposed like a biological specimen or drawing. The ringing of the telephone was loud and startling in the room, and Pyott rushed to answer it as if he were afraid that its noise would waken Quin. Immediately he answered, he glanced at Aubrey, and beckoned him to the desk. It was Cunningham.

" 'C'," Pyott whispered as he handed him the receiver.

"Richard?"

"Kenneth – how is our patient?"

"Not good. Uncooperative, unreliable, withdrawn. Chronically suspicious and afraid."

"I see. No use to you, then?"

"Why? Has the operation been cleared?"

"Yes, it has. The Secretary of State has cleared it with the PM. She's enthusiastic, I gather."

"The Prime Minister obviously wasn't made aware of the difficulties," Aubrey said sarcastically. Cunningham had had to clear the proposed operation with the cabinet minister responsible for the SIS, the Foreign Secretary who, in his turn, had consulted the Prime Minister. The recruitment of another national, Clark being American, the incursion into Soviet territory, and the special circumstances pertaining to the submarine, had removed the operation beyond the sphere of the intelligence service acting alone and covertly.

"She has cleared the operation with the President, if it proves feasible in your judgment. NATO ministers will be informed under a Priority Two order. I have been successful on your behalf, but you now seem to imply that I've been wasting my time?"

"I hope not. I *hoped* not. It does seem rather hopeless, Richard."

"A great pity. Then Clark will have to go in just to get rid of 'Leopard'?"

Aubrey listened to the silence at the other end of the line. Behind Cunningham, there was the enthusiasm, the permission, of the politicians. A chance to give the Russian bear a black eye, a bloody nose, without risking more than one life. Turning the tables on the Kremlin. He did not despise or disregard the almost naive way in which his operation had been greeted with enthusiasm in Downing Street and the White House. It was a pity that the seriousness of the operation's parameters and its possible repercussions had required the political sanction of the two leaders. The NATO ministers, with the exception of Norway, would be informed after the event. They did not matter. The naivety, however, gave him cause to doubt the rationale of his scheme. To be praised by laymen is not the expert's desire. Aubrey now suspected his operation's feasibility.

Cunningham seemed to have no desire to add to what he had said, or to repeat his question. Whatever Aubrey now said, he would, with enthusiasm or reluctance, pass on to the Foreign Office and Downing Street.

"No, he will not," Aubrey heard himself say. The expression created an instant sense of lightness, of relief. It was a kind of self-affirmation, and he no longer cared for pros and cons, doubts and likelihoods. It *would* be attempted. "Captain Clark will be briefed to examine and, if possible, repair 'Leopard', and to instruct the

215

commanding officer and crew of the *Proteus* to attempt to escape from the Soviet naval base at Pechenga.''

Cunningham merely said, ''I'll pass your message on. Good luck, Kenneth.''

Aubrey put down the receiver quickly, as if Clark or Pyott might make some attempt to snatch it from him and reverse his instructions. He had spoken clearly, precisely, and with sufficient volume for them to hear him. When he looked at them, Pyott was fiddling with his moustache again, while Clark was perched on the edge of a foldaway table, arms folded across his chest. He was shaking his head. Then, unexpectedly, he grinned.

Pyott said, as Aubrey approached them, ''You're taking a grave risk with this young man's life, Kenneth. And perhaps with Quin. Do you think it's worth it?''

''Of course he does,'' Clark interposed. He was still smiling. ''He knows I won't refuse, on any count. Uh, Mr. Aubrey?''

''Perhaps, Ethan, perhaps. I'm sorry you have to enact my romantic escapade, but your President is relying on you, too, I gather.''

''That's the last time I vote for the guy.''

Aubrey looked at his watch. Nine-fifteen.

''Giles, get Eastoe and his crew moved down to Farnborough immediately. Ethan, get Quin in here again. We have less than three hours. I want to be at Farnborough, and you must be on your way by this afternoon.'' Pyott was already on the telephone. ''Get that Harrier put on immediate stand-by, and get Ethan's equipment details over to MoD Air.''

''Very well, Kenneth.''

There was no longer a sepulchral atmosphere in the room. Instead, a febrile, nervous excitement seemed to charge the air like static electricity forerunning a storm.

The grocer, Aubrey thought. My immediate task is the grocer. He must meet Clark tonight as near Pechenga as we can get him.

Unexpectedly, it had snowed lightly in the Midlands during the night, and Cannock Chase, where they had stopped at Tricia Quin's request, was still dusted with it. The sky was bright, dabs of white cloud pushed and buffeted across the blue expanse by a gusty, chill wind. Small puddles, some of them in hoofprints, were filmed with ice, like cataracted eyes. They walked slowly, Hyde with his hands in his pockets, relaxed even though he was cold. The girl huddled in her donkey jacket, the one in which she had tried to slip into the NEC unnoticed. She seemed concerned to explain why she had asked him to stop, to have requested him to leave the motorway at Stafford and drive across the Chase until they had passed through a sprawling

216

housing estate on the outskirts of Rugeley and found themselves, suddenly and welcomely, amid firs and grazing land. It was early afternoon, and they were no more than fifteen miles from the girl's mother.

An occasional passing lorry, back on the road across that part of Cannock Chase, caused the girl to raise her voice as she spoke.

"I don't know why I always made their problems mine. They even used to argue whenever we came up here, when I was quite young, and I used to hate that especially."

"Rough," was Hyde's only comment, because he could not think of a suitable reply. He could not join the girl's post-mortem on her parents. His memories of Quin were too recent and too acerbic for him to consider the man either sympathetic or important. He allowed the girl, however, to analyse herself in a careful, half-aware manner. She, at least, had his sympathy.

"I suppose it always sprang from the fact that Dad was much brighter than Mum – much brighter than me, too," she added, smiling slightly, cracking the film of ice over one sunken hoofprint, hearing its sharp little report with evident pleasure, with a weight of association. "He *was* intolerant," she conceded, "and I don't think Mum appreciated what he was doing, after the firm got a bit bigger and she no longer did the bookwork or helped him out. I think they were happy in the early days." She looked at him suddenly, as if he had demurred. "Mum needs to feel useful. I'm like her, I suppose."

"You're a good girl, and you're wasting your time. It's *their* business, not yours. You can't do anything except be a football. Is that what you want?"

Her face was blanched, and not merely by the cold. He had intruded upon her version of reality, casting doubt upon its veracity.

"You're very hard," she said.

"I suppose so." He had enjoyed the drive down the crowded M6 in the borrowed car, after a night's stop which had refreshed him and which the girl had seemed to desperately require the moment her father's plane had left Manchester. Sutton Coldfield for dinner was an amusing prospect. He considered Mrs. Quin's reaction to him as a guest. "Sorry. I'll shut up."

"You don't have to –"

"It's better. It isn't my business."

She paused and looked back. The fern was still brown and stiffly cramped into awkward, broken shapes and lumps by the frost. Birdsong. She wanted to see a deer, the quick flicker of grey, white hindquarters disappearing into the trees. In some unaccountable way, she believed that if she saw deer, things would be improved, would augur well. It would fuse the circuits that existed between present and past. She looked down the perspective of the bridle path, back towards the car park, unaware, while Hyde shivered at her side.

He heard the approach of the small, red and white helicopter first. Its noise intruded, and then it seemed to become a natural and expected part of the pale sky. Tricia Quin knew it would startle the deer, make them more difficult to find, over beyond the line of numbered targets against the high earth bank that composed the rifle range. She looked up, following Hyde's gaze. He was shielding his eyes with one hand. The tiny helicopter in its bright, hire-firm colours swung in the sky as if suspended from an invisible cable, a brightly daubed spider, and then it flicked down towards them.

Hyde's nerves came slowly awake. His other hand came out of his pocket, his body hunched slightly in expectation. The helicopter – a Bell Jetranger he perceived with one detached part of his awareness – was still moving towards them, skimming now just above the line of trees, down the track of the bridle path. The helicopter had hesitated above the car park, then seemed more certain of purpose, as if it had found what it sought. Hyde watched it accelerate towards them, the noise of its single turbo-shaft bellowing down into the track between the trees. Lower, and the trees were distressed by the down-draught and even the stiff, rimy ferns began buckling, attempting and imitating movement they might have possessed before death.

"Run!" he said. The girl's face crumpled into defeat, even agony, as he pushed her off the path towards the nearest trees. "Run!"

She stumbled through frozen grass, through the thin film of snow, through the creaking, dead ferns. Deliberately, he let her widen the distance between them – they wouldn't shoot at her, but he didn't want her killed when they tried to take him out – before he, too, began running.

The first shots were hardly audible above the noise of the rotors. The downdraught plucked at his clothing, his hair and body, as if restraining him. The girl ran without looking back, in utter panic.

ELEVEN:

Flights

The jellyfish bags were gone, except on the port side of the *Proteus*. The starboard ballast tanks had been repaired, and the rudder fin had begun to look like the result of a half-completed, complex grafting operation; spars and struts of metal bone, much now covered with a sheen of new plates. One part of Lloyd, at least, welcomed the surgery. He paced the concrete wharf of the submarine pen, under the hard lights, his guard behind him, taking his midday exercise. The Red Navy had extended the farce even to giving each member of his crew a thorough medical check-up; routine exercise, as much as was permitted by the confines and security necessary to Pechenga as a military installation, had been prescribed. Also permission to use the crew cinema had been granted, alcohol had arrived, in limited and permissible amounts; and fresh food.

Lloyd held his hands behind his back, walking in unconscious imitation of a member of the Royal Family. The diplomat he had requested from Moscow had not arrived, unsurprisingly. Lloyd had made the required formal protests without enthusiasm, realizing their pointlessness. Better news lay in the gossip he and some of the crew had picked up from their guards. Everyone was waiting on the arrival of a Soviet expert, delayed in Novosibirsk by bad weather. He it was who would supervise the examination of "Leopard". It was the one element of optimism in Lloyd's situation.

The fitters and welders were having their lunch, sitting against the thick, slabbed concrete walls of the pen. They looked a species of prisoner themselves, wearing blue fatigue overalls, lounging in desultory conversation, eating hunks of thick dark bread and pickles and cold meat – in one instance, a cold potato. They watched him with an evident curiosity, but only as something belonging to the foreign submarine on which they were working and which was the real focus of their interest.

Lloyd stopped to gaze back down the two hundred and fifty feet of the *Proteus*'s length. Nuclear-powered Fleet submarines possessed a menace not unlike that of the shark. They were long, shiny-sleek, but portly, massive. Three and a half thousand tons of vessel, well over twice the size of a Second World War ancestor. Backed like a whale, but a killer whale. It hurt Lloyd's pride as her captain to have watched, before the hooter sounded deafeningly in the pen to announce the lunch break, Russian fitters clambering and crawling over her; Lilliputians performing surgery on a helpless Gulliver. He turned away, looking over the gates of the pen, into the tunnel which led to the harbour. One o'clock. In the circle of light he could discern a Soviet destroyer moving almost primly across his field of vision. The view was like that through a periscope, and he wished, with clenched fists and an impotent rage, that it had been.

Pechenga harbour lowered under heavy grey cloud, and he resented the weather as an additional camouflage that aided the Red Navy.

He turned to look back at his submarine once more, and Ardenyev was standing in front of him, hands on his hips, a smile on his face. The smile, Lloyd saw, was calculated to encourage, to repel dislike rather than to sneer or mock. With a gesture, Ardenyev waved the guard away. The man retired. The stubby Kalashnikov still thrust against his hip, barrel outwards. The guard swaggered. A Soviet marine, entirely satisfied with the guard-prisoner relationship between them. Young, conscripted, dim. Ardenyev's amused eyes seemed to make the comment. Yet the wave of Ardenyev's hand had been that of the conjurer, the illusionist. *There is nothing to fear, there are no guards, we are friends, abracadabra –*

Lloyd suddenly both liked the man and resented him.

"Come to gloat?" he asked. For a moment, Ardenyev absorbed the word, then shook his head.

"No." There was a small satchel over his shoulder, which he now swung forward, and opened. "I have food, and wine," he said. "I hoped you would share lunch with me. I am sorry that I cannot invite you to the officers' mess, or to the only decent restaurant in Pechenga. It is not possible. Shall we sit down?" Ardenyev indicated two bollards, and immediately sat down himself. Reluctantly, Lloyd joined him, hitching his dark trousers to preserve their creases, brushing at the material as if removing a persistent spot. Then he looked up.

"What's for lunch?"

"Caviar, of course. Smoked fish. Georgian wine. Pancakes." He opened the plastic containers one by one, laying them like offerings at Lloyd's feet. He cut slices of bread from a narrow loaf. "Help yourself," he said. "No butter, I'm afraid. Even Red Navy officers' messes sometimes go without butter."

Lloyd ate hungrily, oblivious of the greedy eyes of the nearest fitters. He drank mouthfuls of the rough wine to unstick the bread

220

from his palate, swigging it from the bottle Ardenyev uncorked for him.

Finally, he said, "Your people seem to be taking their time."

"Our workers are the best in the world," Ardenyev answered with a grin.

"I mean on the inside of the hull."

"Oh." Ardenyev studied Lloyd for a moment, then shrugged. "You have heard rumours, it is obvious. Even Red Navy marines cannot keep anything to themselves." He chewed on a slice of loaf liberally smothered with black caviar. "Unfortunately, our leading expert in naval electronic counter-measures – the man designated to, shall we say, have a little peep at your pet – is delayed, in Siberia." He laughed. "No, not by his politics, merely by the weather. He was supposed to fly from his laboratory in Novosibirsk three days ago. He is snowed in."

"You're being very frank."

"Can you see the point of being otherwise?" Ardenyev asked pleasantly.

"It was a clever plan," Lloyd offered.

"Ah, you are trying to debrief me. Well, I don't mind what you collect on this operation. It has worked. We're not likely to use it again, are we?" His eyes were amused, bright. Lloyd could not help but respond to the man's charm. "It was clever, yes. It needed a great deal of luck, of course – but it worked."

"If your Siberian snowman arrives."

"Ah, yes, Comrade Professor Academician Panov. I have no doubt you will also be meeting Admiral of the Red Banner Fleet Dolohov at the same time. He is bound to come and see his prize."

"You sound disrespectful."

"Do I? Ah, perhaps I only feel annoyance at the fact that an old man with delusions of grandeur could dream up such a clever scheme in his dotage." He laughed, recovering his good humour. "Drink up. I have another bottle."

"They intend removing it, then?"

"What?"

"I'm obliged not to mention sensitive equipment. May I preserve protocol? Their Lordships will be most anxious to know – on my return – that I gave nothing away." Lloyd, too, was smiling by the time he finished his statement.

"Ah, of course." Ardenyev rubbed his nose. There were tiny raisins of caviar at one corner of his mouth. His tongue flicked out and removed them. "No. I doubt it will be necessary. I am not certain, of course. I have done my bit, the balls and bootstraps part of the operation."

"I'm sorry about your men."

Ardenyev looked at Lloyd. "I see that you are. It was not your fault. I would have done the same, in your place. Let us blame our separate masters, and leave it at that."

"When will they let us go?"

Ardenyev looked swiftly down the length of the *Proteus*, taking in the repairs, the fitters slowly getting up – the hooter had blasted across Lloyd's question, so that he had had to shout it, making it seem a desperate plea rather than a cool enquiry – the new plates, the buckled hull plates, the stripped rudder, the skeletal hydroplane below them in the water.

"Twenty-four hours, assuming it stops snowing in Novosibirsk," Ardenyev said, turning back to Lloyd.

Four days, Aubrey thought. It is four days – less than one hundred hours – since I became involved in this business. I have slept for perhaps fifteen of those hours. I have been out of that damned room beneath the Admiralty for even fewer hours. And now I am consigning myself to another box, something even more uncomfortable, something much more evidently tomb-like.

He took the crewman's hand, and allowed himself to be helped up the last steps of the passenger ladder into the fuselage of the AWACS Nimrod. He did not feel, despite his reflections on age, mortality, sleep and habitat, either tired or weary. True, the adrenalin was sufficient only to forestall such things rather than to invigorate him, but he was grateful, as he ducked his head through the crew door near the tail fin and directly adjacent to the huge RAF roundel on the fuselage. Then the bright, quick-clouding windy day was exchanged for a hollow, metallic interior. And Eastoe was waiting for Quin and himself.

"Here you are, Mr. Aubrey. You and Mr. Quin here, if you please." He indicated two seats, facing one another across a communications console from which thick wires and cables trailed away down the fuselage floor, in a channel that might have been a gutter in an abattoir, the way in which it riveted Quin's fearful gaze. Other swivel chairs, bolted to the floor and the curving sides of the fuselage, stretched away down the untidy, crowded interior of the Nimrod towards the flight deck. For Quin's benefit, Eastoe added as Aubrey seated himself, "You're wired into *all* our communications equipment, sir, and the principal sensors. We'll do a full test with Clark when we're airborne. Your equipment operates through this central console –"

"Yes, yes," Quin said impatiently, like someone interested only in the toilet facilities provided. Eastoe's face darkened. His patience was evidently running out. The door swung shut on a gleam of sunlight, and a hand clamped home the locks. Quin appeared physically startled, as if suddenly awoken, and he protested, "I can be of no use to you!" His voice was high-pitched. He held his hands out in front of him, demonstrating their uncontrollable quiver. "I am no use to you!"

"Quin!" Aubrey barked. "Quin, sit down! Now! None of us is here to be self-indulgent, especially you. We all have a task to perform. Kindly see to it that you do yours, when the time comes."

Eastoe studied both civilians like a strange, newly-encountered species. There was an easy, adopted contempt around his mouth which Aubrey had met before in military officers. Pyott was an expert at it, when he chose. No doubt even Lloyd in his confinement was employing the sneer *militaire*. Aubrey almost smiled. The French, of course, had always been world champions. He remembered the young de Gaulle of London-exile days, when Aubrey had been at SOE. The nose had helped, of course.

Aubrey thrust aside the memory, almost with reluctance, and confronted Quin and the RAF Squadron Leader who, he well knew, considered his scheme to rescue *Proteus* wildly incapable of success. Quin slumped into his seat, swivelling in it instantly like a sulking child; there was a moment of debated defiance which only reached his hands as he clenched them into weak fists. He rubbed a nervy hand through his wiry, thinning hair which stood more comically on end as a result of the gesture. The inventor of "Leopard"; the machinery made of silicons, plastics, metal, the man constructed of straw. It was easy to feel contempt, hard to dismiss that emotion. For Eastoe, it was evidently impossible to remove that attitude from his calculations. Aubrey spent no time in conjecture as to Eastoe's more personal feelings towards him because of the crashed Nimrod and its dead aircrew.

"Squadron Leader Eastoe," Aubrey said levelly, "how long before we are ready to take off?"

Eastoe looked at his watch. "Fifteen minutes."

"You will make that ten, if you please," Aubrey said, treading with a delicate but grinding motion of his heel on all forms of civilian-military protocol. Eastoe's eyes widened in surprise. "As I said, Squadron Leader. Ten minutes. Please see to it."

"Mr. Aubrey, I'm the skipper of this –"

"No, you are not. You are its pilot. In matters of flying, I shall consult you, even defer to you. But I am in command here. Please be certain you understand that fact."

Eastoe bit his lip, and choked back a retort. Instead, he nodded his head like a marionette, and went forward to the flight deck. Aubrey, controlling the tremor of weakness he felt in his frame, sat down again opposite Quin, who was looking at him with a new kind of fearful respect.

Aubrey calculated his next remarks, then observed: "It was MoD who originally cocked-up this operation," he said casually, confidentially. "I do not intend to let them do so again. Damn fools, playing war-games with 'Leopard'. It simply showed little or no respect for – or *understanding* of – your development."

Aubrey watched Quin's ego inflate. He had suspected a balloon of self-admiration in the man, and was not disappointed; except in the arcane sense that Quin was so readily comprehensible, so transparent in his inner self. Whether the ego would keep him going, make him sufficiently malleable and for long enough, remained to be seen. Quin had talked to no one except his daughter for weeks. He required the conversation and the admiration of intelligent men; of men rather than women, Aubrey suspected. A deal of chauvinism there, too; Mrs. Quin would have been useful in the early days, but not a sufficient audience for the man's intellect and achievements. It cast a new light on why Quin had allowed the take-over of his small firm by the Plessey giant. It had enlarged his audience of admirers.

"You understand?" Quin asked, almost in surprise.

"Of course. Don't you think I get tired of dealing with these people, too?" Aubrey relaxed, offering Quin a cigarette. The man's right forefinger was stained brown. Quin reached for the cigarette case, taking one of the untipped cigarettes. He used his own lighter, and inhaled deeply, exhaled loudly. Confidence was altering his posture in his seat. He did not slump now, he relaxed.

"I see," Quin said. "I advised them against using 'Leopard' so early, and relying on it so totally. They wouldn't listen." There was self-pity there, just below the surface of the words.

"Arrogant," Aubrey murmured. "They're all so arrogant. This time, however, they do as *we* say, Quin, my dear fellow. They do exactly as we instruct them."

It was six minutes later – Quin had just stubbed out his second cigarette – when the Nimrod reached the end of the taxiway, turned, then roared down the main Farnborough runway, lifting into the patchily cloudy sky, the ground shrinking away from them at a surprising speed. As the buildings and aircraft had sped past his porthole-like window, Aubrey had reminded himself of the delicacy, the weakness of his control over Quin. Laving him with the oil of flattery; no grounds for confidence there, he remarked to himself, watching the man as his hands gripped the arms of his seat and he sat with closed eyes. No grounds for confidence at all.

*   *   *

The Harrier was a T.4 two-seater trainer, and it was unarmed because of the load it would have to carry and the extra fuel tanks, each of one hundred gallons, beneath its wings. There were no circumstances in which it would require cannon, bombs or missiles, for its mission would be aborted unless it could avoid all contact with Soviet aircraft or ground defences. Despite being a training aircraft, however, it was fitted with the latest type of laser range-finding equipment in the nose.

Ethan Clark was able to move only with difficulty in the pressure suit with which he had been supplied, because of the immersion suit he already wore beneath it. It made him waddle awkwardly, flying helmet under his arm, giving him the appearance of a circus clown imitating a pilot. The pilot of the Harrier, an experienced Squadron Leader whose response to his mission was shading to the cautious side of excitement, walked in front of him across the tarmac of Wittering RAF base, in Lincolnshire. Clark's packs of communications equipment, explosives, sensors, meters, spares and tools had been stowed beneath the wings in two pods where bombs might normally have hung.

Clark had been transported by helicopter to Wittering, and he had briefed the pilot, in the presence of the station commandant and Giles Pyott, who had provided the MoD authority appropriate to the commandeering of an aircraft and a pilot. Now Pyott strode alongside him, the wind plucking at his thick grey hair, his bearing upright, his form cloaked in the camel-coloured British warm.

The pilot clambered up the ladder, and swung himself into the cockpit, looking down immediately from behind the face panel of his helmet as Clark paused before his ascent. Pyott extended his hand at once, and Clark took his cool, tough grip.

"Good luck, Clark," Pyott said stiffly, as if avoiding the real subject of a conversation that was both necessary and important.

"Thanks, Colonel." Clark grinned, despite the gravity of the moment. "Here goes nothing, as they say."

"If you can't make it – if you can't *repair*, you *must* abort," Pyott warned solemnly. "Remember that. No heroics over and above the required minimum."

"I appreciate your concern, Colonel."

"Right. Get on with you. I think we're keeping your pilot waiting." Clark glanced up. "Sure."

He released Pyott's grip, and began clambering awkwardly up the ladder. It was difficult to swing his unaccustomed weight and bulk over the lip of the cockpit, and hot and strenuous work to ease himself into the narrow rear seat. Eventually, he achieved a degree of comfort, strapped himself in and adjusted his flying helmet. The pilot reached up, and closed the cockpit cover. Instantly, nerves raised his temperature, and he felt a film of perspiration on his forehead. He looked down, and the ladder was being carried away by a member of the ground crew. Pyott was striding after it like a schoolmaster harrying someone for a breach of school rules, his walking-stick accompanying his strides like a younger limb. Clark had never noticed Pyott's limp before.

When he reached the grass margin of the taxiway, Giles Pyott turned, almost posing with the little knot of the ground crew.

"Fingers in your ears, sir," a flight sergeant informed him.

"What? Oh, yes."

Pyott did as instructed. The Harrier was using the runway in a standard take off, instead of its unique vertical lift, because of the extra weight of fuel that it carried. Lights winked at wingtips and belly, suddenly brighter as a heavy cloud was pulled across the early afternoon sun by the wind. Then the aircraft was rolling, slowly for a moment, then with an accelerating rush, passing them – Pyott could see the helmeted blob that was Clark's head, turned towards him – and racing on down the runway. The heat of its single twenty-one and a half thousand pound thrust Pegasus 103 turbofan engine distorted its outline like a heat haze might have done, so that the aircraft appeared to have passed behind a veil, become removed from them. It sat back almost like an animal for an instant, then sprang at the sky and its low, scudding cloud and patches of gleaming bright-ness. The runway was still gauzy, but the Harrier was a sharply outlined silhouette as it rose then banked to the east.

Pyott took his hands from his ears, realizing that the ground crew had already begun making their way towards the hangar area, leav-ing him a somewhat foolishly isolated figure in an overcoat, a retired officer out for a constitutional who had strolled by mistake into a military installation. He turned on his heel, and followed the others, his imperative now to return to the room beneath the Admiralty.

The Harrier had already climbed into the lowest of the cloud and was lost from sight.

The safety offered by the trees had come to seem a kind of privileged imprisonment, the further they ran. Hyde had seen figures, three of them, drop out of the helicopter into the buffet of the rotors' down-draught in the moment he had paused at the first trees, and knew they were cut off from the car. By now, someone would have driven it out of the car park and hidden it and removed the distributor. The trees masked them – they heard the helicopter roaming in search of them every few minutes – but they bordered a long, higher stretch of barren heathland where summer fires of a drought year had exposed the land even further. Dull, patchy with snow and fern, treeless, exposed. A minefield as far as they were concerned.

When they first stopped, he had held the frightened, shivering girl against him, but even before her breathing calmed and she had drawn any comfort from the embrace, he was asking her urgently, "How well do you know the area? Can you see it in your mind's eye? Where's the nearest road? How far? Can you run? What's the shape of this plantation? What *do* you know? *Anything?*"

Roads? No, she didn't know, she couldn't explain the shape of Cannock Chase, she'd never seen a map of it –

A childhood place, he understood even as he fumed silently. She remembered it as a series of snapshots, the sight of deer, high blue skies above whitened landscapes, the fall and rise of the land only as a viewer who wished the ability to paint would perceive and remember. Useless to them now.

They followed the edge of the plantation north for almost two miles, further and further from the road and the car park and the town of Rugeley. Then the girl announced that she did not know that part of the Chase. They were north-east of the rifle range, but it was hidden from them by the trees.

"The road from Stafford to Lichfield," the girl said, her face screwed up in thought, her chest still heaving with the effort of their last run.

"What?" he said.

"It runs through the Chase." She looked up into the dark trees, as if for inspiration. She was painfully trying to remember turns in the road, bearings from her childhood, signposts. "Past Shugborough Hall – Wolseley Bridge, turn right . . ." She shook her head while he slapped his hands against his thighs in exasperation. Then she was looking at him, a sense of failure evident in her eyes. She added, hesitantly, "I think if we continue north, we'll hit the main road."

"Trees all the way?" he snapped, unable to restrain the sense of entrapment that glided out of the dark trees and accompanied them at every step. They were like her precious deer, confined to the trees.

She shrugged hopelessly. "I don't know."

"Oh, Christ!" She looked at if he had struck her. He added, in a tone that aspired to more gentleness, "Any wardens', gamekeepers' houses around here?" Again, she shook her head.

Beyond the trees, the afternoon was bright, dazzling off the last paper-thin sheet of snow on the higher, open ground. The chilly wind soughed through the upper branches of the firs. To the north and west, the direction of the weather, there was heavier cloud. It was a weekday afternoon, and they had seen no other people since they left the car park, which had contained just one other car. Once,

227

they had heard a dog bark, but they had seen neither it nor its owner. A distant vehicle's engine had sawn into the silence at another point, but again they had not seen it. Hyde had never realized before how isolated he could feel in a part of the cramped island that had become his home.

"I'm ready," Tricia Quin offered.

"OK, let's go."

Their feet crackled on fallen twigs, or crunched through the long winter's frosty humus and leaf litter. An eerie, dark green, under-water light filtered through the firs, slanting on the grey and damp-green trunks. Hyde had time to think that he could not imagine how it had ever been a magic place for the girl, before he dragged her without sound off the narrow, foot-pressed, deer-run track they were following, behind the mossy trunk of a fir. Deep ravines in the bark, its hardness against his cheek, his hand over the girl's mouth, his breath hushing her before he released her; the movement of an insect over the terrain of the bark, almost so close as to be out of focus. He held the girl against him, pulled into his body. She was shivering, and her head was cocked, listening. Her breath came and went, plucking at the air lightly yet fervently; an old lady dying. He dismissed the inappropriate image.

She reached her face up to him in a parody of intimacy, and whispered in his ear, "What is it? I can't even hear the helicopter."

He tossed his head, to indicate the track and the trees in the direction they had come.

"I heard something. I don't know what. Let's hope it's an old lady out for a brisk stroll." The girl tried to smile, nudging herself closer against him. He felt her body still. He listened.

Footstep. Crack, dry and flat as snapping a seaweed pod. Then silence, then another crack. Twigs. Footstep. The timing was wrong for an old lady, a young man, even a child. Wrong for anyone simply out for a walk, taking exercise. Sounds too careful, too slow, too spaced to be anything else than cautious, careful, alert. Stalking.

His heart began to interfere with his hearing as he stifled his breathing and the adrenalin began to surge. He should have moved further off the track. It was *their* tracks that were being followed, easy to do for a trained man, too much leaf-mould underfoot not to imprison the evidence of their passage, along with the deer prints, the hoof prints, the dogs' pawmarks, the ridged patterns of stout walking shoes.

Crack, then a soft cursing breath. Close, close. He pushed the girl slightly away and reached behind him, feeling the butt of the gun against his palm. She watched him, uninitiated into that kind of adulthood, looking very childlike and inadequate and requiring him to be responsible for her.

She pressed against the fir's trunk beside him. The tree was old enough, wide enough in the trunk, to mask them both. He nudged her when he could not bear the waiting any longer and substituted nerves for knowledge, and she shuffled two small paces around the trunk. He remained where he was, his hand still twisted, as if held by a bully, behind his back.

Breathing, heavier than the girl's, the sense of the weight of a heavy male body transferring from one foot to another, the glimmer of a hand holding something dark, the beginnings of a profile. Then they were staring at one another, each holding a gun, no more than seven yards apart, each knowing the stalemate for what it was, each understanding the other's marksmanship in the extended arms, the crouch of the body into a smaller target. Understanding completely and quickly, so that neither fired.

A heavy man in an anorak and dark slacks. Walking boots, the slacks tucked into heavy woollen socks. A Makarov pistol, because a rifle couldn't be hidden.

The man's eyes flickered, but did not look up, as the noise of the helicopter became apparent to both of them. A slow, confident smile spread on the man's face. Not long now. The stalemate would be broken. Hyde concentrated on watching the man's eyes and his hands. Perspiration trickled from beneath his arms, and his mouth was dry. His hand was beginning to quiver with the tension, beginning to make the gun unsteady. The noise of the helicopter grew louder, and the trees began to rustle in the down-draught. He could not kill without being killed, there was no advantage, not a microsecond of it –

A noise in the undergrowth, a small, sharp stamping pattern. The brushing aside of whippy low branches and twigs. High, springing steps. Then the deer was on them.

Hyde it was who fired, because it had to be another pursuer, even though the subconscious was already rejecting the idea. The Russian fired too, because he had been startled out of the confidence that it was a friend, another gun against Hyde. Tricia Quin screamed long before reaction-time should have allowed her to do so, as if she had foreseen the animal's death. The small, grey deer tumbled and skidded with cartoon-like, unsteady legs, its coat badged with dark new markings, then it was between them, veering off, then falling slowly, wobbling as when new-born, onto the crisp, rotting humus, where it kicked once, twice –

Reaction-time, reaction-time, Hyde screamed at himself, even as a wrench of pain and guilt hurt his chest. He swung his pistol, the

Russian doing the same, a mirror-image. Reaction-time, reaction-time; he hadn't totally ignored the deer, kicking for a third, fourth time, then shuddering behind the Russian –

Hyde's gun roared, the split-second before that of the Russian. The man was knocked off balance, and his bullet whined past Hyde's left shoulder, buzzing insect-like into the trees. The man lay still instantly, unlike the deer which went on thrashing and twitching and seemed to be making the noise that in reality was coming from the girl, a high, helpless, violated scream.

He ran to the deer, placed the gun against its temple – the dark helpless eye watching him for a moment, the red tongue lolling – and pulled the trigger to shut out the girl's screams which went on even after the report of his gun died away.

"Shut up," he yelled at her, waving the gun as if in threat. "Shut up! Run, you stupid bitch – run!" He ran towards her, the noise of the helicopter deafening just above the treetops, and she fled from him.

Thirty thousand feet below them, through breaks in the carpet of white cloud, Aubrey could make out the chain of rocks that were the Lofoten islands off the north-west coast of Norway. Clark was perhaps a hundred miles away from them at that point, to the south and east, near Bodø, linking up with the RAF Victor in order to perform a mid-air refuelling of the Harrier. Until that point, both the Nimrod and the Harrier had maintained strict radio silence. Now, however Aubrey could no longer delay the testing of the communications equipment that would link Clark and Quin together when the American reached the *Proteus*.

Quin was sweating nervously again, and a swift despisal of the man passed through Aubrey's mind, leaving him satisfied. The emotion removed doubt, even as it pandered to Aubrey's sense of authority in the situation he had created. The man was also chain-smoking and Aubrey, with the righteousness of someone forced by health to give up the habit, disliked Quin all the more intensely for the clouds of bluish smoke that hung perpetually around their heads, despite the air-conditioning of the Nimrod.

"Very well, Flight Lieutenant," Aubrey instructed the radio operator assigned to monitor the communications console Quin would be using, "call up our friend for us, would you?" Aubrey could sense the dislike and irritation he created in the RAF officers who were crewing the Nimrod. However, having begun with Eastoe in a testy, authoritarian manner, he could not now relax into more congenial behaviour.

"Sir," the young officer murmured. He flicked a bank of switches, opening the channel. There was no call-sign. Clark's receiver would be alive with static in his earpiece. He would need no other signal. The maximum range of the transceivers was a little over one hundred miles, their range curtailed by the need to encode the conversation in high-speed transmission form. A tiny cassette tape in Clark's more portable equipment recorded his words, speeded them up, then they were transmitted to this console between Aubrey and Quin. As with the larger equipment in the room beneath the Admiralty, tapes in Quin's receiver slowed down the message, then replayed it as it had been spoken – whispered, Aubrey thought – by the American. And the reverse procedure would occur when Quin, or himself, spoke to Clark. Clumsy, with an unavoidable, built-in delay, but the only way the signals could not be intercepted, understood, and Clark's precise location thereby exposed.

"Yes?" Clark replied through a whistle of static, his voice distant and tired, almost foreboding in its disembodiment. Clark was a long way away, and alone.

"Testing," Aubrey said, leaning forward. He spoke very quietly.

"Can't hear you," Clark replied. There had been a delay, as if old habits of call-sign and acknowledgement waited to pop into Clark's mind.

"This is a test," the flight lieutenant said in a louder voice.

"That's too loud. Clark, I want you to speak quietly." The RAF radio operator evidently found the whole business amateurish and quite unacceptable. Even Aubrey found the conversation amusing, yet fraught with weaknesses. He would have liked to have taken refuge in established routines of communication, in batteries of call-signs and their endless repetition, in jargon and technicalities. Except that this communications network was simply about being able to communicate in a whisper over a distance of one hundred miles, Clark lying on his back or his stomach in a dark, cramped space, out of breath and perspiring inside an immersion suit, working on a piece of incredibly complex equipment he did not understand, trying to locate a fault and repair it. Call-signs would not help him, even though they seemed, by their absence at that moment, to possess the power of spells and charms. "What?" Aubrey said, craning forward towards the console. "I didn't catch that." There was an open sneer on the flight lieutenant's face. "Yes, I heard you clearly. Now, I'll hand you over to Mr. Quin, and you can run through that technical vocabulary you worked out with him. Random order, please, groups of six."

Aubrey sat back, a deal of smugness of manner directed at the radio operator. Quin looked like a nervous, first-time broadcaster or interviewee. He cleared his throat and shuffled in his seat, a clipboard covered with his strange, minuscule, spidery writing in front of him. Then he swiftly wiped his spectacles and began reading – Aubrey motioned him to lower his voice.

For five minutes, as the Nimrod continued northwards towards North Cape and her eventual station inside Norwegian airspace off the coast near Kirkenes, Clark and Quin exchanged a complex vocabulary of technical terminology. Aubrey remembered occasions of impending French or Latin tests, and the last minute, feverish recital of vocab by himself and other boys, before the master walked in and all text books had to be put away. The dialogue had a comforting, lulling quality. When Quin indicated they had finished, he opened his eyes. Quin appeared drained, and Aubrey quailed at the prospect of keeping him up to the mark.

"Thank you, Clark. That will do. Maximum communication, minimum noise. Good luck. Out."

Aubrey cut the channel, and nodded his satisfaction to Quin and the flight lieutenant. Out of the tiny round window, he could see the herringbone pattern of a ship sailing north through the Andfjord, inshore of one of the Vesteralen islands. The Nimrod was perhaps little more than half an hour from North Cape, and the same time again from their taking up station on the Soviet border. In an hour, they would be committed. "Plumber" would really be running, then.

Clark flicked off the transceiver, and shook his head as if he doubted the reality of the voices he had heard. The Harrier was seemingly about to settle onto the carpet of white cloud beneath them, and the tanker, the old Victor bomber, was a dot ahead and to starboard of them. Below the cloud, where the weather had let in small, almost circular viewing ports, the grey water and the slabbed, cut, knife-carved coastline were already retreating into evening, north of the Arctic Circle. Half an hour before, he had looked down between clouds and seen the vast sheet of the Svartisen glacier, looking like a huge, intact slab of marble fallen on the land, tinged by the sun into pinks and greens and blues.

The Harrier moved forward, overtaking the Victor tanker. The pilot changed his position until the tanker was slightly to port, then the probe that had needed to be specially fitted aligned with the long trailing fuel line from the wing of the Victor and its trumpet-bell mouth into which the pilot had to juggle the Harrier's probe. Bee and flower. Clark considered another, more human image, and smiled. Not like that. This was all too mechanical, and without passion.

The Victor's fuselage glowed silver in the sunlight from the west. The RAF roundel was evident on her side as the Harrier slid across the cloud carpet, and there seemed no motion except the slow, dance-like movements of possible combatants as the two aircraft matched speeds and height. The probe nudged forward towards the cone, the fuel-line lying on the air in a gentle, graceful curve. The probe nudged the cone, making it wobble, and then the Harrier dropped back slightly. Too high, too much to the left. Again, the probe slid forward towards the flower-mouth of the cone. Clark watched its insertion, felt the small, sharp jerk as it locked, then saw the glimmer of the three green locking lights on the instrument panel. The fuel began to surge down the fuel line.

Six and a half minutes later – it had become noticeably more evening-like, even at that altitude – the refuelling was complete, and the probe withdrew, the cone slipping forward and away as the speed of the two aircraft no longer matched. The gleaming, part-shadowed fuselage of the tanker slid up and away from them, the fuel-line retreating like a garden hose being reeled in. In a few more moments, the Victor had lost its silhouetted identity and was little more than a gleaming dot. The cloud brushed against the belly of the Harrier.

"Ready?" the pilot asked in his headset.

"Yes."

"Hang on, then. This is where it gets hairy. Don't look if you've got a weak stomach." The pilot chuckled.

"I can stand it."

Even before he finished speaking, the nose of the Harrier dipped into the cloud, and white turned grey and featureless and dark immediately. Clark felt the altitude of the Harrier alter steeply as she dived through the clouds, descending from thirty-five thousand feet.

They emerged into a twilit world, and the pilot levelled the Harrier and switched on the terrain-following radar and the auto-pilot which would together flick and twist them through the mountainous Norwegian hinterland. Clark watched as the dark water of the Skerstad-fjord rose to meet them, then flashed beneath the belly of the aircraft. The pilot was flying the Harrier at five hundred miles an hour. The tiny lights of fishing hamlets flickered along the shore, and then were gone. Small boats returning from the day's fishing, the main north-south highway, then the dark, high, sharp peaks of the mountain range engulfed them. Clark winced, despite his experience, as the tiny insect of the Harrier flicked between two peaks, then followed the snail-like track of a narrow fjord, a smear of lighter grey in the gloom.

The aircraft lifted over the back of a line of hills, then dipped down to follow the terrain again. A huge glacier seemed to emerge suddenly from the darkness, gleaming with a ghostly, threatening light. The Harrier banked, and slipped as buoyantly and easily along its face as a helicopter might have done. Clark had never flown in one of the US Marine Harriers, built under licence by McDonnell Douglas, and it was the only means of comparison he could apply; a demented, speeded-up helicopter. Then the glacier was behind them, one eastern tip of it falling into a small, crater-like lake.

"Sweden," the pilot announced.

"Nice view," Clark replied drily.

"Want to go back for your stomach?"

"I'm OK." Clark noticed the change in his own voice, the subconscious attempt to discourage conversation. He had moved into another phase of "Plumber". Already, he was alone, already it was another, different border they had crossed.

There were lakes as the terrain slowly became less mountainous, the peaks less sharp against the still lighter clouds and the few patches of stars. Grey, almost black water, the jagged lilies of ice floes everywhere. A rounded space of mirror-like water, a few dotted lights, then two companion stretches which the Harrier skimmed across like a stone. Then a long ribbon of lake, almost like a river because he could not perceive, at that altitude, either end of it, which the Harrier followed as it thrust into the centre of Swedish Lapland.

A village, like one dim street lamp at their speed, even the momentary flicker of headlights, then the Harrier banked to port, and altered course, following the single road north through that part of Sweden, the Norbotten, towards the Finnish border. The sheer rock faces closed in again, and the darkness seemed complete, except where the swift glow-worms of hamlets and isolated farms and the occasional gleams of car or lorry headlights exposed the whiteness of snow in the narrow valleys through which the road wound. Then, lower country, and a gleaming, humped plain of whiteness stretched before and beneath the aircraft.

"Finland," the pilot announced, but added nothing else.

Clark attempted repose, sensing like a man with a severely limited water supply, the waste of adrenalin his tension betokened. The shadow of the aircraft raced over the snow less than a hundred feet below them as the Harrier skimmed under the radar net. Bodø radar would have reported a loss of contact immediately they had finished refuelling, and the matter would not have been taken further. Neither neutral country, Sweden nor Finland, had been required to know of the passage of the Harrier, nor would they have sanctioned its incursion into their airspace.

A herd of reindeer, startled by the roar of the engine, scattered at the gallop beneath them. Then the darkness of trees, then whiteness again. The cloud cover above the cockpit was broken, mere rags now, and the moon gleamed. They were so close to the ground, it was like impossibly fast skiing rather than flying. It was a mere seventy minutes since they had ended their refuelling, and their flight was more than half completed. Clark glanced to port and starboard, and considered the packs in the two underwing pods. Right hand good, left hand bad, he told himself with a smile that did not come easily. Right-hand pack, repair equipment, meters, spares. Left-hand pack, explosives, detonators, the end of "Leopard". He believed that it was the left-hand pack that he would be forced to use. He did not consider his own fate. He would be arrested as a spy, naturally. Prison, interrogation, exchange for a Russian agent. It was a pattern of events that was predictable and not to be considered. The trick was, not to get caught, even when walking – swimming – into a Russian naval base; don't get caught.

The quick, easy toughness amused and comforted him. There was always a persistent sense of unreality about field operations, until the clock started ticking and the adrenalin became uncontrollable, and he knew, from experience and from training, that there was no alternative but to exist within that spacious immortality. It was the state of mind the CIA called "concussive readiness". It was the state of mind of the successful field agent.

Lake Inari, the sacred lake of Finnish Lapland, began to flow beneath them, illuminated by moonlight, the town of Ivalo a smear of light, then a mild haze, then nothing. The occasional lights of boats, the carpet of ice-dotted water persisting for mile after mile, an unrelieved, gleaming expanse where only the few black humps and spots of islands relieved its unreflecting mirror.

Before they reached the north-eastern shore of Inari, the Harrier banked to starboard, altering course to the east and crossing the border into Norway, a tongue of NATO thrusting southwards from Kirkenes and the coast between Finland and the Soviet Union. A tidier, smoother landscape – though he wondered whether that was not simply illusion – well-dotted with lights, then within a mile they were skimming the treetops of well-forested country, and there was a sullen, hazy glow to starboard.

The pilot throttled back, and the blur of the landscape became a dark flowing movement. Clark could not see the trees themselves, not even small clearings in the forest, but the landscape now possessed a life of its own. It was no longer a relief map over which they passed, or a three-dimensional papier-mâché model.

The lights to starboard were from the watch-towers and the rows of lights along the wire of the border fence separating Norway from the Soviet Union. Clark swallowed, then breathed consciously at a relaxed pace, spacing the intervals between each inhalation and exhalation exactly and precisely. Right hand good, left hand bad, his mind recited again.

He saw the lights of a string of hamlets along the one good road north to Kirkenes. Kirkenes itself was a dim glow on the horizon ahead of them. Then the Harrier flicked to starboard, altering course eastwards to run along the Norwegian border. Pechenga was eight miles beyond the border. Eight miles, and they were perhaps now twelve miles from the border as it swung north to the coast. The Harrier was at little more than one third speed and well below the radar net. Four miles per minute. Three minutes. No, already two minutes fifty. The landscape seemed to take on more vivacity, as if he were studying it in order to remember it. The ribbon of a road, dark patches of trees, vague lights, sheets of white snow. Lumpy, softened white hills. Then the sullen, ribbon-like glow, enlarging to a string of lights, decorating the darkness beyond. A gap in the trees, after a narrow strip of water no more than a pool at that speed, where the two fences and the lights marched north and south, and then the glow was behind them, fading.

He was inside the Soviet Union.

The pilot flicked off the auto-pilot and the terrain-following radar, and assumed manual control of the Harrier. The plane's airspeed dropped. Pechenga was a bright, hazy globe of light ahead. The Soviet Union. Fortress Russia. Clark had never taken part in a penetration operation before.

"Ready? It's coming up to port."

He saw the water of a lake and an uninhabited landscape of woods and open stretches of snow. The Harrier slowed even further, almost to a hover, above a tiny white space between the trees. The image of a helicopter came to Clark again. The sound of the Pegasus engine faded, and the pilot modulated the air brake. Then he increased the engine's thrust once more, directing it downwards through the four nozzles beneath the fuselage, putting the Harrier into a hover.

Snow blew up round the canopy, and the dark seemed to grow above them by some freak of fertilization. More snow, obscuring the canopy, then the final wobble, the dying-away of the engine, and the heaviness of the aircraft settling into the snow and slush.

"Right. You're on your own. Don't waste time."

"See anything?"

"No."

Clark opened the canopy. Snow powdered his upturned face. He hefted himself upright, and then swung his body awkwardly over the high sill of the fuselage, beginning his burglary of the Soviet Union. He looked around him, the sudden chill of the early night and the wind making his teeth chatter. He scanned the area of trees around the clearing three times, then he saw the pale, easily missed wink of a torch signalling.

"Right. He's there," he said to the pilot.

"Good luck."

"Thanks." He placed his feet firmly in the foot-holds on the side of the fuselage, and climbed down. He moved beneath the port wing and snapped open the clips on the underwing pod. He lifted out the pack – left hand bad – and laid it on the snow. Then he unloaded the starboard pack.

He picked up the two packs and moved away from the Harrier, dragging the heavy packs through the snow, which was deeper outside the half-melted circle caused by the downthrust of the Pegasus engine. When he looked up, a small, bulky figure was hurrying towards him. There was the inevitable, electric moment of doubt, was it the right man, was it the KGB, almost bound to be the KGB? Then the man spoke.

"Welcome, my friend –"

The remainder of what he said, Clark could see his lips moving, was drowned by the increasing whine of the engine. Clark, still gripping the man's hand tightly, turned to watch as the Harrier rose above the level of the trees, lurched forward, then smoothly accelerated. He was inside the Soviet Union, a couple of miles from the naval base of Pechenga, and on his own, except for the help of a grocer. It was difficult not to feel a sense of hopelessness nibbling at the feeling of concussion which he required if he was to succeed.

The grocer picked up one of the packs, and hefted it onto his back.

"Come," he said. "Come."

Leper. The girl wanted to get up, talk to the two people passing twenty yards away below them, but he held her down, his hand now almost out of habit over her mouth. Fortunately, they didn't have a dog with them. The man wore an anorak and carried a camera, swinging by its strap, and the woman was wearing a fur coat that looked almost like camouflage, white with dark patches. Hyde listened to them talking, watched the man put his arm around the woman because she remarked on the cold of the evening, watched them, too, look up at the fading light and the gathering clouds; finally recognized that they were heading back towards the car park.

Two reasons. He didn't know them and therefore he distrusted them, and also he could not risk enlisting anyone on their behalf. He'd killed now. Anyone who came into contact with him was thereby endangered. Leper.

He released the girl, and she shuffled away from him, rubbing her arms, touching her mouth where his hand had been clamped.

"Why?" she almost wailed. "Why not?"

"Because you could get them killed, or us killed. Take your pick." The wetness of the ferns was soaking into him. He was hungry, his

237

stomach hollow and rumbling. He was thirsty. He scooped up a thin film of half-melted snow, and pressed it into his mouth. Then he rubbed his wet hand over his face in an attempt to revive himself. The girl looked no fresher than he felt.

"They were out for a walk," she said sullenly.

"Maybe. Look, just let it rest, will you? We're on our own, and that's all there is to it."

"Why – *why* are they chasing us?" the girl asked, her face recovering earlier anxieties, past terrors.

Hyde studied her in disbelief. "What?"

"My father's safe – why do they want us?"

"Oh, Christ – don't you understand the simplest moves in the game?" Hyde shook his head. "Perhaps you don't. Obviously, Petrunin has had new orders. You're as valuable to them now as you were before. If they have you, they can trade you off for your dad. See?"

"How? You've got him, for Christ's sake!"

"He's not in prison. If he knew they had you, he'd take the first chance of walking out to join you. On a plane to Moscow."

The girl appeared about to ask another question, then she fell silent, watching her hands as if they belonged to someone else while they picked at the stiff, rimed grass.

"You ready?"

She looked helplessly, tiredly at him, then got slowly to her feet. "Yes."

"Come on, then."

After the death of the deer and the Russian, they had worked their way east across the Chase, assuming that other men on foot, and the helicopter, would pursue them north, towards the Stafford road. The helicopter, blinded by the shroud of firs through which they ran, drifted away northwards, its noise following it like a declining wail. They saw no other Russians.

Hyde waited until this moment, when it was almost dark and the thin, half-melted sheen of snow had begun to gleam like silver, before attempting to make the car park and the road where they had first stopped. The rifle range was behind them now, to the north.

They trod carefully down the slope of dead ferns, then began to ascend slowly along a tiny deer-track through the tightly growing, restraining heather. Almost dark. Perhaps they could risk this open slope –

The shout was alarming, but almost as unnoticed, except by Hyde's subconscious, as the bark of a dog. The girl looked round slowly, but only because he had stopped. A second shout brought him out of his lassitude. A figure on a rise, perhaps two hundred yards away, waving what might have been a stick. Rifles now. No easy-to-hide handguns. They had put them less than equal with him. His body protested at the effort required of it. The girl bumped into him, staggering as though ill or blind. He took her hand. A second figure rose over the edge of the rise, outlined against the pale last gleam of the day. Cloud pressed down on the open bowl of dead heather in which he had allowed them to be trapped.

The helicopter. Almost too dark to see them, too dark for them to make it out until it blurted over the rise and bore down on them, its noise deafening by its suddenness. He did not have to tell the girl to run. The deer track was not wide enough for both of them and he floundered through wet, calf-high heather keeping pace with her.

Shots, deadened by the noise of the rotors and the racing of his blood. Wild shooting. The helicopter overshot them, and began to bank round.

"Over there!"

The land folded into a deeper hollow. Deer scattered out of it as they approached it, startled by the helicopter. A hallucinatory moment as the grey, small, lithe, panicking forms were all around them, and Hyde remembered the pain-clouded eye into which he had looked that afternoon before he squeezed the trigger; then the deer were gone and the hollow was dark and wound away in a narrow trench which they followed. It led northwards, back towards the higher ground and the rifle range, but he had no alternative but to follow it. They ducked down, keeping below the level of the ground, then the trench petered out and they were left almost at the top of the rise.

Hyde threw himself flat and looked over the lip of the ground. Nothing. The light had gone. In no more than a few minutes, there was nothing. The noise of the helicopter was a furious, enraged buzzing on the edge of hearing, as if already miles away.

Couldn't be –? He turned onto his back, and groaned. Worse than he thought. He had imagined a flesh wound, a scratch, but it was throbbing. His whole arm was throbbing. He tried to sit up, and then lay back, another groan escaping him.

"What is it?"

"Nothing –"

"What's the matter?"

She touched his shoulder, and immediately the pain was intense, almost unbearable, and then he could not decipher her expression or even see the white blob of her face any longer. It rushed away from him at great speed, down a dark tunnel.

TWELVE:

Access

"On station." Eastoe's communications with Aubrey were now of a single, close-lipped, unhelpful kind, the RAF officer providing only a grudging assistance. Aubrey, knowing it would not interfere with the pilot's efficiency, was prepared to allow the man his mood.

The Nimrod had begun flying a box pattern over an inshore area of the Barents Sea which would take her to within a few miles of the Soviet border at the end of each eastward leg of the pattern. Travelling westward, the Nimrod would pass up the Varangerfjord, then turn north across the block of land jutting into the Barents Sea known as Varangerhalvöya, then turn onto her eastward leg which would again take her out over the Barents. A rigid rectangle of airspace, at any point of which the Nimrod was no more than seventy miles from Clark's transceiver in Pechenga.

Aubrey glanced once more through the window in the fuselage. A red, winking light to port of the Nimrod, a little behind and below. A Northrop F-5 of the Royal Norwegian Air Force, one of three somewhat outdated fighter aircraft that provided their screen. The arrangement had been considered necessary by MoD Air, and by the Norwegians, but Aubrey considered it mere window-dressing. He did not anticipate problems with Soviet aircraft, and if there were any such problems, the F-5s would be immediately recalled to the military airfield at Kirkenes.

"Thank you, Squadron Leader," Aubrey replied to Eastoe. "Would you come forward to the flight deck, Mr. Aubrey?" Eastoe added, and Aubrey was immediately struck by the conspiratorial edge to the voice. He removed his headphones and stood up, not looking at Quin.

He moved down the aircraft gingerly, an old man moving down a bus or a train, hands ready to grab or fumble for support. He paused between the two pilots' chairs, and Eastoe turned to him. His face was grave, that of a messenger with bad news to impart; some battle lost.

"What is it, Squadron Leader?"

"This." He handed Aubrey a sheet torn from a message pad. "It's for you, Eyes Only. No good letting Quin hear the bad news."

The message was from Shelley, and it informed Aubrey – who felt his heart clutched by a cold, inescapable hand – that Hyde and the girl had disappeared somewhere between Manchester and Birmingham, without trace. Shelley had organized the search which was now proceeding. Aubrey looked up from the sheet, and found Eastoe's gaze intently fastened on him, as if demanding some human frailty from him by way of reaction.

"Thank you, Squadron Leader," Aubrey said stiffly. "You were quite right to keep this from Mr. Quin. You will continue to do so."

"Makes things a bit awkward, mm?" Eastoe sneered. "Any reply?"

"Nothing I could say would make the slightest difference," Aubrey snapped, and turned on his heel, retracing his steps down the tunnel of the aircraft, composing his features and silencing the flurry of thoughts and images in his mind. Now all that mattered was that Quin functioned like a machine, when the time came.

He regained his seat. Quin seemed uninterested in his reappearance. Aubrey studied him.

Quin, under scrutiny, became quickly and cunningly alert. His posture was totally self-defensive. Then he attempted to achieve the academic trick of distracting attention by vigorously polishing his spectacles. Aubrey's features wrinkled in impatience, and this seemed to further embolden Quin.

"Your man hasn't called in, not since he left the aircraft," he said.

Aubrey was incensed. "His name is Clark," he remarked icily.

"But, the time factor?" Quin persisted. Aubrey realized that the man's silence for the last hour had led to a consolidation of truculent fear. He had, as it were, husbanded his bloody-mindedness until they arrived on station. Every minute that Clark had not reported in satisfied Quin that there would be a premature, and not long delayed, end to his confinement aboard the Nimrod. Clark, in fact, because of the short range of his transceiver, had not signalled them since the test. The Harrier pilot, making for Bardufoss to refuel had sent one brief, coded signal to inform Aubrey that Clark had landed safely and without trouble. That had been forty minutes before.

Aubrey looked at his watch. Eight-thirty. He knew that in two, at most three, hours, he would cancel the operation. "Plumber" would be over unless they heard from Clark within that time. He would have been caught, or killed. Aubrey composed himself to wait, wishing that he could do it somewhere where he did not have to confront Quin across a silent communications console in the skeletal, untidy fuselage of a Nimrod. It was, he considered, rather too much like sitting inside a television set. At least, its screens and wiring and circuitry and sensors gave much the same impression as did the innards of his set, whenever the engineer from the rental company had to come to his flat to effect a repair.

241

But it was Quin, more than anyone, who angered and threw him into doubt. Clark had to depend upon this pompous, cowardly, indifferent man, and it seemed unfair.

Abandon that line of thought, Aubrey instructed himself. You will have to make the man helpful, when the time comes. He felt the Nimrod, at twenty thousand feet, make its turn onto the eastward leg of its flight pattern, out over the Barents and towards the Soviet border. Somewhere to the north of them, perhaps no more than twenty or thirty miles away, was the location of the attack on the *Proteus* and the ledge where she had rested until the Russians had raised her to the surface.

He found his fingers had adopted a drumming, impatient pattern of movement against one side of the console. Guiltily, he stopped the noise immediately. Quin seemed wreathed in self-satisfaction. He had evidently decided that Clark would fail, even had failed, to penetrate Pechenga. He was like a man sheltering from the rain. The shower would stop, soon, and he could make his way home.

"What about the air tanks?"

"Those I have stored for you with a friend. No, not one of us, but he can be trusted. It is lucky I had them still. I have not been asked to make a – what do you say, reconnaissance – ?" Clark nodded, smiling. "Yes, a reconnaissance of the harbour for a long time. My old wetsuit – perished, alas. But the tanks are good, my friend, I assure you."

"And I believe you."

They were seated in the small, cramped room above the grocer's shop. The Pechenga agent-in-place for SIS was a short, rotund man with a stubble on his jaw. His eyes were small and black, like raisins folded into the sallow dough of his flesh. When he smiled, he showed remarkably white dentures. Clark trusted his ordinariness as much as his thoroughness. His name was Pasvik. Once, generations before, his family had been Norwegian. Whether that had been before the war, before the first war, before the Revolution, even Pasvik did not know.

Pasvik owned the grocery shop himself. His father had acquired the contract for supplying eggs and flour to the naval base, for use in preparing officers' meals. It was his patronage, his "By Appointment" that had enabled him to retain control of his shop, collect the naval intelligence London required and used, and which gave him freedom of movement and access. Also, it provided him with what Clark suspected was a thriving black-market business involving smuggling from Scandinavia and supplying to the naval base and Pechenga's Party officials modest but lucrative luxury goods. Pasvik had made only passing mention of these activities, as if he felt they qualified his status as an accredited agent of London, but for the American it only increased his awareness of the man's intelligence and nerve.

Clark studied the large-scale map that Pasvik had laid on the wooden table between them. A large brandy glass stood near Clark's right hand. The odour of the liquor mingled with the smell of bacon and flour and washing powder – one of the modest luxuries, Clark supposed, since he had seen the brand-name Persil on one shelf of the store-room behind the shop.

Much of the map was originally blank, but the censored, sensitive areas of the town and the naval base had been pencilled in, and labelled, by Pasvik. Pechenga lay at the neck of a narrow inlet in the coast where the river Pechenga reached the Barents Sea. It was a thriving northern fishing port as well as an important subsidiary base to Murmansk, headquarters of the Soviet Union's most important fleet. The fishing harbour lay on the northern outskirts of the town – Clark had smelt it on the wind, even locked in the back of Pasvik's delivery van – while the naval base, as if hiding behind the civilian port, seemed from the map to be entrenched across the neck of the inlet, behind its massive harbour wall. The submarine pens, his mission target, were arrayed and dug in along the southern flank of the base, farthest from the fishing harbour.

It was evident to Clark that Pasvik regarded himself with some reluctance but without evasion as expendable in the cause of "Plumber". Clark, however, realized that he could not efficiently exploit the man to the degree of endangering his life, and was pleased at that fact. Pasvik making a late, night-time delivery to the base would be a transparent pretext, and the van would undoubtedly be searched. Clark would have to go in by water, not with the groceries.

"We could easily do it," Pasvik said hesitantly, as if he had read Clark's thoughts. Clark shook his head.

"Uh-uh. That's the obvious way to get caught. The water is the only way."

Only then did Pasvik display his full fear and pleasure, in the same instant that exposed his dentures, creased up the dough around his eyes, and brought beads of perspiration to his forehead. These he wiped away with a red handkerchief.

"Thank you," he said.

"No problem. This," he added, dabbing his finger on the map, "the net?" Pasvik nodded. "Here, too?"

"Yes. You will need to go over, or beneath, two nets."

"Mines?"

Pasvik pulled a leather-bound, slim notebook from his pocket. It seemed misplaced about his person. It required an executive's breast-pocket, in a grey suit. Pasvik laughed at the expression on Clark's face.

"One of a consignment that I kept for myself," he explained. "They are very popular with junior officers." He opened the book. "This, you understand, is a digest of gossip and observation collected over some years." He fished in the breast pocket of his shirt, and hitched a pair of wire-framed spectacles over his ears. Then he cleared his throat. "The mines are of different types – proximity detonated, trip-wired, acoustic, magnetic. They are set at various depths, and the pattern is very complicated. I do not have any details. Indiscretion in Red Navy officers goes only so far, you understand?"

"The mines I don't worry too much about. Except the contact stuff. Are they marked? Do you have any idea of their shape and size?"

"Ah, there I can help you, I think." He showed a page of the notebook to Clark. The sleeve of the old dressing-gown that he had borrowed from Pasvik brushed the brandy glass, spilling what remained of the drink across the map in a tobacco-coloured stain.

"Damn!" Clark exclaimed, soaking up the liquid with the sleeve of his dressing-gown. "Sorry." Some of the neatly written labelling on the map had smudged.

"No matter."

Clark studied the drawing. A small mine, probably, activated by direct contact with the horns. To deter and destroy small vessels venturing into the restricted waters of the inner harbour, even to kill a swimmer. He handed the notebook back to Pasvik. The stained map absorbed his attention like an omen.

"OK. Where's the *Proteus*?"

"Here are the submarine pens. This one, as far as I can make out. Gossip, as you will imagine, has been rife." He tapped at one of the numbered pens. There were two dozen of them, and *Proteus* was supposedly in the fifth one, measuring from the eastern end of the pens. "Many of them are empty, of course."

"Where will you be?" Clark asked.

"Ah – here," Pasvik replied, "you see, in a direct line. It is, or was, a favourite picnic spot in summer." He sighed.

Clark looked at his watch. "Nine-forty. Time to get going?"

"Yes."

"Will you be stopped on the road?"

"Yes, but it's not likely I will be searched. Not going in the direction of the fishing harbour. Anyone who knows me will assume I am making a pick-up of some smuggled goods from a freighter. On the way back, they may be more nosey. So I will have some of the old favourites – stockings, perfume, chocolate, cigarettes, even sex books from Sweden – in the back of the van. I make a habit of free gifts, once in a while. You are ready?"

Clark found Pasvik studying him. The raisin eyes were deep in their folds, but bright with assessment and observation. Eventually, Pasvik nodded and stood up. "You will make it," he announced, "of that I am reasonably sure."

"Thanks."

Clark took off the dressing-gown and laid it on Pasvik's narrow, uncomfortable-looking bed. Then he donned the immersion suit again, heaving it up and around his body, finally pulling on the headcap.

"Another brandy?"

"No, thanks."

As they went down the bare wooden stairs to the store-room and the small, noisome yard where Pasvik had parked his van, the grocer said, "So, Mr. Aubrey is not very far away at this moment, up in the sky, mm?"

"He is. At least, he ought to be. I'll signal him before I take to the water."

"I can do that."

"Better me than you." In the darkness, Clark patted the side of his head, then the tiny throat-mike beneath his chin. "This stuff has got to work. I don't want to find out it doesn't after I get aboard the *Proteus*."

Pasvik unbolted the door and they went out into a wind that skulked and whipped around the yard. Clark looked up at the sky. A few light grey clouds, huge patches of stars. The clouds seemed hardly to be moving. Almost a full moon, which he regretted. However, the improvement in the weather would mean a less choppy surface in the harbour, and he might need to conserve the air in Pasvik's tanks. Pasvik, he noticed as the man crossed to the van and opened the rear doors, moved with a leg-swinging shuffle. Presumably the limp explained why he no longer carried out immersion-suited surveillance of the harbour.

Clark climbed into the rear of the van, and the doors slammed shut on him. He squatted in a tight, low crouch behind stacked wooden crates, near the partition separating the rear of the van from the driver. He watched as Pasvik clambered into the driving seat, slammed his door, and then turned to him.

"OK?"

"OK."

Pasvik started the engine, and ground the car into gear. A moment later, they were turning out of the narrow lane behind the row of shops into a poorly lit street on which a few cars and one or two lorries were the only traffic. Clark felt tension jump like sickness into his throat, and he swallowed hard. He squeezed his arms around his knees, which were drawn up under his chin. His two packs – right hand good, left hand bad – were near his feet. Without conscious thought, he reached out and unsealed one of the packs. He reached into one of the small side pockets and withdrew a polythene-wrapped package, undid the elastic bands, and removed the gun. A small, light .22 Heckler & Koch pistol with a ten-round magazine, effective stopping range less than thirty metres. He unzipped the neck of his immersion suit and placed the re-wrapped pistol inside. If he ever needed the gun, he was close to being finished.

The grocery van trailed a tarpaulin-shrouded lorry along the northbound road, through a dingy, industrialized suburb of Pechenga. Pasvik seemed to have no desire for conversation. Perhaps, Clark admitted, he thought talk would make his passenger more edgy. Pechenga was little more than a ghost town after dark. There were few pedestrians, fewer vehicles. The town seemed subdued, even oppressed, by the security that surrounded the naval installation. The place had a wartime look, a besieged, blacked-out, curfewed feeling and appearance which depressed and yet aggravated his awareness.

There was a haze of light to be seen over the low factory roofs from the naval base, a glow like that from the border lights as he had seen them from the Harrier. Then he felt the van slowing. The brake lights of the lorry in front of them were bright red. There was a squeal of air brakes.

"A checkpoint – outside the civilian harbour. Get down," Pasvik instructed him. "Cover yourself with the tarpaulin."

White light haloed the bulk of the lorry. Clark could hear voices, and the noise of heavy military boots, though he could see no one. He slid into a prone position, and tugged the tarpaulin over him, which smelt of cabbage and meal. Once underneath, he unzipped the neck of his immersion suit once more, though he was able consciously to prevent himself from unwrapping the gun. Nevertheless, through the polythene his finger half-curled around the trigger. His thumb rested against the safety catch. He could not prevent finger and thumb taking what seemed a necessary hold upon the pistol.

A voice, very close. Clark's Russian was good, but he reacted more to the interrogative tone. A guard leaning his head into the driver's window. Pasvik's voice seemed jocular, confiding in reply.

"Hello, Pasvik. Out and about again?"

Pasvik smiled, showing his dentures, opening his hands on the wheel in a shrugging gesture.

"You know how business is, Grigory."

"Keep your voice down, Pasvik – the officer'll hear you."

"Then you'll be in trouble, eh, my friend?"

"You want me to search your van, have everything out on the road, now and on the way back – eh, Pasvik?"

"Don't be irritable, my friend."

"Look, I've told you – I'm not your friend. Just keep your voice down."

"You want to see my papers?"

"Yes – quick, here's my officer. Bastard." Grigory uttered the last word almost under his breath.

"What's going on here?" the officer enquired above the noise of the lorry moving off and pulling into the docks. Beyond his short dapper figure Pasvik could see the outlines of cranes, the silhouettes of cargo and fishing vessels. "Are this man's papers in order?"

"Yes, sir."

The officer took them from Grigory, perused them in a showy, self-satisfied, cursory manner, then handed them back. He turned on his heel and strutted away. Grigory pulled a scowling face behind his back, then thrust the papers back at Pasvik. He bent near to the window again.

"I want some more," he whispered.

"More what?"

"Those books."

"You sell them off again, eh, Grigory?"

"No!" Grigory's face changed colour.

"I'll see what I can do. Stop me on the way back, get in the back of the van then. I'll leave some for you, under the tarpaulin. OK?"

"OK. I'm off duty at midnight, though."

"I'll be back before then."

Grigory stepped back, and waved Pasvik on. The red and white pole between the two guard huts swung up, and Pasvik drove the van into the civilian harbour. In his mirror, Pasvik could see the officer speaking to Grigory. The posture of his body and the bend of his head indicated a reprimand rather than an enquiry as to Pasvik's business. He would have to be careful when Grigory collected his sex books from the back of the van on the return journey. Perhaps he needed something for the officer, too?

He drove out of the string of white lights along the main thorough-fare of the docks, turning into a narrow, unlit alley between two long, low warehouses. Then he turned out onto a poorly illuminated wharf, driving slowly past the bulk of a Swedish freighter. Music from the ship, a drunk singing. A head peering over the side. Two armed guards patrolling, leaning towards each other in conversation, stultified by routine and uneventfulness. Pasvik stopped the car in the shadow of a warehouse, beneath the dark skeleton of a dockside crane.

"Very well, my friend. You can get out now."

Pasvik slipped out of the van, and opened the rear doors. The two guards, unconcerned at the noise of his engine, were walking away from him, into and then out of a pool of light. Clark sat on the edge of the van, stretching. Then he hefted the two packs onto the concrete of the wharf.

"Thanks," he said.

"You have everything in your mind?"

Clark nodded. "Yes. What about the tanks?"

"One moment." Pasvik limped off swiftly, towards the door of the warehouse. He appeared to possess a key, for Clark heard the door squeak open, then the intervening moments before the door squeaked again were filled with the singing of the Swedish drunk, who had become utterly maudlin. Clark heard, as the door closed again, the reassuring metallic bump as the tanks struck the concrete. Then Pasvik came scuttling out of the shadows, hefting the two air tanks over his shoulder. He placed them, like game retrieved, at Clark's feet. The American inspected and tested them. The hiss of air satisfied him. Both gauges registered full.

"Good."

"The patrol will be back in five minutes. By that time, I must be aboard the freighter and you must be in the water. Come."

Pasvik helped Clark strap the tanks to his back, lifting the mouthpiece and its twin hoses gently over his head like a ceremonial garland. Then they carried the packs across the wharf, slipping quickly through the one dim patch of light into the shadow of the freighter. Pasvik make a lugubrious face at the singing, still audible from above. The water was still and oily below them, against the side of the ship. Clark could smell fish on the windy air. He unwound short lengths of nylon rope from each pack, and clipped them onto his weighted belt. As he did so, he felt he was imprisoning himself. An anticipation of utter weariness overcame him for a moment, and then he shrugged it off. He would make it, even with that weight being towed or pushed, since the packs would become buoyant in the water.

"OK," he said, about to slip the mouthpiece of his air supply between his lips. "Thanks."

"Don't forget the landmarks I described – don't forget the patrol boats – don't forget the contact mines, some of them are small enough, sensitive enough . . ." Pasvik halted his litany when Clark held up his hand.

"OK, OK." Clark grinned. "I'll take care, Mom."

Pasvik stifled a delighted laugh. "Goodbye, my friend. Good luck."

He lifted one of the packs as Clark moved to the iron ladder set in the side of the wharf, leading down to the water. Clark, holding the other pack, began to climb down, his back to the freighter's hull. Then he paused, his head just above the level of the concrete, and Pasvik handed him the second pack. Clark appeared almost to over-balance, then he stumbled the last few steps and slid into the water. Pasvik peered down at him. Clark waved, adjusted his mouthpiece and facemask, then began swimming out and around the bow of the freighter, pushing the two packs ahead of him, slowly and awkwardly.

Pasvik watched until the swimming man was hidden by the hull of the Swedish ship, then softly whistled and shook his head. Then he slapped his hands together, shrugging Clark away, and headed for the boarding ladder up to the deck of the freighter.

Clark swam easily, using his legs and fins, his arms around the two packs, guiding them through the water. Their buoyancy made them lighter, easier to handle in the water. After a few minutes, he trod water, and opened the channel of his transceiver. The ether hummed in his ear.

"All is well," he said.

Aubrey's voice, slowed down from the spit of sound in his ear-piece, replied a few moments later. "Good luck."

Clark switched off, and began swimming again. Ahead of him, there was a rippling necklace of lights along the harbour wall, with one dark gap like a missing stone in the middle. The water was still calm, its surface only riffled like pages quickly turned by the wind. He headed for the dark gap in the lights, keeping the flash of the small lighthouse to his left, and the steering lights of a small cargo ship to his right. It was a matter of some seven or eight hundred yards – or so he had estimated from the map – to the harbour wall. He moved with an almost lazy stroke of his legs, using the buoyant packs like a child might use water wings. The mouthpiece of the air supply rested on the packs just in front of his face.

It was twenty minutes before he reached the choppier water of the inlet beyond the fish and cargo harbour. Suddenly, as he passed between the lights, the water confronted him instead of allowing him easy passage. The packs began to bob and move as if attempting to escape him. He checked his compass, took a sighting on the lights above the twin guard towers at the entrance to the naval installation, and rested for a few moments, accustoming his body and his breathing to the choppy sea. Then he swam on.

The wall of the harbour curved away from him, as if enclosing him, then it rose in height and the lights along it were brighter and closer together. He was paralleling the wall of the Pechenga naval base.

His awareness, despite his experience and his desire that it should not be so, began to retreat into the confines of his immediate surroundings and experience – the packs behind him like brakes moving sluggishly through the water, the choppy little wavelets dashing against his facemask, his arms moving out in front and then behind, even the tight cap of his suit seemed to contain his senses as well as his mind. Thus the patrol boat was a light before it was a noise, and a light he could not explain for a moment. And it was close, far too close.

A searchlight swept across the surface of the water. The boat, little larger than a motor yacht, was a hydrofoil. Clark, catching the high-bowed outline behind the searchlight as he was startled out of his dreamlike state, saw its forward and aft gun turrets, its depth charge racks. It was paralleling his course, moving along the harbour wall. Even though startled, he continued to observe the patrol boat move lazily across his vision. The searchlight swept back and forth, moved closer to the wall, swept back and forth again, moved closer . . .

Clark panicked into acute consciousness. He fumbled with the two packs, hauling them into his embrace. He ripped clumsily at the valve on the first one – the light moved towards him again – and failed to turn it at the first attempt, and his hand hovered towards the valve on the second pack – the light swung away, then began to swing back, the patrol boat was sliding past him sixty metres away – then he turned feverishly at the first valve, hearing above the panic of his breathing and blood in his ears, the hiss of air. The bag sank lower in the water, and he grabbed at the second valve, telling himself ineffectually to slow down – the light moved forward, closer, like lava flowing over the wrinkled water, almost illuminating the pack that remained afloat – he twisted the valve, heard the air, watched the light swing away, then back, then begin its arc that would reach his head. The pack slipped beneath the water, and he flicked himself into a dive – the light slid across the distressed water where he had been, hesitated, then moved on.

Clark thrust the mouthpiece between his teeth, bit on it as he inhaled, and drove downwards against the restraint of the two packs from which he had not released sufficient air. They pulled like parachute brakes against his movement. The twin diesel engines of the patrol boat thrummed through the black water. He looked up. Yes, he could see the light dancing across the surface, as if it still searched for him. Slowly, it faded. The vibration and hollow noise of the boat's engines moved away. He allowed the buoyancy of the two packs to slowly pull him back to the surface. When his head came out of the water, he saw the patrol boat some hundreds of yards away, its searchlight playing at the foot of the harbour wall.

He lay in the water, the packs bobbing just beneath the surface on either side of him, until his breathing and his heart rate had returned to normal. Then he embraced each of the packs in turn, pressing the button on each small cylinder of oxygen, refloating the packs on the surface. Having to drag them through the water would have exhausted him long before he reached the *Proteus*.

He swam on, still resting his frame on the packs as he clutched them to him. Ten minutes later, he reached the entrance to the harbour. The guard towers on either wall, apart from beacon lights, carried powerful searchlights which swept back and forth across the dark opening between them and swept, too, the water of the harbour and the basin beyond it. He trod water, absorbing the pattern of movement of the searchlights. He saw the silhouettes of armed guards, the barrels of anti-aircraft cannon pointing to the night sky. He felt cold, the chill of water seeping through his immersion suit. Thought seemed to come slowly, but not because of the cold; rather, because he already knew the dangers and the risks. There was no necessity to discover or analyse them. The submarine net stretched across the entrance to the harbour, perhaps fifteen feet above the water. He would have to climb it.

He edged with furtive strokes of his fins around the base of the harbour wall, touching its barnacled sliminess with his hand, reaching the steel net directly beneath one of the guard towers. The packs had begun to resist him, he imagined, as if they had lost their buoyancy. He let them drift behind him as he clung to the mesh, watching the lights. Thirty seconds. He lowered his arm as his watch confirmed the gap of darkness between the passage of each light across the harbour entrance for the second time. He had thirty seconds in which to climb the net, mount it like a rider, drag his packs after him, and climb down again to the water. He could not wait for the chance of the net being opened on its boom to admit a vessel.

The light of the searchlight on the opposite wall slid down the concrete and swung away into the harbour. His fins hung round his neck, and his mouthpiece dangled between their strange necklace. He felt clumsy, burdened. He reached up, and began climbing. The heavy steel cords of the submarine net did not even vibrate with his effort.

Seven, eight, nine, ten, eleven –

The seconds began racing away from him. His mind was blind and indifferent to the progress of the light, hearing only the moving numbers in his head. The numbers ran ahead of him, as his breathing did. *Thirteen, fourteen.* He felt the weight of the packs thrum lightly through the steel net.

Top. One leg, *sixteen,* other leg, packs holding him back, *seventeen,* swing the other leg over against the restraint of the two packs, *eighteen*, his stomach was stretched and pressed painfully along the steel boom, *nineteen*, stand up, *twenty*, five seconds behind already, lift the packs, lift the first one over, drop it, *twenty-three*, hold on, hold on, as the inertia of the pack tried to pull him from the net, arms full of pain as he resisted the pack's weight, *twenty-five*, other pack now, easier, drop it, hang on, pain again, *twenty-seven*, go now, go –

He scuttled down the net, feeling it vibrate now, his breath ragged, his body as tense as a spring, as vulnerable as an insect's. He was aware of the light on the opposite side of the entrance swinging back now, a hazy blur at the corner of his vision. *Thirty-one*. The light slid down the net, opening the shadow beneath the harbour wall, slipping across the small blur of bubbles his entrance into the water had made.

Clark clung to the net, forcing the mouthpiece back between his teeth, trying to calm his breathing, feeling the packs tugging him lazily back towards the surface. He held on to the net with one hand, and reduced their buoyancy with the other, his hand completing the task robotically. They bobbed beside him in the darkness, nudging him as if to remind him of their presence, or to ingratiate themselves because they had almost betrayed him.

He clung to the net until the searchlight's wavering globe of light had passed over his head another four times. Then he further adjusted the buoyancy of the packs so that they began to pull at him, drag him down. He fitted his fins, and let go of the net, moving smoothly down into the darkness.

The mines, now. Magnetic, electronic contact. Pasvik had been unable to provide the pattern. MoD had had some detail, but not enough. There did not seem to be channels through the minefield, since the mines would all be armed or disarmed by remote signal. If a Soviet vessel entered the harbour, the mines would be switched off. Simple. Effective. Clark reasoned that he must dive deep, almost to the bottom, to avoid the contact mines which would be set off by a touch, and which would have been laid at varying depths. He swam down, levelling off when his depth gauge registered a hundred feet. Time closed in on him immediately as decompression became a determining factor. He flicked on his lamp. The packs idled alongside him as he trod water. Compass direction checked, together with the time and the depth, he began swimming, moving rapidly now, ignoring the sense of isolation in his system like an antidote to adrenalin, and which assailed him for the first time since he had left the cockpit of the Harrier. The weak glow of the lamp illuminated the dull silver of fish and the strange forest of cables growing up from the harbour bed below. Above him, invisible, the mines sat at their determined depths. He jogged one cable, then another, and occasionally the packs snagged against them, operating like brakes. He had guessed correctly. He was too deep for the mines themselves.

He swung the lamp from side to side, however, in a precautionary swathe. The mine that came suddenly out of the darkness still surprised him. He flicked aside, remembering the two packs only as he did so. He stopped himself. The chill disappeared from his body. He flicked the light of his lamp behind him. One of the packs rubbed against the cable. It seemed to be sliding upwards towards the mine's old-fashioned, deadly horns. A small contact mine, almost too small to do any damage, but enough to pull a human frame into shreds. He moved slowly. The mine seemed to bob and weave like a fighting animal watching him. The water distressed it and wafted around the pack, moving it upwards. It was only inches from the mine.

He reached forward, trying to keep the light of the lamp steady. The mine bobbed, the pack imitated it. Inches. He reached forward, hardly moving his fins, feeling his body sinking away from the mine and the pack. He could not tread water any more violently. He reached forward along the short line which attached him to the pack. Touch. The buoyant pack crumpled then reshaped as he touched it. Inches. He swept at it, banging his hand down past the horns of the mine onto the pack. It bobbed away like a struck ball, and he reeled it in on its line, clutching it to him like a child who had avoided a road accident, feeling weakness envelope his body.

Eventually, he moved on, holding the packs closer to him by their lines, making slower progress but gradually sensing some kind of courage return. He ran up against the inner net, separating the outer basin of the harbour from the submarine pens, almost before he saw it in the light of his lamp. He clung to it with a kind of desperate relief which surprised him. He realized how much his nerves had been strained already. He released the net eventually, dropping down towards the bottom, dragging the unwilling packs with him. His lamp searched ahead of him. The mud and silt, its lightest elements disturbed and lifted by his movement, drifted up to meet him and almost obscured what he sought. The net ended some four or five feet from the bottom. He gripped it and slid under, pulling the packs after him.

He swam on immediately he had checked his bearings and the time. The mine cables were fewer, as if he had moved above the tree-line for these growths. Soon, they straggled out. The water became slightly warmer, and it appeared lighter. He checked his watch, then ascended twenty feet. Here, he waited, then climbed another twenty feet, waited again. Nerves began to plague him now, the need for action, for arrival, nudging at him, irritating him.

253

His head bobbed above the surface. The packs lay below him at the end of their lines. The row of concrete pens was in front of him. He counted. Fifth along. Lights, noise – no, no noise, just plenty of light. The gates of the pen were closed.

Proteus was in there. He had got to within fifty yards of his destination.

Pasvik the grocer studied the harbour through his night-glasses. He squatted on a blanket which protected his buttocks from the cold of the damp ground. Beneath the blanket he had spread a ground sheet. He had a hamper of food beside him, and he had his back to a tall, old tree.

He moved the glasses up, and the dim, night images blurred and smeared until they were lit with the glow of the submarine pens. He refocused, and he could see, with some degree of clarity, the lights in the fifth pen and a shadowy bulk beyond them that must be the British submarine behind the high gates. Good.

He lowered the glasses. No one would come up here in this weather, but he had a spare blanket to throw over the small dish aerials he had set up alongside him. Clark would be unable to communicate with the Nimrod from within the concrete pen without his messages, and those of the Nimrod, being relayed through the two aerials situated on a small knoll overlooking the harbour of Pechenga, the one with narrow beam facility directed towards Clark, the other, capable of handling broad-beam signals, directed towards the Nimrod.

Pasvik had no fear as he sat there, waiting for the first transmission. He was patient, warmly dressed, and he was engaged in a flatteringly important piece of espionage. However, a dim and long-past regret seemed to move sluggishly in his awareness like a tide coming slowly in. He realized it would be his companion while he remained on the knoll, hidden by the trees. He voiced it.

"Ah, Ivan, Ivan," he murmured, "remember the times we used to come here, eh? Remember?"

A chill, gusty wind plucked his sighs away and scattered them over the darkness of the harbour.

Clark bobbed in the water beneath the repaired propeller of the *Proteus*. He was exhausted after climbing the gate into the pen, exhausted in a subtler, more insidious way by the tension of waiting, of absorbing the routine of the guards patrolling the pen, of choosing his moment to slip over the gate and down into the water. The good fortune that no one appeared to be working on the submarine did little to erase his weariness.

254

Despite their buoyancy, the packs were like leaden weights beneath the surface. His arms ached from them and from the dead-weight of his own body. Now he had to climb the stern of the *Proteus*, to the aft escape hatch. He did not even want to try, could not entertain the idea of beginning. His air tanks and weighted belt he had left on the bottom of the pen. Yet it was the weight of the packs that unnerved him.

The repairs appeared almost complete. There were a number of scarred and buckled hull plates, but the propeller possessed new blades, the rudder fin and the hydroplanes gleamed with new metal. He looked up. The hull of the *Proteus* loomed above him. He groaned inwardly. His feet, flipperless again, rested on a rung beneath the surface, his hands had hold of another rung of the inspection track up the rudder. Tiny, separate *pitons* in the rock-face of the hull. He looked around him. A guard, bored and dulled by routine, turned at the end of his patrol, and walked back out of sight along the pen. Clark heaved his body out of the water and into the irregular rhythm of his ascent. His wet feet slipped, his hands wanted to let go, but he climbed up the rudder, level with the huge fifteen-bladed propeller, until he could clamber onto the hull, dragging the two packs behind him. There, he paused. Along the smoothness of the hull, on the whale's back, was the impression of the escape hatch, a circle cut in grey, shiny dough with a shaping knife. It was sixty feet from where he crouched.

He raised himself, pressing back against the high fin of the rudder, in its shadow to escape the white lights glaring down from the roof of the pen. The guard he had seen, on the starboard side of the *Proteus*, was half-way along its length, back to him. The other guard, on the port side, had almost reached the extent of his patrol, in the dimness of the other end of the pen. He would not make it to the hatch, open and close it after him, before that guard turned and was able to see him. He waited, the tension wearing at him immediately and violently. He felt inadequate to the demands made upon his physical strength, his nervous system.

A voice called out, and he believed for a long moment that a third guard, one he had not spotted, had seen him and was addressing him. But the voice was distant. He watched, heart pounding, as the port guard moved out of sight behind the bulk of the *Proteus*, presumably having been hailed by his companion on the starboard side. It was his chance, perhaps his only one. He weighed the two packs, one in either hand. An obstacle race. He remembered basic training from long ago; fatigues and punishment and discipline like a thin crust of ice over sadism. He gritted his teeth. He'd run up sand dunes carrying two packs then.

Then he began running, hunched up with fear and the weight of the packs, his feet threatening to slide on the smooth metal of the hull. Fifty feet, forty, thirty –

The packs began to slither on the hull, restraining him. His breath began to be difficult to draw, his heart made a hideous noise. Then he slid like a baseball player for the plate, legs extended and reached the hatch. Feverishly, he turned the wheel, unlocking it. Two turns, three, four. His head bobbed up and down like that of a feeding bird. No one. He raised the hatch, and slid into a sitting position on its edge. His feet fumbled for the ladder, and he climbed into the hatch, packs pushed in first and almost dragging him with them; then he closed the hatch behind him, allowing his breath to roar and wheeze in the sudden and complete darkness. He slipped from the ladder and landed on the lower hatch of the chamber. He rubbed his arms, and his body remained doubled over as if in supplication. It was another five minutes before he could bring himself to move again. He unsealed one of the packs – right hand good – and rummaged in one of its pockets. He removed a bundle, and flicked on his lamp to inspect it. Blue, faded blue overalls. He stood up, unrolling the bundle, taking out the socks and boots and putting them on. Then he donned the overalls. His immersion suit was still damp, but the effect might look like sweat, with luck. He patted the breast pocket, feeling the ID there. If the repair and maintenance crew had a specially issued ID for this pen and this job, he still would not be blown as soon as he was challenged. Not with that ID.

He stowed the two packs in the chamber, deflating the second one, securing them to the ladder in the wall. If someone used the hatch, they would be found. He, however, dared not be seen carrying them inside the submarine. His watch showed twelve-fifty. He switched out the lamp, and stowed it with the packs. He would be back within an hour. They should be safe.

Cautiously, he turned the wheel of the lower hatch, then lifted it a couple of inches. He peered into the room housing the electric motors. It appeared empty. He pulled back the hatch and stepped onto the ladder – imagining for a moment Ardenyev or someone like him making his entry in the same manner – closing the hatch behind him and locking it.

He looked around the engine room, rubbing his hands tiredly through his short hair, untidying his appearance. He looked at his hands. They possessed that wrinkled, white, underwater deadness. He thrust them into his pockets as he stared down at the main turbine shaft running across the length of the room. There appeared to be little or no sign of damage. *Proteus* was almost ready to go. She could be taken out of Pechenga and into the Barents Sea on her turbines,

256

even on the electric motors whose bulk surrounded him now. If "Leopard" worked –

He cautiously opened the bulkhead door into the turbine room. Empty. The submarine was silent around him, huge, cathedral-like, unmanned. Clark presumed the ratings were being kept in their accommodation under guard, and the officers in the wardroom. Lloyd would be in the control room, more likely in his cabin, also guarded. He looked down at his creased overalls. A uniform would have been an impossible disguise to have transported in one of the packs. A pity.

He entered the manoeuvring room, aft of the nuclear reactor. For a moment he thought it, too, was empty. Then a figure appeared from behind one section of the computer housing. He was short, almost bald, and dressed in a white laboratory coat. He carried a clipboard, and when he saw Clark, adjusted his glasses and studied him.

"What do you want?"

"Who are you?" Clark replied in Russian. There was an instant, well-learned wariness behind the thick spectacles. Clark continued, "What are you doing here?"

The man was already proffering the clipboard, but then resisted the craven instinct. He did not recognize Clark, and would, presumably, have known which ones to be wary of. Clark appeared officer-like, perhaps, but he did not suggest KGB. He lacked swagger, the birthright.

"Who are you?" the man in the white coat insisted.

Clark reached into his breast pocket. Aubrey had insisted, pressing it upon him like a talisman. A red ID card. Clark tried to remove it insolently, and waved it briefly at the other man.

"OK?" he said. "Or do you want my birth certificate as well?" He laughed as coarsely as he could. "Don't say you don't think I have one."

"I wasn't going to –" the man said. Clark took the clipboard. He understood enough to realize that the technician was from a naval laboratory or testing centre. He riffled the sheets of graph paper. He was checking to make certain that none of the machinery in the manoeuvring room was essential to, or part of, "Leopard". Perhaps – Clark suppressed a grin here – he was even trying to locate the back-up system. He handed the clipboard back to the technician.

"I don't understand all that bullshit, Comrade Doctor," he said in a belligerently unintelligent voice. The technician succeeded in quashing the sneer that tried to appear on his face. "See you."

Clark, hands in pockets, tried a swaggering, lazy, confident slouch out of the manoeuvring room into the tunnel through the reactor. Pausing only for a moment to register that the reactor had not been shut down, he opened the door into the control room. As he had expected, it was not empty. There was no sign of Lloyd or any of the British officers, but white-coated men and a handful of armed guards had occupied the control room, like terrorists in a foreign embassy. Undoubtedly, every piece of machinery and equipment was being tested and examined during the hours when the crew were confined to their quarters. *Proteus* would be a known, familiar thing by the time they had finished. A dog-eared book, a faded woman lacking all mystery. They would possess every secret, half-secret and secure piece of design, knowledge and equipment she had to yield. The computers would be drained, the sonars analysed, the inertial navigation system studied, the communications systems and codes learned by rote.

Clark did not believe that Aubrey had envisaged how much and how valuable would be the information gained from the temporary imprisonment of the *Proteus*. However, Aubrey was right to believe that "Leopard" was the cherry on the cake. This was the present, "Leopard" was the future. He slouched his way across the control room. No one paid him more attention than to look up, and glance down once more. He had acquired the swagger. *Exaggerate it,* Aubrey had said, fingering the red ID card. *However ridiculous and opera buffa you think it is, it will work. You are an immortal.* And then Aubrey had smiled, cat-like and with venom. The red ID card claimed he was a KGB officer.

Clark stepped out of the control room into the corridor. There was a single guard opposite a door, no more than a few yards from him. The guard turned to him. Clark waved the red ID and the guard relaxed at once. He was a young, conscripted marine.

"I want a word with our gallant British captain," Clark drawled. "See we're not disturbed, OK?" The marine nodded. He had probably never met a KGB man of any rank in his life. He had an entire and trusting awe of the red card. Aubrey had been right. Clark opened the door without knocking, and closed it behind him.

Lloyd had been reading, and had dropped off to sleep with the light above his bunk left on. He awoke, startled, fuzzy-eyed.

"Who are you –?" The book resting on his chest slipped to the floor as he stood up. Clark bolted the door, then leaned against it. "Who are you?" Lloyd repeated, more irate than disturbed.

"The Seventh Cavalry," Clark said softly, then put his finger to his lips.

"What? You're an American –" Lloyd studied Clark, his manner, features and dress. His face went from shock to hope to suspicion. "What is this?" he asked with surprising bitterness. To Clark, the man looked tired, dull, captive.

"No trick." Clark sat on the end of Lloyd's bunk. The captain of the *Proteus* hunched away from him. Clark said, in a louder voice and in very accented English, "Just a few simple question about your sailing orders." Lloyd looked as if Clark had proved something to his satisfaction. "I'm here –" Clark grinned, despite himself, "– to repair 'Leopard' and help you get out of here."

Lloyd appeared dumbfounded. "Rubbish –" he began.

"No kidding. Look, I can spend hours trying to convince you who I am. How about one simple thing, to prove my credentials?" He paused, but Lloyd remained blank-faced. "Your daughter has a pet tortoiseshell cat called Penelope and a white rabbit called Dylan."

Lloyd's mouth dropped open, then he smiled and tears prompted by relief and remembered domesticity welled in his eyes. He took Clark's hand. "Who are you?" he asked.

"Ethan Clark, Navy Intelligence."

"Assigned to 'Chessboard Counter'?"

"Right."

"We didn't meet."

"I don't think it matters – uh?"

"No. How the devil can you repair 'Leopard'? Alone? In these surroundings?"

"First, I talk and you listen. Then you tell me everything that happened and everything your people think might have gone wrong. OK?"

"OK. You begin, then."

"Just a moment." Clark raised his voice, and again produced the heavy accent. "Your sailing orders. We already know a great deal. Just fill in a few details, OK?" He smiled and tossed his head in the direction of the locked door. "Now listen," he said.

"We will be with you before first light, Valery. I want *you* to conduct me around your prize." Dolohov was in a mood that Ardenyev could not match and which did not interest him. Behind him, through the glass doors into the mess, Balan and Teplov and the others were raucously into a round of obscene songs and another crate of vodka. The drink and the noise whirled in his head, separating him as surely as static would have done from the admiral's voice.

"Yes, sir," he said as enthusiastically as he could.

"Panov's weather has improved. He's reached Moscow. He'll be here in a few hours' time. Then we'll fly up to you by chopper." The old man might have been a relative reciting his holiday travel arrangements. Ardenyev almost giggled at the thought, and the image it evoked. Old thin legs wrapped in a travelling-blanket, back bent under the weight of a suitcase, and the admiral's mind full of worries about the toilets, obtaining food in transit and would he be there to meet him with the car. "What's all that noise?"

"A – small party, sir."

"Excellent, excellent. Polish vodka, I presume."

"Yes, sir." The old man's voice sounded boringly full of reminiscence. Ardenyev hoped it was not so.

"Good, good." Dolohov sounded offended. Ardenyev cursed the casualness of his tone of voice, his lack of control. Even when half-drunk, he should be able to pretend respect. "Make sure you're sober by the time I arrive, Valery. Understand?" The question was a slap across the face.

"Yes, sir."

"See you in, say, seven hours' time? Enjoy your party."

The receiver purred in Ardenyev's ear. His mood was suddenly, inexplicably deflated. He felt sober and dry-mouthed. He looked at his watch. One o'clock. Dolohov and his scientist from Novosibirsk would be here by eight. Shrugging, he pushed open the door to the officers' mess, to be greeted by a roar of welcome and insult.

The two packs were still in the aft escape chamber. He removed his overalls, rolled them into a bundle, and stowed them in the pack containing the explosives. This he took with him as he climbed back through the hatch into the room below. He hid the pack in a steel cupboard containing repair equipment. Then, he once more closed himself into the darkness of the chamber. He flicked on his lamp, and checked the second pack. He removed a tool-kit already clipped to a belt, and two bulky packages which he strapped to his thighs. He had an image, for a moment, of his ridiculous appearance if he were seen and caught on top of the hull of the *Proteus*, and then it vanished in a rush of nerves and tension. He had trembled, and the pool of light cast on the floor of the chamber wobbled.

He turned the wheel of the hatch, and lifted it. The hard light of the pen poured in and he felt exposed and vulnerable. His legs felt weak, despite the reviving swallow of rum Lloyd had given him, and the coffee he had ordered from the galley in his KGB persona. He waited, but the nerves did not seem to abate. He cursed them silently. He wanted to drop from the ladder to the floor of the chamber. He held on, grinding his teeth audibly, his eyes squeezed tight shut. It was like a malarial illness. His whole body was shaking, revolting against the idea of leaving the dark in order to climb into the spotlit brightness of the submarine pen.

Then the mood passed. The illness retreated, and he was able to swallow the phlegm in his throat, and to feel strength returning to his legs. He lifted the hatch once more, and raised his head above it. The

260

curve of the *Proteus*'s hull prevented him from being able to see either of the guards, and he waited. Two minutes later, the port guard appeared, his head bobbing along the horizon of the hull. He was smoking a cigarette. Clark waited until he had turned in his patrol, with hardly a glance at the submarine, and the starboard guard had come into view, making for the seaward end of the pen. Still only two of them. He was able to diminish what opposed and endangered him to these two men. two against one, that's all it was. He felt calmed.

He waited, but without the bout of nerves returning, until the two men had passed out of sight, and returned. Each patrol, from the point opposite the escape hatch back towards the bow of the submarine and returning to the escape hatch, took three minutes and a few seconds. The time, however, when they both had their backs to him was less, since they were not on identical courses. Two and a half minutes of running or working time.

He watched them, heads down, one of them whistling tunelessly and the other slouching with both hands in his pockets, Kalashnikov slung over his shoulder, until they passed out of his vision towards the bow of the *Proteus*. Then he climbed out of the hatch onto the smooth curve of the hull, crouching like a sprinter on his blocks for a moment as he looked over his shoulder. Neither man had turned, and he straightened and ran for the rudder fin sixty feet away.

He hid in its shadow, hardly breathing more rapidly than normal, then climbed swiftly down the *pitons* in its smoothed, repaired surface to the water. He held one of the propeller blades and trod water gently.

Lloyd had given him Hayter's assessment of the damage to "Leopard". The submarine officer had said, in simpler and clearer terms, what had sprung instantly to Quin's mind when he heard the estimate of damage the submarine must have sustained. Clark, by seeing for himself the repairs and hearing Lloyd's account of his experiences and his conversations with Ardenyev, agreed with Hayter and Quin. At least one, and possibly as many as three or four, of the hull sensors must have been damaged. In themselves, Clark knew with a heavy sensation in his stomach, they would not account for the manner and degree of "Leopard's" malfunction, but without their being repaired the equipment would never work effectively. Before investigating the back-up system which had never cut in, Clark had to inspect and repair the sensors on the outer hull.

When Lloyd had described his conversations with Valery Ardenyev, Clark had sat listening with a faint smile on his lips. He had known it, all along. It had to be Ardenyev. Even the wine and the caviar would have been in character, just as would killing Lloyd if it had proven necessary.

Clark watched the two guards approach the seaward end of the pen once more. The whistler was now being echoed by his companion, who provided a shrill descant or counter-melody as the fit took him. They laughed at their musical antics frequently, the noise having a hollow quality under the bright roof. Lloyd had confirmed that work on *Proteus* had stopped early the previous evening, as a delaying tactic. The repair crew might return at any moment, just as the man from Novosibirsk might also arrive in minutes or hours. Clark felt the weakness pass through him once more, like the debilitation of a stomach infection, and he realized that it was Lloyd's report of Panov's expected arrival, learned from Ardenyev, that had struck him more forcibly than anything else. It all hinged on the weather in Siberia; everything. It was that random, uncontrollable element that had thrown him.

One of the guards began telling a joke. The two men loitered at the seaward end of the pen, giggling at each other across the stretch of imprisoned water. Clark ducked further into the shadow of the propeller, only his head out of the water. Clark's impatience began to mount. Then some vestigial fear of a *michman* or even an officer arriving seemed to prompt the storyteller, and they began to move again, the storyteller's voice rising in volume as the bulk of the *Proteus* interposed itself between himself and his audience of one.

Clark ducked beneath the surface of the water, and switched on his lamp. Its weak beam would probably not be noticed, reflecting through the water, unless someone looked very hard. The two guards wouldn't. He swam along the hull, only a few feet below the surface, holding in his mind as clearly as a slide projected upon a screen a diagram of the hull showing the locations of the numerous sensor-plates. His left hand smoothed its way along the hull, and his lamp flickered and wavered over the metal. Eventually, as his breath began to sing in his head and his eardrums seemed to be swelling to fill his head and mouth, he touched against one of them. A shallow tear-drop dome of thin metal protected the sensor beneath. It was intact, undamaged.

He rose to the surface, breathed in deeply three times, then ducked beneath the surface again. He began to locate the sensors more quickly now, as if he had found the thread that would lead him through the maze. Surprisingly, and to his relief, the wafer-thin titanium domes over the sensors seemed to have withstood damage from both the torpedoes. Beneath each dome lay either sonar or magnetic or thermal signal detectors and, within the domes, baffles like those in a stereo loudspeaker guided and channelled any signals, whether from enemy sonar or other detection equipment, into a transducer. The signals were then fed via fibre optics into "Leopard", where they were analysed, reverse phased and then returned to the transducer. The process was virtually instantaneous. The effect of this was to nullify or deflect any enemy's detection transmissions. The signals returned to the enemy vessel unaltered, thereby confirming that they had not registered or been deflected off another vessel. In addition, some of the hull sensors worked to damp the noise emissions from the *Proteus*'s propellers and hydroplanes, rendering the submarine ninety-eight percent immune to detection. Clark had to assume that some sensors, at least, would be damaged.

Four of them undamaged, then five. It had taken him almost thirty minutes, working on the starboard side of the hull and avoiding the patrol of the guard, who now had a tiny transistor radio clasped to his ear. Clark had heard a sliver of pop music once as he ducked beneath the surface. When the man had gone again, Clark dived and swam down, following the curve of the hull until he surfaced on the port side. Checking the sensors on that side took him twenty minutes. He worked with greater and greater confidence and speed. He moved towards the stern of the submarine, where the damage was more evident to the lamp and to his fingertips. Then he found the first damaged sensor-cowl. The titanium skin had been torn away, whether during the attack or the subsequent repairs he could not guess, and beneath it the delicate transducer had been torn, smashed, rendered useless. In the light of his lamp, he saw the tangled mess of wiring within; it looked like a ruined eye. He cursed, bobbed to the surface, exhaled and drew a new breath, then flipped down towards the bottom, his lamp flickering over the rust-stained, oil-smeared concrete until he saw, to his left, the huddled bulk of his air tanks.

He strapped on the weighted belt, then the tanks, and began swimming back towards the surface. As soon as the short helical antenna clamped to the side of his head broke surface, he spoke into the throat microphone. He described the damage to the hull sensor and its location, and only moments later Quin began speaking excitedly in his ear, sounding very distant and obscured by static.

"You'll have to replace the transducer unit, of course – that will be quickest. You have three of those units with you. As to the cowl, you'll have to do without that. It should be OK. The domes are normally water filled."

Clark acknowledged the instructions, and swam down again to the damaged sensor. Immediately, he began to clear the mass of loose wiring and circuitry and fragmented glass and metal out of the hole, which was no more than a foot in diameter at its widest point. A small shell-hole.

The cleared depression in the hull looked merely empty, of no purpose. He released the locking ring and prised the transducer from

263

its seat. Once he had to surface and request Quin to repeat part of the procedure, but he worked swiftly and with a keen and sharp satisfaction. The new unit plugged directly into the box of the signal converter. It took him no more than ten minutes to complete the task. He swam back to the stern of the *Proteus* and rose slowly and cautiously to the surface, once more in the shadow of the propeller.

The guard was looking at him, looking directly at him. He had to be able to see him.

Clark waited, his hand holding the zipper of his immersion suit, ready to reach for the Heckler & Koch .22. Then the guard blew out his cheeks and spat into the water. The noise was sufficient for Clark to grip the handle of the small pistol tightly, and almost draw it from his suit. The guard seemed to watch the small blob of spittle intently, then he began his desultory walk back to the other end of the pen. He had been staring absently at some point on the hull, some part of the stern, and had not seen Clark's head bob to the surface. Clark zipped up his suit once more, as quickly as his nerveless hands would allow, then he removed the air tanks from his back. They clanged softly, like a sounding bell, against one of the propeller blades, and he held his breath. There was no sound from the guards, and he hooked the webbing of the tanks over one of the propeller blades so that they hung below the surface.

He looked up, then at his watch. Two-fifty-seven. Shaking away the tiredness that seemed to have insinuated itself behind his eyes while he studied his watch – an intent, staring moment which seemed hypnotic, sleep-inducing – he began climbing the hull again, ascending the rudder fin until he could see both guards, backs to him. He had perhaps a minute before the port side guard reached the limit of his patrol. He scuttled out along the hull, unreeling a fine nylon line from around his waist. He had to check every sensor on the stern of the hull in full view. One head had only to turn, one figure emerge from the sail of the *Proteus*, one officer or *michman* come into the pen to check on the guards, Panov to arrive, eager to inspect "Leopard" –

He placed the magnetic pad at the end of the nylon line against the hull, jerked hard on the line, then abseiled down the curving hull, watching the port side guard continually. The sensor was beneath one of his feet, then level with his eyes. He ran one hand over the titanium tear-drop. Undamaged. He looked at the guard, almost out of sight behind the swelling midships section of the submarine, then clambered back up the line to the top of the hull. One.

He saw the starboard guard little more than half-way up the pen, his feet jigging unconsciously to the noise coming from the tiny radio. He swung down on the starboard side until he was level with the tear-drop dome. It was loose, and he cursed silently. He pulled a screwdriver from his kit, and prised at the thin titanium. Beneath it, the sensor appeared undamaged. He juggled his lamp in his hand, and switched it on. He checked, feeling the arm that gripped the line begin to quiver with nerves – guards nearly at the end of the pen, moving into the shadows beyond the hard lights – and his body heating with the tension. Undamaged – yes, undamaged. He loosened his grip on the lamp, and it dangled from his wrist again on its thick strap. He made to replace the screwdriver in his belt, and it slipped from his fingers – the guard was out of sight behind the swell of the midships, and in the shadow – and slid down the hull with a rattling noise that sounded deafening in the intent silence. It plopped like a large fish into the water. They must have heard it. He clambered, feet slipping, then able to grip, body hunched, almost jerking upwards on the line as if he were a fish and was hooked, waiting for the challenge, the shout of recognition at any moment.

He flattened himself on the hull, bunching the nylon line beneath his body, feeling his whole frame quivering. Another malarial attack. He could not stop himself shaking.

"Progress report," he heard in his earpiece. The port guard was in sight again, meandering down the pen towards him. Then the starboard guard came into sight, chewing and cocking his head into the tinny noises of the transistor radio at his ear. "Progress report", Aubrey requested again in his ear, this time with more asperity. Clark wanted to howl into his throat mike for the crazy old man to shut up.

The guard passed beneath him on the port side, then the starboard guard was level with him again. The radio made tiny, scratchy noises. A Western pop station, beamed in from Norway or Sweden.

"Lend us your fucking radio," the port guard called across to his companion in a not unamiable manner. "Bored stiff."

"I'm not," his companion replied, facing him. "You bloody Ukrainians are all the same – scroungers."

"Clark – progress report." *Shut up, shut up –*

"Fuck off." Clark craned his neck. The port guard, the taller of the two with the cropped haircut and the stooping shoulders, had unslung his rifle, and was pointing it at the man on the starboard side. "Hand over your radio, or I'll fire," he demanded.

The man on the starboard side laughed. He wore spectacles and a thin, weak moustache and looked no more than fifteen. He, too, unslung his rifle, and pointed it across the water with one hand, the other still pressing the radio to his ear. "Bang, bang," he said, hooting with laughter when he had done so.

"Piss off."

"Progress report, Clark. Clark?" *Shut up, shut up –*

Clark knew what would happen next, and knew it would be audible. Sharp, painful bleeps of sound, like morse dashes, to attract his attention, then a continuous tone like that of a telephone that has been disconnected because the subscriber has moved. Both guards looked up. Clark squeezed himself flatter against the top of the hull, praying for the curvature to be sufficient, to hide him like high ground or a horizon.

"What's that?"

"Dunno. Fucking radio. Our lot trying to jam it." The starboard guard laughed again, a thin high cackle as if his voice had not yet broken.

"Race you to the other end, you skinny, underfed Ukrainian!"

"What about –?"

"Ready, set – *go*!"

The noise of their boots echoed off the concrete walls and roof of the pen. The tone stopped, and then began again in his head. Clark whispered intently into his throat-mike.

"For Chrissake, get off my back, Aubrey!" He went on quivering, his body seeming to jump with the detonations of their footsteps bouncing off the roof, until Aubrey replied.

"Clark – what is wrong?"

"I'm lying on the fucking hull, man, with two goons training for the Olympics right below me. I can't *talk* to you!"

A few seconds later – he could hear a thin, breathless cheer from the far end of the pen as the taller guard won the race – Aubrey replied stiffly and formally, "Very well. Report as soon as you can."

"OK, OK."

"And again?" the shorter guard called angrily.

"You're on. Ten roubles on this one?"

"Twenty, you Ukrainian bullshitter!"

"Ready, set – *go*! Hey, you jumped the gun, you cheating sod!"

Then the bootsteps rained down from the roof again as they charged towards the seaward end of the pen. Clark lay icily still now, his tension expended with his anger, his sense of time oblivious to anything but the slow passage of seconds on the watch-face he held in front of his eyes.

The starboard guard won, by virtue of a flying start, and crowed and pranced. His companion, now his deadly rival, challenged him to a return. They regained their breath, watched each other like combatants for a fortune in prize money, crouched into sprinting starts, and then began running on the call of the taller man. Clark got to his knees. Their row would bring someone, soon. He scuttled along the hull, careless of the noise he made, fixed the pad, and lowered

266

himself feverishly down the nylon rope, checked the undamaged sensor, climbed the rope again, imagined the ragged breathing of the two runners, waited until he could hear them arguing with out-of-breath shouts, and swung down the port side of the hull. He was elated by the clownish behaviour and the stupidity of the two young guards; almost reckless with confidence. Undamaged. He climbed the line again.

They were still arguing, their voices coming from the far end of the pen. He could dimly discern them, shadows in shadow. He moved back along the hull, lowered himself on the port side again – the two men had moved slightly to starboard of the bow of the submarine – and checked another sensor. The titanium blister was dented, but undisturbed. Then the starboard side, his luck beginning to extend beyond the point at which it was simply acceptable and becoming instead a source of anxiety, where he checked two more sensors. He was almost level with the rudder fin again, almost finished –

Another voice, a snarling petty-officer voice, and silence from the two guards. Berating, angry, loud. Their parentage was stripped from them, then their maturity, then their manhood. Layers of the onion, until they would be left with nothing but total humiliation and punishment duties. They would be replaced, the new guards would be fearfully alert, punctilious in their patrols. The crushing reprimand went on and on.

Clark lowered himself down the port side of the hull again. The plates were scarred, as if the metal had been lashed with a giant whip. He knew what he would find. A weal like a furrow lay along one hull plate, and whatever had caused it had crushed the wafer-thin titanium in upon the sensor beneath it. He reached into his belt, moving with feverish haste now as the *michman's* voice rose again, perhaps towards a peroration. He drew a smaller, stubbier screwdriver and jabbed it into the slot on the locking ring and heaved. It moved, and then turned. He lifted it clear and snapped it into a hook on his belt. As he prised out the transducer he could see the damage clearly. Shattered fragments fell from the transducer and rattled and slid down the hull to the water.

Bare wires. The sheathing was cut through, and half the wiring was severed. Dangling from the end was an ABS multi-pin plug. Half of it. Half a smashed multi-pin plug. He registered it with helpless fury. Silence. The *michman* had finished. Christ –

A door slammed, and then there was silence again, a heavy, ringing silence. He was alone in the pen for perhaps a few minutes at most. Perspiration drenched him. He wiped the back of one hand over his face.

"I got problems," he announced. "Stern sensor fourteen – one of the sonar signal nullifiers. The wiring behind the transducer's a hell of a mess."

He continued to lever at the wiring with the screwdriver while he waited for Quin to reply.

"What extent is the damage?"

The rest of the transducer slid away with a noise like the claws of a crab on metal. Then it plopped into the water. Clark hefted his lamp and shone it into the hole.

"Bad. Most of the wiring has been sheared; but there's worse. The connector's smashed."

"Can you check beyond the breaks?"

"Maybe."

"Can you see the socket and the box?"

"Yes."

Clark peered into the hole. He tidied the sheared and twisted wiring to one side and looked again. The wires reached the fibre optics converter box on the underside of the outer hull.

"Remove it complete," Quin instructed. "Fit a new one. And Clark – "

"Yes?"

"There is a second plug, for the fibre optics. A bayonet fitting. Be careful. The first has forty pins, and it fits only one way."

"Right."

Clark looked at his watch. One minute since the door had slammed. He reached in, pressing his cheek against the hull, feeling the activity within the submarine as a slight vibration. His fingers flexed in the narrow space, snagged and cut on the exposed, shorn wires, and then his fingertips had hold of the upper section of the box. He pulled. Nothing happened. He pulled again, surprise on his face. The converter box would not budge.

"It's jammed," he said. "Jammed."

The door slammed. Marching boots, double time, the voice of the *michman* savagely drilling the two replacement guards. Clark clung to the nylon line and the converter box and prayed for the fifty-fifty chance to work in his favour.

The boots clattered down the starboard side of the *Proteus*. He had a moment or two yet –

"Have you got it? Can you see what's wrong?" Quin was frightened.

Clark heaved at it, curling his fingers round the edge of the converter box. Nothing moved. One finger touched the clip – *clips, strap*, he'd forgotten the clips and the strap securing the box – he flipped open the catch with his thumb, felt it loosen, and then gripped the box again. He gritted his teeth and strained. His arm shot out of the hole and he wriggled on the nylon line, holding on to the dangling wires and the box as the velocity with which he had jerked them free threatened to make him drop them. The *michman*'s voice snapped out orders to the new guards. In a moment, they would appear on the port side –

He ripped open one of the two thick packs and drew out a replacement converter box already wired to the transducer. He fed the complete unit into the hole as carefully as he could. He pushed it forward. Then he let go of the rope, dangling by its tight, cutting hold on his armpits, and shone his lamp. The *michman* had stopped shouting. He was watching the two guards doubling on the spot. Push – no, slight adjustment – push, get it into the clips – push home, feel for the strap ends, yes – hook them over, clamp the catch. He fitted the fibre optics plug, then fastened the transducer into place, and fitted the locking ring to holding it. The *michman* had ordered them to stop doubling.

Clark's arms felt lifeless and weak. He heaved at the nylon line, but his body hardly moved. His feet scrabbled on the smooth hull. The *michman* ordered the second new guard to follow him. It was like a yelled order to Clark. He clambered back up the line. Fifty feet to the hatch. Seconds only.

He ran. He heaved open the hatch, not caring any longer whether or not he had been seen, and tumbled into darkness, the hatch thudding softly shut on its rubber seals behind him. He lay breathless and aching and uncaring in the safe, warm darkness of the escape chamber, every part of his body exhausted.

"Well done, Quin," Aubrey offered, and watched the slow bloom of self-satisfaction on the man's face. He was difficult to like, but Aubrey had ceased to despise him. Quin was back in the land of the living, as it were. Flattery, cajolement, even threat had all played a part in his rehabilitation. Finally, however, Aubrey had seen the danger to his invention, his project, overcome and prompt Quin. The man would not surrender "Leopard" without some effort on his part.

"Thank you," Quin returned. Then his face darkened, and he shook his head. "It's almost impossible, " he added. "I don't know whether Clark has the necessary concentration to keep this up –"

"I understand the strain he must be under," Aubrey said, "but there's no other way."

"I'm – I'm sorry – stupid behaviour earlier – apologies –" Each word seemed wrenched from Quin, under duress. Aubrey respected the effort it was costing the cold, egotistical man to offer an explanation of himself.

"Quite all right."

"It's just that, well, now I don't want them to get their hands on it, you see —"

"Quite."

"It is the only thing of importance to me, you see." He looked down at his hands. "Shouldn't say that, but I'm afraid it's true." He looked up again, his eyes fierce. "Damn them, they mustn't have it!"

"Mr. Aubrey?" There was something trying to force itself like a broken bone through Eastoe's frosty reserve.

"Yes, Squadron Leader?"

"We have some blips on the radar. Four of them."

"Yes?"

"Coming up rapidly from one of the airfields on the Kola Peninsular. Not missiles, the trace is wrong for that. Four aircraft."

"I see. Range?"

"Not more than thirty miles. They'll be with us in three minutes or even less."

"With us? I don't understand."

"They've already crossed into Norwegian airspace, Mr. Aubrey. They didn't even hesitate."

THIRTEEN:

Concealment

They were MiG-23s, code-named Flogger-B, single-seat, all-weather interceptors. Four of them. Even Aubrey could recognize them, in a moment of silhouette that removed him more than forty years to basic aircraft recognition tests at the beginning of the war. A vivid streak of lightning to the north, and the brassy light illuminating the night sky, outlined the nearest of the MiGs. Slim, grey, red-starred on its flank. One wing-tip rose as the aircraft banked slightly, and Aubrey could see the air-to-air missiles beneath the swing wing in its swept-back position.

Immediately, Eastoe was talking to him. "Mr. Aubrey, they're MiG-23s, interceptors. The flight leader demands to know our mission and the reason for our invasion of sensitive airspace."

"What is their intention, would you say?" Quin was staring out of the window of the Nimrod, watching the slim, shark-like silhouette that had begun to shadow them.

"Shoo us away."

"What course of action do you –?"

"Just a minute, Mr. Aubrey. I've got the Norwegian flight leader calling me. Do you want to listen into this?"

"I don't think so," Aubrey replied wearily. "I am sure I already know what he wishes to say."

"Very well."

The headset went dead, and Aubrey removed it. It clamped his temples and ears, and seemed to cramp and confine thought. He did not like wearing it. Quin did not seem disappointed at Aubrey's decision.

There was another flash of lightning, streaking like bright rain down a window towards the sea. The blare of unreal light revealed the closest of the Northrop F-5s turning to port, away from the Nimrod. Their Norwegian fighter escort had been recalled to Kirkenes. Norway's unwritten agreement, as a member of NATO, with the Soviet Union was that no military exercises or provocative military manoeuvres were undertaken within a hundred miles of the Soviet border. Evidently, the Russians had registered a protest, and their protest had been accepted.

271

Aubrey replaced his headset. "Has our Norwegian escort gone?"

"Yes, Mr. Aubrey. We're on our own."

"Very well. Our signals cannot be intercepted, nor their origin traced so far as Clark is concerned?"

"No. Mr. Aubrey, how long do we need to hang around?"

"For some hours yet."

"Very well." Eastoe sounded grim, but determined. "We'll do what we can. I'll try not to get shepherded out of range."

"If you would."

Aubrey stared at the console on the table between himself and Quin. The hull sensors had been inspected and repaired, yet the achievement of that task had been the completion of the easy and least dangerous element. Clark now had to inspect and, if necessary, repair the back-up system of "Leopard". Aubrey suddenly felt alone, and incompetent.

Eastoe spoke again in his ear. "They're demanding we leave the area. They'll see us off the property."

"You are on our eastbound leg at the moment?"

"Yes. But that won't fool them. They'll have been watching us on radar for a long time. They know we're flying a box pattern."

"But, for the moment, we're secure?"

"Yes –"

The window seemed filled with the belly of the MiG-23. The sight was gone in a moment, and might have begun to seem illusory, except that the nose of the Nimrod tilted violently as Eastoe put the aircraft into a dive.

"Shit –" the co-pilot's voice cried in Aubrey's ear. The Nimrod levelled, and steadied.

"They're not in the mood to waste time," Eastoe commented. "You saw that?"

Aubrey remembered the underbelly, almost white like that of a great hunting fish, and even the red-painted missiles beneath the wing.

"Yes," he said. "What happened?" He ignored Quin's worried face, the man was frightened but there was a determination in him now, replacing the former cunning that had sought only escape.

"One of them buzzed us – and I mean buzzed. Crazy bastard!"

Aubrey paused for a moment. "The aircraft is in your hands, Squadron Leader. All I ask is that we never pass out of range of Clark's transceiver. The rest is up to you."

"*Thank you*, Mr. Aubrey."

The MiG – perhaps the one that had buzzed them – was back on their port wing, slightly above and behind. Shadowing them. It was, Aubrey considered, as unpredictable as a wild creature.

272

Tricia staggered under Hyde's weight, slipped, and fell against the long, high bank. Her breath roared in her ears, but she could feel it in her chest – ragged, loud, heaving. Hyde, unconscious, rolled away from her, slid until he lay at her feet looking sightlessly up at her and was still. Tricia was simply and utterly relieved that she was no longer bearing his weight against one side and across the back of her neck where she had placed his arm. She loathed and hated Hyde at that moment, and even feared him; as if he might wake and attack her himself. She blamed him totally, for every fragment and element of her predicament.

Her body was bathed in perspiration, and her limbs were shaking with weakness. Hyde continued groaning, like a murmured protest at his pain.

"Oh – shut up," she whispered fiercely. "Shut up." The repetition was bitten off, as if she admitted he was not to blame.

She had helped Hyde, often supporting his unconscious weight when he slipped once more from pain into stillness, as they moved north, then west. There had been no effective pursuit. The helicopter had lost sight of them after she had half-dragged, half-shouldered him away from the rise where he had first passed out, into a small copse of trees. A tiny dell, where the dead ferns were long and curving, like the roofs of native huts, had concealed them. Terrified, she had heard legs brushing through heather and ferns, voices near and more distant, the crackle of R/Ts. She had kept her hand over Hyde's mouth, in case he babbled in delirium.

The wound had been ugly, and she knew nothing of medicine or nursing. It had bled a great deal. It seemed that the bullet had not lodged in Hyde's shoulder or chest because there was a small hole near his shoulder blade and a larger hole near his collar-bone. She had seen sufficient television wounds to assume that the bullet had passed straight through. Her knowledge of anatomy was sketchy, and she watched anxiously for blood to appear around his lips. When it did not, she assumed the lungs were undamaged. She did not know what other bones, muscles or organs might reside in the area of the wound. She bound the wound with a torn length of Hyde's own shirt.

Now, under the looming shadow of the long, high bank, she knew she could go no further. Hyde's weight had become intolerable. She could bully him no more, support him no longer. She was hungry, and cold, and impatient of Hyde's helplessness. His repeated groans of pain enraged her.

She knelt by him because he would not quieten. She shook his head carefully, as if it fitted only loosely, her fingers holding his chin. His eyes flickered, but then closed again, as if he wished to exclude

273

her and what she represented. She shook his head more violently. A great weariness possessed her, and she sat instead of squatting on her haunches.

"For God's sake, wake up," she pleaded.

"Uuh," he grunted. She looked at him. His eyes were open.

"You're awake."

"Oh, *Christ!*" he cried in a broken voice, his breath sobbing. "My bloody shoulder." He groaned again.

"You're not delirious?"

"My bloody shoulder won't let me. Where – where are we?"

"Behind the rifle ranges. Are we going to stay here?"

"I'm not going anywhere." Hyde looked at the stars. "I can't go anywhere, Tricia."

"I know."

"Have a quick look around. See if you can find some dense under-growth, a ditch, a trench, a hole in the bank, anything. If we can get under cover, we –" He groaned again.

"Where are the police?" she asked plaintively.

"Searching Cheshire probably," he replied, coughing. She looked anxiously for signs of blood as he wiped his lips. There were none. "Trouble is, we're in Staffordshire. They'll get round to us. I hope."

"They must be looking, surely?"

"I bloody well hope so, darling. I pay my rates and taxes so they can pull me out of holes like this. I'll be writing to my bloody Pom MP if they don't turn up."

She almost laughed at the pronounced accent and the sentiments it expressed. Something lifted from her; not her weariness, but some-thing of her isolation. Hyde sounded more like a human being, less like a liability.

"I'll look," she said, and got up. He turned his head slowly and watched her. He felt tears in his eyes which might simply have been the result of pain and weariness. He did not understand them, and for a few moments he could not prevent them. The pain in his shoulder subsided now that he was resting, but he felt his body could make no further effort, not even to defend itself or the girl. He needed to hide.

The girl came back quickly, almost running.

"No –" he protested, sensing her pursued.

"What? No, it's all right, I've found a hollow, scooped out of the bank. It's almost masked by a bush. Can you come?"

He sat up, rocked, then steadied himself. "Give us a hand, mate."

She tottered, but pulled him to his feet. She hitched his arm across her aching shoulders again, and dragged him along the gully behind the bank, which loomed thirty feet or more above them.

It was less than fifty yards, but she was staggering with tiredness when they reached the bush growing out of the bank. Hyde felt its stiff, resisting branches, the sharp ends and points of old thorns. It had spread and flourished for many years, but he could see behind its present leaflessness the outline of a hole in the bank.

"How far in does it go, do you think?" she said, shivering as she realized she would have to investigate.

"It's all right. No bears left, and no wolves. And no bloody snakes like we've got in Aussie biting your arse when you climb in. Go on, then." He sounded genuinely impatient.

She heaved and struggled with the branches of the leafless bush, then went head-first into the hole. "It smells," he heard her call hollowly.

His cackle degenerated into a cough. "It's those bloody rabbits from Watership Down," he said. "How big is it?"

Her head emerged. "Just big enough for two, if you don't mind a crush."

"You'll have to push me in," he said.

She climbed out, snagging her jacket on thorns, then she helped get him to the bush, lifted some of the whippier branches aside like a curtain, then got her shoulder beneath his buttocks.

"Ready?"

"Yes."

She heaved, and he disappeared into the hole.

"Are you all right?"

"Yes," he answered faintly. "Rearrange the bush when you climb in."

She squeezed into the hole, then turned with difficulty, putting her foot into his back at one point, and reached out, tugging and pulling the bushes back into place as well as she could. Then she slithered backwards until she was bunched up against him.

"Wait a minute," she said, and fumbled in the pockets of the donkey jacket. She rattled the box of matches, fumbled with it, then struck one. "There you are."

Hyde's face looked grey and ill, but he managed to say, "Now I get you alone at last, some bloody Russian puts a contraceptive through my shoulder."

"Yes," she said thoughtfully, already finding the light of the match much too bright and wanting to close her eyes. She shook it out and dropped it. "Are you all – right?" she asked faintly. The darkness closed satisfyingly around her. She was not certain whether his reply was positive or negative, and she did not really think it mattered. She heard him groan once before she fell asleep.

Clark closed the tiny hatch into the space between the outer and the pressure hulls, leaving his helical aerial attached to the surface of the outer hull. The darkness was sudden and intense after the hard lighting from the roof of the pen. He could not stand upright, but bent his head and hunched his back as he waited for his breathing to return to normal, or to an approximation of normality.

He had emerged from the aft escape chamber knowing that the new guards on either side of the submarine would be self-consciously, fearfully alert for any and every unexpected noise and movement. Their peripheral vision would be enhanced by the threats of the senior *michman*, and they had been on duty for only twenty minutes. Yet he had to risk it.

When he recovered in the escape chamber, his arms full of cramp and pain, his whole body exhausted with the effort of abseiling down the hull and climbing it again, he first collected the second pack – left hand bad – from the electric motor room and took it into the chamber. He would have to take both complete packs with him. He was on the point of incarcerating himself between the twin hulls of the *Proteus* until he either repaired the back-up system or was forced to abort and plant the explosives which would melt it into a lump of useless metal.

The hatch fitted to the *Proteus* which allowed access to the inner hull where the blister containing the back-up system was fitted lay thirty feet from the aft escape hatch. He had eased open the hatch a matter of inches, listening with his whole body. When the guards' footsteps moved out of range, precise and regular and unconcerned as clockwork, he opened it fully, climbed out, closed it again, and moved along the hull. He had opened the other hatch, and lowered the first pack in. Then he had closed it and returned, waiting until the next patrol of the pen took the two guards towards the bow before moving the second pack along the top of the hull, dragging it after him as he slithered on his belly, into the space between the hulls.

In the darkness now, the two packs rested at his feet. He was aware, as his breathing calmed, of the way in which the pressure hull curved away on either side of him. He was on a narrow ledge, a metal bridge across a chasm, and he must never forget the fact.

He paused for another moment, his bearings uncertain then assured, and then he hefted the two packs until they no longer dragged on the pressure hull before moving forward. He pushed his feet forward, disregarding the lamp for the moment because his hands were full and because it seemed necessary to establish some sense of mastery over his new and alien environment. Behind him, he paid out the wire from his transceiver to the aerial outside the hull. He felt the hull slope slightly upwards, in ridged steps. Unlike the smooth outer hull, the pressure hull of the *Proteus* did not follow exactly the same outline or shape. His shoulders bent lower as the two hulls narrowed the distance between themselves. Another three steps, and he dropped lightly to his knees. The outer hull seemed to press down upon him in a moment of claustrophobia, and the pressure hull beneath his knees and toes seemed thin, uncertain, narrow. The chasm waited for him on either side.

He switched on the lamp. Ahead of him, where the space between the hulls narrowed like a thin, deep shaft where a miner would have had to work on his back or his stomach to dig the coal, he could see, like the pit-props appropriate to the analogy his mind had discovered, the stanchions growing like grey metal trees between the two hulls, separating and binding them. He moved the torch around him, pressing back the thick, blind darkness. It smelt old, and damp, and empty. The sounds thrumming lightly and occasionally through the pressure hull, the murmur of machinery and air-pumps and filters and voices and electrics and ovens and toilets, seemed completely removed from him and not of human origin.

The outer hull sloped away like the roof of a dome to either side, falling sheer out of sight. He could see the lip where the pressure hull followed its shape on either side. The ledge seemed narrow and fragile. He flicked the torch's thin beam deliberately forward again. A hump like a turtle shell or the scaled back of an armadillo hunched in the shadows beyond the stanchion trees. The sight of it relieved him. He fixed the packs to his belt by their clips once more, and lay flat. He began pushing the packs in front of him, slithering awkwardly forward, alarmed by the noise he seemed to be making.

He began to weave through the stanchions, thrusting and pushing the packs in turn ahead of him, then using his elbows and knees to moved his body forward behind them. Whenever he flicked on the lamp – needing its light now as reassurance as well as a guide – the grey humped back of the turtle shell remained ahead of him in the shadows at the edge of the pool of light.

Push. The left-hand pack was fumbled round the next stanchion. Push. The right-hand pack moved. He then moved his body forward. His cheek rested for a moment against the cold, wet-seeming metal of the stanchion, then he pushed the left-hand pack forward again. His lamp clanged against the pressure hull. He cursed the noise, momentarily distracted, and the left-hand pack slid away from him. He felt it tug at his body, urging it sideways. The pack slithered into the chasm. His right hand grabbed the stanchion, and his arm was almost jerked from its socket. He suppressed a cry of pain and held on, reeling in the heavy pack with his left hand. He gripped it to him, shaking.

When he had swallowed the fear in his mouth, and his legs had seemed to recover some of their strength, he moved on, passing the

277

last of the stanchions, slithering more quickly the last few feet to the shell of grey metal, the tumour on the pressure hull.

He was able to kneel, just, with his back arched like a frightened cat's, and shine his lamp over the surface. His first task was to remove it. He placed the packs carefully beyond it, where he would not disturb them accidentally, and began removing the bolts from the sealing gasket of the grey carapace. He was aware that he was above the ceiling of the turbine room, crouching in shadow, alone and even ridiculous, taking his first steps to cure an illness he was unlikely to be able to diagnose. Below him, from what he had seen when aboard the *Proteus*, it was likely that engineers and technicians from the naval base would be inspecting the giant turbines. He had to presume that they were there, assume that the slightest carelessness with regard to noise would betray his presence to them.

"I'm in the tunnel," he said softly, aware of the point on the relief map which Pasvik had pointed out and where he now hid. Pasvik was in the bushes with his dish aerials, the one fragile link between himself and Quin aboard the Nimrod.

"Good." Aubrey's voice.

"Beginning to remove the cowling," he said.

He reached into a pocket of his immersion suit and removed a rubber suction cap. He fixed it to the lamp, and pressed the other side against the outer hull. He jiggled the lamp, but it remained fixed. The pool of light fell upon the grey metal shell.

He loosened the final screw, pocketed it, and lifted the carapace away. Inside it were the carbon fibre braces to withstand pressure at depth. Beneath the carapace were a number of further box-like housings with neoprene seals. He half turned a spring-loaded catch, then lifted the first of the inner covers. What he saw, as he had suspected from the diagram but which still surprised and daunted him, resembled a dug-out, exposed telephone junction box he had once seen beneath the sidewalk of Pennsylvania Avenue in Washington. The telephone engineers had exposed a mass of bright, spiderish wiring, incomprehensible, baffling. He shook his head, and began to learn the nature of what he looked at, remembering Quin's voice guiding him through the wiring diagrams and the "Leopard" manual. Printed circuit boards, a sickly grey-white and green where the copper was coated with anti-corrosion varnish; on the boards, resistors with bright bands of colour in the lamplight, capacitors in tubes of various sizes, some sheathed in coloured plastic, some like sucked cough lozenges. He nodded to himself. His eyes recognized the number of small boxes set out as regularly and rigidly as units of some eighteenth-century army drawn up for battle. Pins like defences protruded from the boxes, glinting gold. Microprocessors.

278

It was no longer mysterious. Merely a collection of components. He breathed easily, with satisfaction. He was now the telephone engineer, not the passer-by. The sheer mass of wiring, however, prevented complacency; all colour coded, lashed into ropes with fine cords. Each circuit board had a serial number, which he would read to Quin or Quin would instruct him to test, and each component, however tiny it might be, fitted in its place in company with a reference number.

His finger traced across the bulk of large power transformers, mounted on blocks of metal and used to dissipate heat from the system. Then his eye began to register the miniature switches labelled *Self-Test Facility* and the multi-pin sockets labelled *Input Tester Socket Type 27 P3D*. They were his heart of the matter, all he really needed to recognize.

He hefted the carapace away from him, together with the inner cover, and placed them gingerly on the pressure hull beyond his packs, steadying them until he considered neither of them would slip into the chasm. Then he removed his special test kit from the pack, and clipped it to his belt. A bead of wetness ran down his cheek, then dropped from his jaw. It would take hours, just the checking. The thought made his hands almost nerveless and caused a cramp in his arched back and neck.

"OK," he said in a whisper.

Quin was back almost immediately, the eagerness evident in his voice. "Begin with the Opto-Electric Converter," he said. "You can identify that?"

Clark studied the exposed boards. "Yes, got it."

"Good. Switch SW One off, and SW Two on."

"Right."

"Rotate SW One to Test."

"Yes."

"Look at the two rows of LEDs – describe the sequence of lights to me."

Clark watched the two rows of light emitting diodes. The top row lit up one by one, accompanied by a low hum. As the last one illuminated, the first light of the lower row lit up, followed by its companions, the top row of lights going out immediately. When the second row was complete it, too, went out, and the first light of the top row lit up once more, repeating the sequence.

When Clark had reached the end of the sequence in his description, Quin interrupted him.

"Switch off. Everything's working properly there. The transducers, the wiring, the fibre-optics and the connectors are all working as they should."

279

"Uh," Clark grunted, disappointed in a childish, impatient way. Nothing wrong. He sighed.

The Nimrod banked sharply to starboard. Eastoe was trying to come round onto the northern leg, across Varangerhalvöya, and two of the MiG-23s had crossed the nose of the aircraft as soon as he began to change course. Aubrey gripped the sides of his seat fiercely, but he did not allow any expression to appear on his face. He could hear the Russian flight leader, speaking in correct, unemotional English, demanding that Eastoe continue on his former course, west along the Norwegian coast towards North Cape. Eastoe remained silent.

The Nimrod, however declared his intention. It dipped violently as the two MiGs banked up and away, flicking with the agility of flies across the darkness, illuminated by a flash of lightning only when they were already more than a mile away, and beginning a turn to bring them back alongside the Nimrod. Eastoe levelled the big aircraft below the flight level of the Russian interceptors.

"Everyone all right – *you*, Mr. Aubrey?"

"Thank you, yes. No more than unsettled." The console in front of Aubrey crackled, and what might have been a voice tried unsuccessfully to communicate something to them. Quin had turned up the volume to maximum, and was leaning forward.

"What did you say, Clark? Clark, I can't hear you."

"What's the matter?" Aubrey snapped fearfully. "What's happening?" Quin shook his head and shrugged. "Eastoe – we can't hear Clark."

"I'm at the limit, Mr. Aubrey. Over a hundred miles out. I'm sorry, but I'm trying to shave the corner off the northbound leg. You'll have to bear with me." There was no satisfaction in the voice. Eastoe had suspended his personal feud with Aubrey.

"Very well." The storm filled the empty ether that was being amplified by the console. A MiG popped into Aubrey's vision, below and almost beneath the port wing of the Nimrod. It had bobbed there like a cork tossed on rough water. There was only the one. Aubrey bent his head and stared through the starboard window opposite him. He could see two more of the Russian interceptors. They were close in, as if juggling for position in order to refuel from the Nimrod. Dangerously close.

Drawn to what he suspected was happening, Aubrey left his seat and crossed to the starboard side of the Nimrod. The aircraft was sliding into a turn, banking slightly and nose-down so that the metal floor had tilted like the floor of some disorientating fairground tunnel. The closest MiG was edging into the Nimrod like a smaller animal

280

ingratiating himself. Its speed had matched the Nimrod's and Aubrey could already see the helmeted head of the pilot within the bubble of the canopy. The flying was skilful even as it was threatening and dangerous. The Nimrod was being headed off, a sheep being directed by a sheepdog. A collision appeared inevitable as their paths converged. Aubrey could do nothing except watch with an appalled fascination. His old frail body trembled with its sense of mortality.

He dimly heard the Nimrod's four Spey engines increase their power, and he felt the nose tilt upwards suddenly. He hung onto a bracket like a straphanger in a tube train, his body wanting to lurch towards the tail of the aircraft. The MiG-23 appeared, then whisked away from the window, like a fly that had been swatted. Even as the Nimrod climbed it began to bank to starboard, pushing Aubrey against the fuselage and his face into the double window port. He felt the glass against his cheek, and his arm aching from its hold on the bracket. The MiG was below them, the other Russian interceptor above, at a distance that implied respect or nerves. Aubrey felt himself hanging over the chasm of thirty thousand feet, imagined the rocks and the landscape below them.

He heard Clark's voice bellow behind him, reporting a stage of his inspection. Then two hands moved his small, frail body, and he was able to let go his hold on the bracket. He looked round into the face of the young flight lieutenant who was in charge of communications.

"Please don't leave your seat again, Mr. Aubrey."

Aubrey shrugged his clothing to greater tidiness on his form. "I'm sorry," he said. "What did Clark want, Quin?" Aubrey sat down heavily.

Quin shook his head. "Nothing so far," he said.

"He is performing the check correctly?"

"He is."

A livid flash of lightning in the distance. The storm was behind and to the north of them now.

"Mr. Aubrey?" It was Eastoe in his headphones.

"Yes?"

"I'm sorry, Mr. Aubrey. I'm not going to be allowed to fly the eastbound leg. They won't stand for that."

"What can you do?" Aubrey asked in utter exasperation.

"Fly a north-south course, over and over – if we can get away with it."

"You're not hopeful."

"No, I'm not. Our time here is strictly limited, I'm afraid. They're determined to get rid of us, one way or another."

281

"Section completed. All readings positive," Clark's voice announced ominously from the console.

"Damn," Aubrey whispered. "Damn."

They were all drunk now, yelling, bellowing, fighting drunk. Falling down and laughing drunk, too. Disrespectful, abusive, coarse, uproarious. Ardenyev enjoyed the noise, the swirl and shudder of the vodka in his veins and head, while one still sober, cold part of his awareness perceived where their laughter and taunts were leading, and anticipated with nothing more than a shudder of self-consciousness the nature of leadership and what he would now have to do to fulfil their expectations and to maintain his grip on their affection and respect.

And also, he concluded, the drinking party had to end with buffoonery, with the game of the ego and the shallowly physical prowess they required to perform their duties. After the death of Blue Section and the others of his own team, the three survivors had been absorbed and ingested as they drank and ate into the cameraderie of the men from the rescue ship *Karpaty*. Balan had understood the necessity of the merger. So Balan's challenge now to him to demonstrate how he boarded the *Proteus* was that of a shrewd drunk. His men wanted it, a boast and valediction. *He* had survived, become more than ever a necessary figurehead, even to the salvage men. In the absence of an athlete, a football star, an actress, he had to submit himself to their fuddled worship, their drunken amusement.

He was drunk, though. He knew that as soon as he stood up, and swayed as if the vodka had punched him in the temple. Teplov was watching him, he could see, as if weighing whether he should let his officer proceed. Viktor Teplov appeared sober, as ever.

Ardenyev looked up, the two images of the wall and the ceiling of the officers' mess coming together, as if he had correctly, though slowly, adjusted a pair of binoculars. He held the new and single image with an effort of concentration. Teplov nodded at the fuzzy corner of his vision. He was prepared to extricate his officer from whatever situation he found himself in.

"Come on, then!" Lev Balan roared, pointing up at the air-conditioning grille. "From that one, right round the room to that one!" His arm swept round the officers' mess, now deserted save for their own noisy group. The two grilles were on opposite walls. Ardenyev was being challenged to clamber and push his way through the duct until he could emerge with honour. Two of Balan's team were busy, balancing with difficulty on chairs, unscrewing the two grilles. Ardenyev looked at Balan, and then at Teplov, and Vanilov. All that remained of the Special Underwater Operations

Unit. Teplov had the face of a stoical peasant in which his eyes gleamed with memory and with a strange amusement, perhaps even with approval. Vanilov looked as if he had drunk too much to forget. He wanted Ardenyev to prove something, perhaps only to be the adult coming into his child's bedroom, easing away the threatening shadows that had gathered around the cot.

"OK. You're on. Two hundred roubles it is."

"One hundred –!" Balan protested.

"Two."

"All right, two. That means a time limit. OK?"

Ardenyev hesitated for a moment, then he nodded. Balan's man stepped down off his chair, the grille in his hand. Ardenyev flicked the remainder of his drink into his open mouth, feeling it burn the back of his throat, then he reached up and took hold of the rough plaster edges of the square hole where the grille had been. He felt mouse droppings under his fingers.

"One minute," Balan called. "You've got one minute to get at least your head out of that other hole. Five, four, three, two, one – go!"

The cheering was deafening. Ardenyev pushed himself up level with the hole, ducked his head into it, and then heaved himself half into the duct, which bent immediately to the left. His shoulders rubbed against the plaster, and he found he had to angle his body in order to be able to move at all. The cheering behind him was muffled by the bulk of his body and by the plaster wall and the metal. He kicked, and his legs followed him into the duct. Immediately, Balan's voice came from behind him, counting.

"Eleven, twelve, thirteen . . ."

Ardenyev shook his head to clear it. Then he began scrambling, leaning to his left, his body rubbing along the metal channel. The cheering was dim and wordless now, falling away into silence. He reached the corner of the room. The duct was a severe right-angle. He squeezed his head and shoulders around the angle, then tried to bring his thighs and knees after his upper torso. He found himself wedged immovably. He struggled as if panicking, and sweat broke out all over his body. He cursed in a yell, and then lay still. Balan's head appeared further down the duct, in a shadowy patch of light. There was a noise that no longer interested Ardenyev coming from behind him.

"Forty-seven, forty-eight, forty-nine . . ."

"Piss off!" Ardenyev yelled, not even attempting to move again. "I'm bloody stuck!"

Balan's head disappeared with a shriek of laughter. Teplov's head appeared in its place. At the same moment, a huge cheer went up as the minute ran out. "All right, sir?"

"Yes, thank you, Viktor."

"Bloody silly game, sir."

"Yes, Viktor."

"I'll come in the other side and give you a shove, sir."

"Thank you, Viktor."

Ardenyev smiled, then relaxed. It didn't matter. Nothing did. The air conditioning duct enclosed him more surely and tightly than the aft escape chamber of the *Proteus*, but there was similarity of darkness and confinement that pressed itself upon him. He allowed a congratulatory sense of memory its place in his fuddled awareness. He'd done it, he'd done it –

No one else, he told himself. No one else could have done it. Then, more sharply, he thought, if I could, someone else could. Most of the team, the dead team –

His thoughts had swung towards a maudlin, drunken horizon. He heard Teplov moving along the duct behind him, grunting with effort. He giggled drunkenly. Anyone could have done it, he affirmed in a mood of quick and sudden self-deprecation as he imagined those who had died. It wasn't anything. Then, through a connection of which he was not aware, he wondered, Why is that Nimrod hanging around? What is it doing?

Teplov's hand tapped his calf. He called back to the *michman*: "What's that Nimrod doing up there, Viktor?"

"Beg pardon, sir?"

"That Nimrod – they were talking about it earlier."

"Oh, that one," Teplov said indulgently. "I wouldn't know, sir."

If I could do it, he thought, anyone could. That Nimrod –

He was aware of himself, stretched out on the pressure hull, held there by the mesh of nerves that covered his body. He had heard the footsteps clattering along the hull from the stern. The boots had stamped to a halt directly over the hatch through which he had entered the space between the two hulls. He had immediately switched off the lamp, as if the outer hull had been no more opaque than a curtain, and he had turned onto his back. He seemed to himself to be less vulnerable, facing the direction of the noises. Evidence, evidence? he asked himself repeatedly. Why? Why now? Noise, suspicion, *evidence*?

He stared up at the outer hull as if he could really see it, almost as if he could see the armed man whose boots had clattered up on him. He listened. Tiny noises now, almost mouse-like. The irresolute shuffling of feet, the claw-like scratching of nails and metal heel-tips. The darkness pressed in, unwelcome, bringing its unexpected and disturbing claustrophobia with it. He reached up and flicked on the lamp. It shone in his eyes. He inspected his watch. Six o'clock, almost. He had been working on the back-up system for over two hours. And he had found nothing. Every circuit, every resistor, every capacitor and microprocessor and wire and pin *worked* –

There was nothing wrong with it, at least not with the sixty-five percent of the back-up system that he had checked. There was something less, or something more mysteriously, wrong with the complex lump of junk near his head than was the matter with the Nimrod. Sure, Aubrey kept reassuring him, but the communications black-outs and the poor reception and the constant re-requests and repeats of instructions told him everything.

The boots shuffled, then moved, on the hull. They were over his face now, only a couple of feet from stamping on it.

The Nimrod was at the fringes of, and at times beyond, the communications range. Which meant that the aircraft had company, Soviet company. MiGs were shadowing the Nimrod, maybe even playing shepherd games with her –

As he rehearsed the conclusion once more, a chill coldness seized him. They suspected, even knew, about him. The boots on the hull, and the silence which he had noticed from the turbine room beneath him. They were listening, too. Everyone was listening for him, waiting for the mouse behind the wainscot to move again. He held his breath, one part of his mind explaining with a weary patience that he was behaving ridiculously, the remainder of his consciousness believing that the hull above him and beneath his back and head and legs was no more than a sounding-board, a corridor of whispers eager to betray his whereabouts.

The boots moved away, forward along the hull towards the sail. Almost immediately, Lloyd was speaking in a voice muffled by the pocket of his immersion suit, through the tiny R/T Clark had left with him. Relief overcame Clark, and he felt the renewed perspiration cool almost at once on his skin, making his flesh shudder.

He removed the R/T from his pocket and pressed it to his cheek. "Yes?"

"I've seen Hayter and Thurston. They know what to do."

"Good."

"Any luck?"

"None."

"It's six now."

"I know."

"Is it still on?"

"Eight o'clock, on the button."

"I heard my guard and another talking. The man from Novosibirsk has arrived in Murmansk."

"Damn. Is he on his way?"

"I don't know."

"OK – I'll call you."

Clark replaced the R/T set in his breast pocket, and zipped the pocket closed with a real and savage anger. He rolled onto his stomach, and the turtle without its shell was humped on the edge of the pool of light from the lamp, still baffling him, still apparently undamaged.

"You heard that?" he whispered. There were noises now from the turbine room. He had imagined the silence.

"Yes," Aubrey replied. His voice was gauzy and faint, a smear of distant sound. Flying on the limit again.

"What trouble are you in?"

"None."

"Tell me."

"Four MiG-23s. They're keeping us as far away from Soviet airspace as possible –" The voice blacked out, then Clark heard an additional smear of sound some seconds later which he could not decipher. Then two more spits of sound which the cassette recorder slowed down and replayed. He could understand neither of them. The cool part of his brain suggested a storm might be adding to the difficulties, but the remainder of his awareness was raging with the same kind of helpless, impotent fury his body felt. He was shaking as he knelt in front of the "Leopard" back-up system. He was in a mood to break, damage, throw. The rational part of him understood, and mocked at, the emotions he felt and his desire for their expression, and gradually he calmed himself. Then, suddenly, Aubrey was speaking again, clearly.

"Can you hear me now?"

"Yes."

"Eastoe has dodged them, ducked inside," Aubrey said. Clark could even pick out the irony of the old man's tone. "Quin suggests it will take only hours to dismantle 'Leopard', if that is what they intend, and the same amount of time for a full analysis, with the resources they have available. Once they begin the work, they will be searching for the back-up system. You must not be where you are when that happens. 'Leopard' must not be intact when this expert steps aboard. Do I make myself clear?"

"Yes."

"It will take an hour from Murmansk by helicopter."

"All right, all right. I'm moving on – what next?"

"Very well. You have *both* packs with you?"

Clark looked up and into the gloom beyond the lamplight. "Yes," he replied with a sense of defeat. "Both of them."

286

"Keep me informed."

"Clark?" It was Quin's voice now, not so irritating, not so pessimistic as that of Aubrey. Quin allowed the fiction of success to be entertained. "You should move on to the spectrum analyser, noise generator and phase reverser unit."

"Right."

"You need the special test kit."

"Sure." Clark unclipped it from his belt. A dial, various scales, a rotary switch, buttons, a small grille. Quin had to instruct every step of the way; every switch, every light, every reading. "All right, I'm ready." He studied the exposed maze of wiring, microprocessors and circuits in front of him. For a moment, his mind was a blank and the system before him was a puzzle to which he had no clue. Then, sighing, he shrugged off his numbing reluctance, and reached out and waited for Quin's instructions.

It was six o-five.

"It's almost six, Admiral – perhaps we can now be leaving for Pechenga. Too much time has already been wasted."

"Comrade Academician, you say it will take a matter of no more than three or four hours to complete your work on 'Leopard'. What is your hurry? You waited at the airport in Novosibirsk for almost three days." Dolohov was expansive, and mocking. He was almost drunk, Panov decided, and had abandoned most of his dignity. Panov did not like the military, especially the older representatives, the officer caste. As a man who was an honoured member of another élite, one without the stain of imitating those that existed before the Revolution, Panov disliked, even loathed, the upper echelons of the military.

Panov glanced again at his gold Swiss watch. He had purchased it in Paris, while attending a scientific congress, and that had added to its potency as a reminder of his identity. The large-faced clock on the wall behind Dolohov, which Panov would hardly have admitted to his wife's kitchen in Novosibirsk, jerked its hand past another minute. The drunken old fool remained in his chair.

"Admiral – I must insist that we leave for Pechenga at once. My colleagues will be waiting for me. I must study their preliminary findings before I can specify what needs to be done." Panov stopped at this point, feeling the asperity in his tone raising his voice beyond the point of acceptable masculinity. He despised his own too-high voice. The admiral growled and huffed like a bear.

"I see. You insist?"

Panov cleared his throat. "I do."

Dolohov reached across his desk and flicked the switch of his intercom.

"Get my car to the door at once, and warn the tower I shall want an immediate take-off." He switched off, and stood up, his arms extended in a bear-like embrace. The image made Panov suppress a shudder, and smooth dislike from his bland features. "Come, Comrade Academician Panov – your carriage awaits." Then Dolohov laughed. Panov had to endure a large hand slapping him on the shoulder, and the log-like fall of an arm across his neck, as he was ushered to the door. Dolohov's voice was like a caress when he added: "Don't you think *I* am anxious to see our prize, too?" Then he laughed again.

The hand of the clock on the wall clicked again. Six o-five.

Clark moved the rotary switch on the test kit for the final time, the needle on the dial flickered away from zero, and he cursed as he unclipped the kit's leads from the last of the test pins on the power supply units. Each and every one of them worked, gave a positive reading, had nothing wrong with them.

"OK, that's it," he said, glancing at his watch. Seven-o-two. Another hour had passed, and he was still at the moment before beginning. Everything he had done during the past three hours had been necessary, and pointless.

"Very well, Clark, you'd better run a check on the power lines, from TP Seventeen, Eighteen and Twenty-Four, using the cable adaptor with the yellow sleeve, marked BFP 6016 –"

"I got that," Clark snapped, wiping his forehead, then letting his hand stray to his eyes. He rubbed at them. They felt gritty with tiredness and concentration. He squeezed them shut and opened them again. He wanted another perspective. "Hold it, I want to talk to Lloyd again."

He took the R/T from his pocket, and pressed its call button.

"Yes?" Lloyd said quietly a moment later. Clark pressed the R/T to his cheek.

"What's happening?"

"I've just been on my rounds." Lloyd almost chuckled. There was a crackling, electric excitement in the man. He had swung away from the helpless depression of the prisoner. Now he was the schoolboy escapee. "I managed to brief one of my chief petty officers while I was doing it."

"What about the gates?"

"There's a minimal guard outside, always has been. The repair crew won't be here before eight. The gates can be opened by two men, one to throw the switches, the other to guard him. I'll detail men as soon as we free the wardroom. Then they can smash the switches so the gates can't be closed again."

"I agree."

"Clark – can you give me 'Leopard'? I can't risk my men and my vessel unless you do."

"Can you kill the first guard, Lloyd, the one outside your door?" Clark snapped back at him. "Because if you can't, then *Proteus* goes nowhere!" Clark, in the silence which followed, imagined Lloyd reaching under his pillow for the tiny Astra pistol he had left with him. Everything depended on Lloyd being able to kill the guard outside his cabin, retrieve the man's Kalashnikov, and release his officers from the wardroom along the corridor from his cabin.

"I – think I can," Lloyd replied eventually. "I'll have to, won't I?"

"And I have to repair 'Leopard', don't I?"

"Very well. Rumour has it that Panov, the scientist, is expected at any moment. The technicians on board have been informed to that effect. No later than eight o'clock."

"It's all coming right down to the wire, uh?" When Lloyd did not reply, Clark merely added, "I'll call you." He replaced the R/T in his pocket. Even as he did so, he heard Aubrey's voice in his ear.

"Clark, you must begin preparing to abort 'Leopard'. It will take you at least thirty to forty minutes to place the charges. You must begin at once."

"No, dammit!"

"Clark, do as you are ordered."

"Mr. Quin gave me a job to do – maybe after that."

"*Now!*"

"Not a chance."

Rapidly, he fitted the cable adaptor to the first of the power lines Quin had designated. Positive. He cursed under his breath. Then the second. Positive. Then the third. Positive. He sighed loudly, in anger and frustration.

"Fit the charges, Clark – please begin at once," Aubrey commanded with icy malice.

Ardenyev watched the MiL-8 transport helicopter sag down towards the landing pad. The down-draught, exceeding the wind's force, stirred the dust on the concrete. Behind it, the sky was beginning to lighten, a thin-grey blue streak above the hills, almost illusory beyond the hard white lighting of the helicopter base. Ardenyev glanced at his watch. Seven-ten. The admiral and Panov were almost an hour early. Viktor Teplov – face-saving, loyal Teplov – had picked up the information somewhere that Dolohov was on his way, and revived his officer with coffee and one large vodka, which Ardenyev had felt was like swallowing hot oil. Then he had commandeered a staff car and driver and accompanied Ardenyev to the helicopter base.

The MiL-8 hovered like an ungainly wasp, then dropped onto its wheels. Immediately, ducking ground crew placed the chocks against the wheels, even as the noise of the rotors descended through the scale and the rotor dish dissolved from its shimmering, circular form into flashes of darker grey in the rush of air. Then they were individual blades, then the door opened as the rotors sagged into stillness. Dolohov's foot was on the ladder as soon as it was pushed into place for him. He descended with a light, firm step, inheriting a kingdom. Men snapped to attention, saluting. A smaller, more rotund figure in a fur-collared coat stepped more gingerly down behind him. Panov. Dolohov waited for the scientist, then ushered him towards Ardenyev.

Ardenyev sucked spit from his cheeks and moistened his dry throat. He saluted crisply, then Dolohov extended his hand and shook Ardenyev's warmly.

"May I introduce Captain Valery Ardenyev," he said, turning to Panov. The scientist appeared intrigued, his face pale, almost tinged with blue, in the cold lighting. He shook Ardenyev's hand limply.

"Ah – our hero of the Soviet Union," he said with evident irony. Dolohov's face clouded with the insult to Ardenyev.

"Thank you, Comrade Academician Professor Panov," Ardenyev replied woodenly. He was enjoying fulfilling Panov's prejudices, meeting one of his stereotypes. "It was nothing."

Dolohov appeared bemused. "Shall we go?" he remarked. "Directly to the submarine pen, I think?"

"If you please," Panov said primly.

"This way, admiral – professor. The car is waiting."

"I'm sorry you lost so many men," Dolohov murmured confidentially as they walked towards the car. Panov, who was intended to overhear the remark, appeared at a loss, even embarrassed.

"So am I, sir – so am I." Teplov came to attention, then opened the rear door of the Zil. Ardenyev smiled wearily. "A ten-minute drive, sir, and you'll be able to see her. HMS *Proteus*, pride of the fleet!"

Dolohov laughed uproariously, slapping Ardenyev on the back before getting into the car.

FOURTEEN:

Running

Hyde woke, and reacted instantly to the cold air that had insinuated itself into their burrow. It was damp. He knew there was a fog or heavy mist outside, even though he could not see beyond the bush. There was greyness there, which might have been the dawn. He felt his shoulder protest with a sharp pain as he tried to rub his cold arms, and he stifled his groan as he remembered what had roused him. The running feet of deer along the track behind the rifle range, past the bush and the entrance into their hole. He looked immediately at the girl. She was soundly asleep.

He listened. And tested his shoulder, moving fingers and wrist and elbow and forearm. Slightly better. He touched the crude, dirty bandage. Dry and stiff. He investigated his resources. His body felt small, shrunken, empty and weak. But not leaden, as the previous night. His head felt more solid, too, less like a gathering of threads or misty tendrils. There was some clarity of thought, some speed of comprehension. He would have to do as he was. He was all he had, all they had.

The hoofbeats of the three or four deer who had fled past their hiding place died away, swallowed by what he was now convinced was a heavy mist. He listened to the silence, slow and thick outside the hole. He stretched his legs carefully, not disturbing the girl, felt the expected cramp, eased it away, rotated his pelvis as well as he could while hunched in a seated position. His back ached. He flexed his fingers once more, aware of the small of his back where the gun had been. Having completed his inventory, he pronounced himself incapable, with a slight smile. Some stubbornness had returned during the few hours' sleep he had had.

Noises. Slow, regular, cautious footsteps outside. He reached up and pressed his palm flat against the roof of the hole. The sand was damp. He levered himself out of his sitting position, and stepped over the girl's drawn-up knees. Her head rested on her chest, and her blonde hair, dirty and hanging in stiff, greasy tails, was draped like strands of cloth over her knees. He leaned forward, then slid towards the entrance to the hole. The branches of the bush became clear, as if he had focused an inward lens on them, and beyond them the heavy mist was grey and impenetrable. One chance. Don't wake up, darling –

The figure of a man emerged from the mist, bent low to study the track, the slim, pencil-like barrel of the rifle he carried protruding beyond the bulk of his form. He was little more than a dark shadow in the first light seeping into the mist. Then he saw the bush, and might have been staring into Hyde's eyes, though he registered no sign of having seen him. The gun moved away from his body, and Hyde recognized it, with a chill of danger and a strange greediness, as a Kalashnikov. Stubby, with a folding steel stock and plastic grip and the curving thirty-round ammunition box beneath the magazine. It was infinitely desirable, and deadly. The small R/T set clipped to the pocket of the man's anorak was similarly desirable and dangerous. Hyde coveted them both.

He held his breath as he felt one of the girl's feet touch his shin. Don't let her wake up, not now –

The man moved closer to the bush, the Kalashnikov prodding out in front of his body. Hyde flexed his fingers, keeping his head as close to the lip of the hole as he could, watching the man intently. The girl's foot stirred again, and Hyde prayed she would not make a noise in the last moments of her sleep. He felt her foot shiver. The cold was beginning to wake her. The stubby barrel of the rifle moved among the leafless branches, disturbing them, brushing them to one side. He squashed himself flat against the damp sand. He felt, through her foot, the girl's whole body stir, then he heard her yawn. Immediately the man's head snapped up, alert, cocked on one side as he listened, attempting to gauge the direction of the sound, waiting for its repetition. His eyes glanced over the bank, the rifle's barrel wavered in the bush, pointing above the hole. The girl groaned with stiffness. Hyde reached out, grabbed the stubby rifle, one hand on the barrel the other on the magazine. The man jerked backwards in surprise and defence, and Hyde pushed with his feet and used the man's response to pull him out of the hole and through the bush. He cried out with the sudden, searing pain in his arm and shoulder, but he held on, twisting the barrel of the rifle away from him, rolling down the sand to the track, pulling the man off balance.

The man almost toppled, then jerked at the rifle. Hyde had to release the grip of his left hand because the pain was so intense, but he had rolled almost to the man's feet. He kicked out, using his grip on the rifle as a pivot, and the man overbalanced as Hyde's shins caught him at the back of the legs. The Russian held on to the rifle, and Hyde felt the heat before he heard the sound of the explosion as a round was fired. Hyde used the rifle like a stick, an old man assisting himself to rise from a deep armchair, and as the man made to turn onto his side and get up, Hyde kicked him in the side of the head. The grip on the Kalashnikov did not loosen. Hyde, enraged and elated, kicked the man once more in the temple, with all the force he could muster. The man rolled away, his head seemingly loose on his shoulders, and lay still. Hyde could see the man's chest pumping. He reached down for the R/T, and a hand grabbed at the rifle again as Hyde held it still by the barrel. The man's eyes were glazed and intent. Hyde staggered away, taking the rifle with him. He had no strength, he should have killed the man with one of the kicks, it was pathetic –

The man was sitting up. He heard Tricia Quin gasp audibly. He fumbled the rifle until it pointed at the man, who was withdrawing his hand from his anorak and the hand contained a pistol, heavy and black and coming to a bead. Hyde fired, twice. The noise of the shots seemed more efficiently swallowed by the mist than the cries of rooks startled by the gunfire. The man's pistol discharged into the earth, and he twitched like a wired rabbit. Hyde, angry and in haste, moved to the body. He swore. One bullet had passed through the R/T set, smashing it. Tricia Quin's appalled groan was superfluous, irrelevant.

Hyde knelt by the man's body, searching it quickly with one hand. He had had to lay the rifle down. His left arm was on fire, and useless to him. He hunched it into his side, as if he could protect it or lessen its pain by doing so. He unzipped the anorak. No papers. The man didn't even look Slavic. He could have been anybody. He patted the pockets of the anorak. Yes –

Triumphantly, he produced a flask of something, and a wrapped package of sandwiches.

"Food!" he announced. "Bloody food!"

The girl's face was washed clean of resentment and fear and revulsion. She grabbed the package eagerly. The sandwiches had some kind of sausage in them. She swallowed a lump of bread and sausage greedily, then tried to speak through the food.

"What –?" was all he heard.

Hyde looked around him. "Help me get this poor sod into the hole. It might hide him for a bit. Come on – stop stuffing your face, girlie!"

Tricia put the sandwiches reverently, and with much regret, on the track, roughly rewrapped. He took hold of one arm, she the other, averting her eyes from the man's face, which stared up into the mist in a bolting, surprised way. They dragged the body to the bank, hoisted it – Tricia would not put her shoulder or body beneath the weight of the man – and Hyde with a cry of pain and effort tumbled the body into the hole.

"His foot," the girl said as Hyde stood trembling from his exertions. Hyde looked up. The man's walking boot was protruding over the lip of the hole.

293

"You see to it."

Reluctantly, the girl reached up, and pushed. The man's knee seemed locked by an instant rigor mortis. The girl obtained a purchase for her feet, and heaved. The foot did not move. She cried with exasperation, and wriggled and thrust until the foot disappeared.

"Bloody, bloody *thing*!" There was a crack from inside the hole. She covered her mouth, appalled. She turned accusing eyes on Hyde.

"We can all be shitty when we try hard," he said, eating one of the sandwiches. Then he added, "OK, pick the rest of them up –" He thrust the Makarov pistol into his waistband, and hefted the rifle in his good hand. The girl pocketed the sandwiches, looking furtively sidelong at him as she ate a second one. "Come on, then." He looked around him. "Bad luck and good luck. No one's going to find us in this."

They walked up the track behind the bank. The girl looked guiltily back once, still chewing the last lump of the second sandwich.

Clark ground his teeth in frustration, and clenched his hands into claws again and again as if to rid them of a severe cramp. The sight of what he had done enraged and depressed him. The plastic charges were taped and moulded to the back-up system, lying across the wiring and the circuitry like slugs, the detonator wires like the strands of a net that had dredged up the equipment from beneath the sea. He had done as Aubrey asked – commanded – and then he had requested Quin to set him another task, like an over-eager schoolboy. More power lines, and still nothing.

"Clark?" For a moment, he was tempted to curse Aubrey aloud. Part of him, however, admitted the correctness of Aubrey's decision.

"Yes?"

"It's time for you to rig the main 'Leopard' system. Good luck." There was no sense of possible argument or disobedience. Aubrey assumed he would behave like the automaton he was intended to be.

The bleeper on the R/T in his pocket sounded. He pulled the set out and pressed the transmit button. "Yes?"

"Clark? I think Panov's about to make an appearance. The technical team are streaming out of the *Proteus*, lining up like a guard of honour. I've just seen them."

"Where are you?"

"Hurry, Clark. You do not have much time –" Aubrey said in his ear.

"The officers' bathroom."

"Your guard?"

"Clark, listen to me –"

"Outside."

"Mood?"

"Pretty sloppy. He's waiting for his relief at eight."

"Clerk, you will abort 'Plumber' immediately and proceed to destroy 'Leopard'. Do you understand me?"

"Well?" Lloyd asked with a nervous edge to his voice.

"Get as close to him as you can, preferably the side of his head or under the jaw, and squeeze the trigger *twice*."

"Clark, you will rescind that instruction to Lloyd –"

"What about 'Leopard'?" Lloyd asked.

"I'll give you 'Leopard' in working order!" Clark snapped. "Where is Thurston, where's Hayter?"

"The First Lieutenant's in the cabin next to mine, Hayter's in the wardroom with the others."

"Then –"

"Clark –!"

"Time for Quin to earn his money!" Clark almost shouted, with nerves and relief and the adrenalin that suddenly coursed through his system. "Help me get this fucking back-up working, Quin!"

"Clark – *Clark*!"

"Go or no go?" Lloyd asked.

"Go – *GO*! Kill the bastard!"

"I'll be in touch."

"Clark – you are insane. You will never get out of Pechenga without 'Leopard'. You have not, you *cannot* repair it. You have just sentenced Commander Lloyd and his crew to imprisonment, possibly even death. You are *insane*." The last word was hissed in Clark's ear, serpentine and venomous.

Clark felt a heady, dangerous relief, and a pressing, violent anxiety. "For Chrissake, Quin – help me get this fucking thing to work! *Help me!*"

Aubrey stared at Quin. He could not believe in what Clark had put in motion, could not apprehend the violent and dangerous half-motives that had prompted him. In its final stage, the *Proteus* business was escaping him again, running on its own headlong flight unhindered by reason or caution or good sense. In a split-second over which he had had no control, Clark had made the decision not to abort. Now, everyone would face the consequences of that decision.

"Quin? *Quin*?" he snapped at his companion. The scientist tossed his head as if startled from sleep.

"What?"

"Can you help him?"

Quin shrugged. "We've tried everything we can. There's nothing wrong –"

"There must be, dammit!"

"I don't know what it is!" Quin almost wailed.

Aubrey leaned towards him. "That bloody American has set the seal on this affair, Quin. Lloyd will either kill his guard, or be killed. If the former, then they will kill others, picking up weapons at each death, until they can open the gates and sail *Proteus* out of Pechenga. Without 'Leopard' in an operational condition, they will be a target for every naval unit in the port. I would not wish to assume that the Russians will be prepared to let her sail away scot free! What can you do? Think of something!"

Quin began flipping through the "Leopard" manual, most of which he had written himself. Aubrey recognized an unseeing, desperate gesture. Quin *knew* the manual, nothing would come from it. The man's hands were shaking. He had collided with a brute reality. Aubrey shook his head with weariness. Tiredness, the sense of being utterly spent, seemed the only feeling left to him. Clark had renegued on reason, on authority. He could understand how it had happened. The American had simply refused to acknowledge defeat.

He heard Eastoe's voice tinnily in the headphones resting around his neck. He placed the set over his head. The microphone bobbed in front of his mouth.

"Yes, Squadron Leader?" He had not meant his voice to sound so waspish and dismissive.

"Mr. Aubrey. We're out of range again. I can try to get back, but I won't be able to hold station for very much longer. I can give you a couple of minutes, perhaps."

Aubrey wanted to rage at the pilot, but he acknowledged the weariness in the man's voice. The MiGs – there was one on the port wing again, turning silver in the beginning of the day – were making patterned flying impossible. Slowly, inexorably, the Nimrod was being shepherded away from the Soviet border.

"Do what you can, Squadron Leader. We're in your hands."

"Very well, Mr. Aubrey. I'll give you as long as I can."

The nose of the Nimrod dipped, and then when Eastoe judged he had lost sufficient height, the aircraft banked savagely, rolling away towards the east and the sun. The porthole in the fuselage became a blaze of gold, blinding Aubrey. He felt as old and thin and stretched as a ghost. Transparent in the sudden light.

"Quin, come on, man – suggest something. We don't have much time."

Quin groaned aloud, and rubbed his face with his hands, washing off his present circumstances. He looked blearily at Aubrey, and shook his head.

"There is nothing."

296

"There must be. Some faulty system, something you disagreed with Plessey about, something you've always suspected or disliked about the system – anything!" Aubrey spread his hands around the communications console, which hissed at him. It was as if he were about to jettison it as useless cargo. A MiG, gold-bright, popped into his view, just off the port wing. Craning his neck, Aubrey could see the grey sea, the misted coast below them. The MiG ducked beneath the Nimrod, and Aubrey saw it bob like a cork into the starboard porthole opposite him. "Something – *please*?"

The console crackled. Clark's voice was faint. The coast and sea below moved, and Aubrey could hear the Spey engines more loudly. Eastoe was running for the border with the Soviet Union in a straight, desperate line.

"You must help –"

"For Chrissake, Quin – say something!" Clark bellowed from the receiver.

Quin's face was an agony of doubt.

"Come on, Quin, come on, come on," Aubrey heard himself repeating.

"I can hear shooting!" Clark yelled. Aubrey knew it was a lie, but a clever one. And perhaps it only described events that had already occurred. Lloyd dead, a guard dead, two guards, three?

"Change-over – automatic change-over," Quin murmured.

"What's that?" Clark snapped.

The MiG on the starboard wing – two of them now, one above the other, moving on a course to head off the Nimrod. There was a slim shadow taking and changing shape on the port wing. One of the MiGs was above them, appearing almost as if it might be lowering itself onto the wing, to snap it in half. Eastoe dropped the nose of the Nimrod again, dropping towards the sea and the rocky coast that seemed to lurch up to meet them. The port wing and the starboard window were swept clean for a moment. Aubrey felt Eastoe begin to turn the aircraft. He'd given up. They were on their way back, and out of range.

"The automatic change-over from the main system to the back-up. I argued time and again, with the Admiralty. No trust in completely automatic systems. They insisted –"

"Tell him!"

Quin leant towards the console. "Clark," he began, "you must check the automatic change-over on the power supply from the main system to the back-up. Locate the power supply box . . ."

Aubrey ceased to listen. The Nimrod had completed its turn, through the brief blinding sunlight on the porthole, and was now heading west once more. Eastoe had dropped the aircraft's speed, but it was a matter of mere minutes until they would no longer be able to talk to Clark.

And, in Pechenga, with whatever outcome, the killing had undoubtedly begun.

One of the MiGs bobbed back into view, off the port wing. The Russian interceptor appeared to be flying a little further off, as if its pilot, too, knew that the game was up.

Lloyd hesitated for a moment, on the threshold of the bathroom, straddling the body of the guard who had only had time to half-turn before the small Astra, pressed against his side, had exploded twice. Lloyd had had to take him into an embrace, feel the man's final shudder against him, and lower him to the deck. One guard only in the corridor. Lloyd had been surprised at the small, muffled sound the gun had made when pressed into the spare flesh the man was carrying. It was as if the pistol had been fitted with a silencer.

He saw the guard outside the wardroom door at the end of the corridor, and hoped, as he studied the man's movements and saw the Kalashnikov turn in the guard's hands and draw a bead on himself, that Thurston would not blunder into the line of fire out of the cabin next door to his own. Then he prayed his hands would move more swiftly to bring the small pistol up to the level of the guard's trunk. He could not believe that he would move more quickly than the trained marine, but some realization that the clock was ticking away precious seconds only for him, came to him as he fired. He had moved inches faster, reaction had been milliseconds quicker, because he had an imperative the Russian did not share. The guard thudded back against the wardroom door, and slid down, feet out, to a sitting position with his head lolling. The pistol now made much more noise, and would have attracted attention.

"Come on, come on!" he yelled, banging on Thurston's door as he passed it. Then he was stooping to retrieve the Kalashnikov, which felt immediately bulky and menacing in his grip. He flung open the wardroom door. Surprised faces, half a dozen of them, mostly unshaven, were grouped around the table above mugs of steaming coffee. Thurston was behind him now. He passed the Astra back to his first lieutenant. "Get the others out – *now!*" he snapped, feeling the dangerous, elating adrenalin running wildly through his body.

Seven twenty-one. Clark had recognized, almost subliminally, the two shots, then the third after a slight delay. He imagined that the same small Astra pistol had made all three reports, but he could not quite believe it, until Lloyd's voice could be heard plainly, coming from the R/T which was clipped to the breast of his immersion suit, ordering his officers to remain in the wardroom until the control room had been recaptured. Then there was the awful, cloth-ripping stutter of the Kalashnikov on automatic – Clark presumed feverishly that it was the one Lloyd had taken from the wardroom guard. It was. Lloyd yelled at Hayter to recover the gun of the man he had just killed. Clark nodded to himself. Lloyd would go on now until he became exhausted or until someone shot him. He was high on escape, even on death.

Clark lifted the lid of the power supply box, as Quin had instructed him. LIFT HERE ONLY. He had unclamped the lid, and obeyed its command, stencilled in yellow.

"Clark?"

"Yes. The box is open," he told Quin. Communications were already weakening as the Nimrod moved towards the fringes of reception. Aubrey had told him what was happening, then patched in Eastoe. The pilot did not enjoy admitting his weariness, his loss of nerve, his failure, but he had done so. The Nimrod was shot, finished. It was on its way home. Eastoe had dropped the airspeed as much as he could, but they were gradually moving out of range, taking Quin with his manual, his diagrams and his knowledge with them. He had, at the Nimrod's present speed, no more than five minutes. Seven twenty-two.

"Switch SW-Eight-R should be off." Clark followed Quin's instruction. Lloyd's breathing was audible to him in the confined, lamplit darkness from the R/T against the submarine captain's chest. Running –? Cries, yells –? *Come on, Quin –*

"OK."

"Press the yellow button marked PRESS TO TEST. Have you got that?" A faint, weak voice, like a man dying in the next room.

"OK?"

Firing.

"Lloyd, what's happening?" He knew he should not have called, that it might be fatal to distract Lloyd now. Yet the sounds tormented him, made his body writhe with an uncontrollable tension and anxiety.

Firing.

Quin said something he did not catch. He prayed it was only his inattention. ". . . through top . . . cover?"

"Repeat, please," he requested loudly, holding his breath. Lloyd's breathing roared on his chest like an illness he had contracted.

" . . . contacts move . . . clear top . . .?"

"Repeat, repeat!" Clark shouted, almost as a relief for the hours of whispering and silence he had endured and partly because he was panicking. The irreversible had begun. Lloyd had killed, the officers were armed with two Russian Kalashnikovs and were in the control room of the *Proteus*. He had begun it – *he* had. "Repeat. I say again, repeat your message." The words were formal, the voice running out of control.

"Right. Hold them over there – no, get them off my ship, *now!*" Lloyd's elation, his success, drummed in the cramped space between the two hulls. "Clark?"

"Yes?"

"What's wrong?" Even in his excitement, Lloyd was responsive to tone, to nuance.

"Nothing."

"We have the control room in our hands again."

"Good –" Clark paused. There was a spit of sound, but when the tape had been slowed, there was only the ether, mocking him. A gauzy, sad, distant voice mumbled behind it. *Christ, what have I done?* "Outside?"

"Thurston's taking a look. I've despatched three men, two of them armed, to the control booth for the gates. A couple of minutes now – ?" The statement ended as a question. Another spit of sound, Clark's heart pounding as he waited for it to replay more slowly in his earpiece, Quin's voice broken and racked by the interference.

"Can you see . . . through top . . . moving?"

Contacts, *contacts*, he recalled. Can you see the contacts moving through the clear top of the cover?

"Got you!" Then, immediately, he cried, "They're not moving!"

"Clark, what the devil's wrong?"

"I *can't* –!" Clark cried despairingly. "I don't know what's wrong!"

"For God's sake . . ." Lloyd breathed. "Oh my God!" Clark stared desperately at the contacts, which remained unmoving. Then he jabbed his finger on the test button again and again.

Spit of sound in his ear. What is wrong? What is the matter?

"Examine the relays," he heard Quin say quite clearly in a calm, detached voice. Then the interference rushed in to fill the small silence after he had spoken.

Relays, relays –

"What do I do?" Lloyd asked peremptorily, a sense of betrayal in his voice.

"Open the fucking gates!" Clark snarled. "You got nowhere else to go!" Relays, relays –

One of them is unclamped, *one of them is unclamped*!

"Chief – get the men to their stations, immediately. Engine room?"

"Sir, we're clear down here."

"Run up electric power. Well done, Chief!"

"Thank you, sir."

300

"Sandy, clear the ship of all Soviet personnel – all of them, mind you."

"One of them is unclamped!" Clark yelled into his throat-mike, as if he expected Quin to be able to hear him in an identical freak reception spot.

"What?" Lloyd asked.

"You do your thing, Lloyd – let me do mine!"

"Is it go?"

"It was go a long time past! Let's get out of here!"

"What about 'Leopard'?"

"I'll give you 'Leopard', dammit!"

"What about you? You can't be outside the pressure hull when we dive."

"You worry about your business, I'll worry about mine."

"Very well. Thurston's opening the gates now."

"Get with it."

Faulty fitting, he told himself. The relay, one single fucking relay, lying there on the base of the case. His fingers trembled as he reached down to it, touched it almost reverently, fearfully. His fingers stroked, embraced, lifted it. The vibration caused by the torpedo damage had shaken it out of place, disabling the back-up system, preventing the automatic change-over from working.

There was another spit of sound in his ear, but he ignored the slowed-down, true-speed voice of the storm and the air. Quin was invisible, inaudible somewhere behind it, but he no longer mattered.

Clark pressed home the detached relay, flipped over the retaining clamp, then removed his fingers from it. They came away clammily. The electric motors of the *Proteus* thrummed through the pressure hull.

His back ached. He groaned with the sudden awareness of it and of his cramped and twisted body and the rivulets of perspiration running down his sides and back.

Lloyd's stream of orders continued, murmuring on his chest like the steady ticking of his heart, slower and calmer and younger than his heart felt.

"Slow astern."

"Slow astern, sir." Thurston's voice was distant, but Clark could still hear it repeating the captain's instructions. They'd got the gates to the pen open, they'd cast off their moorings at bow and stern. How many men had they lost, just doing that?

"Clark?"

"Yes."

"Have you finished?"

"Yes. I hope to God, yes."

301

"Get back in here – now."

"Aye, aye, sir."

Clark turned, still on his knees. He could hear a siren through the outer hull of the *Proteus*. "Leopard" had to work –

He turned to look at the back-up system – the grey carapace lay behind it. He tore at the wiring and at the wads of explosive, huddling them into his chest then thrusting them back into the pack in pure elation. Then he lifted the grey metal casing, fitted it, fidgeted in his pocket for the screws, fixed them one at a time, feeling the submarine moving slowly backwards on her batteries, out of the pen. Yes, yes.

Pack, pack – left hand bad. The other could stay. Whatever happened, he would not be coming back. He took hold of the pack, and turned once more to make his way back to the hatch following the wire of his aerial. He shunted the pack and his lamp in front of him, hurrying now, winding through the tree-like stanchions like an obstacle course.

The *Proteus* lurched forward, as if freed from some constraint.

Clark slipped, and began to slide into the abyss, into the dark. His lamp slid away, wobbling its light back at him for a moment before leaving him in entire darkness, his body weighted by the pack in his right hand – left hand bad – beginning to pursue the fallen lamp. He crooked an arm round one of the stanchion trees, heaving his body into stillness, into a quiver that was devoid of downward movement. He felt sick. He felt exhausted.

"Clark – Clark, where are you, man?"

Clark groaned. He swung the pack until it rested on the level top of the pressure hull, then grabbed the stanchion with his right hand, changing the agonizing hold of his crooked arm for a two-handed grip. He heaved at his leaden body, feeling the revolutions of the motors rise in speed. *Proteus* must be almost out of the pen.

He pulled himself up, aided by scrabbling feet and knees, and lumbered along the top of the pressure hull, reached the hatch and thrust it open. He hefted the explosives through, and let them roll away down the outer hull. Then he clambered after them, closing the hatch and locking it behind him.

The stern of the submarine had already passed into the concrete tunnel leading to the harbour. On her docking prop. *Proteus* was sliding through the tunnel, out to sea.

He watched as the sail of the submarine slid into the shadow of the tunnel. Above the bellow of the siren, he could hear shooting in the distance, like the pinging of flies against a windscreen. Then he ran crouching along the hull, almost slipping twice, until he reached the aft escape hatch, lifted it, stepped onto the ladder inside the chamber, closed the hatch and locked it. Then he felt his legs go watery and he stumbled to the bottom of the escape chamber, bent double with effort and relief.

"Prepare to dive," he heard Lloyd saying, then: "Clark? Clark, where are you?"

"Inside."

"Thank God. Well, does it work?"

"Switch on, and pray."

"You don't sound too hopeful –"

"Switch the damn thing on!" Clark bellowed with rage and relief and tiredness.

Valery Ardenyev instinctively placed himself in front of Dolohov and Panov. The scene in the pen had no precise focus, nor did it possess a great deal of movement – certainly not sufficient to suggest panic – yet Ardenyev knew what was happening. One guard was firing, the technicians who must have been lining up like an honour guard to await Panov's arrival were shuffling like a herd smelling the first smoke of the grass fire. Also, there was someone clambering up the side of the *Proteus*'s sail, making his way back into the submarine. Ardenyev had the immediate sense that events were already minutes old, even though the white-coated group of figures seemed only now to be reacting to them. Yes. The gates were wide open, and there were two uniformed bodies lying dead on the concrete, alongside the *Proteus*.

He heard Dolohov say, in a strangled old voice, "No –!", and then he ushered them back through the door by which they had entered the pen, pushing them against the officers who had accompanied them, then had stood deferentially aside so that the three of them might be the first of the party to see the captured British vessel.

"Close the door – give the alarm!" he snapped, then he was pushing through the jostle of technicians towards the submarine.

The *Proteus* slid away from him. As he passed the huddled bodies he believed he recognized the face of the guard on Lloyd's cabin, the man who had patrolled behind the British officer when he had brought Lloyd lunch and told him about Panov.

He ran faster. The *Proteus* shuddered against the side of the pen, then was free. The bow was still moving away from him as he raced to overtake it. He could not believe the panic appearance of the break-out. There had to have been help, and hope. Lloyd or someone else had been given a gun. He *knew* 'Leopard' must have been repaired. Lloyd would not have risked lives, and his submarine, without knowing he could rely on the protection of the anti-sonar equipment.

The bow was behind him now. He ran closer to the hull. It rose smoothly above him. He was half-way down the pen, the only

303

moving figure. There was rifle fire behind him, pointless but noisy. The *pitons* of a ladder climbed away from him. He reached for the lowest one, felt his feet lifted and dragged, his stride extending to great lunar bounds as his arms protested. Then he was pressing himself against the side of the submarine, watching the concrete wall of the tunnel approaching. He might have been half-jammed into the door of a metro train, watching the end of the platform racing at him.

He clambered up the hull, feet slipping, hands sweaty, onto its upper section. He climbed the last few *pitons* and stood on top of the hull as it slid into the tunnel. He ran to the forward escape hatch, unlocked it, lifted it, and clambered down into the chamber, closing the hatch behind him.

"Did he hear you, man? Did he?"

Quin shook his head. "I don't know," he admitted. "I really don't know."

Aubrey looked at his watch. Seven twenty-seven. They were out of range. The link between Clark and the Nimrod had been broken as certainly as if Pasvik had been shot, and his dish aerials smashed. There was nothing more to be done. As if he saw clearly into Aubrey's mind, Eastoe's voice sounded in the headset.

"That's it, Mr. Aubrey. Sorry."

"Thank you for your efforts, Squadron Leader," Aubrey replied.

Aubrey looked through the porthole, out beyond the sun-tipped port wing. Ahead of the Nimrod, the sky was darker, and the land below them was tumbled and cracked in shadow. Cloud and mist wound like white, unsubstantial rivers through the peaks and the fjords. The MiG-23 on the port wing waggled its body like an athletic silver insect, dipping its wings in turn, and then it dropped away and out of sight. The Nimrod was more than a hundred and fifty miles from the Soviet border, making for North Cape.

Aubrey groaned with disappointment.

"I'm sorry," Quin said.

"Do you think he would have found anything?"

"There seemed no other place to look –" Quin shook his head and stared at the still-open manual in front of him. He closed the wire-bound book. "I don't know. I could think of nothing else."

Behind them, *Proteus* and her crew would be breaking out – to what purpose? With what reprisals? There was blood now, instead of diplomacy or an intelligence game. People had been killed, Soviet citizens. It did not bear consideration. Aubrey surrendered instead to his utter and complete weariness of mind and body; a comforting numbness.

Seven twenty-nine.

Then the signal, in clear, that he no longer believed to be possible.

"Mr. Aubrey?"

"Yes?"

"A signal from *Proteus*, in clear."

"No –"

"It reads – 'At one stride comes the dark' – end of message. Do you understand it? Shall I ask for a repeat?"

"No thank you, Squadron Leader. Let us go home."

"Very well, sir."

A beatific smile wreathed Aubrey's features, inflating his grey cheeks, forming his lips, screwing up his eyes. Coleridge's *Ancient Mariner*. "At one stride comes the dark". The signal he had told Clark to make in a moment of amusement, a moment of looking for the right, witty, portentous thing for Clark to say if and when he repaired "Leopard". Somehow, he had done it.

"What is it?" Quin asked.

"It's all right. It's all right," Aubrey repeated, opening his eyes, slouching back in his seat, almost asleep already. "Clark has done it."

"Thank God," Quin breathed.

The man's daughter, Aubrey thought, his body immediately chilled. Tricia Quin and Hyde. What of them? Alive, or dead? If the latter, how would he tell Quin?

"Admiral, we have no units capable of detecting and stopping the British submarine – not in the inner harbour," the officer commanding the defences of Pechenga explained to Dolohov, nervously standing to attention before the older, more senior man. Inwardly, he wished himself a great distance from the defence control room, set beneath thick concrete and lit by strip-lighting, but he struggled to preserve a form of dignity and an impassive expression on his face. Dolohov was evidently beside himself with rage.

"Nothing? *Nothing*?" Turning, Dolohov waved at the sheet of perspex marked in a grid, displaying coloured lights and chinagraph markings. The two anti-submarine nets were bright red strings of beads, the mines, represented by colours according to type, were like the knots in a fine skein, ready to be drawn about the *Proteus*. Beyond the first net, the units of the Red Banner Fleet at present in Pechenga appeared as a host of bright lights.

"Everything is cold, Admiral – reactors, diesels, turbines all need time to run up to operational readiness. We have been caught flat-footed –" He cut off his explanation as Dolohov turned to him again.

"Where is she? *Where is the submarine?*" he bellowed.

"She disappeared from our screens two minutes ago – here." The defences commandant hurried to the perspex screen in the centre of

305

the operations room and gathered up a pointer that rested against its base. The perspex flexed and dimpled as he tapped with enthusiasm at it. A chinagraphed dotted line ran from the fifth of the submarine pens to a point marked with a circled cross, in the inner harbour. "We think she was already turning at this point –" A junior officer beside the perspex screen nodded in agreement.

"What do you intend to do about it?"

"There are two patrol boats in the inner harbour now – the mines, of course, are all activated. However, the inertial navigator memory aboard the submarine may have tracked their course when they entered the harbour, if it had been left on. Even so, it is unlikely they will be able to avoid the mines with any degree of success –"

"Switch them off! Switch off all your mines, at once!"

"But, Admiral –"

"Do as I order! That submarine must be stopped, not destroyed. We cannot take the risk of doing permanent or irreparable damage to her." Dolohov paused. The political consequences would be enormous, and possibly violent, he considered. In making that judgment, he gave no thought to London or Washington or Brussels, only to the Kremlin. His political masters would not forgive the international repercussions of the destruction of the British submarine in Soviet territorial waters. That had been made clear to him, from the outset.

The commandant nodded to one of his juniors, and the order was given. Almost immediately, the fine skein of lights blinked off, leaving great areas of the perspex screen blank and grey. Every mine in the inner harbour and in the outer basin was now disarmed. The fleet vessels which had before glowed in tiny pockets of greyness, their safe anchorages clear of the mines, now beamed out in isolation; single, unmoving lights. Dolohov hated the blank areas of the screen, like areas on a map still to be explored.

"Now," he said heavily, "I want every unit in the outer basin to be prepared. You have a minelayer in port?"

"Yes, Admiral."

"With low power mines?"

"Yes, Admiral."

"Then they must be instructed to sow fresh mines along the seaward side of the inner net. Proximity fuses, or magnetic. But they *must* be of sufficient strength only to cripple, not destroy. Understand?"

"The inner net, Admiral, will not be opened?" The man evidently did not understand.

"You will lay the mines, by aircraft if you have to, and you will do it at once," Dolohov said with a passionate calmness. "The British captain has torpedoes, wire-guided with television cameras. He can

306

blow a hole in the inner net. If there are mines waiting for him when he escapes through his own hole, he will go to the bottom, or be slowed down, or be forced to the surface. Now do you understand?"

"Yes, Admiral. I will issue the orders at once."

"Good." Dolohov thought once, and briefly, of the fact that Ardenyev was aboard the *Proteus*, and then dismissed his image in favour of self-congratulation. In the midst of his fierce rage and disappointment, there was room for satisfaction. He had anticipated what the British captain would do to escape, and he might already have made the move that would frustrate his efforts.

He studied the perspex screen intently.

"Torpedo room – stand by."

"Aye, aye, sir. Standing by."

Lloyd studied the sonar screen in front of him. As its arm circled the screen, washing the light-pattern behind it, the bright spots and lines of the submarine net appeared on the screen. It was, as Clark had originally outlined, the only way out – through both nets.

"Range?" he said.

"Eight hundred, sir."

"Torpedo room – load number one tube."

"Number one tube loaded, sir."

The Tigerfish wire-guided torpedo was ready to be fired. Lloyd looked at his watch. Four minutes and thirty-six seconds since they had cleared the pen. Speed was the essence, Clark had said. Just like killing the two guards, he reminded himself with a sick feeling in the pit of the stomach. Speed, surprise. And the gamble that Pechenga would switch off and disarm its minefield in order to preserve "Leopard".

"Range seven-fifty, sir."

"Torpedo room – fire one!"

"One away, sir."

Lloyd crossed the control room to where Thurston was studying the tiny, blank television screen set alongside the fire control console's other screens and panels of lights. The screen flickered on. Both men ignored the voice over the intercom calling the range and speed and functions of the wire-guided Tigerfish. They seemed mesmerized by the stir and rush and billow of grey water illuminated weakly by the light on the torpedo. Lloyd's wrist with its curling, dark hairs was at the edge of his eyesight. He saw, conjointly with the image on the screen, the second hand ticking round, moving up the face of the watch, a red spider-leg.

The flash of something, like a curtain or a net though it might only have been an illusion created by the moving water. Then the screen blanked out as the torpedo operator registered the correct and chosen proximity to target and detonated the warhead of the Tigerfish. The shock-wave was a dim, rumbling shudder along the outer hull a few moments later. Lloyd grinned at Thurston.

"Let's see if you can find the hole, John, mm?"

"Aye, aye, sir."

The mist had lifted, remaining in small, thin pockets only in hollows and folds of the ground. The sun had resolved itself into a hard, bright circle, and the sky was palely blue. Hyde was sweating with effort and the rise in temperature as he pulled the girl up the steep bank behind him. When they stood together on the top of the bank, Hyde could see the Chase sloping away from them. He pulled the girl down beside him, and they lay on the wet, dead ferns, staring down through the silver-boled, bare birches towards the tiny figures making their way with laborious effort up towards them. The rifle ranges were behind them, the line of huge, numbered targets perhaps six hundred yards away.

Three of them – no, four. Somehow, Hyde knew there were no others. He checked the magazine, weighing it. Perhaps ten rounds left of the thirty it had originally contained. He thrust the folding double-strut stock against his good shoulder, and looked through the tangent rear sight and the protected post foresight. The action gave him confidence. The mist had been their patron, then their betrayer. Now, the clear air and the bright, warming sun were on their side. Hyde held the high ground. The effective range of the AK-47 was three hundred metres. The four men were at twice that range. He was required to wait.

"You all right?"

"Yes."

The situation became increasingly unreal the more he considered it, the closer the Russians drew. He was in the middle of Staffordshire, these men were either accredited diplomats of the Soviet embassy or they were casuals called out from the woodwork to assist Petrunin. They were the ones on alien ground, and only now that he looked down on them, armed with one of their rifles and with the mist evaporated, could he perceive the situation in those terms. He had already won. The men down there pushed other men under buses, poisoned them with tiny metal pellets in the tips of umbrellas, pushed them onto the live rail of the underground. Maybe in the north of Scotland they could go on playing this hunting game, but not here. In a minute, a portly matron would appear, exercising a small dog, or someone from the Forestry Commission would pass them in a Land Rover.

Stop it, stop it, he instructed himself. It was still four to one, and the police would be out in force on the M6, but not necessarily on Cannock Chase. Perhaps four hundred yards now. The four men had spread out, but until they reached the trees on the slope below they had no cover. They moved more cautiously now, probably afraid.

"Not long now," he offered to Tricia Quin.

"What isn't? What won't be?" she asked in a sullen, tired voice. "Christ, I'm tired and scared and hungry."

"That's two of us." He opened his squinting eye, and removed the gaze of his other eye from the sights of the Kalashnikov. He studied her. She had become girlish again, and his attitude to her hardened. The rest of it, anything warmer, belonged in the burrow where they had hidden and in his disordered imagination as he half slept. Now, he could not say that he even liked her particularly. She, evidently, disliked him. Their former attitudes had re-emerged, as if they both understood that they were already on the other side of their experience. "We've got the advantage now."

She shook her head, staring at the rifle. It alienated her from him. He accepted her distance. She was about to climb back into the feckless skin which he had forced her to shed. She already resented the sloughing of her past self for the last few days.

He looked back. Still the four men, clambering through the wet ferns and the dead heather. A Land Rover passed along a distant, open track behind them, and he grinned. He put down the rifle and cupped his hands.

"Petrunin! Can you hear me, Petrunin?" he bellowed. The men stopped immediately.

"Yes," came the faint reply. Petrunin remained just out of effective range of the Kalashnikov. And he knew he was out of range.

"I've won, you stupid joker!"

"Not yet."

"Admit it. You're finished. You'd better start making arrangements to fly out before they catch you. You're finished in England, mate!"

The four men remained standing, looking like an irresolute group of hikers. Just over three hundred yards away. There was nothing they could do, no way in which they could move forward into the trees without coming into range. Stalemate. Stand off.

"I think not. We are four to one." Petrunin's voice was faint, unthreatening. The Forestry Commission Land Rover had turned into a wide, sunlit ride, and was moving away. The normality it represented did not, however, diminish. Petrunin was bluffing, his words empty.

"Piss off!" Hyde yelled with a quick, sharp delight. "You're beaten and you know it! Go home to Mother –"

The girl's gasp was inaudible, the beginning of her scream merely scratched at his attention, far below the volume of his own voice, but the slump of her body at the corner of his vision attracted him, caused him to turn, his hands reaching instinctively for the rifle. It was kicked away from him, and then a second kick thudded into his wounded shoulder as it came between the walking boot and the side of his head. Tricia Quin, he had time to see, had been struck by the man's rifle stock on the temple, and her head was bleeding. He heard himself scream with pain, his whole body enveloped in the fire which ran from his shoulder. He raised one hand feebly as the man kicked again, then drove the wooden stock of his AKM rifle down at Hyde's face, an action as unemotional as stepping on an insect. Hyde attempted to roll away, but the stock of the rifle caught him between the shoulder blades, winding him, forcing all the air from his lungs so that he felt transfixed to the ground.

He went on rolling, and the man who must have doubled around behind them before they had reached the top of the slope came after him, rifle still pointed stock-first towards the Australian. There was a set, fixed smile on the man's face. The man wasn't going to shoot him, he was going to beat and club him to death. Petrunin and the others would already have started running, reaching the bottom of the slope, beginning now perhaps to labour up it to the top, through the birch trees.

Hyde kicked out, struck the rifle but not the man, who stepped nimbly aside and then came forward again. Hyde tried to get to his knees, aware of himself offering his back and neck for more blows, for execution. He could not catch his breath, which made a hollow, indigestible noise in his throat. The rifle swung to one side, then the stock swung back. Hyde fell away from it, and kicked out, catching the man on the shin, making him exclaim with the unexpected pain. The rifle stock sought his head. He pushed himself half upright on one arm, and dived inside the intended blow. His head snapped up into the man's groin, making the man's breath explode, his body weakly tumble backwards. Hyde grabbed the man's legs, squeezing them together, aware of his back exposed to the next blow. Broken back, his imagination yelled at him. Broken back, lifelong cripple in a chair. He heaved at the man's thighs against his shoulder, and they tottered in that supplicatory embrace until the ground dipped and the Russian lost his balance and fell onto his back. Hyde clambered along the man's body, aware of the shadow of the rifle and the man's arm moving to his right, holding his belt, then his shirt, then his throat as if he might have been ascending a sheer slope. He raised himself above the man, blocking the swing of the rifle with his shoulder and back, pressing down as he levered himself up on the man's windpipe.

Then he released his grip, bunched his fist, and punched the man in the throat. The man's tongue came out, his eyes rolled, and there was a choking, gagging sound from his open mouth. His body writhed as if at some separate pain.

Hyde scrambled back to the lip of the slope, dragging the man's AKM behind him by its strap. He fumbled it into his hands, and flicked the mechanism to automatic. He knelt, unable to climb to his feet, and squeezed the trigger. The noise deafened him. Bark flashed from the scarred birches, ferns whipped aside, one man fell just as he emerged from the trees, twenty yards from Hyde; a second man was halted, then turned away.

Hyde released the trigger, and inhaled. His breath sobbed and rattled, but it entered his lungs, expanded them, made him cough. He swallowed phlegm, and crouched down, breathing quickly as if to reassure himself that the mechanism of his lungs now operated efficiently. When he could, he yelled at the hidden Petrunin.

"Tough shit, mate! Nice try!"

Silence. He waited. The man behind him was making a hideous noise that somehow parodied snoring, or noisy eating. Otherwise, silence. He looked at the girl, and thought he could see her breasts rising and falling in a regular rhythm. He hoped it was not an illusion, but he could not, as yet, summon the strength or the detachment to investigate. Silence.

Eventually, he raised his head. Beyond the trees, three tiny figures were moving away. One of the dots supported a second dot. The one in the lead, striding ahead, Hyde took to be Petrunin, his mind already filled with images of his skin-saving passage out of the country. A small airfield in Kent, after he had arranged to be picked up by car and driven down the M1. Hop across the Channel, then Aeroflot to Moscow direct.

Hyde lay back exhausted, staring up at the bright sun in the almost cloudless, pale sky. He began laughing, weakly at first, then uncontrollably, until his eyes watered and his back and ribs were sore and his shoulder ached.

He heard a noise, and sat up. The girl was wiping her head with a dirty handkerchief, pulling grimacing faces, seeming surprised at the blood that stained the handkerchief. Hyde wiped his eyes, and lay back again. The sky was empty, except for the sun. He waited – he decided he would wait until he heard a dog bark, and then raise his head and check whether it was indeed a portly matron out exercising a runt-sized, pink-bowed dog in a tartan overcoat.

Clark looked up at the ceiling of the wardroom pantry with an involuntary reaction. A forkful of scrambled eggs remained poised an inch or so from his lips. The cook had disliked his insistence on eating in the pantry rather than the wardroom proper, but the rating now seemed almost pleased at his company. What was it Copeland had said? *They'll have to be careful, like small boys scrambling under a barbed wire fence into an orchard. Lloyd could get his trousers caught.* Clark smiled. Evidently, they had found the hole they had blown in the net, but not its exact centre. The starboard side of the *Proteus* had dragged for perhaps a hundred feet or more against some obstacle, some bent and twisted and sharp-edged remnant of the net, and then the fin had clanged dully against the net, jolting the submarine, which had then altered its attitude and slipped beneath the obstruction.

Clark registered the scrambled egg on his fork, and opened his mouth. He chewed and swallowed. The food was good, and it entirely absorbed his attention and his energies. He picked up his mug of coffee, and washed down the mouthful of egg. He was eating quickly and greedily and with an almost sublime satisfaction. The responsibility was no longer his. "Leopard" worked. Immediately, his concussive readiness had drained from him while he lay slumped in the aft escape chamber, and he had gone into a doped and simple-minded superficiality of awareness and sensation. He realized how dirty he was, how much he smelt inside the immersion suit, how hungry and thirsty he was, how tired he was. A junior officer had escorted him to the wardroom. By that time, food had become the absolute priority, after removing his immersion suit. They gave him the disguise of his overalls to wear until he had taken a shower.

What was happening, in the control room and outside the submarine, was of no interest to him. He could not, any longer, have recited the instructions he had given Lloyd when he first boarded the *Proteus*. Some tape in his mind had been wiped. He could not have seen the loose relay in the back-up system now, without having it pointed out to him.

"Like some more, sir?" the cook offered, holding the saucepan out towards him.

Clark grinned, and patted his stomach. "That'll do, I think, don't you? Very good."

"Thank you, sir. More coffee, sir?"

"Please."

The senior rating brought the jug of coffee towards the table where Clark sat. Then he seemed to wobble sideways, and lurch against the stove. A stream of dark coffee flew from the jug, cascading down one of the walls – at least, Clark knew that would be what the coffee would do, but the lights went out before he could observe it happen, and he was flung off his chair and bundled into one corner of the pantry. His head banged sickeningly against some jutting piece of kitchen furniture, and he rolled away from it, groaning. He sat up, rubbing his head, his ears ringing with the concussion and the noise that had accompanied the shudder of the submarine, as the emergency lights flickered on, then the main lights came back almost immediately after.

"All right?" he asked.

The cook was wiping coffee from his apron, and rubbing his arm. He still had the empty jug in his hand.

"What happened, sir?"

The *Proteus* was maintaining course and speed, as far as Clark could apprehend.

"Mine." Someone in Pechenga was thinking fast. He got to his knees, head aching, and the second mine threw him forward as the submarine rolled to starboard with the impact of the explosion. Darkness, slithering, the clatter of utensils, the groan of the hull, the terrible ringing in his ears, the thud of the cook's body on top of him, winding him, then the lights coming back on. He felt the *Proteus* right herself through his fingertips and the rest of his prone body. Over the intercom, Lloyd requested an all-stations damage report immediately. The senior rating rolled off Clark and apologized.

"OK, OK. I think I'll just go see what's happening." The cook appeared disappointed at his departure. "You OK?"

"Yes, thank you, sir."

Clark left the wardroom pantry, his body tensed, awaiting a further explosion. He entered the control room at the end of the short corridor from the living quarters, and immediately sensed the mood of congratulation. *Proteus* had not been seriously, hamperingly damaged.

"Contact at green three-six closing, sir." Someone had got the Soviet ships moving in double-quick time.

"Increase speed – nine knots," he heard Lloyd say.

"Nine knots, sir."

"Net at two thousand yards."

"Contact at red seven-zero also moving. Range one thousand."

"Contact at green eight-two closing, sir."

The hornet's nest had been poked with a stick. Clark realized that the Russians needed less luck in the confined space of the harbour than they needed out in the Barents Sea, and then they had found a crippled *Proteus*.

"Contact at red seven-zero making for the net, sir."

"Contact at green three-six closing, sir. Range seven hundred."

Lloyd saw Clark from the corner of his eye. Clark waved to him, and grinned. Lloyd returned his attention at once to the bank of sonar screens in front of him. Moved by an impulse to see the equipment he had repaired actually functioning, Clark crossed the control room softly, and exited through the aft door. The "Leopard" room was directly behind the control room.

As he closed the door, he heard Lloyd speak to the torpedo room after ordering a further increase in speed.

"Torpedo room – load number two tube."

They would make it. Just, but they would make it.

The door to the small, cramped "Leopard" room was open. Clark, as he reached the doorway, was instantly aware of the rating lying on the floor, and the officer slumped against one of the cabinets containing the main system. And he recognized the dark-jerseyed man who turned towards the noise he had made, knocking on the door-frame in the moment before he had taken in the scene in the room.

Valery Ardenyev. It *was* him. Clark knew he had killed Hayter and the rating.

Seven forty-three. He saw the clock above Ardenyev's head as he took his first step into the room and the Russian turned to him, a smile of recognition on his face. Ardenyev's hand moved out, and threw the switch he had been searching for before Clark disturbed him. As the switch moved, Clark knew that "Leopard" had been de-activated. The *Proteus* moved through the outer harbour of Pechenga, registering on every sonar screen of every Soviet ship and submarine.

"I knew it had to be you," Clark said in a surprisingly conversational tone, warily skirting the rating's body near the door. Ardenyev had apparently killed both of them without a weapon.

"I didn't reach the same conclusion about you." Ardenyev's back was to the control console of the "Leopard" equipment, protecting the switch he had thrown. "Perhaps I should have done." The Russian shrugged, then grinned. "It won't take long. I only have to keep this stuff–" He tossed his head to indicate "Leopard", "– out of action for a few minutes."

"Sure." Clark shook his head, smiling. "You're beaten. We're on our way out, you're alone on an enemy submarine. What chance do you have?"

"Every chance, my friend. That's the Soviet Union a few hundred yards behind you –"

Clark sprang at Ardenyev, who stepped neatly and swiftly to one side, bringing his forearm round sharply across Clark's back. The American grunted and collapsed across the console, his hand reaching instinctively for the switch above him. Ardenyev chopped the heel of his hand across Clark's wrist, deadening it, making the hand hang limply from his forearm. Then Ardenyev punched Clark in the kidneys, making him fall backwards and away from the control console,

314

doubling him up on the floor. Ardenyev leaned casually against the console, watching Clark get groggily to his knees, winded.

"You're tired, my friend," Ardenyev observed.

Mistily, Clark saw the red second hand of the clock moving jerkily downwards. Fourteen seconds since Ardenyev had thrown the switch. He staggered, then tried to lean his weight against the Russian and hold onto him. Ardenyev rammed his knee into Clark's groin, and then punched him in the face. Clark fell backwards again, groaning. He did not want to get up, and did not feel he had the strength to do so. The clock just above Ardenyev's head obsessed him. Twenty-two seconds. *Proteus* must almost have reached the net.

He seemed to feel the submarine hesitate, and saw the attentiveness on Ardenyev's face. He heard a noise scrape down the hull. The net –

The mine exploded beneath the hull, rocking the submarine, blinking out the lights. In the darkness, Clark struggled to his feet and groped for the Russian, feeling his woollen jersey, grabbing it, striking his hand at where the Russian's face would be. He felt the edge of his hand catch the man's nose, below the bridge, felt Ardenyev's breath expelled hotly against his cheek as he cried out in pain, and grabbed the Russian to him in the dark. The room settled around them.

Ardenyev thrust himself and Clark against one of the cabinets. A sharp handle dug into Clark's back, but he hooked his leg behind Ardenyev's calf and pushed. The lights came on as they rolled on the floor together. Clark drove his head down into the Russian's face, but the man did not let go of his neck. Clark felt his throat constrict, and he could no longer breathe. He tried to pull away from the grip, but it did not lessen. Blood ran into Ardenyev's mouth and over his chin, but he held on. The fin of the submarine scraped beneath the holed outer net, the submarine jerked like a hooked fish, shuddering, and then *Proteus* was free.

Clark's thoughts clouded. Ardenyev was interested only in killing him. Nothing else mattered. He beat at Ardenyev's face and neck and shoulders, his punches weak and unaimed and desperate. Consciousness became more and more fugged and insubstantial, then Ardenyev's grip on his throat seemed to slacken. Clark pulled away, and the hands fell back onto Ardenyev's chest, lying there, curled like sleeping animals.

Clark looked at his own hands, covered with blood, bruised, shaking. In one of them he held something that only slowly resolved in his watery vision until he was able to recognize it as the R/T set from his overalls pocket, the one he had used to communicate with Lloyd. He leaned down over Ardenyev's chest, listening. He avoided looking at

315

the man's battered face. He had slapped the R/T set against Ardenyev's face and head time after time with all his remaining strength, as if the movement of his arm would pump air into his lungs.

Ardenyev was dead.

Clark clambered up the cabinet, then lurched to the control console, flicking the switch back to "On". "Leopard" was activated. It was seven forty-five. "Leopard" had been switched off for almost two minutes. Long enough for *Proteus* to have been spotted, not long enough for her to be attacked.

He sensed the increased speed of the *Proteus* through the deck, as she headed for the open sea. He avoided looking at Ardenyev's body. He dropped the blood-slippery R/T to the floor and hunched over the console, wanting to vomit with weakness and disgust and relief. He rubbed at his throat with one hand, easing its soreness. He closed his eyes. Now, he wanted only to sleep, for a long time.